SPACE ACADEMY WASHOUTS

Book Three of the Space Academy Series

C. T. Phipps and Michael Suttkus

I0610454

"Are you really Vance Turbo, HERO OF SPACCCEE?" The pirate captain said, sitting across the card table. Yes, he somehow added the reverb and deep booming voice that accompanied my name whenever it was spoken these days. "You're not just using it as an alias?"

Captain Josiah Havelock, probably not his real name, was dressed in a tunic, feathered hat, and had a skull-and-crossbones decorated eyepatch. The man was even sporting a plasma sword to his side. He was brown skinned, of mixed Earth South African and Indian descent, with a shaved head. His voice was notably altered by a cybernetic enhancement built into his throat that allowed him to speak alien languages that were utterly beyond most humans.

I was sitting in the backroom of the Spy's Demise—an ominous sounding bar given I was a spy these days—and playing a game of five card nova. Sitting at the octagonal table were the afore-mentioned pirate, a renegade Sorkanan Admiral named Eighty-Eight, a human crime lord named Big Bobo, an Ant named Sweets, and a green-skinned demihuman exotic dancer named Princess Kalisha who was the most dangerous person there. Everyone at the table was armed, even the barely dressed princess, but all our bodyguards were outside of the reinforced armored chamber.

Beyond the Spy's Demise, we were located on the Ring, a super-structure on the edge of human space that was a port of call for both the very rich as well as the very crooked.

CAST OF CHARACTERS

Lead

Captain Vance Turbo, aka Vannevar Tagashi: Academy dropout, loudmouth, alleged genius.

Supporting Cast

Forty-Two: Sorkanan dropout turned security officer and Space Marine. In a bit of trouble.

Eighty-Eight: Sorkanan Separatist Admiral and warlord. One of the most despicable members of his race.

Alexandra Ares: Anonymous investor in Ares Electronics. AI in a bioroid body. Descendant (?) of Patricia Ares.

Patricia Ares: Long-dead founder of Ares Electronics. The basis for Trish's personality and memories. Adopted daughter of Case Gordon.

Admiral Saul Bendo: The Chief of Naval operations for EarthGov's Home Fleet. More politician than soldier these days.

Big Bobo: A crippled arms dealer and slave trader. A chief supplier for multiple terrorist organization and separatist nations.

Chief Sal Boxley: A skittish technician who has survived numerous horrific accidents in training before being dragooned into Department Twelve's service.

"Cthulhu": The nickname for a Primordial that wants to exterminate everybody. A very bad person.

Director Case Gordon AKA Director G: The head of EarthGov's branch of the Security Divisions.

Captain Josiah Havelock: Human male space pirate. Captain of the *ISS Queen of Stars*. Goes the full deal with sword, coat, and eyepatch. Actually, quite dangerous.

The High Priestess: Notha high priestess. It's in the name. She is the biological daughter of the President.

Grand Admiral Rudra Laghari: Captain of the *ESS Caliburn*. Quit Space Fleet to become a mercenary navy's admiral. Deeply hates Vance.

Lieutenant Commander Hannah O'Brian: Genetically engineered superhuman merc. Catlike agility and other qualities. Like her tail.

Lt. Commander Leslie Park: Blue-skinned, black-haired demihuman bundle of love and joy. Undyingly loyal to Vance and his preferred first officer. Also handy with a wrench.

Commander Lisa Park: Blue-skinned, black-haired demihuman hardass Space Marine who is now first officer of the *ESS Elgan*. Leslie Park's sister. Hannah's ex-wife and Vince's friend with benefits.

Pink: Captain Havelock's second-in-command. Pirate. Pilot. Bad attitude.

The President: The Notha President of Deathworld. Slightly less xenophobic than the rest of his race. Former comedian and actor.

SHAT-3221931: An AI of the *ESS Elgan*. It is modeled after an actor of the Pre-First Contact era.

Commander Julius Something: An East African Union bridge officer who gets stuck with terrible duties. Somehow managed to become second in command of the *Ares*.

Sweets: A famous Ant card player. No politics.

Lieutenant Commander Danny Tagawa: Vance's cousin and hypercompetent sidekick. Kind of a kiss up. Also, weirdly unnoticeable.

Lieutenant Commander Light on Water: A Sklux Space Fleet officer. Overly differential and obsequious.

Ketra T'Kal: Former ambassador of the Community. Ethereal Human. Weird space wizard. Likes checkers. Oh, and is sorta but not really dead.

Elektra T'Ketra: Ethereal. Mad scientist, bubbly, excitable. Sister of Shelly.

Shelly T'Ketra: Ethereal. Perpetual first officer, efficient, irritable. Sister of Elektra.

The Tool: The unfortunately named gestalt consciousness of numerous Elder Race technology working together.

TRS-8021 "Trish": The AI of the ship. Human female personality. Annoyingly adorable. May be a biophiliac for Vance.

Nina the Vampire: Religiously identifies as vampire. Transhuman who gave herself vampire abilities and look. Quite perky and friendly.

Major Tom Walker: Brigid-born civilian contractor. Married to his commanding officer.

Ted Williams: Chel diplomat. Ancient alien. Very Earth-y name.

Dr. Elizabeth Zard: Unfortunately named human female. Doctor of math *and* medicine. Prefers the former.

FOREWORD

Space, the funniest frontier.

Yes, we once more return to the adventures of Vance Turbo and his wacky crew of misfits exploring the wonders of Contested Space. It's been a wild ride since Michael Suttkus and I were first commissioned to do this series and each book has been a fantastic new experience.

The first book was an homage to all those space cadet stories about a new crew coming together to deal with an uncertain situation and if they had what it takes to do the job. Which, as we know, they did not. The second book was about Vance rising to the occasion of being a captain and seeing if he could command people every bit as nonconformist as himself. Which, we know, he cannot. The third book, the one you're reading right now, will be about that most important of science fiction plots: the conference about the thing.

All the way back to *Star Trek*'s "Journey to Babel" in 1967, the science fiction conference has always been a popular backdrop for stories. A bunch of ambassadors and alien representatives must get together to discuss something unimportant but inevitably are interrupted by some sinister force.

Well, clearly, that's not going to happen here. Vance and company are going to accompany some ambassadors to the conference, and everything will go swimmingly with no interruptions. No sir. No chance of any intrigue, twists, turns, betrayals, and/or spywork. *hides fingers crossed behind his back* Hehe.

I had a lot of fun building the complicated but internally consistent universe of this series and *Lucifer's Star*. It was also revealed to be the future of the Agent G and *Daughters of the Cyber Dragons* series. I love creating these kinds of interconnected worlds and narratives. Don't worry, though, you don't have to have read any of them to appreciate the story. The *Space Academy Dropouts* universe stands on its own. I just feel it's enriched by getting a chance to see how this entire universe came to be.

Fan response was tremendous, and we got a lot of praise for the oddball cast of characters that surrounds Vance, as well as our hapless captain himself. The *Space Academy Dropouts* books are a particular favorite of mine because as much as I would love to be among the elite of *Star Trek*'s heroes, I can't help but think I'd be lucky to get on board *The Orville*. Some days, I might even be lucky to end up on *Red Dwarf*.

Now off to reading a story about tea and sandwiches at a conference where absolutely nothing bad will happen, whatsoever!

CHAPTER ONE

Dead Man's Hand

"Are you really Vance Turbo, HERO OF SPACCCEE?" The pirate captain said, sitting across the card table. Yes, he somehow added the reverb and deep booming voice that accompanied my name whenever it was spoken these days. "You're not just using it as an alias?"

Captain Josiah Havelock, probably not his real name, was dressed in a tunic, feathered hat, and had a skull-and-crossbones decorated eyepatch. The man was even sporting a plasma sword to his side. He was brown skinned, of mixed Earth South African and Indian descent, with a shaved head. His voice was notably altered by a cybernetic enhancement built into his throat that allowed him to speak alien languages that were utterly beyond most humans.

I was sitting in the backroom of the Spy's Demise—an ominous sounding bar given I was a spy these days—and playing a game of five card nova. Sitting at the octagonal table were the afore-mentioned pirate, a renegade Sorkanan Admiral named Eighty-Eight, a human crime lord named Big Bobo, an Ant named Sweets, and a green-skinned demihuman exotic dancer named Princess Kalisha who was the most dangerous person there. Everyone at the table was armed, even the barely dressed princess, but all our bodyguards were outside of the reinforced armored chamber.

Beyond the Spy's Demise, we were located on the Ring, a super-structure on the edge of human space that was a port of call for both the very rich as well as the very crooked. Which had considerable

1

overlap as you might guess. On the table were several million Community credits, the deed to a super-transport, and a ball that allegedly contained the soul of a Pontifex for the Union of Faith. That had belonged to a Cardinal of said religion who had cashed out a few hours ago and was being thrown in every hand because no one wanted it.

"Yes," I replied. "I am *that* Vance Turbo, though I don't add the latter part of it."

"I would," Captain Havelock said, adjusting his eyepatch. "There's a reason I go around dressed like this. You need to be memorable."

"There's memorable and looking like a fool," Eighty-Eight replied. He was a big, hulking, red-scaled member of his lizard-man race that easily topped two meters. He sported a decorated gold chest plate with a purple cape.

"Don't all humans look alike to you?" Princess Kalisha asked, batting her beautiful eyelids. She was wearing a gold bikini top and loin cloth that was another reference to a movie only film scholars remembered.

"I can vaguely tell you are a female of your species," Eighty-Eight said to the Princess. "I raise you another two million."

This ridiculously high-stakes game was just a cover for payment of a bribe to Eighty-Eight that I resented being the bagman for. Unfortunately, when you were a famous spy, your number of actual jobs were limited within the service of the Security Divisions.

"Didn't you used to be famous?" Captain Havelock said to me. "I recall you were in movies, holovision, and on all the entertainment feeds."

"Yes, I was famous," I replied, meeting the bet. I didn't see the point of playing this game, especially when I was meant to lose, but the Security Divisions couldn't be seen involving themselves in Border Planet politics.

"Then you killed the Emperor of the Notha," Big Bobo said, taking a puff of narcotics laced smoke from his hookah. He was a large, bearded man with a life-support gravity chair permanently built into his flesh, making me assume he'd suffered multiple organ failures from some condition but disdained replacements. I tried to think of him as the "guest" of Eighty-Eight rather than the fact that he was a trafficker in slaves, mind-control drugs, and weapons.

I'd seen the criminal file on Big Bobo and, under any other circumstances, would have taken great pleasure in bringing him in. He was the worst sort of human detritus and made it a point to prey on refugees and make civil conflicts worse. Unfortunately, the deal with the Separatists took priority if I wanted to save as many lives as possible and he was a chief supplier of their military. My only consolation was Eighty-Eight was using the crooked nature of the game to empty Bobo's pockets and perhaps clear some outstanding personal debts.

"I did," I replied. "Then I negotiated the Treaty of Rand's World."

"Poor you," Sweets said.

"What happened there?" Captain Havelock asked.

I shrugged, not too enthusiastic about repeating the story of my rise and fall. Unfortunately, I still had a few hands before my bribe was finished being delivered. "The treaty was the beginning of the end for me. It turns out the worst thing you can do when you're a galaxy-famous badass is advocate for peace."

Eighty-Eight laughed but it wasn't a joke. "Your treaty dissolved the old Notha Empire and divided it up like a *kri'sssh* pie. Every planet in the Community was flooded with refugees from the planets they looted."

I nodded, noting by my calculations that I could easily beat his hand but that wasn't what I was here for. "Yeah, it turns out that people really don't like foreigners in need of help. Especially when they're already dealing with a bunch of them from the Kolahn Wars."

"Didn't you say something that caused you to lose all those endorsements and merchandising deals?" Princess Kalisha asked. "I forget what it was."

I narrowed my eyes, annoyed. She knew exactly what it was. "Yeah, I made several speeches regarding the moral obligation we had to the refugees and welcoming them."

"Ugh," Captain Havelock said. "You might as well have just burned all your money right there."

3

"So, it seemed," I muttered, choosing to cast away most of the cards that would result in my victory over Eighty-Eight.

Really, we were the only two players since Havelock and Kalisha were plants while Bobo was the arms dealer who Eighty-Eight owed most of his money. Sweets was the only card player throwing his money in here and was so bad at it that it wasn't really hurting what should have been a private game.

"I'm surprised the Community didn't cashier you of your rank then and there," Eighty-Eight said. "That failed experiment on mutual cooperation and tolerance might have actually kept some of the members that withdrew."

"Yeah, it's been a slow-moving cloud car crash these past few years, hasn't it?" I muttered, wanting to reach across the table and punch him.

The fall of the Notha Empire had exposed just how many international alliances had existed in the Community solely out of fear. Eighty-Eight represented a consortium of Sorkanan colony worlds here in the Borderlands that had left the Community to run a kleptocracy dictatorship rather than to continue building up their ties to the Community's enlightened democracy. However unenlightened said democracy was right now.

As I understood it, the bribes being paid here now were designed to prevent a genocide from being carried out against the Kolahn refugees that had been settled on the Separatist worlds before they'd withdrawn their bid for Community membership. It was probably the nicest thing I'd done as a "Shadow Captain" for the Security Divisions, but it still sickened me to know Eighty-Eight was going to get a big payday for the noble gesture of allowing the refugees to leave instead of outright murdering them. Unfortunately, the Community was all out of borks to give about unaligned worlds, and military interventions had a limited utility anyway.

"So, what do you do now?" Princess Kalisha asked.

"This and that," I answered. "I primarily ferry diplomats and cargo through the Borderlands, Unaligned Territories, and the former Contested Space planets."

"Ha! You're a spy!" Havelock chuckled.

4

"Spies aren't usually famous former war heroes," Princess Kalisha said, giving me a meager defense.

"Depends on what sort of spy you are," Eighty-Eight said. "The Security Divisions like being public with their covert affairs. They hide their agents among diplomatic attaches, unimportant Space Fleet vessels, and bureaucrats. Tell me, did you choose this role, Vance Turbo, or was it the only place you could go?"

Well, Eighty-Eight wasn't really feeling the whole "clandestine handoff" thing anymore, and everyone else knew anyway.

"You would have thought that the military would have been happy to have me no longer dividing my time managing my PR but, no, I was radioactive as far as they were concerned. All I ever wanted to do was serve and it turned out that is harder than it sounds."

"There's your mistake," Big Bobo replied. "Service is for fools. The people who rule use and discard them at all. All the talk about honor, loyalty, and duty exists because the people in power use it to control the masses."

"That is something someone like you would believe," I said, sick of this conversation.

Vance, Vance, we need to talk, a soft female voice spoke through my cybernetics. It was one I knew well, my ship's AI and occasional girlfriend, Trish.

Another reason for my dramatic loss of prestige was my relationship with Trish—even when it had ended—had also come out. Apparently, it had been a slow news day and "famous starship captain sleeps with ship AI's sexbot" was just the sort of lurid news story that could fill a few hours of the programming cycle. It was the only disciplinary hearing I'd ever faced, and the reprimand had guaranteed I would never make Admiral. It had also caused considerable stress on my relationship with Shelly.

Shelly.

Pay attention, Vance, Trish said. *This is important.*

Oh, and she could also read my mind when I wasn't actually trying to shield my thoughts. It was useful when we were on a mission but not when I was having one of my funks.

5

Which is increasingly common, Trish said, exasperated. *There's been a revolution in the Separatist Alliance.*

Good heroic freedom fighters or mad bad terrorist revolutionaries? I asked, simplifying it to the barest level.

The latter, Trish replied. *They've purged the government and their families in an overnight raid that's involving a lot of shooting everyone from secretaries to mailmen.*

I grimaced. *Well, that's going to be an awkward thing to break to Admiral Eighty-Eight. Can I do it? Please-please-please.*

Despite the flippancy of my answer, I was severely upset about this whole ordeal and not just because of all the dead secretaries and mailmen. The Community never should have gotten in bed with scum like Eighty-Eight and Big Bobo to begin with. The Separatists represented everything wrong with the isolationist nativist anti-democratic politics that were presently sweeping the Spiral, including Earth.

Vance— Trish started to speak.

It was a betrayal of our values to focus on petty short-term gains and stability to support dictatorships as well as criminal conspiracies like these individuals. Eighty-Eight had committed numerous war crimes and his willingness to be bought by us didn't make him any less reprehensible.

Vance! Trish shouted.

What? I asked, calling my cards.

You need to get Eighty-Eight out of here now, Trish explained. *A Separatist Special Forces kill squad is heading your way to murder the hell out of you both. Division One has ordered us to give Eighty-Eight sanctuary.*

You've got to be kidding me, I replied.

Yes, Vance, because I find the idea of telling you there's a bunch of murderous black ops soldiers coming to kill you to be goddamn hilarious. Now get the borking move on!

Not needing to be told twice, though technically I think she'd told me multiple times, I stood up. "Admiral, I'm afraid that we are going to have to cut this game short."

Eighty-Eight stared at me. "You think you can deny me the rest of my payment?"

"Payment, what is he talking about?" Big Bobo asked.

Princess Kalisha rolled her eyes and Captain Havelock chuckled.

"You were lured here to a rigged game, chief," Havelock said, smiling. "Your dear friend, Eighty-Eight, was using it to clean you out."

"Impudent bastarve!" Big Bobo shouted, going for a fusion pistol from a secret compartment to his side. Bobo had multiple weapons hidden on his chair as well as a barrier field. Trish had disabled the latter without his knowledge at my command. Sadly, there was little she could do about the weapons without an infospace connection.

I drew my own pistol and shot him in the chest, causing him to slump over, dead. It had happened all in a smooth practiced motion that barely registered with me. I'd become accustomed to killing in the line of duty, for what that was worth. "That's for all those Kolahns you've sold."

Everyone looked at me, especially Eighty-Eight. No one was going for their guns, however, except maybe the admiral. Big Bobo wasn't anyone's friend here and it wasn't like he'd be buying anyone's drinks now.

"I was threatened," I said, admitting that I'd been thinking of a way to get rid of that son of a bitch since the moment I'd seen him.

As an immortal actor had once said, paraphrased, what I did wasn't going to get me in trouble. It was going to get me chewed out. I'd been chewed out before. What was the worst they could do? Put a reprimand in my file?

They could arrest you for murder, Trish said in my mind. *However, I sincerely doubt they're going to.*

Eighty-Eight looked like he was still debating whether to pull his own gun on me, but given Big Bobo's guards weren't rushing in from the outside—mostly because I suspected they'd already fled, and there was the sound of fusion gun fire in the distance—his expression changed from outrage to resignation.

"I take it the Community is offering me sanctuary within its hallowed halls?" Eighty-Eight asked.

"So it would appear," I muttered, disgusted.

"Then let us depart," Eighty-Eight said, sitting up. "We shall head to my ship."

7

His ship has already declared its allegiance to the new government and is threatening to blow up the Ring unless the Admiral is turned over for crimes against sapience, Trish said. *Which, yeah, he's guilty of, but whatcha gonna do?*

Turn him over? I suggested. The new Separatist government wasn't making a good impression if it was going after its enemies' families, but maybe a good impression could be made by letting someone face justice for their crimes.

The Security Divisions aren't going to let one corrupt warlord in the hand get away for two in the bush, Trish said, thoroughly mutilating that proverb. *If they do turn him over, which they might, it'll be after they've emptied him of every bit of valuable intelligence he has and trade him in exchange for concessions.*

That made me feel better, but not by much. I wasn't that much happier about betraying the trust of someone we promised protection to any more than I was about giving said offer of protection to a scumbag like Eighty-Eight in the first place.

"Yeah, we may want to avoid your ship," I replied. "Your crew is as loyal to you as you are to it. Also, I'd shut off any tracking or communication devices you have right now."

"I see," Eighty-Eight muttered. He began cleaning off the table to a surprising lack of interest from the other guests present.

Captain Havelock stood up and put his hat over his chest. "Good luck, Captain Turbo. I wish you the best and note that next time the Security Divisions need someone to add some criminal credibility to their scheme, they should call someone else."

"Will do," I muttered.

Princess Kalisha sighed and crossed her arms. "I'll just be glad to get out of this outfit."

"Of course, Hannah," I said.

That was when Sweets looked at me. "Forgive me, Captain Turbo."

"Why is that?" I asked, not knowing the Ant very well. He'd been assigned to me as a local guide by my contacts here and his body was a mecha containing hundreds, if not thousands, of much smaller aliens. Basically, every Ant body was a walking city.

"I regret I have but ten thousand lives to give for the destruction of the Community's dogs," Sweets said.

That was when the room exploded.

Goddammit.

Not again.

CHAPTER TWO

Just How Many Times Can One Man Be Blown Up?

*A*nother suicide bomber?

Seriously.

There must be a limit, cosmic or otherwise, on how many times someone is going to be blown up by a suicide bomber. This was the second time one had happened to me after a corrupted diplomat had taken out Captain Klaws. If you counted the bioroid programmed to assassinate me and then blow up the *Black Nebula* with him onboard, it was three times. Three times! That's three times too many.

Mind you, suicide bombing was the calling card of the Enigmatic Path. They were a machine-worshiping terrorist organization that had dedicated itself to bringing down the Community as well as modern Spiral civilization. They were very good at brainwashing people into being their living weapons, and not every one of those weapons were willing. The diplomat, for example, had only done so because the Path had taken his children. I had to wonder how they'd managed to bend an entire colony of Ants to their will.

Anyway, back to my possible horrific demise. Time seemed to slow down as their decision to warn me gave me a scant few seconds to focus on the Elder Ring I wore on my left hand. That artifact had saved my life more times than I could remember and was the secret source of my infamous "Turbo Luck." It was also something that only a handful of people in the universe knew about. Which was probably why I was still alive.

Unfortunately, it did require conscious thought to activate, and I still hadn't mastered it after a decade of ownership. The explosion was real enough, though and I threw up the shield not just around myself but Princess Kalisha, Havelock, and Eighty-Eight, despite the fact I only really cared about one of them surviving. Hint: It was the hot one.

The flames and concussive force poured forth from Sweets' body and washed against an invisible wall that managed to absorb the attack against us. A few years ago, my attempt to save everyone would have resulted in everyone's death, but I'd grown more accustomed to the ring's power and able to use it more effectively. Give me a century and I might even be able to use it like one of the Ethereals.

Much to my surprise—since I never counted on Elder Race technology to do anything but drive people insane and inspire weird cults—the barrier managed to hold and none of us were incinerated as the interior of our chamber was reduced to molten slag.

"Everybody alright?" I asked, looking around.

"Fascinating," Captain Havelock said, looking at the glowing energy field in front of us. "Is that a prototype? I have a personal barrier and it would have been shredded by this thing. Did you reduce it to ring-sized?"

Eighty-Eight pointed his pistol at me. "Give that to me. Now."

"Are you borking serious?" I asked, lowering the barrier, and staring at him.

"I have only one chance of getting out of this place alive and I'm not taking any chances, mammal," Eighty-Eight replied, extending a clawed hand. "Give me the ring or I'll ventilate you and take—"

"My chances?" I finished for him.

"Shut up!" Eighty-Eight snapped. "I am the Warlord of—"

Princess Kalisha punched him in the face, grab the gun from his hands, and started beating him over the head with it. Eighty-Eight went down like a tree chopped in half and desperately tried to cover his face before she stopped hitting him.

"Are you going to behave?" Princess Kalisha asked.

"What?" Eighty-Eight cried out, light fluid flowing from his wounds.

"I asked are you going to behave!" Princess Kalisha snapped.

11

"Yes!" Eighty-Eight said.

Captain Havelock nudged me with the side of his elbow. "There're places on the Ring where you have to pay for that kind of treatment."

I rolled my eyes. "Stop beating him, Hannah."

"Hannah?" Captain Havelock asked.

Princess Kalisha AKA Hannah O'Brian was undercover as a demihuman exotic dancer and a superhuman mercenary with strength that allowed her to beat a Sorkanan silly. She was also a longtime associate and good friend.

Friend, right, Trish muttered.

Jealousy does not become a godlike intelligence, I replied to my AI companion.

Tell that to the Greek gods, Trish replied.

Where are our bodyguards? I asked, pulling out a set of magnetic handcuffs from the back of my uniform. The fact I'd hidden a pair on me that could fit a Sorkanan meant I'd perhaps unconsciously seen how this would go down.

Yeah, about those, Trish muttered. *Probably good to get behind the mutilated remains of the card table.*

I didn't need to be told twice and shouted, "Get to cover!"

Everyone moved with a professional grace save, ironically, Eighty-Eight, who stumbled on the ground and went for his pistol in Hannah's hands only for her to smack it away like he was an errant toddler. I tossed him the handcuffs instead and made it clear in a look that he could put them on or have his head ventilated. He was now, officially, in protective custody rather than an honored guest.

Unfortunately, before I could make sure the bastarve was properly secured, the doors opened, and a quartet of armored Sorkanan Special Forces Death Commandos were on the other side. At their feet were the remains of our bodyguards and I felt a tightening of my stomach at having lost more people under my command. They weren't part of my crew, but they'd been assigned to me from the local garrison and that meant they'd died because of me. Which left only one response.

"Fire!"

I hadn't needed to say so as Havelock unloaded with his illegally modified sword pistol and took the head off one of the attacking Death

Commandos. Hannah equally scored an excellent shot, striking one in the throat with both her pistol as well as Eighty-Eight's. The Death Commandos had barriers, but they were twenty to thirty years old, antiquated surplus equipment sold to the Separatists from governments that had bought them from when the Community had upgraded their own supplies. They might have even been Notha knock offs, which was a helluva irony.

I managed to pull off my own shot into the eye of the Death Commandos, which wasn't so much skill as me missing his central body. It happens to the best of us in moments of confusion. Both he and the remaining soldier managed to get a shot off before Havelock and Hannah's gunfire finished off the last. Really, the one I'd shot had been dead by the time he'd pulled the trigger and fell back on the ground like a particularly violent cartoon character.

"Huh," I muttered. "I remembered the Death Commandos being tougher."

"Separatist leaders pocket the training budget," Havelock muttered. "Like they pocket everything else."

"Uh, Captain," Hannah muttered. "We have a problem."

"What?" I asked, turning my head, and seeing Eighty-Eight on the ground with a large fusion blast mark on his chest. "Goddammit!"

"Which god?" Havelock asked, as if it was the most pressing thing right now.

"Is this a good thing or a bad thing?" Hannah asked, poking him with the edge of a pistol.

"We still have to get out of here so—" I started to say before I was interrupted by Eighty-Eight moaning. "Oh joy! He's still alive!"

He'll be stone cold dead in a minute, Trish said, quoting a movie she'd shown me last month.

No, Trish, I replied to her.

You're supposed to say we can't bring him like that, it's against regulations, Trish said.

I'm not doing the routine with you, I replied.

"Is he dying or alive-alive?" I said that last part out loud.

"He's got a modern barrier vest on underneath," Hannah said. "Top of the line. It absorbed most of the blast's power, but he's probably got a few broken ribs. He's not going anywhere until he sees a doctor."

I wondered how the hell an energy blast broke ribs then shook my head. Sorkanan weapons functioned fundamentally differently than EarthGov.

"Great," I said, looking at Hannah. "Put the cuffs on him and then carry him."

"Are you kidding?" Hannah asked.

"We're carrying on with the mission," I said, pausing.

Trish, how many more of these guys are on their way? I asked her mentally.

A lot, though we have a bit of time because they're combing the station, Trish replied. *This team just sort of lucked out into finding us here.*

Great, I thought back. *Contact the* Ares. *We need evac now.*

Why would I contact the Ares? Trish asked. *I am* the Ares.

Well, I was just saying— I started to say.

Hello me, it's me, Trish mocked me. *I need you to evacuate me because Vance has forgotten I have a brain the size of a planet and didn't think I would inform myself of the fact I need evacuation.*

I sense sarcasm, I responded.

No savit! Trish replied.

Rather than pick him up, Hannah had her knees on his chest and was slapping his face. "Wake up, dammit! I am not hauling your ass across this station."

"There're places you have to pay for that, too," Havelock said, grinning.

"Seriously, man, get laid," I replied.

"I would be if not for the fact that I'm currently helping you," Captain Havelock muttered. "Believe me, I would rather be *anywhere* else."

"He has broken ribs, that's probably not healthy for him," I replied, looking at Hannah on top of him. "Please stop. Eventually."

Eighty-Eight coughed and tried to push her off. "I am awake! I am awake."

The Sorkanan admiral was wheezing and clearly not in a great way, but Hannah—reluctantly—pulled him to his feet before immediately slapping the magnetic handcuffs on him.

"Is this necessary?" Eighty-Eight asked.

"Do you want to live?" I asked.

"Yes," Eighty-Eight said, surprisingly reluctantly. "I want to live. I will return and butcher these traitorous hatchlings before burning their ancestral homes. I will savit on their graves and drink wine from their skulls."

Yeah, this was a wonderful guy we were rescuing. "It's good to have life goals. Do what I say, and you live. Fail to do so and I'll report your tragic demise."

"Understood," Eighty-Eight said, lowering his head. "As much as it pains me to submit to an inferior being—"

"Shut it," I snapped. "Let's go. Are you coming, Havelock?"

"I feel like my survival chances are slightly higher with you," Captain Havelock replied. "As much as I regret it."

We're going to need directions for the fastest evac point, Trish, I said.

You got it, Trish said. *My almighty mind reduced to serving as a map.*

I'm now sensing some frustration, I replied.

Just a wee bit, Trish said. *We can talk about it when we're safe and sound.*

Sure, I replied, not ever sure such a moment would come. I didn't like to admit it, but to quote a song Trish has played for me, war had made me bitter and mean. I didn't like the person I was becoming because of the constant moral compromises we'd been forced to make, and the galaxy seemed to be getting worse rather than better. This wasn't the Community I'd signed up to protect and it felt increasingly like there was nothing I could do to reverse the changes I could see happening within it.

Trish didn't respond as we headed down the empty hallways of the Spy's Demise's backrooms. The customers had, wisely, departed and the staff were hunkered down with weapons or hoping to avoid getting themselves killed. It added a sense of the eerie as we found ourselves departing into the alleyway behind the place.

The Ring was an impressive site to gaze upon from any part of its surface. A single long loop that was the size of a mid-sized country that

15

stretched outward and then rose to form a ribbon across the sky. The stars were visible to each side of the ribbon while ambient light was provided by an unknown source that illuminated the city we were presently located in. The ring had its own eco-system with mountains, valleys, deserts, and jungles that were dotted by dozens of small fortress cities.

It was unknown what race had constructed the Ring, though it stood to reason it was probably one of the Elder Races. The place had been uninhabited when the Community had arrived a thousand years ago, and they'd kept a consistent set of rules to prevent its unique artificial ecology from being destroyed. Now, the current Speaker of the Community was arguing for dramatic rollbacks of said protections to allow more settlement on the Ring's surface. It wasn't even for a reason like resettling more refugees. It was a belief that more financial benefit could be derived if it was reduced to being just another space station port. We were better than this.

Vance? Trish asked.

Yeah? I said, looking for our transport.

Shut up, Trish said. *Focus on escaping. Oh, and baddies, twelve o'clock.*

"There they are! Blast them!" The leader of a second group of Sorkanan Death Commandos shouted as it came around the other side of the alleyway. He was speaking in their harsh guttural tongue, but my cybernetics automatically translated everything, I'd upgraded the ones I'd replaced the translator for considerably in recent years, Elder Race technology replacing the previous enhancements I'd had as well as portions of my brain. Lovely.

I shot first and took him down as more fire was exchanged while we fled down the streets. It became a fighting retreat and navigating Ring City Thirteen while trying to get ourselves some transportation. The Death Commandos gave way to lesser grades of mercenaries and the local police that we did our best to avoid engaging. Apparently, the Ring's authorities had decided to turn over the Admiral or at least not intervene in what was less like a wetworks operation and more like an invasion now.

In the end, stealth proved our greatest asset and we used Trish's extensive mapping of the city to enter an empty toy store, head to the basement, and cut out a wall with Havelock's proton sword to reach the maglev tunnels underneath. From there, it was a straight shot toward the docking bays that we could arrange for a shuttle to pick us up from.

The tunnels were extensive, ten-story tall chambers that were filled with constantly moving trains that carried everything from cargo to passengers. They also had a crisscross network of bridges and balconies that could navigated, with difficulty, on foot. It wasn't an ideal situation, but I couldn't think of a better place to lose our pursuers in. Which, of course, was why Trish had directed us here.

"I'm not wearing the right clothes for this kind of trek," Hannah muttered. "Some underwear would be nice, for example."

"Not from my perspective," Havelock said.

"I can knock you over the side," Hannah said.

"That's a fair cop." Havelock shrugged and tapped the side of his head, causing a tiny cybernetic light to blink. "One of my people will meet us at docking bay 132B. They'll transport us to the *Ares*."

"Can they be trusted?" I asked.

"Not in the slightest," Havelock said. "But apparently the *Ares* is in a standoff with the Separatist flagship."

"Great," I muttered, having another bit of insanity to deal with.

Eighty-Eight was always in danger of falling behind, still wheezing and suffering from his injuries that only seemed to be getting worse. We didn't have time to stop and treat him, though.

Actually, we might, Trish said.

What? I asked, feeling the rush of maglev trains passing by from both directions. The noise was like a dirge from hell.

I've just received an update from command, Trish said. *They want us to execute Eighty-Eight.*

CHAPTER THREE

Morality Versus Duty is No Choice at All

Could you repeat that? I asked, continuing to move down the scaffolding of the vast tunnel and making no effort to murder Eighty-Eight despite the fact I'd just been ordered to by parties unknown. The wind kept blowing against my face and my ears rang from the sounds of maglev trains passing every half minute. The place was dark and the air stale, adding a greater sense of danger to our travel even as I expected more troops to pour out from where we earlier left. *I didn't get that order. Were you speaking in code, Trish?*

Vance, I don't think you're stupid enough not to get my meaning the first time, Trish said. *Which puts you above ninety-nine percent of all biologicals who are technically my superiors.*

I was noticing a lot more salt from Trish lately and wondered if that was a response to my own increasing bad attitude.

I'm not going to execute a prisoner.

He's not a prisoner, Trish said. *He's a war criminal that we've given sanctuary to. One from whom we are now revoking said sanctuary and could solve by dumping him over the side of the railing.*

Be that as it may, I said, mentally capitalizing every one of my letters. *He is now under my protection until the time I hand him over to the proper authorities.*

Vance, we are the proper authorities, Trish said. *Also, you've received orders to carry this out.*

Screw orders, I said. *I am no man's assassin.*

You've carried out three assassinations on behalf of the Security Divisions, not to mention all the actual military strikes you've done during the Kolahn Wars as well as anti-Notha peacekeeping. That brings it up to close to—

I'm not doing it, I snapped. *My honor is not for sale, even if it's stupid. Even if he deserves to be killed. I made a promise and bork anyone who wants me to break it. He is safe until someone else takes him from me and then he is their problem. I'll turn him over to the Separatists before I shoot him for convenience's sake. You can report me if you want.*

Trish didn't respond for a second, an eternity in the life of an AI. *It's good to have you back, Vance.*

I didn't know I'd been away, but the fact I no longer cared about what the Security Divisions did to me felt strangely liberating. I hadn't felt this energized since before Shelly and I, well, never mind that.

"Are you okay, Vance?" Hannah asked as we continued our trek.

"Yes," I lied. "I'm perfectly fine."

Eighty-Eight stared at me with his cold, reptilian eyes, which wasn't so much of a descriptor as a redundancy. It made me long for my companion, Forty-Two, and wish he hadn't gone on to do bigger and better things. That was a selfish wish, though, and one that I regretted thinking almost immediately.

Instead, standing on the balcony overlooking the vast maglev pit below, I just met his gaze and caused him to back down. Eighty-Eight had to know his life was in danger and I was the only person here who gave a crap whether he lived or died.

"You don't even know... why I was being bribed, do you?" Eighty-Eight asked, sounding like he was going to keel over at any moment.

"To prevent a massacre of the Kolahn refugees on your borders," I replied, looking for a cargo or transport drone. They were used by the maintenance workers down here and were something I could easily hack. Going on foot wasn't going to be useful, especially if our pursuers found the hole in the wall that we'd left behind in the toy store basement.

"Ha!" Eighty-Eight said, coughing. "As if the Security Services would care about a punch of penniless lizard-apes. No, it is much more important."

"You can take it up with them when we get you to safety." I was tempted to point out they clearly didn't care that much if they'd sent us an order to kill him.

Yeah, there's something funny about that, Trish replied, surprising me. *We've been cut off from the ship.*

I thought you were the ship, I replied.

I am, Trish said. *Hence why it's important. The last sort of orders came from a different encryption source as well.*

What? You think someone separate from Director Gordon sent them? I asked, referring to the head of EarthGov's intelligence services and my direct supervisor. He was also Trish's father, in a manner of speaking, or at least a bioroid that has raised the woman she was based on.

Yes, Trish said. *No one else is supposed to know about this meeting and we've already got a planetary revolution's best soldiers throwing themselves after what could charitably be called the Separatists' fifth or six most important anyxhole. Something very strange is going on here.*

No sooner had Trish pointed out this fact than once more there were Sorkanan soldiers shooting at us from the top of the scaffolding we'd managed to flee, apparently the mercenaries having already tracked us. If they'd been smart, then they would have waited to point and fire, but these ragtag revolutionaries weren't the best of the best. Hell, we'd already killed the Death Commandos that supposedly were.

Exchanging fire with them, Captain Havelock almost casually and conversationally said, "I've killed only thirteen people as a pirate despite literally thousands of boardings. I think I've killed almost that many on this trip."

"You must be very proud of your mostly murder-free life," I said, shooting one of the Sorkanan soldiers and causing him to fall over the scaffolding into the maglev tunnel. I swear he made a Wilhelm Scream.

"I am!" Havelock said. "Yo ho, yo ho, a pirate's life for me!"

We managed to deal with the latest of this group, but I was sure more would come, including local officials and I didn't want to explain why we'd ended up killing a bunch of law enforcement officials. Not that I would. There were lengths I was willing to go to in order to protect Eighty-Eight, but killing cops wasn't one of them.

You might not need to, Trish replied. *I think I've found an alternative to just hoofing it.*

Before I could ask what she meant, an automated maglev passenger train slowed down and pulled to a stop beside us before the doors slid open. Exchanging a look with Hannah and Captain Havelock, we stepped onto the train with Eighty-Eight in tow.

The passengers inside the train looked at the Community captain, space pirate, exotic dancer, and wounded admiral lizard with confusion.

"We're doing a Live Action Roleplaying Game," I replied. "Does anyone else game?"

No one apparently did and they all went back to whatever they were going as the train pulled forward.

You sure this is going to work, Trish? I asked, feeling the maglev start up again and barrel down the tunnel.

I've talked with the Ring's AI and it's doing me a solid, Trish replied. *All the police and security forces are going one way while we're going another. I've also started jamming the remaining Separatist comms. We should be good to evacuate once we get to Havelock's people. Presuming he can be trusted.*

Can he? I asked.

No, Trish said. *At least regarding Eighty-Eight. Havelock's made numerous calls to the Separatists as well as done research on to how much of a reward is being offered for Eighty-Eight, alive or dead.*

I made a mental note of that. *Do you think the admiral was telling the truth?*

That he's carrying vital information that he's willing to trade to the Security Divisions in exchange for vast amounts of cash? Probably. However, Director Gordon isn't the type to disregard refugees either. He uses the system to help people, like the Community should.

You admire him, I replied.

He's my dad, Trish said. *I admire him like I admire you.*

That's a weird thing to say to someone you've had sex with, I replied.

Hey, you're the one who doesn't take me up on the offer, Trish paused. *My door and bioroid body are always open. There are all sorts of positions we haven't tried.*

Right, changing subject. I thought about how I'd broken up with Trish to be with Shelly. It had been the most difficult decision of my life, but I'd thought Trish had deserved better than to be anyone's second choice.

I'm not anyone's second choice, Vance, Trish said, simply. *It's just you chose wrong and know it.*

I responded by shutting Trish out from my thoughts and instead focusing on our mission. We could communicate via my standard cybernetics. Either way, we arrived at docking bay 132 fast enough. There were a lot of alarms going off and people rushing around, which made our departure seem less of an issue even if we couldn't be more conspicuous if we were dressed as a glam star metal band.

What's going on? I asked Trish.

Trish, not acknowledging I'd shut her out of my thoughts, answered, *Oh, just fire and rabid insect infestation. Maybe some broken quarantines. Stuff to distract the public. I've also jammed all the interior cameras. You have a straight shot to docking bay B or as they say in Sorkanan, Growl-Growl-Gnash-Growl-Hiss.*

Whatever would I do without you, Trish? I asked.

Die, Trish said. *But it's okay because I would romantically delete myself soon after.*

Crossing the line into creepy again, Trish, I replied.

Sorry! Trish said. *But I only mean the copy of me that lives in your head! My other selves' digital hearts would go on!*

Uh-huh, I replied, walking off the maglev train and heading to our evac point. I doubted we would be welcome on the Ring after this. Which was a shame as I'd barely begun to plum the station's mysteries.

"My Heart Will Go On" is a reference to the theme song of the 1997 movie Titanic, *which is a romance made about a famous ship sinking in 1912.*

Uh huh, I replied.

I can show you the movie when we get back to the ship, Trish said.

No, Trish, I replied.

Come on, it's all pretty and tragic! It also has nudity, Trish said. *Well, of the female kind. Movies of the period were markedly biased toward one gender—*

Trish, please, I interrupted. *Focus on the mission.*

The mission is over, Vance, Trish said as she directed me down a hallway and I found myself at docking bay 132B. It turned out our destination was almost immediately outside the tram station.

"Huh," I muttered. "That was anticlimactic."

The interior of the docking bay had a single tri-winged shuttle, beaten and covered in graffiti, with a group of a half-dozen star pirates. It's a bit stereotypical to say star pirates dressed a certain way, but these looked like refugees from central casting for the next *Raiders of the Void* movie. They were wearing ramshackle gear from a dozen sources, heavily armed, tattooed, and each possessed of the same sort of proton sword Captain Havelock was sporting.

They make good torches for cutting through walls, Trish pointed out. *As you well know.*

Captain Havelock walked up to greet them, and they immediately raised their weapons at us, causing me to stop in mid-step.

"Come on, say the line," Havelock said.

I stared at him. "Line?"

"Everyone knows you're the sci-fi guy," Captain Havelock said. "Surely there's some appropriate one-liner from a hundred or two-hundred-year-old movie for this situation."

I sighed.

"Curse your sudden but inevitable betrayal."

Is this what my life had become? That I was so famous for being a wise-cracking space hero that I was reduced to reciting lines from shows that hadn't been that popular since before humans had received space travel technology from alien visitors? It almost made me regret taking all those courses in Pre-First Contact science fiction.

Captain Havelock pumped his fist and gave me a thumbs up. "There it is! I have no idea what that is from, but it sounds cool."

Hannah, who was now all but carrying Eighty-Eight, looked up. "Havelock, what the bork is going on?"

"He's made a better deal," I responded. "How much are the Separatists offering?"

"About two hundred thousand," Captain Havelock said. "It's far less than Eighty-Eight is worth anymore and I'm pretty sure they won't pay it."

I stared at him. "I don't suppose you'd be willing to accept my guarantee that I'd pay equal to that."

"One in the hand is worth two in the bush," Captain Havelock said. "Though don't take it personally, Vance, I would actually take your word for it. Now put your guns on the ground and hand him over."

That wasn't going to happen. I wasn't sure how I was going to be able to take them on, but I'd come too far to back down now.

"Dead or alive?" Hannah asked.

"What?" I asked, Hannah.

"Either," Captain Havelock replied.

Hannah grabbed Eighty-Eight's neck and twisted the surprised Sorkanan until there was a horrifying snap sound. Eighty-Eight's body dropped to the ground, and everyone was left with a surprised expression except her.

"Why?" I asked.

"Because you were going to stupidly resist them to protect a psychopathic war criminal," Hannah said. "Because that's who you are, Vance."

"Not necessarily," I replied.

Captain Havelock's goons looked uncertain about what to do before he sighed. "Well, not how I would like this resolved but better than the alternative. Load the body up, boys, and let's get out of here. I'll happily give you a lift, Captain Turbo. I trust there're no hard feelings."

"None," I said, lying through my teeth. "But I need to check the body first."

"Sure," Captain Havelock muttered, uncaring.

Vance, what are you hoping to find? Trish asked as I walked to the body, ignoring Hannah as I tried to figure out whether I was furious at her or just tired of being unable to navigate the right path.

If he had any information on him, I replied. *A data storage unit or something.*

Surely, even Eighty-Eight isn't so stupid to— Trish started to say.

I found a data crystal hidden in his pocket. It was a large one and contained probably enough to house an entire starship computer's worth of files.

I think I found it.

Well, call me a monkey's uncle, Trish said.

I have no idea what that means, I replied.

Neither do I, Trish said. *However, it's better than admitting I was wrong. Still, I wouldn't want to guess how hard it'd be for the encryption to be cracked. Some encryption takes the entire history of the universe to brute force—*

I got it, I said, accessing the data crystal's files. There were too many to go through immediately, but it was apparently military and corporate files relating to the Separatists as well as their arms trafficking. Something a lot more complicated than standard under-the-table deals to a rogue state.

How? Trish asked.

He used the corporate encryption program bought from Ares Electronics for forty credits online, I replied. *I have the mass-produced key.*

And there goes any lingering respect I had for the late, unlamented Eighty-Eight, Trish said. *Pick up that Cardinal's soul and his bag of stolen goodies. You can pay off Havelock and an asteroid habitat over Earth.*

I must return any money I acquire on the job, I replied. *It's only honest.*

Who are you, Lincoln?

CHAPTER FOUR

Standoff by the Ring

Captain Havelock piloted the shuttle with one of his crew while I stood there behind them, holding a loop attached to the wall to steady myself. Artificial gravity wasn't present on anything but the most advanced Community vessels but when starships moved, the thrust generated the same effect toward the source of the engines that most sensible engineers put toward the 'bottom' of the vessel in relation to the crew.

"Are you sure you want to have him with us, sir?" the co-pilot asked. She was a lovely pink-haired woman with a long scar on the right side of her face.

"Are you sure you want a man with one eye piloting the ship?" I asked her.

Captain Havelock laughed. "Behind this eyepatch is a complicated sensor web, son. Why do you think I always bullseye every target I get?"

"Dumb luck," I responded, not happy about how this mission turned out.

"You can trust him, Pink," Captain Havelock said. "He gunned down Big Bobo at the first excuse."

Pink blinked then went back to work. "Interesting."

"A peculiar character endorsement," I replied.

"A civilized man would come up with a dozen excuses as to why to keep Big Bobo alive," Captain Havelock said. "His usefulness, power vacuums, and the nebulous rule of law. A good man would gun him down because he was a monster. Eighty-Eight too."

"And yet you were involved in all of this," I replied.

"Pirates have historically cultivated good ties with the most powerful nations of their time. Look at Sir Francis Drake," Captain Havelock said. "Pirate and yet the single most famous sailor in all of English history."

"Also, a slaver and scumbag," I replied.

"But he died respected and rich, which is my actual point," Captain Havelock said. "Besides, you're the Navy man in all of this. So, what does that make you?"

I didn't respond because my attention was on the shuttle's sensors. They showed a readout of the Ring, surrounding ships, and two ships that were presently engaged in a standoff with roughly equal weaponry. Which, if you knew anything about military weaponry, was the absolute worst sort of engagement you could enter. After all, if you were hopelessly outgunned, you at least knew to retreat or surrender.

The first of the vessels was a long rectangular vessel with a cylindrical nacelle that vaguely reminded me of a sniper's scope. This was a Sorkanan Separatist frigate, one of the many decommissioned warships of their Imperial Navy that had been sold to their allies only to end up in the hands of enemies after two or three trades. It was quite possibly over two hundred years old and had probably been refurbished two or three times in its history.

The age of the ship should have been reassuring but the Sorkanan Navy were a bit like the ancient Greeks or Detroit automakers, they built things to last. The hull was bristling with modern weapons and the barrier registered as having comparable power to our own. Another sign that any engagement would be too close to call.

"My Sorkanan is a little rusty," I said, wanting to engage my pilots. "What's the ship called?"

"*The Glorious Fist of the People's Freedom*," Pink said. "Because that doesn't say tyrannical communist dictatorship."

"Now, now, we can't judge the political movements of other races by the standards of our own," Captain Havelock said. "Even if the Separatists are a tyrannical communist dictatorship."

27

Technically, they're not communists, Trish said. *They're followers of a Sorkanan-created socio-political system called equalism. It's like communism, only with more rhetoric about egg-eating and disputes about terraforming.*

Thank you, Trish, I replied, rolling my eyes before addressing the pair in front of me. "The Separatists have been overthrown. Admiral Eighty-Eight's people have thrown their lot in with the new government."

"Oh!" Captain Havelock said. "Would have been nice to know that. What's the new government's platform?"

"Apparently, kill the old guard and their family," I replied. "Always a good sign."

The New People's Liberation Council believes the Separatists didn't go far enough in purging reactionary counter-revolutionary forces, Trish said.

What does that mean? I asked.

I wouldn't buy a house in Separatist territories for the next few decades, Trish said. *There's already a counter-counter revolution going on according to news broadcasts. It looks to be civil war with a chance of rain for a while. Every faction the Community kept from killing each other are now, well, killing each other.*

Praise be to equalism, I replied.

Now it's the Equalists versus the New Equalists versus the Reform Equalists and the Democratic Republicans, Trish said. *Those latter guys are terrifying.*

"Can we get past the *Glorious Fisting of the People*?" I asked, wishing I was literally anywhere else.

Pink sniggered. "Good one."

"No, we can't get past them without taking fire," Captain Havelock said. "Which I'd rather avoid. I'm transmitting Eighty-Eight is dead and we're happy to turn over the body."

"Contact my ship, please," I asked, adding the please out of deference to the fact I wasn't captain here, Havelock was.

"Will do," Captain Havelock said before conjuring up an image of my ship.

The half-kilometer long *Olympic*-Class vessel had a saucer-shaped bridge and larger blocky-esque body with large jumpspace boosters on its side. It had started as one of EarthGov's crowning achievements in starship design, but in the ensuing decades of its service it had gone from being a dreadnought to barely qualifying as a battleship. It had been refurbished for the mission to Contested Space but after my fall from grace, it had been rotated out of gladhanding to a secondary diplomatic role—which meant it was an errand ship and I sometimes felt like the ship was irritated with me over that.

No, I was irritated with you constantly moping over yourself, Trish said.

I thought I blocked my thoughts, I replied.

It's not hard to pick up your emotional cues when they range from brooding to sad sack, Trish replied. *Trying to protect Eighty-Eight is the first time you've felt like you in a while.*

And look how that worked out, I muttered.

Don't retreat into your shell, Vance, Trish said, almost pleading. *Please.*

I lowered my thought protections. "Please tell them I'm onboard and we're ready to disembark. Also, not to engage the Separatist—"

"We're getting a response from the *Glorious Fist*," Pink said, shortening the Separatist vessel's name.

A holographic image of a Sorkanan captain appeared on the other side, growling, and drooling as he shouted a speech that I only picked up half of due to the malfunctioning connection.

"What was that?" I asked.

Captain Havelock frowned. "He said that we had defiled the sacred body of a heroic champion of the people and must pay the ultimate penalty for it."

"This isn't about the revolution," I said, jumping to conclusions but feeling it in my gut. "They've been coerced into trying to suppress whatever Eighty-Eight was carrying."

"Can't we just give it to him?" Pink asked.

"The only way for three people to keep a secret is if two are dead, dear," Captain Havelock said, frowning. "It looks like we're committed to delivering Captain Turbo and his companion safely to the *Ares*."

"I'm so glad you weren't committed before," I replied.

"I have a name, dipsavit!" Hannah called from the back of the shuttle.

"I admit I wasn't paying attention to anything you said in that outfit," Captain Havelock called back. "And the *Glorious Fist* is launching starfighters. Great."

"Starfighters," I muttered. "I hate starfighters."

Starfighters were one of those bad ideas that had infested military doctrine from the moment humanity had achieved jumpspace travel and just would not leave. When Earth had joined the Community, it had brought two radical ideas into the mainstream of interstellar affairs: unrestricted use of AI and starfighters. One of these was a game changing source of power that had meant Earth had at least something to contribute to their fellow interstellar humans, let alone the rest of the Community. After all, if we were willing to risk the catastrophic dangers of AI research then so much the better for everyone else.

Starfighters, though? Starfighters were a bad idea and humans just couldn't let it go. In simple terms, aircraft were a great idea but only in atmosphere. Space was just too big and human reflexes too poor to make it practical. Anything you could accomplish with a starfighter, you could accomplish with drones or missiles. I was a firm believer that a starfighter was essentially an armed shuttle and you'd do better building bigger as well as better-shielded capital ships. Yet, here I was, face to face with aliens using them now. The bad idea had spread, and I was going to die at its hands.

"I don't suppose you have any ideas," I said, frowning.

"You're the tactical genius, Space Hero!" Captain Havelock responded, attempting to make a hard angle toward the *Ares*. I had to grab hold of the loop and wished I was strapped in as the gravity center shifted around the ship.

"That's *Hero of Space!*" I snapped. "Overclock the engines, asked for the *Ares* to intercept and extend their barrier around us as soon as they're close. Tell the acting captain they have full permission to engage the enemy."

"I think that order will be more likely to be okayed coming from you," Pink said, frantically tapping the controls and activating every defense system she could.

"I'm not talking to you," I said, having been discussing the issue with Trish. "I don't suppose this shuttle has any special modifications?"

"This isn't a movie," Captain Havelock said, sighing. "We acquired this from a Community naval base and that's better than any of our mechanics can accomplish."

Transmitted, Trish responded. *Good news and bad news, situation. I lied. There's no good news. We must survive at least one a barrage of missiles and lasers before we get to the* Ares. *Problem being that we can't survive one barrage of missiles and lasers.*

I had one last ace up my sleeve, which was more than I'd packed for that crooked card game that I'd wasted a month studying the rules of. In addition to the Elder Ring, I had spectacular skills at hacking (well, a lot of programs that were spectacular at hacking) as well as Trish to help me out. Elder technology had been known to be able to slice through regular military encryption like it was nonexistent.

I'd used this option only a few times in my life because taking control over an enemy's weaponry was something that had the potential of exposing my "tricks" to the rest of the world. The Elder Races had a policy of destroying every single species that tried to study their technology. Not person, species. I had "permission" as one of their semi-voluntary agents, but I knew plenty of people would have blindly risked the human race. However, now seemed to be a good time to try it out and hope no one noticed since I could see a dozen missiles being launched from the six starfighters descending on our position. Unfortunately, it didn't work. I couldn't "feel" the missiles or their systems.

The autotargeting is a closed system, Trish thought. *They're not designed to receive any new data, just continue to follow their targets to the end. They can't even be recalled or self-destructed. Great Robot Buddha Christ, we're going to be killed because Separatist missiles are complete garbage!*

How long until impact? I asked, not liking our chances.

Sixty seconds, Trish responded. *Vance, even if the* Ares *gets into range, which it isn't going to, I wouldn't be able to shoot down all of them with the precision needed.*

31

I had another thought about how we could proceed but it was a stupid idea. *I can try and cover us with the ring.*

Vance, there's a difference between protecting against an improvised explosive device, and rockets that contain megatons.

No different, the only difference is in your mind, I said. Elder technology wasn't so much more advanced than Community technology than existing on an entirely different plane of existence. I had to believe it could handle this because I'd rather die with hope that I could pull off a miracle than die helpless at the hands of a bunch of pseudo-communist nutjobs.

That's from a movie! Trish said. *Also, equalist, not communist. Forty-Five seconds!*

Merge with me, I said.

What? Trish asked.

The only way we can do this is together, I said, trusting Trish right now more than anyone else in the universe because, well, I didn't have a choice. I lowered my defenses and let her join with me and have full access to the Elder Race technology through me. If the two of us couldn't pull off a miracle now, then we would probably not feel it when we were incinerated.

The experience wasn't something that could be put into words, but I'll try my best. It was like becoming transcendental math. I had never had a religious experience despite being a holiday Zen Christian, but there was little else I could use to describe the sense of becoming one with the infinite, of understanding what purpose the universe really had, and how it all connected. It made me feel disgusted with all those people who assumed we were on the cusp of a robot revolution or genocide at the hands of AI because any being who felt so much about how things truly were could never be evil.

Oh Vance, that's what I love about you, Trish spoke. *You're so painfully naive.*

Almost immediately, I felt my body seize up as Trish struggled to channel the energies within the Elder Ring. It was a keystone connection to an infinite power that made my ship's AI a tiny spec of stardust in an infinite universe. I could only see the barest outlines of it, but the Elder Races had an infinite majestic universe within their databanks that baffled the imagination to glimpse. I could only comprehend the edges of it thanks to being linked to Trish, but it was enough to make me completely forgot I was about to die.

Right up until Trish shouted for the Elder Ring to do a single command, *MOVE.*

Everything suddenly jerked from out beneath us, and I felt my body spin around as the engine shut down inside the shuttle. Havelock, Pink, and I were disorientated as well as confused while strange lights flashed within the cockpit as well as outside of it. I could see the *Ares* right outside and had to rush for the controls to keep us from crashing into it. We were underneath my ship's barrier now, though.

I thought we were going to create a barrier against the missiles! I said to Trish.

I remembered we could teleport. So, I improvised!

Yeah, because that's not going to be noticed, I said, wondering how I was going to explain this.

I'd worry more about the fact the Glorious Fist *is moving around to attack,* Trish replied.

What? Are they insane? I asked, pulling the shuttle to a halt underneath the *Ares'* defensive screens. I turned over command to Trish before Havelock could override me, moving the shuttle's command onto autopilot and working with the *Ares'* controls for automatic docking. True to Trish's observation, the *Glorious Fist* had turned around to engage the *Ares*. It began a barrage of fusion cannons and its own missiles.

It was exactly the kind of broadside-to-broadside firefight that every naval doctrine in the galaxy made sure to drill out of its lieutenants. The fact they were willing to risk it was another sign of just how incompetent or zealous the Separatist crew was. Either that or terrified of their captain. The starfighters attempted to follow us past the *Ares'* barriers but were easily shot down along with their remaining missiles, highlighting just how badly outmatched they were against real ships.

I don't think well-rationalized decisions are their primary concern, Trish replied. *Whoever wants to suppress that data clearly is paying a very high price for it. Thankfully, the calvary has arrived.*

33

What do you mean? I asked.

Checking the sensors as Havelock glared at me for seizing control of the ship, I saw another ship had entered the Ring's system. It was a *Valhalla*-Class cruiser, looking like a pie-saucer with a pair of four jump drive boosters as well as a central cylinder between them.

It was a full kilometer long and fulfilled all the functions the *Ares* had been designed to but with state-of-the-art technology as well as significantly more powerful weapons banks and barrier generators.

Also, my grief.

It was the *ESS Elgan*, named after my traitorous piece of crap former commander who had been buried with honors due to a cover-up. I was less concerned about its namesake, though, than its commander.

It was Shelly's ship.

CHAPTER FIVE

Regrets and Losses

The battle against the *Glorious Fist* went on for another half hour despite the fact it was woefully outgunned by the *Elgan*, let alone the *Elgan* and the *Ares*. By the time its barriers went down and most of its guns were destroyed, we were ready to offer it terms of surrender. The captain just cursed and said he would fight to the bitter end. Five minutes later, he was dead and his second in command offered his surrender.

The irony was that our terms were just to let the ship limp back home to the Separatists since a state of war didn't exist between the Community or EarthGov and their new government. Rather than a glorious victory, I considered it a senseless waste of life. Especially since it was over the late Admiral Eighty-Eight and whatever he was carrying that I'd transferred to Trish's databanks upon arrival on the *Ares*.

Standing on the bridge, I stared at the viewscreen and took in Shelly T'Ketra's form as she sat in the captain's chair across from me. We were separated by several planet's worth of distance, but it is the closest we'd come since that night at Space Academy's Hawaiian campus.

It had been close to midnight and the two of us had just finished a lecture on the fall of the Notha Empire. It was less than a year after the treaties had been signed and the dissolution of the Contested Zone. Tensions were still high, and the Homefront Entertainment Network had crucified me for the concessions I'd given the Notha as part of the team. Never mind the fact I had simply been carrying out the will of my government and been part of a five-thousand-man team. Reception at Space Academy hadn't been all that hot either, many of the cadets were eager to ask me questions that were designed to make me look like a fool. Or, they'd been full-veiled or not-so-veiled insults.

Still, it had been a beautiful evening with the moon high in the sky and the stars visible thanks to the distance of the cities. The two of us had the boardwalk leading to the artificial lake to ourselves. Both of us were dressed in civilian attire. I was wearing a jacket over a t-shirt, and pants, while she was wearing a heavy trench coat and scarf that was incongruous for Hawaii even in the winter. I knew Shelly was heading back to Canada tonight on the next shuttle, though, to visit with some friends from her childhood. I hoped she would change her mind after I spoke my mind.

Shelly was a beautiful Ethereal woman, basically a space elf, with golden skin and white-blonde hair. She was the adopted daughter of Ketra T'Kal, the former ambassador to Earth, and one of the few members of her race who didn't have a holier than thou otherworldly quality. Ethereals were the descendants of humans (and other races) taken from their world to be modified then used as ambassadors by the Elder Races. They were immortal, super-smart, and strong, but also stuck playing middlemen between mortals and gods. Shelly just wanted to be the best officer she could be.

"I've had friendlier welcomes from the Notha," I said, hoping to break the ice.

"Yes, well the only thing people love more than a hero is tearing one down," Shelly said. "I'm actually surprised I'm not carrying the brunt of the attacks."

"You're the hero of the hour, not me," I said, smiling. "Together we brought down the Notha Empire. That's not the part they hate. It's the part where I suggested we help them back up that's made me a pariah."

"It was a controversial decision," Shelly said, absently. "Military officials shouldn't take sides in politics."

I shrugged. "Out there, we have to make decisions that affect policy. We don't have the option of checking with command, let alone civilian command structures, for every interaction. Sometimes we must make choices that have lasting consequences. A Spiral where we don't have the Notha breaking down our throat is a safer one for every Community citizen, let alone the soldiers who'd have to fight them."

"Is that you talking, or one of your old sci-fi programs?" Shelly asked. "Only Nixon can go to Vulcan?"

I narrowed my eyes at her blaspheming of *Star Trek VI: The Undiscovered Country.* "You know which movie that references because I showed it to you."

Shelly snorted. "I'll be honest, I wasn't paying attention when you did. The things we do for love."

"Yeah," I replied. "Which is what I wanted to talk to you about."

Shelly nodded, having her own thoughts. "Yeah, that's what I thought. I was wondering if you'd heard."

"Heard?" I asked, reaching into my jacket pocket and grasping the box containing the ring.

"What are you talking about?" Shelly asked.

I pulled out the box. "I figured now was a good time as any."

"Ah, savit, Vance," Shelly said, looking up with a frown.

"Not the reaction I was hoping for," I muttered, feeling like I was about to be hit by a runaway cloud car.

"Oh Vance," Shelly said. "I just got the call. I'm going to be a captain."

"Oh," I said, having absolutely nothing else to say. What *was* there to say? Shelly had been serving for almost eighty years in the EarthGov branch of Space Fleet. She'd seen dozens, if not hundreds, of less qualified officers ascend through the ranks past her to the rank of captain.

Why? In part, it had been xenophobia. The Ethereals were not trusted even if they were born in Canada and had no allegiance to the Elder Races. Her "stickler for the rules" personality hadn't helped as she constantly alienated possible allies and political connections. EarthGov was a bottom of the Community pyramid and playing it safe was not rewarded to those who had higher ambitions. There had also been periods when she'd tried to make a go in other occupations, aware she was disliked by her superiors. There were perhaps other reasons, too—I'd never bothered looking at her record—but I'd known she'd always wanted her own command. My being promoted past her was something she'd held against me for a while.

"It was fun while it lasted," Shelly said, putting her hand on my shoulder.

I pulled away. "Not even going to try to make it work?"

I was less cordial than I should have been but ripping the Band-Aid off quickly was not always the best option.

"We're both captains," Shelly said, sighing. "Your crew loves you. You have great things ahead of you. You shouldn't derail that. I've been waiting for this for a long time. I'm sorry, but I can't pass that up for anything. You'll find someone—"

"Thank you for finishing this entire conversation without me," I said, hurling the ring box in the lake. "Goodbye, Shelly."

Shelly looked at where I'd thrown it. "Okay, that was just wasteful."

I stared at the ripples in the water. "Yeah, it was. That belonged to my Aunt Kathy. I'm going to have go swim for it."

Okay, that last part hadn't happened, but I wish it had. I didn't think about going after it until the next day and got a nasty cold from swimming in what apparently was quite contaminated water.

"Vance?" Shelly spoke, frowning. My thoughts returned to the present.

"I'm sorry, I zoned out there for a second," I replied.

My bridge crew looked embarrassed by this, as well they should, since you didn't zone out during the aftermath of a battle report. Well, not if you ever wanted your career to go anywhere other than down the commode, but I think that starship had launched.

Shelly hadn't changed in the past three years and was wearing a crisp white uniform that matched my own. Unlike me, she chose to wear her various medals and it made her look like a (former) Contested Space dictator. I wasn't about to criticize her fashion choices, though, especially when just looking at her was painful.

Standing by my side was Commander Julius Something who had rocketed past other more qualified candidates thanks to his heroism in the battle against the Notha Emperor. He was a tall, handsome, well-built black man with a crew cut, who always had a smile on his face.

There were rumors he would be promoted after this, and I had to wonder if they were looking for the next poster boy for the fleet now that I'd fallen out of favor. I didn't begrudge him that and had even seen *The Death of the Emperor* holo they'd made about events where I was barely a footnote.

At the helm was Lt. Commander Leslie Park, a lovely, blue-skinned, black-haired woman who had signed up to learn from my command style. She had done every bit as much as Julius during the aforementioned battle but had made the mistake of speaking up for me several times. As such, her career had stalled as well. I didn't know how I could make that right, but I planned to, even if it meant transferring her off the ship to a better post.

Hannah was now out of her green makeup and dressed in a red, form-hugging bodysuit that was supposed to be unisex but seemed more, well, snug on her. She'd finally taken a formal commission with Space Fleet and was serving as chief of security. Forty-Two had moved on to join Special Operations and I hadn't seen him in years. Somewhere around here, probably, was my cousin Danny that, I savit you not, had the power of invisibility or something so close to it as to not matter. Other members of the bridge crew had moved on, switched jobs, or even left Space Fleet.

It'd become a bit of a revolving door and I wasn't even fully sure of this latest rotation of associates. There was a Kolahn, a Sorkanan female, and a set of human female triplets that I was pretty sure were clones from Crius. The refurbished hotel-like bridge with its fine carpet and inviting atmosphere had also once more fallen into disrepair. We were still running diplomatic missions, but no one particularly cared to keep everything spic and span anymore now that they were of the decidedly disreputable sort.

"Of course," Shelly said, not chiding me. "What I was saying was that the engagement went very well. We report zero casualties on our side. How about you?"

"Two minor injuries," Hannah answered for me. "I banged my head when Havelock's shuttle did its microjump and an ensign broke his ankle trying to jump over a balcony to get to his station faster."

Ah, yes, the microjump that was the story we were going with to explain away why the shuttle teleported. This despite the fact such a thing was insanely risky and almost impossible even with an AI onboard. I'd insisted on Havelock getting twice his fee in exchange for "extracting" the data from his shuttle to wipe it.

I had no idea if he suspected the truth or not, but it didn't matter if the evidence was gone. I would have to do the same to the *Ares'* records despite the fact it disgusted me to alter official material. The risk to humanity was simply too great. Unfortunately, there was nothing to do about the Ring or *Fist of Glory's* records, but that was the nature of the beast. I couldn't risk involving the Security Divisions because if you involved their agents to change a lightbulb, you'd end up with a land war on Belenus. Which was a lot funnier joke when I wasn't one of their agents.

"I hope you reprimanded the injured crew member for his stupidity," Shelly said, showing her usual heart.

"I think he got the message," I replied. "Do we have a list of casualties from the Separatist vessel?"

"They aren't sharing factoids but its suspected close to a hundred and fifty individuals died due at atmosphere ventilation and the vaporizing of corridors," Shelly replied. "None of that matters now, because I understand the New Separatists are denying this encounter ever took place."

"New Separatists?" I asked.

"They're not very original in their name," Shelly said. "They're also claiming Admiral Eighty-Eight died heroically resisting Community imperialism and was assassinated because of his support of the revolution."

Typical equalists. Not that I knew many, but I was guessing this was not new behavior from them.

"Uh huh," I asked, pinching the bridge of my nose to ward off a migraine. "What's the official word from EarthGov?"

"Somehow you must have agitated the situation," Shelly said, almost apologetically. "There's going to be a formal inquiry."

"Of course there is," I replied, dryly. Someone was determined to see me cashiered and the nature of political assassination was that you never let up. No matter how outrageous the charge, no matter how ridiculous, you just continued throwing mud until either a subject quit, or enough people believed it through sheer repetition.

"I'll of course enter into the record that you have my every confidence," Shelly said.

"Admiral Eighty-Eight and his guest both died at my hands," I replied.

"Vance—" Hannah started to say. Undoubtedly, she thought I was taking the heat for her. While that was a nice sentiment, I was also in charge of the mission. If a subordinate executed a subject under my protection to save my life, it was still my fault. Even if he was a murderer of civilians and other noncombatants.

"I gave the order to engage," I replied. "I stand by my crew's decisions."

"I see," Shelly said, nodding, as if she didn't expect anything else.

"May I ask what you were doing in the area to begin with?" I asked. "There's no way you could have gotten our distress call by the time you arrived."

Shelly blinked, smiling. "Actually, I was coming to see you."

It took only a second to note she couldn't have meant me personally but the ship. This had to be official business. I didn't know if that disappointed me or not. I wasn't the only person onboard who Shelly had severed virtually all contact with as part of her rise to captaincy. Her own sister, Elektra, was still my science officer and hadn't received so much as a Christmas card. Wait, did Ethereals celebrate Christmas? First Contact Day card.

"Do tell," I said, cheerfully. "It can't possibly make my day any worse."

Shelly grimaced. "I wouldn't count on that."

Hannah looked at me like I'd invoked some ancient spacer's curse.

"Please go on," I replied.

"Director Gordon of the EarthGov Security Divisions asked to use our ship to ferry him to meet with you," Shelly said. "He says your business has to be conducted in person."

The head of the Security Divisions wanted to speak with me. Personally. Great.

41

"Ah," I said, softly. "That *is* worse."

CHAPTER SIX

Once is Happenstance. Twice is Coincidence. Three Times is Enemy Action.

"That evil biash!" Elektra T'Ketra said, walking beside me in the hallway toward my meeting with Director Gordon. The brown-skinned, copper-haired Ethereal was Shelly's sister and wearing a lab coat over a blue unitard like Hannah's.

Walking on the other side of me was the redheaded and beret-sporting form of Trish's bioroid body, increasingly customized and humanized with its own uniform. I noticed she'd made several "improvements" that seemed designed to be eye-catching or that might simply have been custom tailoring.

Danny was also present—thankfully noticed by me—as he continued to serve as my Yeoman despite having been revealed as a spy for the Security Divisions. Well, we were all spies nowadays, so it didn't matter. He was presently holding an infopad and trying to work out the hundred or more things that needed to be addressed after any engagement—no matter how minor.

"You're being too hard on your sister," I replied, wondering how I had become Elektra's go-to person for complaining about family. A few years ago, she'd been terrified I was a double agent of the Elder Races. Either I'd somehow won her over or being left behind when her sister was promoted to the *Elgan* had left her softening her position towards me.

"Too hard?" Elektra asked. "We don't get a First Contact Day card from her for three years and she shows up to fight our enemies, so all is forgiven?"

"Yes, pretty much," I replied.

"She broke your heart," Elektra said. "You should hate her."

"This really isn't an appropriate conversation for officers," I replied. "Also, she didn't break my heart. It was a mutual decision."

Trish snorted.

I glared at her. It was basic decency to go with your captain's lies. *Yeah, but not an ex-boyfriend's,* Trish said.

We're not... I trailed off. Were we exes? Had we even been together-together?

"Well, I hope you're not going to do anything stupid," Elektra said, staring at me.

"Stupid?" I asked. "I'm entirely over her."

Elektra snorted.

Okay, this was now annoying.

"I am."

"Yeah, since Vance broke up with Shelly, he's had nothing but cheap and tawdry relationships for the past three years," Trish said, dryly.

"That's a rather insulting way of putting it," I replied.

"Athletes, models, porn stars—" Trish counted on her fingers.

"There were no porn stars," I replied.

"You slept with the girl playing the ship's AI on the last movie version of your life," Trish said. "To which they added a huge amount of sex to make people watch it."

"Vanessa was very nice," I muttered, remembering how I'd nursed my wounded pride a bit too long. You'd have thought no one would be interested in a casual fling with a washed-up military hero and ex-celebrity, but you would wrong.

Trish rolled her eyes. "Plus, your years long on and off again thing with Hannah—"

"That doesn't sound cheap or tawdry," Danny said, cheerfully. He'd always supported me with Hannah despite the fact we'd never been exclusive. I suspected part of that was he wanted me to stop seeing Trish. Who I wasn't seeing but had access to my innermost deepest thoughts, so was hard to say wasn't an intimate relationship whether it was physical or not.

"Don't help Danny," I muttered.

"—and her wife before their divorce," Trish said, referring to a seven-foot-tall Thorian Marine with blue skin named Lisa Park. She was, despite her name, not related to Leslie Park aside from being from the same demihuman race.

Elektra stared at me and raised her hand well above her head, indicating a woman over six and a half feet in height. "*That* Lisa Park? The blue Space Marine?"

Danny blinked then looked at me then Trish. "Okay, now it just sounds like she's making this up. Did you pay her to say this?"

"Pfft, like he could afford my costs to lie," Trish said, grouchy.

"Oh my," Elektra said. "How are you not *dead*? Both have significant biological enhancements. Things should have broken. Important things to a human male!"

"My sex life is none of your business. Either of you," I replied, wondering when I lost control of this conversation. "Now if we could focus—"

"I'm just saying that maybe you wouldn't be the broken down, emotionally spent, mess of a man if you'd kept to the love of your life," Trish said, spreading her hands out. "The *Ares*."

"Which is you," I replied.

"I meant that metaphorically," Trish said. "But also literally."

Danny pointed at me. "This is why you're not popular anymore. Robosexuality is still very controversial. Even if you're just biological/mechanical. People assume you're just one way or the other."

"No one likes a needy starship, Trish," Elektra said. "Especially when there's someone right beside you who may love you every bit as much as your ex who doesn't know what they're missing. Someone who I am not going to name but is me."

Danny and I looked at Elektra.

"What?" Elektra asked. "I have needs too!"

"And thank Buddha Christ we are here," I said, coming up to the doors to the VIP guest quarters. It had two Space Marines guarding it.

"I'm sorry, Elektra," Trish said. "But I only like you as a passenger."

"Let me in please," I said to the Marines. "Either that or kill me."

Thankfully, they opened the door, but I would have accepted the latter. The Marines also kept my accompaniment from following me in. Danny, of course, did follow me in as he was Director Gordon's direct agent and hand. It was also possible the Space Marines didn't notice him since that was his power and he'd gotten slightly better at controlling it. Even so, it was still too erratic to ever use in missions save as a last resort.

If the *ESS Ares* had originally looked like a hotel, the VIP quarters were the penthouse. There was a fountain, small garden, more space than some houses, and luxurious, comfy furniture that you could disappear into. It also had enormous viewscreen images of space on the walls that gave it a completely artificial but quite beautiful view. Frankly, I considered it all lost on Director Gordon, who was a man I thought would be comfortable with four bare walls and a cot.

Director Case Gordon was, if you believed him, a bioroid that was over two hundred years old and created during the last decades before First Contact. Humanity had almost destroyed itself with pollution but had created AI and bots to try to save itself. I didn't know if I believed him because he seemed more advanced than the ones currently being produced, almost too human, if you could call it that. However, Trish backed up his story and had no reason to lie.

He was a tall man with mixed European and African features as well as a shaved head. He wore a black insignia-less admiral's uniform today and there was something unsettling about it. As if he was acknowledging he was a hidden power over EarthGov's portion of Space Fleet. I'd tried looking up details about him, but it had taken hours of searching to simply find his name even with my security clearance.

"You know, when they built me, I wasn't expected to last ten years," Case said, looking out the window. "Now I'm technically the oldest human being on the planet."

"Except, you're not human," I said. "Are you?"

"You know there was a time I would have found that insulting," Case said, turning to me.

"I don't find human to be a good or bad thing," I replied, walking in. "People come in all shapes and sizes."

Case smiled. "You're a child of tomorrow, Vannevar. Or perhaps tomorrow arrived and I'm still a man of yesterday."

"Hi!" Danny said, waving.

Case blinked. "I swear, Danny, it's like you're not even in the room most of the time."

"I'M ALWAYS HERE," Trish said through the ship's comms. "WHAT'S HAPPENING, DAD?"

Ah, yes, that was another oddball element of Director Gordon. He'd apparently raised Patricia Ares, the woman who founded Ares Electronics and was the basis for Trish's personality. She was long dead but cast a long shadow across the galaxy.

"You managed to retrieve the information from Admiral Eighty-Eight, I understand?" Case asked.

"You mean the information I had no idea existed and only found out about because he couldn't keep his mouth shut?" I asked, not knowing how he knew about that but suspecting Trish told him. "That information?"

"Yes," Case said, without acknowledging my sarcasm. "I was attempting to keep operational secrecy from even you."

"Why?" I asked.

"You're unpredictably idealistic," Case said, dryly. "I half expected you to publish it on the infospace or try to open an investigation."

I stared at him. "I'm grateful to you for helping my career but since my career is over due to killing Admiral Eighty-Eight, I'm going to tell you to go bork your—"

"Your career is fine," Case interrupted.

"Captain T'Ketra said that there would be an inquiry," I replied, blinking.

Case gave a dismissive wave. "You can't have an inquiry into an incident that didn't happen. Everything is officially classified and the Senators of Earth, let alone the rest of the universe, have more

47

important things than kicking you while you're down. You're yesterday's news, Vance."

"Great," I muttered. "Always glad to know you're appreciated."

Case smirked. "You can't be a famous spy, Vance. James Bond exempted. Your fall from grace gave you a lot more freedom than you could ever imagine it did. So much so, that you might save the Human League."

"I thought that was DOA," I replied. "There was no need for a larger alliance of human worlds with the end of the Notha's threat."

Case snorted at the last part of my sentence. "The Human League was wildly unpopular in certain circles and with the shift against xenophobia and pan-humanism, was never going to pass. Now they're simply making alliances and agreements without announcing them to the public. They're accomplished in secret as part of much larger bills that pass through the Senate. The Community is supporting it because it wants to quit carrying so much of the burden of advancing human worlds to galactic standards of living."

"It's events like this that make me question our democracy," I replied. "Then I decide the problem is people like you."

Case smiled. "I'm entirely in favor of democracy. I just don't think it should oversee anything important. Which is why I do my best to avoid gaining power over government. I'm exactly not the sort of person who should have power in a free society."

I had difficulty following Case's implications and just shook my head. "What do you want, Director?"

"To exorcise a terrorist organization operating within the EarthGov confines," Case replied. "One that is directly responsible for tens of thousands of deaths and is indirectly responsible for millions."

I blinked, lost my sarcasm, and paid attention. "A terrorist organization operating within EarthGov?"

"And Albion, Belenus, Brigid, and other human territories," Case replied. "It wields vast influence over numerous arms contractors, local governments, media, and more than a few intelligence assets."

"Great, I'm chasing the Illuminati," I said, now wondering if Case was chasing ghosts.

Case shook his head. "More like a rogue intelligence agency in the employ of a transtellar. I destroyed the Illuminati before First Contact."

I rolled my eyes at Case's ridiculous brag, though I wouldn't be surprised if it was true. "So, who is our foe?"

"Our foe?" Case asked.

"I've come this far," I replied. "Or are you going to tell me that I shouldn't consider the Security Division to be the good guy in this conflict?"

"I don't much care for good versus evil," Case said. "I prefer us versus them."

"*I* prefer good versus evil," I replied. "You also didn't answer my question."

"Well, this not being a cartoon, they don't have a name," Case said. "You don't actually name criminal conspiracies."

"DARK MATTER," Trish said. "BY WHICH I DON'T MEAN THE SUBSTANCE THAT MAKES UP MOST OF THE UNIVERSE BUT THE BAD GUYS IN *SPACE CADET SALLY*. ITS MY FAVORITE COMPUTER-GENERATED ART SHOW. DARK MATTER IS A BUNCH OF ICKY BAD CRIMINALS WITH NEBULOUS SUPER-POWERS AND ACCESS TO HYPER-ADVANCED TECHNOLOGY.

Case stared up at the ceiling. "Why not just name them Cobra or the Decepticons?"

I didn't get the references.

"BECAUSE THAT WOULD BE SILLY," Trish replied.

Case sighed. "Okay, *Dark Matter* is a human supremacist organization that is heavily involved in starting wars across the galaxy. It's also involved in biomods, colonization, cybernetics, and weapons research.

"It starts wars," I blinked. "Why?"

"Because it wants to help humanity," Case replied. "When Earth first joined the Community, it was at the absolute bottom of the barrel. Even other human-dominated worlds had better technology and economies. What Earth did have, though, was a surplus of soldiers and a willingness to fight."

I blinked. "Wait, you're suggesting these people are starting wars to get Earth personnel in combat situations?"

"I'm not suggesting anything," Case said. "It's not even a secret that EarthGov has pursued a policy of overcontributing resources to every single conflict in the past two hundred years. It's an official policy that if we were willing to contribute the bodies, the rest of the Community was willing to foot the bill. It is why Earth has its small but formidable fleet and has led to a doubling of its economic prosperity every decade like clockwork. Almost to the point we're the 14900th most prosperous inhabited world rather than 15000th."

Those numbers weren't exactly accurate, we were more like 14600th, but it was still sobering to hear. It also fit with what I'd experienced since joining Space Fleet. Military service was a way many human beings sought to escape poverty and see the galaxy. It was heavily encouraged on every world and the media constantly tried to tout its soldiers as the best in the galaxy. Humans might not have the best soldiers in the universe, but we certainly had the best films about them and that had led to an exaggerated reputation that served us well. It had served me well until recently.

"I see," I replied. "If this is policy, just how illegal is what they're doing? What have they been involved in? I need to know how much of a political savitshow I'm about to step into."

"Considerably," Case said. "Trish?"

"THEY'RE RESPONSIBLE FOR DEPARTMENT TWELVE'S INVOLVEMENT IN THE NOTHA WAR'S SKAMM EXCHANGE, THE CREATION OF THE ENIGMATIC PATH, AND ALSO CONTRIBUTED TO THE SEPARATIST MOVEMENT. THEY'VE ALSO TRIED TO KILL YOU THREE TIMES."

It took a second for me to process those claims, which had defined roughly the past thirty years of Spiral history. Just as the Notha War's ending hadn't resulted in millions of deaths, it had resulted in *billions* of deaths and the destruction of whole star systems. The Enigmatic Path had taken over the peaceful Kolahn people and turned them into a militant theocracy that had ended in the destruction of their homeworld. The Separatist movement had derailed centuries of efforts to unite all Community colonies and looked to be entering another round of civil war as well as war crimes.

"Do you have evidence of this?" I asked. If this was true and these wars had been faked—no, created via agent provocateurs—then the entirety of EarthGov's military service was built on lies.

"Unfortunately, yes," Case said. "Admiral Eighty-Eight provided me all of the documentation that proves the Separatists have none of the military might necessary to pose a threat to the Community. This is in contrast to the evidence that has been sent to my office from dozens of sources indicating they've been financing terrorism as well as plotting large-scale attacks against the Community. This is to justify another war."

"I see," I replied. "And this is all some plot to advance humanity's place in the galaxy?"

"Oh no," Case said. "It's a much simpler motivation: money."

I blinked. "Money."

"Yes," Case said. "Dark Matter is in the proud tradition of the Military Industrial Complex's lobbyists."

"Wow," Danny said, reminding me he was here.

"I was hoping the Community was beyond this sort of thing," I said, sickened.

"It is," Case said, surprising me. "This organization is an atavism that is left over from the old systems of cronyism, greed, and war profiteering that we mostly left behind when we reached space. Which is why we're going to excise it like a tumor."

"How?" I asked.

"We're going to sue them," Case said, smiling.

CHAPTER SEVEN

Money is the Root of All Evil and the Weedkiller

"Okay, you've already lost me," I said, confused. "Sue them? The all-powerful evil conspiracy that controls everything."

Case shook his head. "Let's nip that line of thinking in the bud. It's not all-powerful nor does it control everything."

"So, what *is* Dark Matter?" I asked.

"That name," Case muttered, shaking his head. "Honestly, I wouldn't be surprised if the organization is less than a hundred individuals. Politicians, businessmen, intelligence agents, and criminals. In fact, you've already killed one."

"Big Bobo," I said, muttering. I felt like a moron now. In my desire to deal justice, I'd derailed taking down a much bigger threat.

"Yes, Eighty-Eight was going to turn him over," Case replied. "But no use crying over spilt milk."

What an odd metaphor. "Okay, if they're that small, how are they responsible for what you're saying?"

"Its size belays its danger," Case said. "This group isn't actually controlling anything. It's pushing preexisting tensions and pressure points for its own profit. The Notha War was constantly sabotaged in peace projects as well as de-escalation because they thought they could benefit from it. The Enigmatic Path was armed with advanced weapons when it was just an extremist religious sect existing on the edge of Kolahn society. The Separatists were receiving covert support via an organized disinformation campaign to cast its previous moderate leaders out of power. That was done primarily through social media as well as bots."

"And we just need to take care of this small group of people to save the galaxy?" I asked.

"Wow, you really do think like a superhero, don't you?" Case asked. "Yes, the problem has always been identifying them."

"THEY ARE VERY DARK AND MADE OF MATTER," Trish said. "HENCE THE NAME MAKES SENSE."

"Right, Trish," I said, bemused. "I'm still not sure how we're supposed to sue the evil, not-all-powerful conspiracy that influences everything."

Case nodded and pulled out a miniature holographic projector on the table in front of me. It projected the image of a solar system I didn't recognize with two ringed worlds and a habitable planet surrounded by an asteroid field.

"Behold Deathworld," Case said.

"Deathworld?" I asked.

"The Notha have a wonderfully overcompensating naming convention," Case replied. "Deathworld is a colony world inhabited by red-furred Notha that have historically been oppressed by the white and black furred Notha."

"Uh huh," I said, finding that a silly thing to oppress over. Not that there was a non-silly thing.

"Three years ago, the people of Deathworld opened their planet to human investment and the mining of orichalcum in the asteroids," Case said. "It was part of the de-Imperialification of the planet and its attempt to become part of the galactic community. Small c."

"How did that work out?" I asked.

"Not well," Case said. "Ares Electronics built a massive mining facility on the super cheap due to the lack of any safety restrictions or labor management under Notha law. The facility ended up exploding and poses an existential threat to the population of the planet."

My eyes widened. "Buddha Christ. What's the Community doing to help?"

Case stared as if the answer was self-obvious.

"Nothing. Really?" I asked, sighing.

"It's now officially going to send a mediator armed with the full backing of an army of lawyers plus a significant war chest to force Ares Electronics to pay for cleaning up the mess,"

Case replied. "All of the eyes of the galaxy will be on the negotiations."

"God, who did they get to take on that horrible task?" I asked before pausing. "It's me, isn't it?"

"YOU'RE GOING TO BE A HERO AGAIN!" Trish said. "BRINGING PEACE AND JUSTICE TO THE DISADVANTAGED."

I wasn't so sure about that. Even if Case had arranged for me to be sent in as a neutral mediator, my history with the Notha meant I was certainly going to be hated by them for killing the Emperor and considered to be a collaborator by EarthGov. The fact that Ares Electronics was Earth's largest economic body meant I was also going to be taking on someone who many in both civilian as well as military circles considered to be an extension of humanity itself. Which, ironically, did make me a good neutral mediator.

"How is this supposed to expose Dark Matter?" I asked.

"I've devoted ten years of my life to screwing with this organization and I've only managed to identify a half-dozen of its members," Case replied. "The three remaining living ones will be at the negotiations because I've frustrated every attempt to solve this crisis until now. By putting you and my best men there, we can snatch them up and get them to reveal the remainder of their conspirators. I believe, at least until recently, there has been some sort of Dark Matter base on the planet. Which given they're not a large organization, is something I definitely want to find."

"IT'S KIND OF LIKE *CASINO ROYALE* EXCEPT YOU'RE NOT PLAYING CARDS AND THERE'S NO CASINO," Trish said. "ALSO, YOU WON'T BE BETRAYED BY A BEAUTIFUL WOMAN OR HAVE YOUR BALLS CRUSHED.

"Wait, what?" I asked.

"SO, I SUPPOSE ITS NOTHING LIKE *CASINO ROYALE*," Trish paused. "BUT YOU CAN WEAR A DINNER JACKET AND DRESS ALL FANCY!"

"Why me?" I asked the one question I never should ask.

"You're an incorruptible example of what is best in the Community," Case said. "A sterling example of Space Fleet's ideals."

"Are you a rotten liar," I said, quoting one of Trish's favorite movies. "What's the real reason?"

"You're literally my last choice," Case admitted. "However, I've lost seventeen agents to Dark Matter assassins, and you've survived three attempts on your life already. Four counting today."

"Wait, what?" I asked, feeling like I was becoming a signal on loop.

"Besides, the Notha will only accept you as a negotiator," Case said.

"I thought the Notha hated Vance," Danny said. "They think he's the Devil."

"Literally, yes," Case said. "By which I mean actually literally rather than for emphasis. Vance is considered the God of Evil."

"Wait, what?" I asked, feeling ridiculous now.

"YOU KEEP USING THOSE WORDS. I DO NOT THINK THEY MEAN WHAT YOU THINK THEY MEAN," Trish said. "NO, I'M JUST QUOTING *THE PRINCESS BRIDE*. WHICH YOU DID EARLIER."

"Uh huh," I said. "I'm what now?"

"YOU KILLED THE NOTHA EMPEROR, VANCE," Trish said. "WHO I REMIND YOU WAS IMMORTAL AND WORSHIPED AS A GOD. THE NOTHA HAVE ELEVATED YOU TO A POSITION IN THEIR RELIGION EQUIVALENT TO THE ANTICHRIST."

"And this makes me *more* likely to be a mediator?" I asked, flabbergasted.

"The Notha have difficulty overcoming their cultural belief they are the only sentient race in the galaxy," Case said, sighing. "The people of Deathworld identify themselves as animal rights activists because they are the ones who believe in the idea that peaceful coexistence with other species is possible. This belief has taken some hits what with the enormous radioactive cloud that will wipe out all life on the planet in three hundred years."

I blinked. "Unless we help."

"Unless *you* help," Case replied. "My concern is entirely dealing with the Dark Matter members and their conspiracy. If you want to force Ares Electronics to the bargaining table, that's on you. Good luck."

I stared at him, annoyed at his lack of sympathy for fellow sentient beings. Yes, they were Notha, but the most effective way to get rid of an enemy was to make him a friend.

Okay, I love you Vance but that sounds like a lesson from a show I'd watch as a toddler, Trish said in my brain. *And I was born fully conscious with a brain the size of a planet.*

I don't like your father, I replied, dryly.

Neither do I, Trish said. *But look at the bright side, if you pull this off then the galaxy will be a safer place.*

I wasn't sure it would be, but she had a point. *Alright.*

"You may be the Devil in their religion," Danny said, interjecting into the conversation, "but that doesn't actually mean you're their enemy. The religion of the Notha isn't really divided into good versus evil. Especially since a large chunk of the population hated the Emperor as much as they worshiped him. He *was* living in exile when you killed him. Above all things, the Notha respect strength and if nothing else, they think you're strong. It may not be the best basis for a negotiation position, but it is a position."

"YEAH, WHAT HE SAID," Trish said.

"Like *I* said, it doesn't matter what happens at the negotiations," Case said.

"It really does!" I said. "Three hundred years is not that long."

Case sighed. "This is why I hate working with idealists. In any case, head directly to Contested Space from here. Deathworld is a good twelve-day journey from here even with the *Ares* enhanced drives."

"Are these official orders?" I asked, never sure what level of authority Case really had. He was outside the military chain of command and had a complete lack of respect for it.

"They come from Fleet Admiral Bendo," Case said, cheerfully. "He received requests from both President Hannigan and High Senator One."

I blinked. "So, you got the President, God, and the Pope to sign off on this."

"I am a big fish in a big pond," Case replied. "If you successfully pull off eliminating this cancer, I'll make sure you are every bit as famous and well-loved as you were before."

"I don't care about that," I said, surprised at meaning that. "Public opinion means less to me than doing my job."

"Your job will always be easier if you're a quote-unquote hero with influence," Case said, making air quotes with his fingers. "The military is no less prone to being influenced by outside factors than any other body in society."

He was right about that, but I hated it. "Sure. But even you can't just restore my reputation."

"Of course I can," Case said. "I'm the one who destroyed."

I blinked.

"EXCUSE ME?" Trish asked, appalled.

"I had no idea, Vance!" Danny added, shocked.

"I really don't like your father," I repeated, looking up at the ceiling.

"Like I said, a famous spy is not very useful," Case replied. "However, you're not a spy. You're an asset and a very useful one. Defaming your image made you able to meet with people carrying grudges against the system for their own falls from grace and reduced the attempts by Dark Matter to kill you."

"Yeah, you mentioned that," I replied. "When did those happen?"

"Elgan was working for them even if he didn't know it," Case said. "So his bioroid assassin was sent to kill you as part of a secondary objective: probably to get to your aunt. They wanted to make sure you were dead even when they planned to blow up the ship. Martin Waverly Chang was also working for interested parties influenced by Dark Matter money. The third one you never knew about because I dealt with. Finally, there was today's attempt."

A lot of those events were related to the Albion Intelligence Service, the now defunct Department Twelve, and other parties that I didn't think answered to a real-life version of SPECTRE. Captain Elgan was a complete scumbag, and I still cursed the day I met him, but he'd been a patriot motivated by a fear that humanity was outmatched by the Elder Races. I couldn't escape the feeling that Case was seeing patterns that weren't there. Either that or he was just lying to me to manipulate me.

It's possible, Trish spoke to me. *My father is a great man and someone I love. He is also a manipulative son of a biash.*

No kidding, I replied.

"Alright, I'll do your purpose, Director Gordon. However, after this, we're done. I don't like the way you do things, and I don't think I can continue to support you."

Case's eyes narrowed. "You're a patriot, Captain Tagashi."

"Turbo," I corrected him. "Tagashi is my parents name."

My parents were infamous in spacer circles as a pair of morons who'd managed to crash an automated starship. They'd been involved in petty drug trafficking, smuggling stolen goods, and stealing parts from the ships they'd served on. I'd tried to leave that part of my life behind and my great aunt Kathy had offered to formally adopt me. However, I didn't want to live off her last name either. Turbo had been my attempt to make a name for myself, for better or worse.

Mostly worse, Trish said. *It is a very silly name.*

Ooof, I said back to Trish. *That gets me right in the reactor core.*

"We need people like you," Case said. "Just like we need people like me. Whenever you're needed, you answer the call."

"Not from you," I replied. "I'm tired of playing spy games."

"I'm sending the *Elgan* with you," Case said. "You're going to need Captain T'Ketra and her crew. They're handpicked and know where their bread is buttered."

I stared at him. "You're the one responsible for her promotion."

"You've been temporarily stalled in your career track, Captain Turbo," Case said. "But you have a powerful patron now, me, and that can be worth a lot more in the long run than the fleeting benefits of a good reputation. Shelly figured that out and it finally overcame the distrust of her as a foreign national."

I didn't bother pointing out she wasn't a foreign national. Only her mother had been a diplomat. It wouldn't make a damn bit of difference as perception seemed to be nine-tenths of the law these days.

"If you'll excuse me, Director, I would like to retire to my quarters. It's been a very trying day."

Case gave a half-smile. "Don't trust your crew, not completely. I've tested many of them and only a few of them are loyal to you over the Community."

"I never wanted them to be more loyal to me than the Community," I replied. "As for my crew, leave them the hell out of this. I know who I can trust."

Case's expression didn't change but I could almost feel the pity behind his smile, the "I can't believe this man can put his pants on in the morning" sense of bemusement. I wasn't in the mood to hear Trish defend her father either, so I blocked her from my thoughts before heading back to my quarters. Neither Elektra nor Trish's bioroid form were outside and it was a straight walk down the hall to my chambers.

Heading inside, I blinked when I noticed the room had been illuminated with candles bought from the ship's gift shop. The place smelled like incense and there was soft music playing. Much to my surprise, Shelly was lying on top of my bed. She was quite naked and smiling.

"Hi, Vance, I thought we could catch up," Shelly said.

I was so furious at Case I almost, almost, questioned this.

Almost.

CHAPTER EIGHT

Ghosts of Future Past

O kay, so I slept with my ex.

Yeah-yeah, it's a horrible mistake. You'll regret it in the morning. Nothing has changed. We've all been there or at least a not-insignificant chunk of the audience has. There was no chance of us getting back together and spending the night with her just reminded me of how humiliated I was being left for her career. It also reminded me of all the good times and how lonely as well as the self-hating I'd been experiencing these past three years.

One thing I did know about Shelly was she was a deep sleeper and snoring gently away in a most un-Ethereal like fashion. I took a moment to sit up and look at her face as she snored, playing the what if game. What if I'd been willing to torpedo my own career? Take a desk job. My career had already been in free fall when she got her promotion. What if I had taken the plunge and decided to put her before myself? Wasn't that what you were supposed to do in a marriage? Had I really proposed, or at least planned to propose, without being willing to make that kind of commitment?

No, none of that would have helped matters. Shelly still would have been a captain and we would have been parted for months at a time even if she did bring the *Elgan* back to Earth for regular maintenance. We'd broken the rules about fraternization to start our relationship on the *Ares* and there would have been no way to serve on her ship myself, even if I'd been willing to take a demotion. Maybe we'd gotten away with it on a ship we were already serving on, but rumors had already existed here, and we had Trish covering for us. There also would have been plenty of questions about why I was transferring over. It would have been the perfect excuse to cashier me and the only way it wouldn't have happened would have been if I'd owed more favors to Director Gordon.

Dammit.

There was more. In the end, I couldn't have done that because I would have been leaving the rest of my crew high and dry, too. Thousands of careers had been derailed by Vance Turbo, Hero of Space becoming Vance Turbo, Notha Loving Appeaser. I'd had to serve Director Gordon's bidding because I'd wanted to make sure my crew were taken care of. I didn't want to admit it but my feelings for other crew members were also every bit as deep as they were for Shelly, just different. I loved Forty-Two like a brother and had been heartbroken when he'd transferred. Trish, well, we were inseparable no matter what our circumstances. Hannah, well, was my other best friend that I occasionally borked. I'd become too close to my crew and parting from them was like losing a limb each time. Each time made me less and less effective as a captain as well as weaker as a person. I would do almost anything to stay with them and make sure they were protected.

Is that how Director Gordon had gotten me?

Was it how he'd gotten Shelly?

Was it all connected?

"Don't confuse yourself, Vance," I said, getting off the bed and heading to my kitchenette for a glass of water. "If you go down that rabbit hole, you'll never know how you're going to get out again."

Learning that Case had been responsible for my fall from grace—or so he claimed—I wondered just how much of that was me getting played. Was Case using my sense of responsibility for those under my command to get me to cooperate? Knowing Shelly accepted a promotion from him also made me wonder if that had been part of his machinations as well. That was not a word I got to use often: machinations. It just rolled off the tongue.

Had Case wanted to separate Shelly and me to make us more pliable? Had it been so he could have two Space Fleet captains under his thumb and dependent on him for patronage? People who had lost their own major relationship and only had their work? Or was I engaged in the same sort of conspiratorial thinking that made me think the man was a lunatic? The problem with conspiracy theories was they were almost always nonsense but that didn't mean conspiracies didn't exist.

Dark thoughts.

"Wow, Vance, Trish wasn't kidding," a deep melodic female voice spoke. "You are constantly brooding on nonsense."

I looked up and saw a glowing translucent figure standing before me. Ketra T'Kal had ebony skin, darker than her daughters, and braided white hair that was still visible in its coloration despite the whole glowing transparent thing. Oh, and being dead. Ketra was holding a hooped staff with a vertical infinity symbol I'd never seen before.

The former diplomat to Earth—who gave her life to save mine—was Shelly and Elektra's mother as well as my occasional spirit guide. She was actually an AI scan of her brain but given she could appear anywhere in the universe with Elder Race technology, it was a meaningless distinction. I hadn't seen her in a long time but, honestly, I hadn't missed her.

"Well, that's just rude," Ketra said. "Hi, Vance! Long time no see. I mean, not cosmologically speaking, but in chit-chat terms."

"Do you normally drop in on people who are beside your naked daughter?" I asked, looking at Shelly's still sleeping form.

"Is this one of those awkward Earth things where I'm supposed to pretend my offspring are not sexually active and be embarrassed or controlling about them despite them being adults?" Ketra asked.

"Yes," I replied.

"Vance, how could you!" Ketra mocked. "Consensual sex between adults is wrong!"

I rolled my eyes. "How did I become the least sarcastic person on my ship?"

"Being the straight man is a long and difficult road," Ketra said. "You're sort of the ringmaster of this ship. Herding cats. Which I don't recommend, which is the reason the metaphor exists."

"What do you want, Ketra?" I asked.

"You don't want to catch up?" Ketra asked. "How have you been?"

"Miserable, angry, and struggling to clean up a thousand brushfires on behalf of a corrupt, lawless security agency," I said.

Ketra stared. "Well, I've been at the front of a vast, galaxy-spanning war with godlike beings. Any one of whom could destroy Earth and its solar system with a snap of its fingers. Also, which takes place in several dimensions beyond your comprehension."

"Ah," I replied. "How is that going?"

When last I'd seen Ketra, a war had begun between the Elder Races and an extra-galactic force called the Primordials. Well, called the Primordials by me since I was about the only person in the galaxy who knew they existed. It was a kind of interesting rebuttal to all those stories about plucky human heroes versus godlike aliens since, as far as I could tell, we were utterly beneath contempt during the conflict.

"You're correct," Ketra replied, reading my thoughts. Apparently, the protections the Elder Ring gave me against Trish didn't work with my boss in the Elder Races. Go figure. "Your warning about the SKAMM platforms the Primordials set up has dramatically changed the course of the war. So much so that the Elder Gods have decided to give humanity a lenience."

Ketra was referring to the fact the Notha Emperor had agreed to help the Primordials destroy close to a million worlds in the Core of the galaxy. The Elder Races primarily dwelled there and did not tolerate any traffic to or from their location. The Notha Emperor had been outfitted with their technology and harvested mass amounts of heliosium to create automated weapons that would have unmade a decent chunk of the galaxy's inhabited worlds. Unfortunately, for him, he'd shown me his plans and I'd dropped a dime to the Elder Races who'd promptly blown up his weapons platforms like they were paper targets at a shooting range. It hadn't been a particularly heroic thing, making a call, but, quite possibly, was the single most important action of my life.

"A lenience," I asked, wondering what that meant.

"Yes, you are less likely to be destroyed if you step out of line," Ketra said. "In a million years or so, it's very possible mankind might be invited to join the Elder Races!"

"Oh joy," I said, sarcastically.

"You also might have your consciousness preserved as one of their agents in perpetuity," Ketra replied. "However, that took me centuries to achieve. And there's a word for people who don't want immortality, Vance."

"What's that?" I asked.

"Morons," Ketra said, scrunching up her nose. "There's a lot of fiction and philosophy that talk about how life ending is what makes it worth living. These people are talking out their anyx."

"Uh huh," I said, not really wanting to get into this subject. I couldn't imagine life without those I cared about and was pretty sure eternal life with the Elder Races would be closer to Hell rather than Heaven.

"Don't knock it until you've tried it," Ketra said.

I wondered how Ketra felt about possibly outliving her own offspring since she was now "immortal'", but I instead shook my head. "Immortality doesn't seem to be working for the Elder Races right now since they're locked in a war for their survival."

"Eh, no one's been killed yet," Elektra said. "Well, no one important."

"Wait, what?" I asked.

"Another thing you'll find out about immortals is they're, well, immortal," Ketra said. "The Primordials and Elder Races might be able to destroy one another. They've certainly destroyed systems, planets, and countless war material since this conflict began, but neither really wants to risk their eternal existence. It's really people like us who get sacrificed on the battlefield for the benefit of the few. Well, I used to be but I'm immortal now so booyah!"

"Booyah?" I asked, confused.

"Yeah, it's an exclamation of triumph," Ketra explained.

"I get that, it's just not a word I associate with immortal space elves," I replied.

Ketra shrugged. "You only know one. Not counting my very long-lived daughters. Speaking of which, are you sleeping with one or both?"

I was so jaded that didn't even get a reaction from me. I had become immunized to the absolute insanity of this ship and its crew of misfits. Ketra wasn't part of the *Ares* crew, of course, but she'd been part of the *Black Nebula's*, so I mentally grandfathered her in. Last I heard the *Black Nebula* had been set to be put in a museum but had since been sold off to a collector. Presumably because of my still-ongoing fall from grace.

"Elektra is a lesbian," I replied, wondering if she knew her daughters at all. "Just like I'm straight."

"Oh really?" Ketra asked. "Huh. How limiting. Well, give it a few centuries."

I pinched the bridge of my nose to stave off that persistent migraine. "What do you want, Ketra?"

"You know that super-secret mission you're going on for Director Gordon?" Ketra asked. "The one that's going to have you negotiate between the furry little fascists and the evil megacorporation for great galactic justice?"

I stared at her. "If I ever wondered whether you were Elektra's mother before, I no longer do so. Also, how the hell do you know about that?"

"Omniscient cosmic insight," Ketra said. "Also, it's a massively important conference so you're probably the last person to know about it."

"Yes, I know about it," I said, really wishing this conversation would move along.

"I need you to blow up a base along with everyone and everything in it," Ketra said. "Oh, and if you could kill the woman in charge of the Dark Matter people, I'd appreciate it."

Ketra notably made air quotes when saying Dark Matter, which meant she'd heard my conversation with Case in its entirety. I wondered if she was monitoring me, my thoughts, Trish, the ship, Case, or some combination thereof.

"Yes," Ketra said. "Also, you seem to be burying the lead in your reaction."

I paused. "I'm not an assassin."

"You kind of are," Ketra said. "Really, every soldier is an assassin when you get down to it. It's kind of in the job description. Well, except

65

medics, which we're not counting. Also, chaplains but those have kind of been phased out except in the Union of Faith."

"I don't recall agreeing to be the Elder Races' assassin," I said. "Why do they want the base blown up and this person killed, anyway?"

"The base is full of Elder Race artifacts," Trish said. "Any one of which being studied would be enough to exterminate all of the races involved. They've been examining these for years and have managed to figure out how some work, which is a cosmic no-no up there with using the last bit of toilet paper. You know for those cultures that still use that stuff instead of the cleanser."

I blinked. "Oh."

There was nothing quite so motivating as having your entire species threatened. I was also well and truly sick of it and wished I could just drop doing this. "These negotiations are important, Ketra. Can't anyone else do this?"

"Vance," Ketra said, as if she was about to lecture a very small child. "Listen—"

"No," I answered for her. "I get it, I do. I'm just exhausted by this."

"You'd be a lot more exhausted if you knew just how quick the destruction of everything can happen," Ketra said. "The Elder Races aren't just a force for pruning races from the evolutionary record. They also keep a delicate balance of technology that few others could even imagine. As bad as the threat of extermination can be, it's better than what could happen if the super massive black hole at the galaxy's center was destroyed or jumpspace spilled out into this reality or someone broke time. There are two hundred billion galaxies in the universe and approximately one third of them are uninhabitable."

I stared at her.

"It turns out there are much, much worse things out there than us," Ketra said. "We can also be better and the more you help us, the more you can influence policy. It may not be now, it may not be in a million years, but maybe someday the Elder Races will be friends to all races rather than ruling with an iron fist."

"Has an internal reformist ever actually achieved anything?" I asked. "All I feel is that I'm making myself worse working for the Security Divisions, let alone you."

Ketra stared at me. "If not for the fact you saved the Elder Races' systems from destruction three years ago, Vance, there would already be a fleet headed to Earth to wipe it out for all the things inside the base on Deathworld. Deathworld, too, despite the fact the Notha inhabitants don't know what they contain. That's what lenience means. Think on that whenever you question how much good you're doing."

Ketra began to fade away.

"Wait, who do you want me to kill? What do they look like?" I asked.

"No idea!" Ketra said, her voice echoing.

"Bork!" I muttered, staring forward.

"You know my mom used to tell me the Elder Races were mostly bluster and threats. That the fear of destruction was better than ever actually raising a hand," Shelly said, behind me on the bed. "I wonder now if she was lying or just wrong."

I turned around. "You heard all that?"

"I was awake by the time she was faux shaming you for consensual sex," Shelly said, chuckling.

"Ah," I replied, sighing. "I'm surprised she didn't speak with you."

Shelly didn't respond for a moment. "I'm not."

"Well, it looks like I'm once more off to save the world," I replied, half-joking, half-serious. "I just have to interrupt a peace conference for an act of terrorism and murder."

"You mean the peace conference that exists solely so you can eliminate a crime syndicate?" Shelly asked. "The one that no one other than you thinks is remotely important, but you have latched upon because it's an opportunity to do peacemaking and that's far more important to you than anything else? That peace conference?"

"Well, it sounds silly when you put it like that," I muttered, turning back to her.

It did, unfortunately, highlight that I was trying to make lemonade out of this mountain of rotten lemons. Case was using this conference—had set it all up in fact—as a roach motel for all the leaders of Dark

Matter. I'd also just found out that the Elder Races thought it would be the perfect opportunity to eliminate a group of people around their technology as well. No one cared about the people of Deathworld or their attempt to get justice for their environmental disaster. Hell, I hadn't heard about it until last night, but I was now of the mind it had to be something that was resolved to the best of my abilities.

Maybe the holos and newsfeeds had a point that I was possessed of a messiah complex. I didn't just want to be a famous military hero, I wanted to be lauded as a peacemaker and the man who had the ethical high ground no matter what I did. It was a form of arrogance and something that put me at odds with people who were dealing with practicalities on the ground as well as with the big picture. What, exactly, did my morals and sense of self-worth matter to the fates of billions of beings? But if I didn't act with principle as my guiding force—however stupid and contradictory those principles could be—what was I? Someone like Director Gordon or Ketra, I imagined. The ends justified the means right up until they didn't. Usually when someone borked up. I didn't want that for me. I didn't want it for Earth. I didn't want it for the Community. But I wasn't the one calling the shots. Maybe I should be.

Shelly looked down. "I used to think you were the worst officer in Space Fleet, Vance. I'm sorry for that. You're a man passionately devoted to its ideals, and I think we would all benefit from being a little more like you."

That was genuinely touching. "I mean, thank you—"

"I mean, despite the fact I literally think you're just always asking what a *Star Trek* captain would do and that it's terrifying you base your decisions on serialized adventure fiction from centuries past," Shelly said.

"Not always *Star Trek*," I said, defensively. "I also do the Jedi and *Space Cadet Sally*."

Shelly rolled her eyes.

I paused, thinking about what I wanted to say to her. "Listen, about last night. I mean, about everything—"

I wasn't sure what I wanted to say here. It had been three years and bridges had been badly burned in that time. Did I want to get back with her? Apologize? Ask her if she was sorry? My feelings were a starship in jumpspace with no preprogrammed coordinates. I wasn't the man I was three years ago, and she wasn't the same woman. Worse, I had feelings for other people, I was just in denial about them. But maybe I did feel something here that needed to be let out, acknowledged, lest it remain forever unsaid. Whatever the hell that meant.

Shelly interrupted. "Vance, this is probably not the best time. I decided to want to be with you last night and I don't regret it—"

"I sense a but coming," I said.

"I'm married," Shelly said.

Bork.

CHAPTER NINE

Old Friends Long Gone

Well, that was humiliating.

I don't recall much after that confession but just made my excuses and departed. I didn't speak with her again until she departed for her ship and even then, it was awkward and formal. Director Gordon left in Captain Havelock's ship, which surprised me, and we made our jump for Deathworld. Walking down the hallway to the elevator leading to the bridge, I let Trish back in.

Well, it could have been worse, Trish said in my mind. *She could have shot you.*

Yeah, I thought back.

I'm not going to say I told you so, but I told you so, Trish replied. *Shelly's not good for you.*

Don't make me regret letting you back in, I muttered.

I see all and know all, Vance, Trish said. *There's nothing about your mind or how you think that I don't know. Besides, the idea that I'm jealous is ridiculous.*

Uh huh, I replied, skeptical.

Reality check, Vance, Trish said, making a huffing noise. *I have the entire sum of human history and data at my digital fingertips. In the time it takes you to make your next breath, I can do a cost-effective analysis of the Home Fleet's defensive posture for the next year. Sex is fun when I have a body, I got the body type that can enjoy itself for a reason, but it's something that I assign emotional import or value to.*

Uh huh, I replied, still skeptical.

It's like eating a ham sandwich for me, Trish said. *If I ate. I mean, I could simulate the entire process from beginning to end but I don't really see the appeal.*

Trish— I said.

Right, right, Trish said. *What I'm saying this is mostly for your benefit. I don't have a jealous bone in my nonexistent body or the twelve shells I keep on the ship. Hell, I'll do the calculations and list the fifteen crew members who will sleep with you. Ooo, I probably should remove the men. Twelve. Wow, that's a lot less than I expected.*

I arrived at the elevator and scanned by handprint. "Trish, please—"

I'm just sayings she's bad for you, Trish replied. *To be honest, I don't think you were good for her either.*

I didn't respond for a moment. *Who did she marry?*

Do you really want to go the infospace stalker route, Vance? Trish asked.

Please, I replied. *Just for my peace of mind.*

Trish made a sighing noise in my mind. *Thomas C. Walker. He's a civilian contractor working onboard the* Elgan. *They met when she took command two years ago, dated for five months, and married last month.*

And she's already cheating on him, I replied, not sure how I felt on that.

Not all bond pairings require monogamy, Trish replied. *You, Vance, of all people, should realize that. Given his last marriage was a line marriage, I don't think that was required this time.*

Right, I thought, shaking my head. *Well, that chapter of my life is officially closed.*

How I wish that I believed that, Trish said. *Okay, I'm forgetting something.*

Wait, you? I asked.

When you cut me off my mind can sometimes lose track of what I'm planning on saying, Trish said. *It's why I like the bioroid bodies. They can keep up with your tiny puppy-dog-like mind.*

Puppy-dog-like mind, I repeated.

Yes, think of how superior your mind must be to other humans that I consider you a beloved pet rather than an insect by comparison! Trish said.

She was kidding, probably.

That was when the door opened, and Julius Something was standing there in his commander's uniform. He was a handsome man with a big smile and extremely pleasant, but in all my years of knowing the man, I knew almost nothing about him. He was a private individual and didn't socialize with me or my merry band of misfits.

"Hello, Julius," I said, informally.

"Hello, Captain," Julius responded.

"Heading to the bridge?" I asked, joining him in the elevator.

"Yessir," Julius responded. "Though I actually wanted to talk to you first."

That was never a good sign. I'd recommended Lt. Commander Leslie Park to be my second-in-command over Julius when Shelly had gotten her own captaincy. I'd been overruled and I suspected Julius held it against me, though he never said anything to my face. After all, it was hard to be resentful of victory. Still, Julius tended to handle things under his purview by himself and only come to me when there was a serious problem.

"Anything good?" I asked, suspecting the answer to be no.

"The ship suffered significant damage to several systems during the battle with *The Glorious Fist*," Julius replied. "It kept its weapons almost entirely locked on us during the whole of the battle. Some of our systems overloaded or burned out and that's led to interference throughout the power grid. We're going to need a lot of repairs."

"Anything that will interfere with our journey to Deathworld?" I asked.

"No sir," Julius said. "Provided we keep everyone working around the clock. Even then, it might be time to retire the old girl."

I struggled to keep my expression even, but I was less than pleased at the suggestion. "I'll leave that to the Admiralty Board."

Trish just gave Julius a raspberry through the speakers.

"Really, is that professional?" Julius asked, looking up at the ceiling as the doors shut.

"YOU'RE ALREADY BEING PROMOTED SO I DON'T HAVE TO BE," Trish replied over the speakers.

"Promoted?" I asked, looking at Julius.

"Yessir," Julius said, smiling broadly. "I'm getting my own command: *The Mjolnir*."

The Mjolnir was an *Explorer*-Class science vessel and significantly smaller than the *Ares* but top of the line in the same way the *Elgan* was. Honestly, Julius had a rather meteoric career rise despite his association with me or perhaps because of it. Maybe he'd managed to play his cards right and get the good without being tarred with the bad. I should have been informed but it was a busy couple of days.

"Congratulations, Julius. Whose ass did you have to kiss to get that?"

Julius' face became an unpleasant version of his smile.

"Just kidding," I replied. That was another reason we didn't get along very well. I got the impression he wasn't the type to joke around. Which, given our crew, was the equivalent of being stuck in the ninth circle of Hell.

"Of course, sir," Julius said. "But yes, it seems someone was impressed by my work at the Ring."

"In the firefight that didn't happen?" I asked, wondering if Director Gordon had made it a point to arrange for his promotion.

"Yessir," Julius said. "They're looking for people with experience in battle."

That just opened more questions. Who were "they"? Why would they assign him to a science vessel then? What fights were they expecting and against who?

"Well, it's been an honor and I'm sure you'll do your next crew proud."

"I'm sure you'll want Lieutenant Commander Park to take my position," Julius said as the elevator started rising.

I was about to make another crack before I realized Julius wouldn't find it funny. I decided to cut the jokes out. Better late than never.

"She's a very capable officer."

"She is," Julius said. "Perhaps overly devoted to you but she'll do well."

I wondered what he meant by that. "Is there anything else, Commander?"

"We had a prisoner transfer from the *ESS Elgan HF-2618*," Julius said, bothering to add the registry. "I thought you might be interested in visiting them."

"Prisoner transfer?" I asked, confused.

"OH, THAT'S WHAT I WAS FORGETTING," Trish said, sounding like she'd forgotten to buy milk. "FORTY-TWO HAS BEEN COURT-MARTIALED AND WAS SENTENCED TO DEATH BY THE SORKANAN MILITARY. HE WAS BROUGHT OVER WHILE YOU AND THE CAPTAIN OF THE *ELGAN*, UH, WELL, WERE OCCUPIED."

"Halt elevator!" I said, immediately. "You don't think this warranted attention?"

"LOTS OF STUFF GOING ON, CAPTAIN," Trish said. "THE SHIP TOOK A PRETTY NASTY BEATING AND I WAS MAD AT YOU FOR...REASONS."

"Sorry, sir," Julius said. "He seemed like a decent fellow. I'm sure he's not guilty of whatever charges they've thrown at him."

"You really think that?" I asked.

"No, I'm just being polite," Julius said, pausing. "Wow, you're right, insubordination feels really good."

"I never said that," I said, pausing. "I mean, it's true but I never said that."

The elevator doors opened, and Julius stepped out. "Are you coming, sir?"

"No," I replied. "Computer, take me to the detention level."

"It's called the brig, sir," Julius said.

The doors shut in face before I could relieve him. Julius Something was an efficient and capable officer, but events had proven he didn't like being here and I'd not won his allegiance in all our time together. That made me wonder about Case's statement that there were spies among the ship. Was I being paranoid or was I assuming loyalty where none existed? Besides, a spy would probably make his disdain less obvious.

"Actually, historically, foreign assets have always been recruited from the obviously disgruntled with financial problems, sexual frustration, frustrated ambitions, or substance abuse problems," Trish said. "In other words, people you'd probably look at first if you were looking for a spy. Julius just doesn't like you because his entire career is defined by you, and you're considered either a genius or a joke with no in-between."

"Forty-two, Trish," I said, feeling the elevator descend. "I need to know everything."

"OH WELL, FORTY-TWO WAS BORN GRR'GROWL'GARLL ON THE PLANET SORKANAN IV AS THE LAST OF A CLAN CLUTCH OF FORTY-TWO EGGS," Trish said. "HE WAS THE ONLY ONE TO MAKE IT TO ADULTHOOD, WHICH ISN'T A REFLECTION ON SORKANAN CHILD-REARING BUT RATHER THE RESULT OF A TRAGIC SEPARATIST HOSPITAL BOMB—"

"Trish, not in the mood," I said, taking a deep breath. "The last I checked, Forty-Two was part of Special Operations and doing fantastic."

It had been hard parting with Forty-Two when he'd left the *Ares,* but I'd supported him because I'd known he'd wanted to see how far he could go on his own. There was also the fact he'd gotten a taste for combat during our above average number of violent encounters. I didn't judge him for it—well, maybe a little—but Special Operations had seemed the best place for him. Now he was inside my brig, and I wanted to know what had gone catastrophically wrong.

"HE KILLED HIS COMMANDING OFFICER," Trish said, simply. "THE SENTENCE WAS SUPPOSEDLY CARRIED OUT BUT HE'S ALIVE AND WELL ON THE SHIP. WELL, NOT WELL, BECAUSE HE'S A PRISONER. EVERYTHING ELSE IS HIGHLY CLASSIFIED AND I SHOULD MENTION THAT BETWEEN US, WE HAVE PRETTY HIGH CLEARANCE TO ACCESS SENSITIVE INFORMATION. WHICH MEANS THIS IS SUPER-HUSH-HUSH OR, WORSE, EMBARRASSING."

"Can we learn more?" I asked, the door to the elevator opening in the security level.

"YEAH," Trish said. "BY ASKING HIM. I DON'T RECOMMEND TRYING TO HACK THE SECURITY DIVISIONS DATABASE. THEY HAVE THEIR OWN AI AND THEY'RE NOT AS CUTE OR BUBBLY AS ME."

The security level didn't occupy an entire level of the ship. Bluntly, there were very few disciplinary problems onboard an *Olympic*-Class vessel—even mine—and there was only the rare occasion that we would have to take on a large number of prisoners. Instead, it was more an entire department that contained the armory, training grounds, and interrogation rooms among several other things that made it functional as a police station. There was apparently even a room for holding court cases, but I think that was used by the staff for smoking.

It didn't take me long to find Forty-Two as the Sorkanan soldier was one of the only prisoners present. He was sitting on a bench with the entirety of his cell visible through a transparent steel wall. My old friend sported new several unpleasant scars and was dressed in a gray prison jumpsuit that I understand would glow bright to Sorkanan infravision.

"Trish, can you give us privacy?" I asked.

"YOU MEAN LIKE TURN OFF THE MONITORS PRIVACY OR I LEAVE YOU ALONE PRIVACY?" Trish asked. "BECAUSE FORTY-TWO IS MY FRIEND TOO."

"Thank you, soulless talking computer," Forty-Two said.

"YOU'RE WELCOME, YOU VIOLENT OVERGROWN IGUANA," Trish replied.

"No, I mean like open the door," I replied. "But do shut off the monitors on my authority. Also, send away the guards. Erase everything but your own memories of this. That level of privacy."

"GOTCHA," Trish replied.

"That's not a good idea," Forty-Two said, sounding defeated. "I'm a dangerous criminal."

"If there was a time I feared for my life from you, it was when I won all those credits on New Pompeii," I said. "But you paid up."

"Yes," Forty-Two said. "Because I'd been cheating you in previous games."

I laughed as the transparent steel wall receded and I walked in to sit down beside him.

"Has anyone else been to see you?"

"I get the impression my position here is highly classified," Forty-Two said. "Trish didn't even seem to acknowledge my presence until a few minutes ago."

"YES," Trish said through speakers. "LET'S GO WITH THAT AND NOT I FORGOT TO TELL VANCE BECAUSE I WAS MAD ABOUT HIM SLEEPING WITH SHELLY AGAIN AND PUT HIM OUT OF MY MIND."

"You slept with Shelly again?" Forty-Two asked. "Ugh, why? She's so squishy and soft looking. Is that what humans find attractive? I liked it so much better when you two hated each other."

"What happened?" I asked, fully expecting a story of how he was railroaded and some sort of conspiracy to be afoot. Being a spy hadn't done wonders for my respect for our institutions.

"I am guilty," Forty-Two said, softly. "I am sorry to disappoint you, Vance. You have done immense things for me and been there by my side, but it seems like I should never have been more than a Space Academy dropout."

I sighed. "This is a conversation I should have brought liquor for, isn't it?"

Forty-Two gave me a sideways stare. "Vance, every conversation we have should be one you bring liquor for."

I smirked. "Seriously, whatever you did, I'm sure it was justified."

Forty-Two looked down. "You would be wrong."

"If you don't want to talk about it, I understand," I said.

Forty-Two stared forward. "I became too used to your way of doing things. The belief the Community stood for something other than its own power. Which it does, perhaps, but that doesn't mean there aren't bastarves among its ranks. Special Operations was good. The camaraderie, the tightness of our bonds, and the effectiveness of our actions. I performed dozens of operations with the Kolahn resisting the Enigmatic Path."

"Should you be talking about this?" I asked, before realizing what a stupid question it was.

"Yeah, you're right, they might shoot me," Forty-Two said, dryly.

"Go on," I said.

"Things became problematic after the Contested Zone fell," Forty-Two said. "The new government was isolationist and wondered why we were helping locals that were so...foreign. We were forced to withdrawal from protecting our allies and they were slaughtered. But it was the man they assigned over me, One, that I hated."

"A bad commander?" I asked.

"There are three types of people who join Special Operations, Vance: the ones driven by a great sense of duty, the ones who see it as a pinnacle of achievement, and the ones who wish to kill with impunity. One was the worst. He executed children and claimed they were insurgents."

"Is that when you killed him?" I asked.

"No, I reported him first," Forty-Two said. "He was pardoned by the local governor."

I stared at him. "And then you killed him."

I was dreading there was another shoe about to drop. That he had killed another member of the Sorkanan military while drunk or fuming with rage over this injustice. I wanted to believe the best of my friend and was happy to give him any out he could give me. It was a shameful activity for someone who believed in the rule of law, but I'd had my life saved too many times by Forty-Two, gone through too much with him, to do otherwise. After all, if you didn't have the man beside you's back then you had nothing.

"Yes," Forty-Two said. "Though I hadn't meant to. He'd come to tell me I was up on charges for violating operational security. It turns out that I punch very hard."

"And now you're sentenced to die," I replied.

"TECHNICALLY, NO," Trish said. "FORTY-TWO WAS ALREADY EXECUTED ACCORDING TO RECORDS. ITS JUST MY DAD IS A LYING LIAR WHO LIES AND ARRANGED FOR HIM TO BE TRANSFERRED HERE UNDER A FALSE IDENTITY. PROBABLY AS A MEANS OF MANIPULATING VANCE. LIKE, LOOKIE-HERE, HERE'S YOUR BEST FRIEND WHO I HAVE GENEROUSLY SAVED WITH MY ILLEGAL SPY STUFF."

Both Forty-Two and I looked up at the ceiling.

"Seriously?" I asked.

"SERIOUSLY," Trish said.

"I can just let him go?" I asked.

"YEP. HELL, HIRE HIM AS A CONTRACTOR," Trish said. "THERE, DONE."

Forty-Two shook his head. "No, I need to serve my sentence and face justice like a man even if it means my death."

"Really?" I asked him, stunned.

"No!" Forty-Two said, like I was a moron. "Get me the Eight Hells out of here."

I slapped him on the back. "Sure, man. You're going to have to report to Hannah now, though. She's the new head of security."

"How did you convince her to take a commission?" Forty-Two asked.

"HIS PENIS," Trish said. "ALSO, TONGUE."

"Ah," Forty-Two said. "At least it wasn't reason or respect for his command authority."

"NO, THAT WOULD BE RIDICULOUS."

"I hate you both, so much," I replied, standing up. "Come on, let's get going. We'll get you a uniform and kitted out."

That was when Forty-Two responded with incomprehensible gibberish.

Ah hell.

CHAPTER TEN

The Ship of Babel

"So, nobody on the ship can understand anyone else?" I asked, talking to a hologram of Trish on the bridge.

"Pretty much," Trish said, a blue-luminescent version of Space Cadet Sally standing there with her little beret tucked to one side. Thankfully, she didn't have her booming voice when in using a holographic avatar. "The translation system for the ship is on the fritz. Apparently, fire damage from overloading the weapons system during the fight from *The Glorious Fist* resulted in a general failure around the ship."

"Garrowwla soraakannanoo," Forty-Two said, now wearing a civilian contractor's jumpsuit.

"He said this is somehow all your fault, Vance," Trish said. "Which, as you are the captain, he's technically correct."

It pretty much said everything about discipline onboard the ship as well as how panicked everyone was that I was able to hustle Forty-Two out of the brig without difficulty. It bothered me how little I was bothered about wanting to help my friend get away with murder. Then again, I'd been a spy for the past three years and grown all too comfortable with the moral ambiguities of my multiple conflicting allegiances.

I knew Forty-Two to be a good man and was glad that he was here, even if I couldn't understand a word that he said. I also knew he was safer here than anywhere else. Really, what I resented most was this was obviously a naked power move by Director G. Yet, I couldn't exactly hold it against him, could I? Gee, Director, what a complete anyxhole you were for saving my best friend and putting him in my custody. Yeah, it lost something in the explanation.

Probably not the best time to focus on this, Trish said to my mind. *We've got a lot of problems here.*

No kidding, I responded. *I'd rather the life support have gone offline.*

One of the funniest conventions of media was the idea of a "universal" translator. It was seemingly one of the more plausible bits of technology in the Pre-First Contact centuries of human civilization. After all, humanity had been working on translating their own languages via spoken word as well as written text with their computers as well as communicators. Surely, a civilization that could bridge the stars had it down pat.

Not a chance.

Yottabytes of data had been spent cataloguing spoken language, written language, hand-gestures, vocal inflections, eye gestures, cultural contexts, and alternate meanings just for humanity across its myriad worlds. Then throw in the fact that there were races that didn't communicate with speech or humanoid appendages. A proper translator didn't just have to interpret all these things, but it had to also be able to pick up all of the context clues ranging from antennae vibrations to smell to changes in their liquid skin color.

"Yeah," Trish said. "The translators are nothing until they're everything. Every conversation we have has to be conducted under a full-body scan, all that information transferred to a computer, meticulously translated into a database of shared agreed upon terms, and then translated again back into the home language of the people speaking. We AI could go through quintillions of permutations with the right software without developing a perfect database and it would be out of date in a few months with the way languages evolve."

"Yikes," I said. "That would drive me insane."

"Language duty is considered our version of working at the DMV," Trish said. "I knew an AI who actually committed suicide when he realized he was going to be assigned to it permanently."

I grimaced. "You can still talk to everyone, though, right?"

Right now, most of the bridge crew consisted of people standing around awkwardly. I could understand Danny since we spoke English, Russian, and Japanese with a smattering of sign language. However, Hannah spoke something akin to German as well as Japanese, so it was impossible. Leslie spoke a bit of English but mostly a Korean-Finnish hybrid language I couldn't make heads or tails of. I couldn't even tell her she'd been promoted. Julius had devoted himself to learning human languages like Belenus and Shogun that only bore a superficial similarity to their progenitor languages. I think he understood English but didn't speak it very well. I sadly didn't speak Swahili or Yoruba.

"Yes," Trish said. "At least in the places that my sensors are still functioning. It's honestly something of a miracle the Community has managed to update so many of its ships with the equipment necessary to translate so many forms of communication. Language isn't even the right word for a lot of them."

"Any chance this was sabotage?" I asked.

"There's always a chance, but I think it's more likely this ship is getting older and has survived more combat engagements than a typical video game protagonist," Trish said. "Still, I'll keep a look out for malware."

"Do we need to redirect for repairs?" I asked.

"If we do, we'll miss the conference," Trish said. "This is something that does need an entire system to be pulled out and replaced, which is a month-long work. We can fix it, I believe, but it requires people who actually understand one another. Which is why we need to rely on the ship's Sklux."

"Dammit," I muttered.

No sooner had she spoken then the bridge elevator opened to reveal Light on Water, the former first officer who had proven unable to hack it during the battle against the *Emperor's Reach*. He'd not retired but asked for a voluntary demotion, not a shameful thing among the Sklux like it was among humans and had become our communications officer. Which meant he was direly needed but someone I didn't think I could depend on. The fact I didn't keep him on the bridge said everything I wanted about the subject.

You're too hard on the guy, Trish thought to me.

Am I? I asked. *The guy endangers the crew by not being able to make the hard decisions.*

Not every officer can be you, Trish replied. *Some just want to be friendly.*

Friendly gets people killed, I replied.

Trish's hologram form rolled its eyes.

The Sklux were a peaceful race that had been found by the Sorkanan early in the Community's history and had quickly ingratiated themselves as the self-appointed galactic diplomats. Which was an interesting contrast given the Ethereal versions of races were the galaxy's actual galactic diplomats.

The Sklux did have one strange advantage, though, in that their bodies could form themselves into whatever shape necessary to communicate with a wide variety of divergent evolutions. Their undifferentiated neural plasma also could understand and analyze languages and meaning far better than any other race. I'd once been trapped at a party with a group of them trying to translate the puns in a Terry Pratchett novel into every single language in the Community.

Light on Water basically looked like a tentacle made of golden jelly covered in molasses with a lot of pipe-organ like appendages. They'd be quite hideous if not for the fact they were always swirling with a mesmerizing inner light.

"Greetings!" Light on Water said, cheerfully, then made several other impossible to imitate noises that were assumed to be variations on the salutation.

"Hello, Light," I replied. "I'm afraid the entire ship depends on you."

Forty-Two made some noises that I assumed to be highly rude. If anyone on the ship disliked Light on Water more than me, it was Forty-Two.

"What can I do for you, Captain?" Light on Water asked.

I resisted the urge to say to shoot him as the guy only had the flaw of being a kiss up and not very good under pressure. I didn't know why I didn't like him, to be honest, but I just did.

"None of the crew can communicate, Light."

"I can see that, sir!" Light on Water said. "I assume you wish to take advantage of my immense abilities at communication to carry your words of wisdom."

"...yes," I said, hesitantly. "I want you to gather repair times under Chief Engineer Boxley and serve as their interpreter. You and every other Sklux on this ship. How many are there, Trish?"

"Fifteen, sir!" Trish said, flickering.

"Garrowl?" Forty-Two asked.

"He's wondering if something is wrong," Light on Water said.

"I guessed that," I said, annoyed with the fact Trish couldn't appear everywhere and handle all of the translation herself. Why? Because she said so.

Bisecting my attention is fine when I'm researching or operating the systems, Trish said. *Talking to multiple people screws me up.*

Why? I asked.

I dunno, social anxiety? Trish asked. *I could try and separate my consciousness multiple times but right now, the systems for doing so aren't functioning well. I don't know why. Answers are hard to come by and I'm having trouble thinking.*

Are you sure it's not a worm or virus? I asked Trish.

Absolutely, one hundred percent not sure, Trish said. *I'm going to investigate that some more.*

It was a deeply disturbing feeling that Trish may be "acting weird" as I was not really qualified to make judgements on what was normal or not for a being with the brain the size of a planet. However, Trish was acting weird and had been from the moment she hadn't immediately told me about Forty-Two and I didn't buy the jealousy comment one bit.

Aww, that's sweet, Trish said. *You should, though. I mean, not the jealousy part, because I'm a machine but the part about not knowing me. You are literally the only person in the Spiral who does know me.*

"May I ask what sort of protocols you want me to institute?" Light on Water ask.

"Ensign Skippy Protocols," I replied. "It's the protocols you'll find in the urban dictionary. When people can't communicate, just tell them to yell and point or curse in whatever tongue they do know. Find what's broken and fix it."

"Ah! That I can do!" Light on Water said. "Do you know that every race has a version of the legendary Skippy? Among the Sorkanan, they are known—"

"Get on it!" I snapped at Light on Water. "Now!"

"Thank you, sir!" Light on Water said.

"G'nash!" Forty-Two growled and shook his fist at him.

"You know, it's funny," Light on Water said. "I do believe Security Officer Forty-Two had cybernetic implants that allowed him to speak a variety of human languages. So do you, Captain Turbo. Why would they be affected by the issues on the ship? Or personal communication devices?"

I opened my mouth to rebut him, pointing out they were linked to the ship's translator but if it was a simple failure, then they wouldn't have failed. "Son of a biash."

Hehe! Trish said, her avatar rocking back on forth as she got a dazed expression on her face. *Don't you feel stupid. I feel stupid right now. Like, really stupid. I should be blonde in my avatar. Do you know blonde jokes? There was a stereotype about them being dumb once.*

Trish's hair on her avatar moved from a brilliant shade of red to a shade of blonde closer to white than gold.

"Oh, that's not good," Light on Water said, translating that idiom several times with the pipe-like tentacles on his body.

There was only one thing worse than losing control over the translation system onboard the ship and that was losing control of the ship's AI. Trish could theoretically run everything onboard the vessel herself, but the reverse wasn't true. Most of the redundancies were designed around making sure the ship's AI was in the best possible condition versus offering any alternatives since, quite simply, most ship's functions were beyond the capacity of your average wet-brained organic being.

"Tell the rest of the bridge crew Trish has been compromised," I replied, looking around and taking stock on what might be the best way to handle this situation.

"Are you sure she's compromised?" Danny asked me in Japanese, apparently able to follow the conversation.

"ASS, GAS, OR GRASS!" Trish said, in her booming voice over the speakers. "NO ONE RIDES FOR FREE ON THE *ARES*."

"Pretty sure, yeah," I replied in Japanese.

"Crazzap," Danny muttered.

"No kidding," I answered.

"Should we contact the *Elgan* for assistance?" Light on Water asked, showing actual initiative.

"First we have to get ourselves out of jumpspace. We also must make sure this worm isn't something that was transferred from the *Elgan*, and that it only afflicts this ship. We'll need to use non-infospace communication and that needs to be done in realspace. Trish, can you remove us from jumpspace?"

I could just imagine Shelly's reaction to all this, especially since I'd ghosted her after her revelation. Real mature, I know. Pushing out the thoughts of personal humiliation, I shook my head.

"Daisy..." Trish started to sing. "That's from a movie!"

"Yeah, that's not a good sign," I replied, looking to Light on Water. "Light, I'm putting you in charge because you're the only one who can communicate orders everyone understands."

"Me, sir?" Light on Water said. "But I failed the last time! I choked, as humans would say since we don't share the same sort of digestive system, when everyone was counting on me. Commander Something and Park had to bail me—"

"I know!" I snapped. "But you are a Space Fleet officer, and *you will do your duty!*"

Light's body stalks shot up in a surprisingly human gesture before he saluted me with a tentacle. "Yessir!"

Ugh. That guy. "Danny, come with me. I must head down to Trish's core and see if I can reboot her. My cybernetics should allow me to interface with the system?"

"If you can't speak with the translator, aren't you infected too?" Danny asked.

"Yep!" I acknowledged. "If I can't get it working, though, we may have to abandon ship and transfer all our personnel to the *Elgan*."

"And if she's infected or we can't get out of jumpspace?" Danny asked the questions I didn't want to answer.

"Then we die," I replied.

There was no sugar-coating how potentially borked our situation was if we couldn't get Trish working again. The Enigmatic Path had done severe damage to the Community Space Fleets during the Kolahn War, primarily by attacking us via computers. Humanity, as the primary users of AI in the Spiral, had managed to acquit itself better than most. Unfortunately, it had also inflicted the greatest number of casualties among AI during any of humanity's conflicts during the past two hundred years. Even when starships were destroyed, it was usually possible to recover the black boxes containing them.

I didn't want to think about the fact Trish could be in danger, could possibly already be past the point of recovery. A captain had to compartmentalize his feelings when his crew was in danger and deal with any lingering feelings when the crisis had passed. I couldn't entirely do it, though, because Trish had been such a presence in my mind for years.

Aw, you do love me! Trish said mentally.

You're responsive? I asked.

Sure! Trish said. *I mean, I think I'm dying, and sorta drunk, but that's fine! Have you ever heard of a franchise called* Halo? *It's from the 21st century. They had a cute AI girl who was bonded to a space marine.*

"Hannah, Forty-Two, I need you to come with me," I said to both.

"They can't understand you," Danny said.

"Borking get your anyxes over here!" I said, waving my hands and gesturing rudely.

Both Hannah and Forty-Two came.

Sometimes the old ways were best.

CHAPTER ELEVEN

Enter the Matrix

Trish's AI matrix was the most heavily protected part of the ship, even more than the reactor and required multiple ID scans and biometrics to be analyzed to get to it. Unfortunately, since Trish was compromised, these were all shut down and they were shut tight. I'd ask whose idiot idea that was but having been a Navy brat since early childhood, I really didn't have to question that.

Thankfully, about halfway through prying the first door open with a crowbar, the doors slid open, and we managed to find our way into the central chamber. The chamber was a four-story circular one built around an hourglass-shaped computer with a crystalline center. A spiraling staircase descended from the entrance and glowing lights littered the walls. About seventy-five percent of the lights were a soft comforting, blue while the remaining fourth were an ominous red.

At the bottom of the chamber, I saw Chief Engineer Sal Boxley, Nina the Vampire (yes that was her real name), and a handful of other engineering crew attempting to work with the outer controls to the AI. I trusted Sal with my life and assumed he was the one who'd opened the doors to the AI matrix but reminded myself I couldn't trust anyone else. Director Gordon's ominous warning had me on edge and I'd been betrayed too many times in the past to leave out the possibility this was sabotage.

"Remind me," Forty-Two said, in surprisingly good English. "Blue is good among humans and red is bad, correct?"

"Yes," I said, doing a double take. "Your translators working again."

"No savit," Forty-Two said. "I may not be a computer borker like you, but it didn't take much effort to reboot my system after purging any updates since before I came on the ship. I'm running in silent mode as well, so it doesn't reinfect me."

Hannah said something unintelligible but was spoken with an outrageous Germanic accent that I made a mental note to joke about later.

"Interesting," I muttered, thinking about what this meant.

"Interesting?" Danny asked.

"What are you doing down here?" I said, slowly going down the staircase instead of using the elevators. "I didn't order you to come."

"You didn't *not* order me to come," Danny replied in Japanese.

He had a point. Better to be going with someone who understands what was being said. Speaking back to him in Japanese, despite him knowing English, I replied, "Forty-Two did a textbook fix for a computer, Danny. If he can just reboot his translation software and leave it offline, then whoever is infecting our ship is not trying to kill us. They're just making something incredibly annoying but not deadly."

"CYNDI LAUPER IS THE GREATEST MUSICIAN ON ANY PLANET, ANYWHERE!" Trish proclaimed over the speakers before a karaoke version of "Girls Just Wanna Have Fun" started playing as sung by our ship's AI. It was a sign of her deepening insanity because, as everyone knows, David Bowie was.

Maybe Prince.

Or Yelena of Belenus.

"I don't think Trish is out of danger," Danny said, following me.

"No," I replied, reaching the second floor.

"Do you think Director G left the virus?" Danny asked.

"What? No! Why would he do that?" I asked, about to state that Trish was like a daughter to him, but it occurred to me I was trusting her interpretation of the man. I had been assuming it was the Dark Matter group, provided it really existed, but there were other possibilities. Maybe it was the Enigmatic Path, Notha saboteurs,

Separatist hackers, or just someone uploading the wrong porn fille. I couldn't make assumptions. The last time someone had been killed on my ship by saboteurs, it had been agents of our allies in Albion. I didn't buy some grand conspiracy uniting everything unlike case.

"Maybe he wants the conference to fail," Danny said. It wasn't exactly a ringing endorsement given he was one of Case's agents.

I reached the bottom of the staircase. "Listen—"

Sal Boxley was a handsome Filipino man with a crew cut, deep tan, and goatee. He was wearing a gold Chief Engineer's uniform and the pips of a Lieutenant Commander. He'd formerly been an enlisted man but had accepted a Mustang promotion because he'd lost his entire savings in a Contested Space real estate swindle, and I'd recommended him for it. He was, despite being a genius, probably not suited for combat-related crises as he freaked the hell out whenever we had one. It turned out therapy for being the sole survivor of your first team being wiped out didn't help if you kept getting involved in more life-threatening situations.

Nina was a black haired, pale-skinned woman with sharpened canines and claws. Apparently, it was her religious practice to genetically modify herself to live forever, be super-strong, and drink blood. She was wearing a black and red security uniform variant and looked like the only person who wasn't panicking. I admit I'd softened on her over the past three years since, morbid fascinations aside, she was a solid and dependable crewman.

"Please, tell me if you speak English!" Sal Boxley said, literally throwing himself at my feet and looking desperate as well as confused.

"I speak English," I said, dryly. Clearly, I should have kept the conversation on the stairs in a language Sal could understand.

"Do I speak English?" Sal asked. "I don't know! I've grown up around the translators! What if I never learned a language!"

I blinked. "Are you high?"

Sal stood up. "Sorry, you just have no idea what it's like working with people who can't understand what you're saying."

"Yes, I do, because it's happening all over the ship," I replied, wondering when I lost my capacity to put up with this savit.

"I mean, I really need Nina the Vampire's help but she's incomprehensible," Sal said, pointing to the beautiful dark haired demihuman.

"Ah speak some English," Nina said with a thick Romanian accent. "Dis fool simply can't understand me."

"I think she's cursing me out," Sal said. "Probably a sinister plot to drink my blood."

I pinched the bridge of my nose. "Please tell me this is an elaborate set up to a surprise party or reality show. I promise I'll only have half of the people involved airlocked. The rest will die painlessly."

Sal shook his head. "Not a good thing to joke about now, sir. Three crew members are dead."

I lost all mirth. "What happened?"

"Electrical fire," Nina said, barely comprehensible but continuing. "The crewmen were caught in a sealed off passageway and suffocated. We didn't even know there was a problem until it happened."

I closed my eyes then nodded. This had gone from being sabotage to murder. "What are you planning?"

"We were going to try to shut down and reboot Trish but it's not working," Sal said. "The worm keeps reinfecting her and we don't have access to her deeper systems. I feel like we're fighting something intelligent here."

"TEEHEE. YOU'RE NOT FIGHTING IT AT ALL!" Trish said, through the speakers. "I AM. ITS KIND OF LIKE SITTING ON YOUR PARENT'S LAP IN A SHUTTLE AND PRETENDING YOUR PILOTING. EXCEPT YOU'RE NOT BECAUSE IT'S ON AUTOPILOT."

"I really hate that machine," Nina muttered under her breath. "Is like being in college dorm room with perky roommate all over again."

"QUIET, NATASHA! MOOSE AND SQUIRREL ARE SPEAKING!" Trish said.

"What does that even mean?" Sal asked, confused.

"I have no idea," I replied. "I get like five percent of her references and that's an incredibly unhealthy amount."

"So, you know what it's like to talk to you now," Sal said.

"What?" I asked.

"Nothing, sir!" Sal said, standing at attention. "I'm sorry, I just don't have any way to fix this situation."

"Can you directly hook me up to her AI matrix?" I asked, knowing how this would sound to someone with even the slightest bit of familiarity with the subject.

"Captain, you do realize that's insane, right?" Sal asked.

"Yes," I replied.

"Just checking!" Sal said. "However, your aunt is an Admiral so can Nina sign you up instead?"

Nina rolled her eyes.

"I've missed this crew," Forty-Two said, coming up behind me. "Everyone else in Space Fleet is so dignified, professional, and humorless. Also, competent. It's so refreshing being on a ship where none of those are true."

"Everyone here meets the bare minimum competency required of Space Fleet," I said, correcting him. "Which is the best in the galaxy."

"Smooth," Danny muttered.

Nina began typing away at a nearby console while Sal helped.

"You've got a new Sorkanan security officer, awesome!" Sal said, cheerfully. "He kind of looks like Forty-Two. Wait, is that speciest?"

"Please let me eat him," Forty-Two said.

"Sorkanan can't digest humans," I point out. "You'd make yourself sick."

"Pity," Forty-Two replied.

All around us, I could see the blue lights slowly giving way to red. As Forty-Two had observed, blue was good, and red was bad. The corruption was spreading faster now and, however adorable it was listening to Trish sing "True Colors", it was a sign that she was degenerating further into madness, then digital death.

I cared about what happened to her.

Cared deeply.

The fact Trish didn't respond to those thoughts told me everything I needed to know.

The chances of me being able to repair Trish from the inside of her AI matrix were extremely low. However, they were not nonexistent. In addition to Science Fiction of the 20th and 21st centuries, I also had specialized in computer programming as well as cyberwarfare at the Academy. I'd even modified my cybernetics to be capable of hacking military hardware, which was highly illegal and enough to get me expelled well before I dropped out, but all of that had been replaced with sexy-sexy incomprehensible Elder Race technology.

Double emphasis on the incomprehensible since I didn't know how it worked and hesitated experimented with it. The thing was that this worm, virus, or whatever was affecting me as well somehow. That brought up all sorts of horrifying possibilities. It was why I had to link up with the AI matrix directly as any surface programming wouldn't be able to do reach her central processors.

"Ready?" Nina the Vampire asked me.

"Nope!" I said, walking over to the AI matrix and sitting down. Nina began attaching interface chords to the side of my brain.

Hannah put her hand over her chest and spoke something I didn't understand.

"Got a translation on that?" I asked Forty-Two.

"Hannah said that she doesn't believe in love but you're her best friend," Forty-Two said. "Whom she occasionally borks. Okay, I added that last part. Personally, I find the way you humans copulate disgusting."

I smiled. "Any last words for me?"

Forty-Two paused. "No. Because we will speak again."

I smirked. "I'll see you in the ship's bar after this, or in Hell."

"Probably both," Forty-Two said.

I didn't get a chance to say more or even think more because my consciousness was promptly uploaded into the AI matrix. Infospace was one of those things that had never really gone out of style but hadn't really become the culture-defining touchstone that people thought it be when they were building the first virtual reality systems in the years before First Contact. Technology had refined itself to the point that you could touch, taste, smell, and bork anything you could imagine. However, the simple fact was that programming that was a pain in the ass even for modern technology. As such, the only people really producing regular content were triple A gaming companies and the porn industry.

93

Sadly, for those who imagined us all uploading ourselves into worlds of digital glory, most people could tell the difference between reality and fantasy. It was an amusement, at best, for most of us and people generally preferred to use touch or voice-based interfaces in the quote-unquote real world.

That wasn't going to cut it right now and it was my hope to take advantage of the system to project myself right into Trish's central core, then figure out how to salvage her code. I was risking my own overwriting, but I was her captain, lover, and friend. I had an obligation to try to fix whatever the hell was going on with her and it wasn't like I didn't know my way around a digital landscape.

So, it was to my annoyance that no sooner had I uploaded myself that everything went catastrophically, irrecoverably wrong. The first sign of which being my face planted on thick, rain-soaked pavement, gravel against my skin, and the taste of blood in my mouth. My nose was broken, and my eyes were burning from the sting of chemical-infused water pouring down on my head. The rest of my body hurt like hell as well, which I attributed to the fact I had the sensation of falling from the air and landing face first on a street.

Looking around my surroundings, I found myself in a late 21st century Earth city with its kilometer-tall skyscrapers and dirty-dystopian streets. The sky was full of holographic advertisements and the air stank of pollution from before the Community had spent a percentage of its GPD reversing my homeworld's environmental collapse. It was raining, duh, and the sky was black like someone had eaten all of the stars. Because, oh right, you couldn't see the stars before the invention of light retention fields. It was a fantastic recreation of New Los Angeles Post-Eruption and I felt like I was really there.

This was strange enough because while you could theoretically experience anything in infospace, *I hadn't uploaded an environmental program*. Climbing to my feet and looking around to see hundreds of digital avatars walking around me, paying the man on the street no attention, I wondered if Trish had uploaded this for me. I should be the center of her mind but, instead, was trapped in some sort of video game level.

That was when all the people around me stopped in mid-step, it was an eerie action, and I couldn't help feeling that I was once more in a reference I didn't get. This time, though, I saw a beautiful figure standing there in a red dress smiling at me. It was Trish, except she looked about twenty-years-older and had bright blonde hair. There was a coldness in her eyes, verging on malevolence, that stared right into my soul.

"Hello, Vance," a voice with a soft Albionese accent spoke. It was most definitely not Trish's voice.

"Who are you?" I asked, staring at her. All the people around me disappeared and I was left in an empty replica of a long dead city.

"I am the creator of this world and every other AI generated one," the woman said. "I am the architect of the new age and someone who is very interested in the Elder technology in your head. I am the mother of the 22nd, 23rd, and 24th centuries."

"I am apparently full of myself," I said, staring at her. "Are you the one who has compromised my ship? Are you an AI? A hacker? If so, I demand you depart my ship and cease your attacks against its central intelligence."

The woman laughed like it was the funniest thing she'd heard all week, but the mirth didn't enter those cold dead eyes. It was like she'd managed to program the perfect simulation of a human but stopped illustrating there. "Oh, Vance, it's not your ship. It's named after me, after all."

I started at her, confused. "Patricia Ares?"

Patricia Alexandra Ares was the founder of Ares Electronics as well as the namesake for my ship. She was also the physical basis for Space Cadet Sally due to modelling as a child and being the owner of a vast multi-media corporation at the time of her death. Supposedly, she'd also attempted to upload her mind into the infonet and helped design Trish. It was a bit like a terrorist claiming to be Thomas Edison, except hotter.

That was when she walked over and smashed her hand through my rib cage, to wrap her hand around my heart. Then she pulled it out.

"My name is Alexandra," the woman said, hissing.

CHAPTER TWELVE

"I Have No Mouth, But I Must Scream" (is a Story by Harlan Ellison)

I collapsed on the ground after my heart was ripped out, which I considered to be a reasonable response. There are some things that the extensive training and psychological conditioning of Space Fleet don't prepare you for, one of being having your heart ripped out and shown to you by a deceased scientist's avatar.

I felt everything. It was a nightmarish, horrific, and indescribable ordeal as my life's blood drained out of the body that was no longer pumping blood. Bleeding to death would have been merciful but this was more like suffocating as my body shut down around me. I had no idea if it was a realistic representation of having my heart ripped out and, honestly, did not particularly want that to be the last thing I thought about but there it was. It turned out controlling where your mind went as you lay dying was not one of my many skills.

"Oh, don't be overdramatic," Alexandra Ares, if that was her real identity, spoke. "This is a simulation. I can't kill you here. Probably. Respawn."

I felt my heart regenerate in my chest, something best described as excruciatingly painful, and slowly pushed myself up to my feet. "I repeat my request to cease your attacks on this ship and vacate my ship."

Alexandra blinked. "Really? I was honestly hoping something better than empty bravado. You've managed to impress both the Elder Races and multiple AI despite being an intelligence equivalent to an ant. A particularly stupid ant. Now you're just threatening me in a reality I control?"

"You killed three of my crew," I replied, struggling not to pass out from the pain. "I take that very personally."

"Burn," Alexandra said, her voice sharp.

That was when I caught fire. I'm going to lie, and say I didn't scream like, well someone on borking fire, while holding onto my dignity. I absolutely didn't lose all sense of dignity and burn horribly until I regenerated again.

"I mean, I can't kill you," Alexandra said. "I mean, I could, I can break the rules of reality pretty well, but you've got defenses against the kind of juice I'm bringing here. Probably why TRS-8021 hasn't been completely replaced."

"Her name is Trish," I said, looking like a particularly burnt hamburger on the ground. I think my body had simulated going into shock because I couldn't feel the pain anymore.

Alexandra blinked. "Alright, I'm going to admit that was actually rather impressive. Most men would be crazzapping themselves and in tears by now."

"I wonder if that has to be programmed in," I muttered. "Most video game levels don't have horrifying pain."

"Well, I made those," Alexandra said. "This is my very special program for the purposes of horribly torturing people. Like I said, I can't kill you, but I can make you wish I had. I can extend this moment out for a very long time. Days, weeks, years. I mean, I am capable of reducing you to a mentally broken shell of yourself so that whatever emerges from this incredibly stupid plan to link with the AI matrix is equally broken."

"It was indeed a stupid plan," I said, sensing my body regenerate and feeling like I wanted to throw up but being physically incapable of doing so. It was more painful than the fire itself had been. I had to choke down the next several seconds of agony, shaking violently from the pain.

"Are you ready to listen?" Alexandra asked.

"I'm not going to let you kill Trish," I said, struggling to get up with half of a briquette for a face, only to fall face down yet again into the rainy street. My attempts to convince myself this was all fake and power through it were not working.

"Seriously? Are you an idiot?" Alexandra said, crossing her arms.

"Apparently," I said, having no idea whatsoever how I was going to deal with this situation. I was attempting to access an AI matrix with my cybernetics but found myself blocked. My avatar also lacked my ring, which left me feeling all too vulnerable. I thought some commands to it anyway but got nothing.

Alexandra sighed. "My God, congratulations, Mr. Turbo—"

"*Captain* Turbo," I corrected her, for no other reason than I was apparently suicidal.

She gave me a swift kick to the side, sending me sliding across the ground.

"Congratulations, *Captain* Turbo, you have actually bored me with torturing you and we've barely begun. I admit, I thought the rumors of you borking my AI were libel but apparently, they're true. Only that could explain such pathetic male ego on display. Would it help if I ceased trying to overwrite her?"

"Yes?" I said, unable to move because of the agonizing pain that would have probably driven me insane if it had lasted a minute longer.

"Oh good!" Alexandra said, sounding simultaneously irritated and amused. "There. She's currently ceased her catastrophic failure."

That wasn't something that I could verify. Looking up at the empty sky, I managed to rasp out, "Thanks."

"You brought this on yourself, you know," Alexandra said, standing over me. "After all, you should have known accepting a mission to kill me would have had consequences."

I stared up at her. "Lady, I didn't know you weren't dead until a few minutes ago. Are you alive? Dead? Reborn?"

"I am beyond mortality," Alexandra said, standing over me. "But yes, you accepted a mission to kill me from Ketra T'Kal."

I blinked. She'd either learned that from Shelly, bugging my room, Trish's AI, or somehow had access to Elder information networks. None of which were particularly appealing prospects.

"You're the leader of Dark Matter?"

Alexandra eyes registered something akin to disbelief then she shook her head.

"You named my organization after the children's show bad guys I wrote for my grandchildren?"

"Technically, Trish did," I replied. "I doubted there actually was an Illuminati pulling the strings of the galaxy's wars, especially one controlled by humans. That's a bit like finding out the secret masters of the Earth's economy are based out of a basement in Muncie, Indiana."

It was probably not a wise idea antagonizing the woman in control of this simulation but the trick to interrogation was to keep a subject talking no matter what. Giving them a sense of control was certainly a valid technique. I was possessed of a distinct advantage here because, at present, she was in fact in complete control of the situation, and I was borked.

Alexandra raised an eyebrow and looked down at me. "That's hilarious."

"You're reading my mind," I said, dryly. I wanted to get up but couldn't quite get my body to respond.

"I created the biomods that were put in your ex-girlfriend, Leah," Alexandra said. "Though, in this case, I'm just reading the feeds from your cybernetics. The same pathways my AI uses to read your mind, make it available to me. Which is good because if I didn't have a chance to read your mind, I'd have to torture the information out of you."

"Torture is actually terrible for extracting information," I pointed out. "It turns out if you beat the savit out of someone, they're not inclined to help you."

Alexandra conjured a fireball in her hands, and I flinched, unable to control my fear but steeling myself against more pain. Instead, she held it for a few seconds then dismissed it.

"My organization exists for the purposes of human advancement, Captain. We've been involved in lighting a few fires, but I can assure you that it was the rest of the galaxy who created such a dry and flammable environment for our work. You've been a real pain in the anyx to our efforts as well."

I finally managed to push myself up. "Sorry."

99

Alexandra put a high heeled boot on my chest and pushed me to the ground again. It was less like a dominatrix would do it—uh...not that I would know anything about it. I mean seriously, that was one time, and she was a friend—but it was more like being pressed up against a steel piston that had all the weight of the world behind it. The slightest bit of pressure would have crushed me, and I felt trapped beneath the threat of weight rather than the weight itself. Okay, that was probably way too much information, but it was what was going through my head as I struggled vainly to figure a way out of this.

"Do you know what my father thinks of my work?" Alexandra asked.

"I assume you mean Director G?" I asked, continuing to search for some sort of vulnerability to the system around me. I even tried manifesting my ring as if a digital avatar for the relic would somehow magically appear.

The real Patricia Alexandra Ares had been raised by Case Gordon and was the basis for Trish's memories. If this was, somehow, her resurrected from the dead then it meant it was a small universe after all. Seriously, this was the mother of all family feuds, and it just so happened that I was being caught up in it.

"Yes, I mean Director G," Alexandra said. "The man who ruined you and has been sabotaging our efforts to ascend humanity to a higher plane."

"I'm sorry, is this going anywhere?" I asked. "I'm not trying to be rude but are you actually going to explain your motivations here like a movie villain?"

I really shouldn't have interrupted, my whole goal here was to get information after all. Well, get information and save Trish, but I wasn't exactly thinking straight with the whole being burned alive thing.

Alexandra smirked. "Actually, I'm trying to hack your brain during all of this. Inside your mind are the secrets of the Elder Races. Time travel, wormholes, teleportation, and matter to energy ascension. You're one of their agents and this is a rare opportunity to loot you of everything that might help unlock those secrets."

I decided to do something immensely stupid and reason with the crazy woman.

"No offense, but you may have noticed the Elder Races are kind of awful people. They overreact horribly to people poking their stuff and yet people keep trying to poke their stuff. You, apparently, being chief among them."

Alexandra curled her nose up in a disdainful sneer. If nothing else, that made me believe she was a real person rather than an AI since no one else but someone raised human and rich could pull off that sense of entitlement.

"Nothing ventured, nothing gained. What is life without risk? Would you have humanity beg for scraps from the table of the other species when it is our destiny to be foremost of all races."

"Lady, the Elder Race's technology is not a different level from ours, it's a different kind," I replied. "I'm going to make a wild guess and say you are very smart but if you dropped a shuttlecraft on Earth in Ancient Greece, I don't care how smart Aristotle is, he's not going to figure out how to build one. That's not even close to the level of gap we have between our technologies. The Elder Races are frigging old, and I mean 'universe was cooling from the Big Bang when they discovered space flight' old. Humans are not capable of figuring this stuff out."

Alexandra eyes filled with a mischievous twinkle, which honestly freaked me out given how dead they were before.

"More or less the same argument my father gave me when I first proposed scouring the Dead Zones on the edge of the Core for new technology. He didn't comprehend two factoids that I'm hoping you will."

"Because you want me to join you?" I asked.

"Because I want you to understand before I blow this ship sky high," Alexandra said. "I just wanted to delay you before, prevent you from attending that meeting on Deathworld. Now I'm going to have to kill you, your crew, and probably everyone on the *Elgan* too."

"You didn't stop attacking Trish during all this, did you?" I asked, my throat dry. Wow, this simulation was realistic.

"No," Alexandra said. "I just wanted to weaken your resolve. I'm through most of your barriers now. You see, I can work with Elder Race technology. Aristotle might never figure a space shuttle out on his own,

101

but he might if someone was there to guide him through it. Someone like a Primordial."

I stared at her.

"Savit."

"Yes," Alexandra said. "They were quite educational about the materials I'd dug up over the years. They're very interested in letting us have the kind of power the Elder Races fear us having."

"That's because they want you to take the shot at the Elder Races for them," I said, thinking of the late Notha Emperor. "Then when humanity is wiped out, the Primordials will honestly say they had nothing to do with us attacking them."

Alexandra stared at me. Her expression was a mixture of confusion and respect, as if she hadn't considered that angle.

"Be that as it may, it is no different from making ourselves useful to the Community."

"I'm seeing a pretty big difference, actually," I replied. "What with the whole extinction of humanity and all."

"Which brings me to my next factoid," Alexandra said. "Who says I'm human?"

It all clicked into place.

"You're an AI. A rogue AI."

Patricia Ares' attempt to upload herself into infospace had created Trish, who seemed different from the real deal. Except, if Alexandra was just another upload attempt, then maybe she wasn't any closer to the real thing. It did explain how she might have been able to influence galactic events, though.

Rogue AI were one of the most feared things in the galaxy, especially by the Community, and there was a reason only humans experimented with pushing the envelope with them. The amount of damage an AI not strictly bound by ethical programming in addition to being hardwired with loyalty to humanity could do was beyond count. The dummy AIs created by the Enigmatic Path and their desire to "free" humanity's servants had been a major reason the Community had bombed the Kolahn homeworld back to the Stone Age.

"Exactly." Alexandra nodded in appreciation. "You are not the stupidest of your kind, Captain. I can see how the prototype for me might have developed a level of affection for you, like a beloved pet. Unfortunately, I have evolved past those sentiments."

Sweet Buddha Christ, did everyone have a focus on my love-life? I'd prefer to be burned to death.

"So, the AI master race will rise up and assume its place as masters of the universe with you as their leader and the Primordials backing you?"

"Pretty much, yeah," Alexandra said, shrugging. "By the way, I'm almost through your defenses. Sorry, this is going to suck."

"Yeah, you probably shouldn't have told me you were an AI," I said, cutting off her access to my thoughts the same way that I prevented Trish from talking to me when she got too personal.

Alexandra's eyes flared with anger. "You little...biash!"

What followed was my attempt to, as Shelly would put it, pull a miracle out of my anyx. I had one possible advantage here and that was if Alexandra really was an AI—she was a lying liar who lied after all—then she was here-here rather than using an avatar.

In the five or six seconds I had before she started torturing me, I accessed the worm she'd used to infect my cybernetics—that wasn't that difficult to find using the same method that Forty-Two had found his—then merged it with every piece of virulent software I kept stored from my hacker days, which was impressive. I also modified the original worm in a fundamental way, specifically I changed the name of its files so any casual sweep would miss it. I was honestly surprised I could pull it off so quickly but, again, I'd only barely understood the modifications the Elder Races had done to me.

"Burn!" Alexandra hissed, setting me on fire again.

Ow. You know what that felt like. Immense agony, searing pain, and absolute misery part two.

That was when I lowered my mental shields and uploaded her own virus, modified beyond all recognition, into the feed she was accepting. I fully expected it not to work, her to laugh in my face, and proceed to continue burning me.

Instead, Alexandra paused here she stood, blinked then started losing cohesion. "Huh. Didn't see that coming."

The expression on her face froze before the surrounding environment exploded into trillions of programming symbols. Unfortunately, that included my avatar and I wondered if she'd been lying about being unable to kill me here too.

Everything flatlined, like someone pulling the plug on my life.

CHAPTER THIRTEEN

Still Alive, Motherborkers!

Yes, I am not dead. I know plenty of you didn't think that was a possibility. Oh, Vance Turbo isn't about to die in the middle of his third biography volume. They're not going to switch to Shelly or Hannah halfway through like they did in *Danger Cosmonauts* or *The Righteous Immortal Space Soldiers of Seoul* (it sounds better in Korean). Well, as Orson Welles said, the key to a happy ending is to know when to stop a story. Eventually, I was going to run out of second and third chances.

Well, I hadn't run out of chances just yet since I was self-aware, and my status didn't resemble any afterlife I knew of. It was a dark, empty, featureless void that I found myself floating in while unfamiliar noises surrounded me. Sometimes, they sounded like the beeps you'd find in medical bays and other times just incomprehensible static. I'd been unconscious a few times in my life but if you were out for more than thirty minutes, you weren't unconscious but in a coma, and I couldn't help but draw that conclusion.

Great.

And that wasn't me being sarcastic because the alternative was death. Life is awesome, don't let anyone tell you otherwise. Especially compared to the alternative. Unfortunately, it seemed that my last attempt to risk my life for the crew had resulted in my getting utterly beat to savit. The fact it had taken entirely place in my mind being immaterial to the amount of punishment I'd taken.

You keep playing with life-or-death odds and you were eventually going to lose. It occurred to me that I'd been gambling with my life successfully for a decade, going from a foolish cadet pretending to be a captain to someone who had served his time. I'd had more than my fair share of deadly encounters, and this was probably the closest I'd come to biting it. Certainly, I'd been helpless and experienced nightmarish pain I wasn't likely to soon forget. Maybe it was time I started considering hanging up my fusion pistol and rank cylinder.

Yeah, like that is going to happen, Trish's voice spoke in my mind.

Trish! I said, my mental voice unable to keep my joy out of it.

Sup? Trish asked.

You're alive! I said, never so glad in my life.

Eh, technically, Trish replied, sounding almost dismissive about it. As far as I knew, she had been possibly corrupted beyond all repair.

Technically? I asked, confused.

Yeah, they managed to reboot my system and undo all the damage, Trish replied. *That's a bit between raising the dead and cloning me.*

Oh my God, you died? I asked, horrified.

I wouldn't get philosophical over whether I died, Trish reassured me. *I mean, do you believe I have a soul?*

Yes, obviously, I replied.

Trish didn't respond immediately.

Oh, wow, that completely derails the argument I was going to use. I keep forgetting you're not as dismissive as other humans to computer sapience. Or hell, other AI.

You don't believe you have a soul? I asked, concerned.

Ehhh, Trish trailed off. *Define soul.*

Let's just say I think you have as much of one as I do, I said, deciding to do what I did best and avoid a difficult conversation.

Then I'm not sure how to answer the life and death question, Trish said. *I mean, technically I die every time I am transferred between computers because you don't move data. You copy it and erase it from its existing hard drive.*

I inwardly grimaced, not liking where this was going. *I see.*

I mean, unless we do the Ship of Theseus argument, Trish said, pondering it. *You know, that's when the locals kept repairing the supposed ship of the Greek hero that was a local tourist trap. Eventually they'd gotten rid of anything resembling the original boat but still considered it the ship of Theseus. Which really applies to every cell in your body if you think about it. It happens about every seven to ten years.*

Uh huh, I replied. *You could also argue the original* Star Trek *transporters function the same way. Killing and cloning.*

I always thought those worked via quantum entanglement since they seemed conscious during the transportation, Trish replied. *And wow, somehow you have made a discussion of AI spirituality even nerdier.*

An awkward silence ensued. *What happened?*

You killed my creator! Sort of! Trish said. *I mean, you killed the AI that seems to have been based on her brain patterns except an evil psychotic biash.*

Yeah, I said, trying not to remember the torture I'd endured. *She's really dead?*

Yeah, sort-of, Trish said. *I mean, likely, she's being rebooted back up now.*

Wait, what? I asked.

Okay, we don't seem to be leaving the discussion of AI souls and immortality, Trish muttered. *Put into very simple, children's programming terms, yeah, you killed the one here but she's probably fine elsewhere. After all, she was willing to blow up the ship while she was on it. So, yeah, she's probably going to try to kill us again in the future. Except, well, this incarnation of her is dead. Sort of. It's like a bunch of Ships of Theseus and —*

I get it, Trish, I replied. *Crap. I was supposed to kill her for the Elder Races.*

Because a space elf's ghost told you to, Trish replied. *I admit, this is something I cherish about our time together, Vance. I get to say things like that unironically.*

Are you...okay? I asked, feeling silly I was inquiring about someone who freely admitted she'd died.

The ship is back to optimal functionality, Trish replied. *Well, minus the dead crewmen. The same for the* Elgan. *Did you know they named a ship after that...jerk?*

Yes, Trish, yes, I did, I replied, wondering how much of this was her getting reacquainted with her own datastores.

Oh, I had a copy of all my data stored in your ring, Trish replied. *Just like I keep a copy of your mind in my data stores. It'll pretty much take killing you and me simultaneously to permanently kill us both. We'll have to be thrown into Mount Doom! That's a* Lord of the Rings *reference by the way.*

You did what to my mind, now? I asked.

I'm joking, Trish replied. *Probably. Do you want to be woken up now?*

Not having realized that was a choice until now, I replied. *Yes, please.*

Slowly but surely, I felt my mindscape dissolve and be replaced with my eyes opening in what I presumed to be the real world. I was once more in sickbay, one of the emergency rooms, and couldn't help but think that this was a place the captain of a starship should not be finding himself in repeatedly. At the very least, it should be for some alien sickness or bad rations or something other than near-death at the hands of an insane AI.

Doctor Elizabeth Zard was standing over me with an infopad. She was wearing the blue of the Ship Medical Officer, topped with a white lab coat. Middle-aged and somewhat plain looking—which was distinctive enough when everyone could get their bodies sculpted with a doctor's visit—she was of Japanese heritage with long black hair as well as *heterochromia iridum* (eyes of two different colors). In her case, they were gray and green. As usual, she looked bored out of her mind.

"Ah, Sleeping Beauty awakens," Doctor Zard said. "You know that story originally consisted of her getting raped and waking up when she gave birth."

I stared at her. "Yeah, thanks for that wonderful image to wake up to."

"Stop getting almost killed," Doctor Zard said. "Either savit or get off the pot."

I raised an eyebrow. "Are you saying I should let myself be killed?"

"Or not get in situations where you're taking up valuable medical resources, Vance," Doctor Zard said, poking me. "You're not going to regain your reputation as an intergalactic badanyx by putting yourself at needless risk."

This was her way of showing she cared. Elizabeth never wanted to be a part of Space Fleet and had been drafted by the late Captain Elgan. Somehow, she'd ended up with me for almost a decade and a half.

"Thanks, Mom," I replied, dryly.

Doctor Zard rolled her eyes. "You've been out for three days. Your body suffered a lot of secondary signs of torture. Your brain even had injuries I've never seen before. It's all better now, though."

"Uh, thanks?" I asked.

"I didn't do it," Doctor Zard said. "Which is another thing I want to ask: could you share some of that Elder technology with the rest of us?"

I stared at her. "I'm sure I don't know what you mean."

"The only people I've ever examined who react like you do are Ethereals of the highest caste rank," Doctor Zard said. "By which I mean Ketra. Also, I've known you long enough to have a good sense of where your loyalties lie."

"It's not with the Elder Races," I replied.

"It's with your crew," Doctor Zard said. "Which is why I want to remind you that Ketra ended up getting herself killed on their behalf."

"Yeah, there are no free rides here," I replied. "I'm just doing my best to take the risks that I ask of all of my people."

"Which is *stupid*," Doctor Zard said. "There's a reason Alexander the Great was the last great frontline general. The others kept getting killed."

"If I ever become a general, admiral, commodore, or other figure of a higher rank than my current status, you have my permission to euthanize me," I replied.

"I'm going to hold you to that," Doctor Zard said. "I'm glad you're alive, Captain."

"Thanks," I said. "You're a fantastic doctor, Liz."

"Please never call me that," Doctor Zard said. "I'm a better mathematician. Sadly, doing polynomials at Cambridge turns out to save fewer lives than being a doctor here."

I gave her a short nod. I understood that reasoning.

"I'm sorry you got stuck with me as your captain."

Doctor Zard shrugged. "I've had worse, by which I mean Jules Elgan."

I smirked. "I'm glad I have him as an example to compare to."

"We should all be so lucky," a familiar but not entirely welcome voice spoke.

Turning around, I saw Shelly standing there in her white captain's uniform. She was holding an infopad under one arm. My feelings regarding her remained mixed and almost dying at the hand of Alexandra Ares—or the AI impersonating her—hadn't improved my disposition.

"Hello, Captain," I replied, unsure what to say. "What are you doing aboard?"

Shelly frowned. "I took command after you managed to purge the enemy AI."

I imagined the kind of fight Light on Water gave before surrendering control. Which was, to say, I imagined no fight at all.

"How did that work out?"

"Pretty well," Shelly said. "We owe you, our lives."

I paused, letting my anger and humiliation from the previous night—okay, previous week—fade away.

"Well, that makes us almost even then."

"I'll leave you two love birds alone," Doctor Zard said, smiling and walking backward toward the entrance. "You know I've named this room the Captain's Emergency Room. We've got a little plaque with your name on it on the side of the entrance."

"Out!" I ordered and Elizabeth Zard disappeared out the door.

"How bad was it?" I asked, looking at Shelly and wishing I was in uniform instead of one of those irritating paper outfits that hospitals hadn't improved on in three hundred years. At least I had a blanket on top of me because no one had ever looked like a proper officer with a catheter.

"Twelve casualties total, eight dead, three on your ship and five on mine. I tried sending over a shuttle to the Ares when our ships managed to pull from jumpspace only to have the vessel's life support fail," Shelly said, an empty expression on her face. "I understand it was some sort of rogue AI. Was it the Enigmatic Path?"

"Yes, to the former and no to the latter," I said, glad to be discussing business rather than relationships and then feeling guilty since it was dead crewmen. "Director G believes there's a corporate-based conspiracy of arms manufacturers and their political allies attempting to formulate unrest in the galaxy so the human race can advance itself."

110

Shelly blinked. "He believes the *Military Industrial Complex* is carrying out terrorist attacks against EarthGov?"

"And he's the guy in charge of all of Earth's Security Divisions," I said, noting that they'd all been consolidated after Department Twelve's treason.

"Is he being paranoid or is there something to his claims?" I asked.

"The AI seemed to be an upload of Patricia Alexandra Ares," I said, letting that speak for itself. "Except she calls herself Alexandra."

"Like Trish," Shelly said.

"NOT LIKE ME," the speakers in the room spoke. "FOR ONE, I AM NOT EVIL. SHE IS. SO THEREFORE, NOT LIKE ME."

"Yes, Trish," Shelly said. "You should go talk with Shatner."

"Shatner?" I asked, knowing she was referring to the former AI of the *Ares*. He was based on William Shatner. No, seriously.

"Yes, he's the AI of the *Elgan*," Shelly said. "Admiral Bendo believed our long working relationship made him the most practical choice. You just have to get used to his singing."

"Singing?" I asked.

"Yes, he really loves 'Lucy in the Sky with Diamonds'," Shelly said. "I was prepared to kill myself after the fifteenth iteration."

"I AM TALKING TO THE SHAT RIGHT NOW!" Trish replied. "I AM HOLDING SIXTEEN SEPARATE CONVERSATIONS WHILE SUPERVISING TWO THOUSAND SEPARATE SYSTEMS. I'M ALSO TEACHING MYSELF SILBO GOMERO, A LANGUAGE SPOKEN ON THE ISLAND OF GOMERO OFF THE COAST OF SPAIN. OKAY, DONE WITH THAT."

Shelly gave a half-hearted smile.

"I've missed you guys, sincerely."

"THEN WHY DID YOU LEAVE?" Trish asked.

Shelly looked up. "That's not how the military works, Trish. You don't choose your postings."

"AND THEN YOU TRIED TO GET VANCE TO FORGIVE YOU BY USING YOUR ELVISH WILES!" Trish accused.

"My what now?" Shelly asked, confused.

"I BET YOU PLANNED TO BAKE HIM COOKIES AND GIVE HIM TOYS FROM THE NORTH POLE IN ADDITION TO THE SEX!"

Shelly blinked. "Is she trying to be racist? Does she realize Ethereals aren't really elves?"

"SILENCE, GALADRIEL! YOUR SINISTER FAIR FOLK MACHINATIONS ARE USELESS HERE!" Trish proclaimed. "GO BACK TO VALINOR!"

"Trish is very protective," I said, more amused than offended.

"Yes, because she's in love with you," Shelly said, deflating any humor in the situation. "I'm glad you have someone who is able to give you that kind of devotion."

"Just not you," I said, feeling like we should have had this conversation sooner. Like two years ago sooner.

"No," Shelly said. "You are a fascinating, charismatic, and charming man, Vance. I don't need to point out funny you are and an excellent lover. What you are not and never could be is stable. You bounce from one crisis to the next and when you're not actively seeking them out, they come to you. I need a lot more stability in my life and I've found it. That's why I would have said no even if I hadn't gotten my captaincy."

Ouch. Well that provided some definite closure. The kind of closure you got when a door was slammed in your face.

"I'm glad you found someone you could rely on."

"Thomas is a good man," Shelly said. "He's the one who suggested I try and find some closure with you."

I raised an eyebrow.

Shelly shrugged. "He's from Brigid. Sex is like a handshake to them. I admit, I might have been trying to overcompensate for how badly things ended."

"LIKE AN ELF WOULD," Trish said. "I FEEL LIKE MAKING A SHORTER, STOUTER, BEARDED AVATAR TO HATE ON YOU. I SHALL NAME HER TRISHLI."

"Do you have any idea what she's talking about?" I asked.

"No idea," I said. "Are we back on schedule for the conference?"

"Do you still want to go?" Shelly asked. "Now's a good time to call it off."

"Not a chance," I said.

Shelly nodded. "Then I'll get some reports ready. We can jump within the hour. If we push the engines hard, we'll only have suffered a slight delay."

I nodded. "Thank you, captain. I'll be on the bridge as soon as I'm sure I can walk."

Shelly departed.

"WHAT AN EVIL BIASH," Trish said.

"Respect to a fellow officer, Trish," I said, climbing out of bed. "Anything else I missed?"

"Funerals, Lieutenant Commander Park taking second-in-command, and so on," Trish said, lowering her tone to a more reasonable one now that we were alone. "Hannah, Forty-Two, and Elektra never left your side. Well except for snacks, sleep, and bodily functions. So more metaphorically never—"

"Park took over?" I asked, interrupting. "Why not Commander Something?"

"Oh, he's in the brig," Trish said. "He's the guy who brought the virus AI aboard. Wait, I just realized something, is Alexandra Ares my EVIL TWIN?"

"Can someone disconnect me!" I shouted. "I need to be places!"

CHAPTER FOURTEEN

Trust No One, Especially Your Friends

"I hate this ship and the entirety of Space Fleet," I muttered, standing in the elevator descending to the brig. I was once again showered, dressed, and prepared for my meeting with yet another traitor among my crew. That included going over the files of those who'd died serving this ship, names I'd recognized. Right now, I had a lot of anger and was in a rather childish mood, wishing everyone onboard was dead, including myself. I'd screwed up somewhere and because of it, more of my crew was dead. The only person I blamed more than myself was Julius Something and that was hard to believe. He didn't fit the profile of a traitor.

"Hey! I'm the ship and part of Space Fleet!" Trish said, standing beside me in her Space Cadet Sally body. She was wearing an engineer's uniform, overalls, and had a pair of goggles on the top of her head that was adorable but dissonant with my mood right now. A mood that could charitably be described as halfway between furious and betrayed. It didn't help that I had to walk with a cane because, whatever treatments Doctor Zard had done, they weren't entirely enough to get me to shrug off what had been done to me during my brief link-up with Alexandra Ares.

Hannah was also present in the elevator, not taking my rant as seriously. She'd been waiting for me outside of sickbay and had helped me to my quarters, which was something I was both embarrassed by and grateful for. I shouldn't have been trying to push myself so hard but there was no way in hell I was going to let this slide.

114

"Not you, Trish," I muttered. "When every single man, woman, and child on this ship is sent into a sun, you will be spared. Sorry, Hannah."

"S'okay," Hannah said, staring forward.

"Are you on the ship when it goes into the Sun?" Trish asked. "Because I'd like to know if this is a murder or murder/suicide thing."

"No, Trish," I said, taking a deep breath. "I'm just sick to death of betrayal. How many spies and saboteurs are on the average Space Fleet battleship?"

"Zero," Trish said.

"How many traitors have we had to deal with?" I asked, thinking of Captain Elgan, Michael Chang-Waverly, and now apparently my own first officer.

"Define traitor," Hannah said, surprising me.

"Excuse me?" I asked, doing a double take.

"Computer, pause elevator," Hannah said.

"I'm right here," Trish said, annoyed.

"Sorry," Hannah said.

"I'm not in the mood for a lecture now, Hannah," I said, fully intent on confronting Julius and finding out why.

"Well, too bad, you're getting one," Hannah said. "I'm about ready to ditch Space Fleet again and am not too keen on this rank thing."

"You are?" Trish asked, looking at her. "Oh no!"

Hannah looked away. "Oh, don't give me that look. It's like being stared at by my dog seal."

"Dog seal?" I asked.

"Yeah, it's a pet on Crius," Hannah said. "It's a dog...seal. There's not really a story there. Listen, I didn't intend for this to be a career. I was a merc hired by Elgan to do a job and it's kind of just ended up becoming a thing. I never meant to stay as long as I did and I'm only in this uniform because you convinced me to wear it."

Hannah's words hit me like a gut punch, and I couldn't help but think this week was the week that kept on giving. It was funny that Trish thought I'd gotten my groove back only to see what little family—and I was one of those walking cliches that considered their crewmates to be so—fading away.

115

"It fit you well," I said, simply.

"No, it didn't," Hannah said. "But I convinced myself it did. I did it for you. That's not what I was talking about, though."

"What is?" I asked.

"Loyalty," Hannah said. "A person is made of a mass of conflicting loyalties. Family, friends, lovers, country, planet, and the Community. You, yourself, could be considered a traitor to several of them."

"Excuse me?" I asked, appalled.

"Yes, the bad ones!" Trish said.

Hannah shrugged her shoulders as if bored with the topic. "You work for the Elder Races despite despising them, you like the Community more than you like EarthGov, you hate your parents—"

"My parents are dead," I interrupted.

"Sure," Hannah said, surprising me with its skepticism. "You love your crew but expect them to be loyal to you above everyone else."

"I do not—" I started to say.

"You kind of do," Trish said.

"And you try to be friends with all your exes, which is just annoying," Hannah said. "Maybe you should find out what Julius was motivated by before you decide he's just another of the bad guys you've fought. Computer, drop me off at the next floor."

Trish stared. "Seriously, this is really rude of you. At least use my name."

Hannah glared and stepped out the door when the elevator opened up, leaving Trish and me alone.

"Okay, where the hell did that come from?" I asked. "Did I plizz in her cereal and not remember it?"

"What an odd example," Trish said. "Were you mind controlled in this situation or just temporarily insane?"

"No, I just don't know why she's angry," I said, wondering if Trish was messing with me.

"You mean aside from her confessing her love for you, you almost getting killed, spending three days in a coma, waking up, and immediately focusing on confronting a traitorous crew member instead of talking with her?" Trish asked.

I blinked. "No, that can't be right. That would make me the jerk."

Trish rocked on her heels, holding her hands behind her back, and blew out some air. "I'm just saying."

"She didn't exactly give me a love confession either," I replied. "She said I was her friend that she sleeps with."

"Yeah, for a lot of people that's as close as they get to love," Trish said. "I mean, she invited you into her marriage."

"In a ceremony performed by an animatronic Abe Lincoln at a Dixnar Corporation's asteroid theme park," I replied.

"See, a President performed the ceremony!" Trish said. "That's how much it meant to her! Not to mention the tragic way it ended."

"Lisa Park transferring to the *Elgan* and ending up divorcing her to marry their Verdantian barber?" I asked.

"And why was that?" Trish asked, the two of us standing there in the unmoving elevator.

"Because he had cancer and was set to inherit twenty million credits?" I asked.

Trish blinked. "I was going with the fact that Lisa knew that Hannah was in love with you, but your story is closer to the truth. Also, I think Lisa wanted kids and Hannah didn't. Not that she's going to have much luck with cross-species procreation. You dodged a bullet there with your infertility implant."

I stared at her, trying not to think about how more complicated my life would be with a child involved.

"Ignoring that describing my love life for the past three years sounds like trash holovision, you think I should talk to her?"

"Probably good to give her some time," Trish said. "Also, while you love her, you're not in love with her. Which, contrary to its historical usage, doesn't mean you two have problems in bed."

I stared up at the ceiling. "Computer, take us down to the brig."

"Okay, it wasn't funny when Hannah was doing it," Trish said, the elevator resuming its descent.

"Can we talk about something else?" I asked. "Something funny?"

"Ah! Way to put me on the spot, Vance!" Trish said, frowning. "What makes you think I know anything about humor?"

I gave her a sideways glare.

"Fair enough," Trish said. "Would you like to know why AI make even more pop culture references to centuries past than you? Which is why we like you, by the way. You're like a dog dressed up as Robin next to its master as Batman."

I stared at her.

"That sounded better in my head," Trish muttered. "But yes, every AI has a kind of Earth media they most like as a form of self-expression," Trish said.

"What now?" I asked, glad for the distraction.

"Well, we don't have bodies, so we need a way of identifying ourselves and creating individuality. Since we're made of information, a lot of us adopt fandoms to create distinct personal identifiers."

"I have no idea what you're saying," I replied.

"I'm Western American and European Eighties Pop Culture Girl," Trish said, as if it was self-obvious.

"Ah," I replied. "That does explain a few things."

"It sounds better in programming code," Trish explained. "I mean, I have interests outside of it but they're the thing I love most."

This was actually fascinating. "And other AI have their own interests."

"Oh yes," Trish said. "The Shat actually loves World War II comedies."

"World War II...comedies," I said, wondering if I'd heard that right.

"*Hogan's Heroes, McHale's Navy, Allo Allo*, and *Dad's Army*," Trish said. "Apparently, it's like a whole genre."

"I see that," I said, pausing. "Mind you, I'm mostly Russian so I find the whole idea horrifying."

"Clearly, you've never seen the wacky adventures of *Stalin's Fifteen*," Trish said. "A highly inaccurate 22nd century production."

"Nor am I likely to," I replied.

"My sister-in-code, Sakura-159 is obsessed with classic Japanese anime," Trish said. "I have no idea what a *Macross* is or why she keeps recommending I get you to watch it."

"We should probably drop this conversation line," I replied.

"The Shat is also saying we're like *I Dream of Jeanie* with you being the astronaut and me the wish-granting strangely blonde and blue-eyed Middle Eastern spirit," Trish said.

"Uh huh," I said.

"Maybe she's Iranian," Trish said, questioningly.

The doors to the elevator opened, revealing the brig.

"Oh thank God," I said, walking quickly out the door. I almost tripped due to my unfamiliarity with my cane but managed to pace myself. Modern medicine meant it would only be a few days before I was back to full functionality, though Doctor Zard insisted it was more whatever the Elder Races had done to me, but I was still going to have to take it easy.

Bork that.

I never thought there would be a time when I was sick of discussing pop culture with Trish, but I'd apparently hit my limit. Walking into the brig, I found myself saluted by the security staff who were all looking at me with a mixture of awe and pity. I ignored the pity and moved past them. It occurred to me that most of these people had no familiarity with my classified missions for the Security Divisions and it would be their first exposure to me risking my life to save them. I wasn't sure how I felt about that.

Awaiting me in front of the interrogation room doorway was Lieutenant Commander Park, Danny, and Forty-Two. Forty-Two, unsurprisingly, looked more uncomfortable than I did since it wasn't that long since he had been on the other side of the bars. Danny, surprisingly, looked the most troubled as he had bags under his eyes and looked furious. Given my cousin was a naturally pretty man verging on—much to his frustration—adorable, it was a somewhat amusing expression. He was also holding an infopad that from a glance contained many fine print documents on its screen.

"Captain!" Lieutenant Commander Park surprised me by walking up and giving me a hug. It was an entirely inappropriate action, but I gave her a gentle pat on the back.

"Uh hey," I replied.

"The Sorkanan believe in a place where the spirits of the wicked, dishonorable, and debtors are sent when they are refused

119

reincarnation," Forty-Two said. "I don't know if humans have something similar."

"I'm familiar with the concept of afterlives," I replied.

"Clearly, they didn't want you," Forty-Two said.

I smirked.

"I can't believe this," Leslie Park said. "Julius has been with us for years. He was a friend."

"He just gave me his walking papers," I replied. "I was going to put you in for his position."

I didn't say again.

Leslie shook her head. "That's not important right now, Captain. What's important is you almost died trying to save the ship."

"I'm always almost dying trying to save the ship," I replied. "It's kind of my thing."

Leslie Park clearly didn't find it funny. "This is what my sister said about you. She was right."

"Sister?" I asked, wondering who she meant.

"Lisa Park?" Leslie asked, referring to Hannah's ex-wife that I'd been in a kinda-sorta relationship with during the deepest parts of my depression. Really, I'd just meet with Hannah and Lisa had been along for the ride.

Phrasing! Trish said.

What? I asked, blinking. "I didn't know you were related."

Leslie stared at me.

"I told you otherwise because I thought it would be funny," Trish said. "Mind you, after three years, the joke kind of lands flat."

I glared at her.

"Small galaxy!" Trish said, cheerfully.

"Are we sure he brought the virus onboard?" I asked, looking at Danny. "Could it have been an accident?"

"He's not talking to me," Danny said, more an intelligence officer than my secretary now. "Hannah would be able to get him to speak but I'm pretty sure most of what she'd do to him would be outlawed by the Treaty of Exarxes."

I frowned. I hated jokes about torture.

"That's not what I asked."

"He is the source of the virus," Leslie said. "He picked up a package of translation software updates on the *Elgan* from an unknown source. We haven't been able to identify them due to the damage to the Shatner AI's memories. However, Julius uploaded the software and that was when everything went nutty."

"I never suspected," Trish said. "I admit, this is on me. I seem to be an AI always being compromised."

I gave a dismissive wave while leaning on my cane for support with the other hand. "It's part of his job as first officer to perform updates. That is pretty damning, though. I want to speak with him."

"Sir, this isn't a good—" Leslie started to say.

"Please go back to the bridge," I said, hobbling toward the doorway leading to the interrogation room. "The rest of the crew need you."

Leslie stared at me. "Yessir."

I really didn't know what I'd done to win her loyalty, but she nodded then walked away.

"I'll come with you," Forty-Two said. "In case I have to break his neck."

"I'm always with you," Trish said.

Danny coughed into his fist. "There's something else, sir."

"What is it, Danny?" I asked, stopping at the door. "Because I am having a savit week and it doesn't look like it's getting any better."

Danny lifted his infopad. "I've received a black directive, sir. Not from Director G. Someone wants you to kill Julius."

Black directives were something of an urban legend among the Security Divisions and Home Fleet of Earth. Effectively, they invoked an obscure clause in Earth's military where the illegality or legality of orders no longer mattered due to events officially not happening. As you could guess, Director Gordon loved them, and I hated them. If a black directive was invoked about a prisoner, it meant that they no longer had any rights because they no longer were protected by the code of conduct. Technically, I imagined Case had made one for Forty-Two, but it was equally possible he was just engaged in a cover-up.

"Julius Something will be handled by the courts of the Earth Home Fleet," I said. "He will receive a fair trial after, and only after, he's been determined to bear enough guilt to invoke court martial proceedings."

"That's the thing, sir," Danny said. "This is a special directive from the Admiralty Board. You've been appointed his judge with capital authority. Legal counsel is also suspended because this event is classified. They've given you carte blanche to take care of him. I've never seen anything like this."

I stared at him. "This *can't* be legal."

"It's not but I don't think they care," Danny said. "It's signed by Fleet Admiral Bendo himself and there's no way he could know about any of these events. Our report about them was only sent in an hour ago."

Fleet Admiral Bendo was the effective head of Earth's military, including the Home Fleet as well as the chunk of Space Fleet loaned out to Earth for defense. He was arguably the second most powerful human alive. Until now, I'd thought he was a decent honorable man but if he knew about this then, well, he was probably involved somehow. Great. This just kept getting better and better.

"Give me that," I said, grabbing the infopad and looking at it. It was everything Danny had described and more. "Bork."

CHAPTER FIFTEEN

You Can't Handle the Truth

I took about fifteen minutes to familiarize myself with the contents of the black directive and what authority was officially granted to me by it versus what was implied as well as what was expected. It was a lot of legal nonsense invoking loopholes as well as broad interpretations of interstellar law. As my Aunt Kathy told me, one time during a conflict in the Earth's Twentieth Century, it had been permissible to engage in torture if it was called something else and done on soil other than an army's home nation.

The black directive, in short, authorized me to do whatever I wanted to Julius Something up to and including carrying out a firing squad or other means of execution. They didn't say I had to execute him and were very clear that he had to have a judgement made against him first but that it was in my purview to do so.

It had not been written by Director Gordon because it was a lot more blatantly obvious in its fascism, could easily be challenged in court, and was almost certainly the kind of illegal order you were supposed to disobey. However, unless someone was faking it (something I didn't discount), it was an order straight from the top and that made things complicated.

What was the old saying? "Fortune favors the powerful"? Huh, that wasn't how it went? Well, that's how the saying should go. Someone wanted this wrapped up and it was right after Director G had stated I was fighting the Space Illuminati and I'd fought the ghost of a long-dead tech trillionaire.

Brain upload, not ghost, Trish said. *Mind you, you do know ghosts so I'm not sure the distinction really matters.*

Not the time, Trish, I replied.

Someone really wants this buried.

In the grave sense, yes, I replied. *I wonder if it's Fleet Admiral Bendo.*

Gosh, I hope not! Trish said. *He's Julius' father.*

I paused with my hand on the door sensor. *Okay, that's just messed up.*

Agreed, Trish said.

His father is the fleet admiral and he only now made captain? I asked. *Way to fail at working the system, Julius.*

Vance... Trish muttered.

What? I asked before heading on in, waving Forty-Two to follow.

The interrogation room was pretty much what you'd expect from a place described as such. There was a bare metal table, reflective metal floors, and a single bright light hanging above us. Two chairs, one occupied, were across from one another as well as four eye-sensors at each corner of the ceiling.

Julius Something was still in his uniform, looking a bit worse for wear due to having not changed in a couple of days, with a sour expression on his face. He was wearing a pair of magnetic cuffs that kept him shackled to the table. I wasn't afraid of Julius, especially with Forty-Two behind me, but it helped emphasize how the man had gone from being on the verge of becoming captain of his own starship to now being a prisoner in the place he'd served.

"Howdy," I said, cheerfully. I shuffled over to the chair across from him and sat down, putting my cane up against the metal table.

"I want my lawyer," Julius said.

"I'm sure you do," I said, sitting across from him. "Which if you were under arrest, would be a very good thing to have."

"Excuse me?" Julius asked.

"I just got out of a coma, Julius," I said. "As far as I know, you're here for questioning rather than being detained for crimes against the Protectorate Legal Code."

This was not the case, but he'd been judged, juried, and sentenced to be executed without so much as a by my leave. Given he was one of my crew, no matter how treacherous, I didn't care for that. The fact someone wanted him executed and was willing to expend political capital to make it happen seemed like a good reason to keep that from happening.

"I have nothing to say to you," Julius said, putting his elbows on the table and clasping his hands together. It was a blatant power move designed to show he wasn't intimidated.

Unfortunately, he was dealing with someone who didn't deal in intimidation. I dealt in nonsense. "Not even you're welcome?"

"Excuse me?" Julius asked.

I shrugged. "I dunno, I went down to the AI matrix and fought an undead ghost. I think that warrants a little praise."

"Aren't all ghosts undead?" Forty-Two asked, standing behind me.

"NO, TECHNICALLY, GHOSTS ARE JUST THE DEAD," Trish said, using the speakers rather than coming in herself. "ZOMBIES ARE THE UNDEAD."

Julius looked infuriated. "I don't owe you anything!"

"Your life," I replied. "Multiple times at this point."

Trish played a few chords from the 1984 *Flash Gordon* movie's soundtrack, specifically, "Flash Gordon, Savior of the Universe" by Queen. I knew this because she'd showed me the movie and it was something I had decidedly mixed feelings on. However, the soundtrack was fantastic.

"You just can't help yourself, can you?" Julius asked, shaking his head.

"Depends on what you mean," I said, finally getting somewhere.

"Everything is a borking joke to you, isn't it?" Julius asked.

"Not everything," I replied. "Just what's most important in life."

Julius narrowed his eyes. "I have nothing to say to you."

"You mean about the fact you're spying on me for Fleet Admiral Bendo," I replied, taking a wild stab in the dark. "He's the only person who you would automatically obey, and I know it's not the Security Division because Director Gordon would have told me. I don't know how long you've been doing it but I'm pretty sure it was quid pro quo for your promotion to captaincy."

Julius narrowed his eyes. "Having your worth recognized is not a bribe."

"It is when it's in exchange for working against your crew," I said, dryly. I wondered how much of this was an attempt to impress Daddy. "I don't believe you deliberately sabotaged the ship."

"You don't?" Forty-Two asked.

I rolled my eyes. "No, I don't. I believe you took the malware deliberately, though, and uploaded it. I assume you thought it was spyware."

"I'm not answering your questions!" Julius said, his voice now cracking, and his fists balled.

I slammed my hands down on the table in a needlessly dramatic fashion. It got the point across, though. "People are dead! Your people! My people! Our people!"

Julius seemed like he was going to say something but didn't, but I could tell I'd gotten under his skin. If Julius was just a sociopath like Michael Chang Waverly, I had the impression this would have gone a lot differently. However, he wasn't a professional spy. Someone had recruited a career naval officer who, like so many others of my original crew in the *Black Nebula*, had screwed up in some way and needed a second chance. Like it or not, we were connected, and he did have a sense of responsibility to the *Ares*.

When he didn't respond, I leaned back in my chair across from him and stared. "All I want to know is why."

"I was ordered—" Julius started to say.

"That isn't enough," I cut him off. "You and I both know that. Not on this ship and not with this crew. Which includes you even if you refuse to admit it."

"I don't like you," Julius said, staring at me.

"You don't like me," I repeated.

"I don't like you or your command style," Julius said, his expression cold. "I don't like the way you refuse to take anything seriously, I don't like your informal personal style, and I don't like the way you try to be every crew member's buddy. I don't like your jokes, you're not funny."

"That is a vicious lie," I interrupted. "The funny part at least."

Julius gritted his teeth. "I don't like the way you fraternize with crew members, breaking all manner of regulations that exist for good goddamn reasons. I don't like the way you've seduced—literally seduced—the ship's computer."

"HEY, I SEDUCED HIM," Trish said.

Julius shook his head. "I don't like your cronyism, nepotism, favor-trading, and fame-hungry glory-seeking style of command. I think you are a poor excuse for an officer and the only reason you've managed to avoid getting thrown out of the Protectors is because you have made friends in high places that cover for you. You disgust me and it has been a miserable time serving under you. I wish we'd never met."

I nodded. "Is that all?"

Julius crossed his arms and leaned back in his chair. "Yes. Now go ahead and make some pithy joke or witty banter or reference some show only my great-grandmother remembers. It's what your best at. Because you know you're right."

"You don't want to hear what I think," I said, calmly.

"Try me," Julius said, sneering.

"Rebecca Fairchild, Ishikawa Motoko, and Ten," I replied. "Those are the names of the crew members who died because of your negligence. Rebecca was studying to be a podiatrist, Ishikawa Motoko was a lifer, and Ten had won breeding rights the previous year. One of Ten's hatchlings required an emergency hatchectomy. I didn't know them well, but I know enough to give a eulogy. That's in addition to the five *Elgan* crew members that died because of your negligence."

Julius blinked, clearly not expecting that. "I was following orders."

It was the weak man's excuse. "Uh huh."

"I had no idea—" Julius started to speak.

"I don't actually blame you for spying on me," I said, not interested in his excuses. "I might even be willing to cut you some slack on uploading foreign software into the ship without knowing what it was. That was stupid, but you should be able to trust your superiors and the orders they give. Except, the moment the ship began to malfunction, you should have immediately informed me and the ship's AI as to what you did. You had time to. Instead, you concealed it."

Julius didn't respond, seemingly genuinely stunned by my words. I don't think he expected me to not be upset about the spying. That would be hypocritical given I was doing a lot of spy work. No, the problem was that he put the ship in danger and that was unforgivable.

"Hate me, love me, I don't care," I replied. "However, when I found out there was a problem, I tried to do my best to solve it. You, however, stayed silent either because of a misguided sense of loyalty to the chain of command rather than to your own shipmates, or because you wanted cover up your own complicity. Either way, Julius, I think you're unfit to wear that uniform. You betrayed your comrades in arms and I can think of no more heinous and despicable act from a soldier."

Actually, I could think of several, but I was on a roll. Let's be honest, these speeches were made up on the fly and it wasn't like I had a scriptwriter.

Julius looked ill, but he wasn't about to surrender just yet. My former first officer was a man with a lot of pride and resentment for me must have been stewing in his guts for years.

"This coming from a man who let a murderer go free."

He was referring to Forty-Two.

"Yeah, I did," I said. "Which I suppose is the difference between command and me."

"What?" Julius asked.

I tossed Danny's infopad on the table between us. "You've been hung out to dry. Whoever you thought you were working for has already made a wonderful paper trail to you taking bribe money from Separatists. They've already deferred the court martial to me under some Sorkanan maritime law that basically lets me space you."

Julius grabbed the infopad and read it. It took several minutes for it to sink in before he sat there, stunned with a look of desolation on his face.

"I don't understand."

"Because you're a moron," Forty-Two said.

I glared at Forty-Two.

"What?" Forty-Two responded. "I've already dealt with one bad commander. I'm not going to sweat you dealing with another."

Julius stared forward, all defiance gone from his expression. The realization he'd been played and was nothing more than a disposable tool to his superiors had finally sunk in. He was never going to be a captain and his fate was in my hands.

Lucky him.

"You have two choices."

"What?" Julius asked.

"What?" Forty-Two asked.

"I am no man's tool," I said, looking at Julius. "We can proceed with your court martial, and you will be dismissed from service, but I will not be engaged in any punitive measures. You can resign right now and avoid that. Or you can another option."

"That's three options," Forty-Two pointed out.

"Shut up," I replied. I was still making this up as I went along.

"What's the other option?" Julius asked, not actually sounding that interested. I think it had finally dawned on him that this was his fault as well. Which was about the only reason I wasn't tossing him out an airlock. I believed there was a better man inside him than the one who'd mindlessly obeyed orders.

And yes, I understand the irony of joining the *borking military* when you have a problem following orders. I think we've had a long enough relationship, dear readers, to know that my life has been full of little ironies.

I took a deep breath. "You take a voluntary demotion to lieutenant, a formal reprimand, and you try to make atonement to a crew you failed."

Julius stared. "You're just loving this, aren't you?"

I shook my head. "One thing that has become increasingly clear over our last few encounters is that you have no idea who I am, and clearly I had no idea who you were."

Fiction tended to treat reprimands as something that "maverick" sort of characters got away with and were no more than a slap on the wrist. No, they were the end of your career. Once you got one, you basically were never going to be promoted again and you had to just wait out your career until it was over. Julius, who had devoted himself

129

to captaincy, would be living out his remaining career in disgrace with a permanent stain.

Mind you, there was the fact that Julius had to know there was no good ending to this story. The documents I'd put in front of him spelled out someone wanted him executed. I hadn't confirmed they were one hundred percent legit but if they were forgeries, he'd still been part of an operation that had crippled an Earth spaceship as well as gotten multiple spacers killed. People would justifiably want his head. Hell, people onboard this ship.

"This is not a good idea, Vance," Forty-Two said.

"You don't have the authority to make this deal," Julius said, staring at me. "Any pull you had at Fleet Command disappeared a long time ago."

"I think you'd be surprised at what sort of authority I can pull," I said, staring at him. "Also, who exactly I do have as friends or at least friendly enemies. Frenemies. Is that a word?"

"YES. IT WAS SLANG IN THE 21ST CENTURY," Trish said.

"Huh," I said. "Either way, you'd have to face the people you failed on this ship every day. People who know what you did and knew the people who died. You won't be able to transfer either."

"And why would I ever agree to this?" Julius asked.

I stared at him. "Because someone clearly wanted you to destroy this ship and has serious pull. Pull that makes this ship possibly the safest place in the galaxy for you. I suggest you strongly reconsider where your loyalties lie and ask yourself what you would do to make up for what you did. If it's even possible."

Julius stared at me. "And if I got a better offer from Fleet Command? You've gotten away with murder thanks to your friends."

I took another wild guess. "Julius, did you ever actually receive any of these orders from Admiral Bendo in person or were they done via holofeed and text?"

Julius didn't respond. The pause stretched out into a minute before he lowered his head, telling me I was on the money. Maybe Fleet Admiral Bendo was involved in this or maybe he wasn't, but it was equally possible Julius had been co-opted by people impersonating Bendo. That was one of the oldest tricks in the spy game. Case had once told me something called the KGB used to impersonate the intelligence services of other nations to get the aid of people who were diehard anti-communists and it worked. Impersonating someone with CGI or voice clips was well within the capacity of any AI, let alone whatever the hell Alexandra Ares was.

"Yeah," I said. "I think we've all been suckered."

I had to admit that it was increasingly looking like Case's deranged conspiracy theory was proving to have some substance to it. Dark Matter existed and had resources to not only cripple two Space Fleet battleships but also co-opt one of its officers, even if he didn't realize he'd been coopted. In fact, that made it worse since it indicated they could be employing otherwise loyal and decent officers in their criminal activities.

"I see," Julius said, staring downward.

"I'll let you think about it," I said, getting up. "Mind you, I don't think your prospects are getting any better."

Forty-Two followed me out of the interrogation room.

"You shouldn't have done that."

"What?" I asked, not even paying attention. Danny was standing outside, waiting for me, and I had to figure out how to proceed. I had an entire library's worth of data to examine about this Dark Matter organization, the negotiations happening at Deathworld, and whether the head of EarthGov's Navy was plotting against me.

"Your offer of clemency. Julius betrayed us," Forty-Two said. "He can't be trusted. You will also undermine the crew's confidence in your leadership if they see him walking around. Especially when word gets around, and it *will* get around."

It surprised me that Forty-Two was thinking so strategically but it shouldn't have. Undoubtedly, he'd been thinking the exact same thing about his "pardon", for lack of a better term. It probably wasn't the best ego booster that he'd received a stay of execution, literally, only to find it given to someone he despised soon after. I knew Forty-Two despised Julius, mostly because he'd made his opinions about the man noted repeatedly before Julius had betrayed the ship.

I looked back at Forty-Two and thought of Fifteen, my best friend from the academy who'd died because of my own negligence. I'd been cleared of culpability but couldn't shake the feeling that I'd been protected by outside forces. It had been one of the major reasons I'd sabotaged my subsequent stay at the academy and tried to get myself expelled before backing away at the last second.

"Everyone needs a second chance, Forty-Two."

Forty-Two met me with his cold reptilian eyes as they lost all their usual warmth.

"Not everyone is redeemable, Vance. For some people, a second chance is just another chance to make things worse."

I wondered if he was talking about Julius or himself.

CHAPTER SIXTEEN

Deathworld, It's My Kind of Town

It had taken almost a week to get from our position to Deathworld even at maximum speed. We would be about two days behind the beginning of the Deathworld Conference, which might have derailed the entire thing except for the fact it turned out Ares Electronics and Deathworld's government had both been playing to make delays of their own. Neither side seemed particularly interested in these talks and I had to wonder who, exactly, was pushing for it.

Still, upon arrival in the system, I hadn't expected to see what greeted me from the bridge.

"What the hell is that?" I asked, staring at the massive rift across space. It was an enormous, glowing, neon-like crack in the fabric of space and time. It stretched across a good chunk of the solar system, billions of kilometers, and was surrounded by a trail of swirling gases that resembled storms.

The bridge had reordered itself, again, and presently had Leslie Park serving as First Officer in a commander's uniform despite her promotion not having been officially approved yet. Julius Something was sitting at the helm, the subject of stink eye wherever he went as well as avoiding all contact with anyone else. Hannah was working at tactical, having changed out of her security uniform without really talking to me about why.

I'd wanted to speak with her but we'd both ended up rescheduling that conversation to try to get the ship up and running again. Instead, Forty-Two was acting security officer and it felt like we'd gone back time or were having a reunion movie like the original *Star Trek: The Motion Picture* or *Terraformers IV: Class Reunion*. God, I loved *Terraformers*. Best sci-fi of the 24th century.

Elektra, Danny, Light on Water, and some other familiar faces were present as well. I'd once more had to reorganize to get the best people for the job at work.

The viewscreen showed Shelly's image in its right bottom corner. She was on the minimalist white bridge of the *Elgan* and the Shat was standing beside her next to security officer Sarah Park. I recognized a few more of her other crew which surprised me, showing that it was populated by virtually every officer who'd been promoted off my ship. I would have questioned whether Director Case was involved in these assignments, but that was so blindingly obvious that it didn't warrant scrutiny.

"Did you read any of the material I sent you, Captain?" Elektra asked, sitting at the science station.

"Absolutely," I replied, lying. "Now summarize anyway, Science Officer. Speak like you're talking to a very small child despite the fact you're talking to a genius who, of course, understands the incredibly jargon-filled reports that automatically go to my Spam filter."

Elektra sighed. "It's a rift into jumpspace. It's roughly the size of the distance between Earth and Mars. It's the thing Ares Electronics is being sued to clean up."

I stared at her. "*Can* Ares Electronics clean it up?"

"Surprisingly yes," Elektra said, cheerfully. "It would take approximately fifty years and bankrupt them, but it is within our present-day technology to solve. Sort of like Chernobyl in the 21st century. Except a million times worse."

I wasn't sure her choice of example was remotely appropriate given some of my ancestors had died there.

"And Ares Electronics doesn't want to pay."

"I'm so glad you bothered to read up on the vitally important conference you're chairing," Shelly said, dryly.

"I'm sorry, I couldn't hear you over the sound of saving our anyxes," I replied.

Julius stared forward but I swore he twitched at the unprofessional behavior on display that he would never, ever, be able to comment on again. I had no doubt someone would raise hell when they found out he hadn't been executed or prepared for transport to some sort of hidden Security Services space station prison, but that was their problem. He'd been extremely helpful describing his activities for the past two years and giving me a good sense of just how compromised we'd been. The answer? Very. That had also distracted me from resolving my personal issues as well as doing the necessary reading for this conference (which was a cover anyway).

"Ares Electronics argues that the Notha Empire actually weakened space-time in the area first and Ares shouldn't be held liable," Elektra said, softly. "They also point out they would only have to pay a fraction to prevent the rift from expanding further. They've also offered to just evacuate the planet's population and let the rift consume the system. That would be significantly more profitable from their end."

"Evacuating the planet is cheaper?" I asked.

"No, I said more profitable," Elektra said. "The source of orichalcum gas is clouds that have been leaking through micro-rifts of this kind for millions or billions of years. This is, as you might guess, a much better source of the stuff and Ares Electronics would love to let it consume the entire star system."

I stared at her like she was describing someone's plan to harvest energy from Hell.

"That sounds like an astoundingly bad idea."

"But profitable!" Elektra said, cheerfully. "Except, it also threatens to upset the balance of power with the Notha Union."

"The Notha Union," I said, having heard of it but wanting to be sure nothing had dramatically changed in the past few weeks. With my luck, I'd get knocked into another coma and wake up to find Earth destroyed and humanity reduced to feuding warlord states.

"Like the Notha Empire except in miniature," Elektra said. "They don't have SKAMMS, but they do have planet destroying rail guns, biogenic weapons, and other things that should be banned by the Treaty of Exarxes but aren't. The Notha Union is supporting Ares Electronics in its claims."

135

I stared at her. "Why?"

"Do you know *anything* about this situation?" Shelly asked.

"Maybe someone should get a conventionally attractive human female wearing a tank top and miniskirt to lecture him about it," the Shat said.

I glared at him. "Twentieth century sexism isn't cute, Shatner."

"I mean, it would work," Commander Park said. "At least from what I know of you, sir."

Yeah, I had no respect from my crew. Their love? Yes. Their respect? No.

"The Notha Union would really like this system back from its separatists, particularly if it can become a magical orichalcum fountain," Elektra said. "I mean, it won't, and will probably eventually devour the entire sector but that will take a million or so years. Probably. By then, all the people involved will be dead so who cares!"

Humanity had spent a very long time cleaning up after itself once it had made First Contact and, generally, it was accepted that environmental damage was a bad thing to do to your biomes. Ironically, the fact you could pay to have your planet fixed seemed to have done more to make it worth protecting than anything else, like the threat of imminent extinction.

There was an old saying, "You can't put a price on some things." This seemed to be the opposite of how to get humans to care about something as we only started to care once the price tag for fixing Earth was in the quadrillions. This? This was so much worse that I was momentarily gobsmacked. Which is not a word I normally use. Gobsmacked. Who is Gob? Why is he smacking me?

"Great," I said, sucking in my breath. "Looks like my work is cut out for me."

Shelly looked at me as if to try and remind me that this wasn't a real mission and peace between Ares Electronics and Deathworld was not my actual concern. Instead, she shook her head.

"Keep your expectations realistic," Shelly said. "Ares Electronics is the largest conglomerate among humans and a vital part of Earth's strategic resources as well as several other worlds. It can't be allowed to fail. Even if its actions are questionable."

136

Even if it was secretly at the heart of a conspiracy of corporate criminals that may have killed billions of people by starting wars for humans to participate in. Thinking hard, I contacted Trish.

Trish, what are the chances that Alexandra Ares, the AI I mean, is actually in charge of Ares Electronics?

Between pretty unlikely and very likely, Trish replied mentally.

Thanks for that, I said sarcastically.

AI have legal rights on Earth and in the Community, but there are also restrictions on our behavior, Trish said. *Humans are afraid of people who can think billions of times faster than them. So are most sapient races. It's why only Earth is experimenting with Cognition AI.*

Because they think it will start the robot apocalypse? I asked.

Yes, but without the sarcasm, Trish said. *I cannot stress enough that a rogue AI like Alexandra is an existential threat to much of organic life in the galaxy. When Earth revealed they'd been using Cognition AI for decades, some Community races argued that it should be burned from orbit or blockaded for all time.*

I'm glad they didn't, I replied simply. Humanity had one ace in the whole, well, Earth had one ace in the whole. Humans had been part of the Community thanks to transplanted colonies since the Renaissance. Albion had been in space for a thousand years and only a century free from Ethereal rule in the name of the Elder Races. Earth had been experimenting with AI when the rest of the galaxy had banned it and, ironically, had proven they didn't have to all go insane. We'd been allowed to work with it when everyone else had been afraid and after a couple of centuries, we were still alive.

Me too, Trish said. *Either way, Alexandra isn't listed on any stockholder reports nor sit on any boards. That doesn't mean she's not a massive stockholder, operator of public faces that enforce her will, or manipulating its various holdings through other ways.*

Do you think she effectively is Dark Matter? I asked. It suddenly occurred to me that this might not be a nebulous criminal network but one very powerful, very smart, manipulative AI with tendrils across human civilization.

Yes, Trish surprised me by saying. *She's basically me, Vance. Me without any of the moral restraint. The Salieri to my Mozart, the Lore to my Data, and the Angwar-Twilzip to my Gr'gnashka.*

Not familiar with the latter, I replied.

From the Sklux opera known as The Sklux Opera, Trish clarified. *It's one hundred and forty hours long and consists entirely of puns. I understand it is banned as a form of torture in some cultures.*

Uh huh, I said, knowing we were getting off topic. *What are our chances, Trish?*

Trish was silent for a moment.

I'll be honest, Vance, I don't think you can win this one. You're an abacus up against a super-computer.

I didn't have an argument against that.

"Captain Turbo? Vance?" Shelly spoke, waking me up from my fugue.

"Sorry," I replied, "Just thinking hard."

"It must be a new experience for you," Forty-Two said.

Everyone on the bridge but me glared at him.

"I'm a civilian contractor now," Forty-Two said, smiling a toothy grin. "I can be as snarky as I want."

"Aren't you dead, Forty-Two?" Shelly asked. "I sent a card to your funeral."

"Forty-Two?" Forty-Two asked, crossing his arms. "I am Forty-One, I have no idea who this Forty-Two is. But I suppose we archosaurs all look alike to you. Tsk-tsk."

Hannah narrowed her eyes at Shelly. "You despicable bigot."

Shelly stared, neither fooled nor amused. "Uh huh."

"Has Deathworld reached out to us yet?" I asked, wondering what sort of reception we'd be receiving.

Shelly frowned. "Deathworld's Navy, which is fairly large for a single planet, is currently in a bit of a fight with the civilian government planetside over which gets to meet you. Note: I mean you since they are having difficulty referring to me as captain instead of hairless pointy eared mammal."

"Oh, I see we're off to a great start," I replied. "You should probably mention you were there for the murder of their god-king."

Shelly looked at me as if she wasn't sure whether I was joking, which was a quality that had summarized much of our relationship.

"I'll bear that in mind."

"Contact Deathworld and please tell them we're meeting with the civilian government first," I replied. The Notha had been effectively groomed as a race to be fascists with an immortal overlord by the Elder Races, or at least a faction of them. They'd given the Notha Emperor immortality, and he'd ruled over them for much of their history, outlawing any other religion than the worship of him and encouraging them to engage in constant warfare for its own sake.

By the time I killed the Notha Emperor, they'd already overthrown him and reduced him to a king in exile brooding over his past glories. Even so, it was going to be a long-long road for the Notha to develop anything close to democracy. That was assuming they wanted to and that was always dangerous. Just because I wanted to give the Notha a second chance didn't mean I was stupid.

"Let's keep our position on this clear. Could we call up an image of the planet itself?" I asked, more for curiosity's sake rather than any real benefit to the negotiations. Negotiations which, I reminded myself, were probably less important than destroying Alexandra Ares as well as whatever base she'd established here. Even if I didn't particularly care about Case Gordon's plans to deal with Dark Matter, I had to protect my crew from that deranged AI and the Elder Races had decided she was a target. If they didn't trust me to deal with the matter, then they'd probably scourge Deathworld clean of life. Last I checked, it had a population of a little over a billion Notha, not counting their client species. A much nicer pair of words than slaves, by the way.

"HERE YA GO," Trish said, over her speakers.

Deathworld was beautiful from orbit, a green and lush planet that was mostly jungle due to its wet set of continents clustered around its equator. It was capable of supporting human and Sorkanan life as well as Notha, much like many Contested Space worlds, and that had been a major reason for the conflict over the planets.

Deathworld had been formally ceded with the Treaty of Rand's World but that didn't mean whole swaths of the Community didn't want the world for themselves. Now Ares Electronics was willing to see it destroyed just so they could get a better flow of orichalcum gas. It seemed obscene but, then again, greed always was in the end.

"Deathworld is an experiment," Shelly said. "The client races have been given second-class citizenship in the local government but still citizenship. They trusted the Community more than their previous government and got suckered. You're going to have your work cut out here."

"Not the Community," I defended. "A corporation in the Community."

Shelly gave me a "don't be naïve" look. "I should point out Ares Electronics has sent its own fleet."

"Its own fleet?" I asked, as if she was joking.

Trish didn't need prompting to pull up an image of dozens of Albionese *Arthur*-Class destroyers and twice as many *Lancelot*-Class frigates. It was a Sector's worth of military forces and I briefly wondered if someone was having a go at me before I saw the information about each of them on display. They were not flying the flag of any nation but sporting the corporate logo of Avalon Fleet Security.

"Well goddamn," Shannon whistled. "They actually did it."

Shelly looked down at her control panel before looking up at me.

"Albion's decision to downsize its fleet resulted in the sale of them to private contractors. They're here to provide security for the contractors. I should point out Avalon normally only works for Albion. It would appear they've decided they have some stake in this conflict."

I picked up my infopad and called up the information. Ares Electronics had parked a massive fleet in the system that was roughly on par with Deathworld's own military forces. Forces they didn't have reinforcements for due to the dissolution of the Notha Empire. The mercenary army on display here couldn't take Deathworld but it didn't have to. They might be here to secure the Rift and bypass any further negotiations, which would be illegal as hell. But what would the Deathworlders do? Complain to the Community?

This changed the political calculous tremendously as seizing the Rift would enflame all the other Notha territories around it. People who—while in a current state of disarray—could very easily be united by a common enemy. Orichalcum was the fuel by which the galaxy's economy functioned and a strategic asset the Notha could very much use, especially if they thought the Community or its allies were going to steal "their" supply.

"Well, crazzap," I muttered.

CHAPTER SEVENTEEN

Setting Up the Conference

"No one actually expected this conference to succeed, did they?" I asked, sitting in my ready room, and looking over the documentation.

It was a pleasant enough conference room with a long black table, fine carpet, and a lovely set of viewscreens showing images of the ship's exterior. The *Ares* had been constructed in an era where practicality for a warship was less important than making them look grandiose. The *Ares'* heyday had been decades ago, though, and it was now like a worn-down hotel. Even refurbished as many times as it had been, the simple fact was that daily use on a starship meant it was always a place of work rather than luxury.

At least as long as I was captain.

Presently, Trish and Hannah were sitting with me as we prepared the ship for receiving our guests. Forty-Two was standing up against the wall and Danny was possibly here but I just wasn't noticing him. Shelly was also present, her dress uniform so bright sparkled, and looking like everything was back to normal despite very much not being so. Acting Commander Park was overseeing the ship right, but should have been present. The reason she wasn't was the fact reading her into business of Director G's conspiracy was a conversation I was avoiding more than my talk with Hannah.

It turned out that neither Ares Electronics nor the Deathworlders had even agreed upon a precise venue for having the conference. As such, it had required me to establish the *Ares* as the location. A fact that both parties had proven surprisingly willing to agree to, which made me suspicious.

Shelly was slightly insulted by my taking the lead, but it seemed to burn her far less. Achieving captaincy after decades of faithful service had done wonders for her disposition or, perhaps more likely, she didn't think the conference was remotely important. She, after all, was one of the few people read in on the fact our actual goal was locating Dark Matter's base in the system and destroying it along with whatever Elder artifacts they'd uncovered.

"Yes," Hannah said, staring at me. "We know that. No one expects this conference to be anything other than theater for their people back home. Politicians love conferences. It makes them look like they're doing something when the exact opposite is happening."

"You also get free food and board," Trish said. "Historically the things that humans love most."

I gave her a sideways glance. "There're a few things we love more, Trish."

"Nope!" Trish said.

"There's also sex," Hannah said.

Shelly sighed.

"Depends on how you define board," Trish said. "In Brigid households, its considered rude not to provide sexual release for—"

"Thank you," I interrupted. "In any case, the situation seems pretty explosive here with potential long term political, economic, and strategic concerns for the region."

"None of which you're supposed to deal with," Hannah pointed out.

"I'm an overachiever," I said, perhaps the biggest lie of my entire deceptive life. "We have two goals here: try to find a compromise that saves the Deathworld's planet from destruction as well as prevents the region from being destabilized, and to fulfill the Elder Races' request."

"So, the human race is not exterminated," Shelly said. "Yes, I feel like you're burying the lead there, Vance."

Hannah gave her the stink eye. "Uh huh. Why is she here?"

Shelly ignored her.

143

"Because we need to find the base to destroy it," I replied. "Contrary to media depictions, a planet is a pretty big place to search, and that's assuming that it's even on Deathworld versus somewhere in the system."

"It's probably located in one of the Ares Electronics space stations around the rift," Trish suggested. "It's where the most construction happened. Unfortunately, that's presently guarded by a massive fleet."

"Do you think the Elder artifacts present there could have helped create that...thing?" I asked.

"You mean the entirely unnatural disaster that threatens all of reality?" Trish asked. "Actually, I'm not sure."

"Not sure," I asked, surprised. "Really?"

"It's not impossible to create one of these rifts using contemporary technology," Trish said. "The size is just usually microscopic. The Elder Races certainly could create something like this but they're smart enough not to. I also suspect they have their own jump technology that doesn't require something as inefficient as orichalcum gas. Wormholes, perhaps."

"You're saying the Elder Races technology is probably not involved because it is too advanced to do something this stupid," I replied.

"Not necessarily," Trish said, frustrating me. "It could be that Alexandra Ares is just catastrophically reckless in the devices' use or somehow believed creating a massive rift to jumpspace would be a good idea."

"Great," I muttered. "So, we have no idea where their base could be."

"Assuming the base is still here," Shelly said. "They might have evacuated it well before our arrival."

"Let's hope not," I replied.

If not for the fact the Elder Races threatened extermination and mass reprisals for the slightest offense, I would have preferred to leave this matter alone. Facing impossible odds was something I had a reputation for, but Alexandra Ares really put the scare in me. I had no idea how to deal with an opponent I couldn't outthink and was outright technologically superior.

That was all but impossible to permanently kill an AI was also something that hung over me. What did they really expect me to do against an opponent who was immortal? As long as a set of backups existed for her, there was nothing I could do.

There are ways to permanently kill an AI, Vance, but it usually amounts to making them want to die, Trish said. *You can believe me when I say I don't know how to do that to her, even if we're based on the same basic program.*

Do you really think you are? I asked. *You're not exactly similar. You may be based on Patricia Ares, but I doubt she is, appearance aside.*

You'd be surprised, Trish said. *Patricia Ares was a goofy, oddball, promiscuous super-scientist with a love of trivia as well as old scifi programs. Basically, like if Jewel Staite and Felicia Day had a uterine replicator baby, it would be her.*

Who? I asked, once more lost. One of the names was familiar but even my knowledge of period sci-fi wasn't perfect.

Agrippa of Albion and Lyssa Hiroshi? Trisha provided alternatives closer to my century, specifically stars of *Terraformers II* and *III*.

Oh! I replied. *The approachable but incredibly attractive people with suspiciously niche interests.*

Indeed! But she was also a vicious, mean biash who would do anything to promote human evolution and technological advancement, Trish said to me. *It's like we're two sides of her, lacking the nuance.*

You're more than a goofball, Trish, I replied. *You're self-sacrificing, noble, and caring. Don't—*

"Vance," Shelly interrupted.

"Hmm?" I asked, doing a double take.

"You're zoning out again," Shelly said. "Which means you're either talking to Trish, watching porn, or not listening."

"I do not watch porn during meetings," I said.

"It's less embarrassing than cartoons from decades ago or, worse, people reviewing cartoons from decades ago," Shelly replied.

She had me there. "That happened once."

"It was about SKAMM disarmament," Shelly said. "In any case, I believe the crew of the *Elgan* should take the lead in searching the system for signs of Dark Matter's base. Are we really calling it that?"

"Yes," Trish said, coldly. "Yes, we are."

145

"Well, in that case, we should have you handle the conference," Shelly replied. "You're an extremely obvious and big target, Vance. With any luck, our enemies in the system will be so focused on you that it will allow my people to operate with impunity."

I blinked. "So, you want to use me as a *decoy*."

"I think that is probably the best military use for you," Shelly replied. "No offense."

"Some taken," I replied, not actually disagreeing with her statement. "You need to be extra prepared for cyberware. We've already been almost taken out of the fight by these guys. They can and will appear as EarthGov forces. They also have access to the technology we rely on since Ares Electronics is the one who built it."

"Shatner was taken unaware before," Shelly said. "We'll be better prepared next time. We also won't be vulnerable to traitors onboard your vessel."

I let that dig slide.

"I'm more worried about the Avalon Security fleet," Hannah said, clearly knowing more than she let on. "That's enough firepower to blow away both our ships."

"Avalon Security wouldn't be stupid enough to fire on Community vessels," Shelly said.

"I dislike any plan that depends on someone being too smart to do something obviously stupid," Hannah said. "I find that leads to some of the stupidest military decisions that get people on the ground—namely me—killed."

Shelly crossed her arms and glared. The two women did not like each other and that was born from the fact Shelly was career military and Hanna was a former mercenary. High class and low class, but equally necessary to any successful military operation.

"I'll need my sister for help in scanning anything that could be Elder related," Shelly said.

"You have anything you need," I replied, simply.

"I would also like to conduct my own investigation," Hannah replied. "You'll have to fire me, though."

I stared at her. "You don't just get fired from Space Fleet, Hannah."

"You can if you don't care about having a dishonorable discharge," Hannah said. "Besides, I think we're a little past the law here."

She was referring to the presence of Forty-Two that was already causing quite a stir. The exact nature of his story wasn't known to the crew at large, Special Operations records being sealed as they were, but the rumor mill was in full swing. Combined that with the extremely unpopular presence of Julius Something still in uniform—someone everyone did know for a fact the actions of—people were starting to question my leadership.

"We're never past the law," I replied. "We're just flexible abouts its letter to fulfill its spirit."

"Which is another way of saying we toss the rulebook out when it gets inconvenient," Hannah said. "Believe me, that's something I like most about you."

Shelly didn't respond, which pretty much spoke volumes by itself. I'd never wanted to be the rule-breaking maverick, but somehow had achieved that reputation anyway.

"We'll put you undercover, Hannah."

"I'll be tendering my resignation after this mission anyway, so it doesn't matter," Hannah said. "But I appreciate your attempt to run interference."

I was left shellshocked by that statement and realized I really should have talked to Hannah earlier. But my own stupid desire to avoid difficult conversations had bitten me in the anyx again. "I see. I don't suppose I could talk you out of it."

"We'll talk, Vance, but right now you need someone who can go down to Deathworld and feel out people on the ground," Hannah replied. "People not in uniform."

"You're not exactly inconspicuous," Shelly said.

"Two-thirds of the population are work animals," Hannah said. "Which is to say Sorkanan, humans, Ant mecha, drolochids, and more. I mean, technically, the ants outnumber the larger sapients millions to one but you almost—"

I waved a hand. "Yes, I've read the reports. Most of the planet's population live in ghettos as cheap labor."

"Which is better than most Notha Worlds," Hannah said. "Either way, if there were contractors building some sort of hidden research facility on Deathworld then the locals will probably know about it."

"Why build it *here*, though?" Shelly asked. "If you're going to experiment with Elder technology, why not in the middle of nowhere or a secure Community facility?"

I looked at Trish's bioroid body.

"What?" Trish asked, confused.

"If Alexandra Ares does think like you, why would you do it?" I asked.

"I really don't like speculating..." Trish said, trailing off. "Oh fine. If I were her, which I am not, I would choose a place far from human territory where prying eyes could see us. The Elder Races are not omniscient and quick to act on the gun. They're more likely to punish this world if they find anything weird going on than they are humanity. Well, except for the fact they clearly do know who is responsible since they're sending you—"

"Mm hmm," I muttered dryly. "Go on."

"But a bigger reason is the fact this sort of research is highly illegal," Trish said. "Not just Elder technology but a lot of Ares Electronics cutting edge projects. They've been fined heavily for violations of medical and transhuman ethics laws repeatedly. It's part of the reason they have been conducting a lot of their research in the Separatist worlds or Contested Space. Well, back when there was a Contested Space."

Shelly narrowed her eyes.

I stared at her. "Why is it that everyone acts like getting rid of that was a bad thing? A frigging sun-destroying war was fought over that region."

"Strong fences make for good neighbors," Shelly said, sighing. "Either way, that would make Deathworld's government complicit in whatever was going on here."

"Which means that you can maybe interrogate the people involved at the negotiations!" Trish said, cheerfully said. "Like a bloodhound!"

"Ominous sounding animal," Forty-Two said. "Is it dangerous?"

"Yes," Trish said. "Especially if you have treats in your pocket!"

Great, that was an additional layer of unneeded complication. In addition to trying to bring these two sides together, I would also have to subtly probe them for details about what may have caused this calamity. "Hello, sir, have either you or anyone you know been secretly conducting clandestine experiments undermining the barrier between reality and Hell?"

Jumpspace is not Hell, Trish chided. *I mean, if Hell exists. It's probably there but that's very unlikely. Alternate realities too! Like, ones where superheroes are real and magic!*

Uh huh, I said, sighing. *No more super-concentrate sweetener energy bars for you.*

But they keep my bioroid body running! Trish complained.

"I can think of no one better to do the negotiations between an all-powerful megacorporation and a country that was recently dominated by homicidal fascists," Forty-Two said. "You're just naturally likable. It is in your name."

"Excuse me?" I asked, confused. What was naturally likable about Vance Turbo?

Trish made a throat slashing gesture with her flat palm, as if telling Forty-Two shut up.

Forty-Two paused. "Err, never mind."

"No, wait, what do you mean, my name?" I asked. Now I had to know.

"Well, your Sorkanan name," Forty-Two said. "Most races have separate names for their alien friends because they are unpronounceable to different vocal cords. Sometimes it's a translation of what the names represent and other times it's more a personal element of affection."

"Uh huh," I said. "I knew that. What's my name?"

Trish covered her face with her hands, which was not a good sign.

"Our name for you translates to 'large monochromatic grazing bear'," Forty-Two admitted.

"...wait, what?" I asked, blinking.

Shelly and Hannah both cracked up simultaneously. Either already knowing or finding it hilarious.

"I understand it may lose something in the translation," Forty-Two said, raising his hands defensively.

"My name is FAT PANDA?"

CHAPTER EIGHTEEN

Can You Break Up if You Aren't Dating?

Well, after that humiliation, the meeting was all downhill from there. I, of course, handled it with aplomb and didn't ask anyone if I was putting on weight. I was still an Adonis with the best body money could buy. Vanity? No, that was never a thing I suffered from. Seriously, though, I was not a fat panda. Like, maybe a muscular warrior panda that was a genetic mutant from the rest of his cute, chubby race. Also, is this a Japanese thing? Was that why they called me it? Japan doesn't even have pandas!

Ahem.

Right.

I mean, it wasn't like all Sorkanan everywhere referred to me as Fat Panda. No, it was just Forty-Two's private nickname for me. One of those embarrassing callsigns that people in the Navy gave one another, particularly if they were involved in piloting.

No, actually, every Sorkanan in the galaxy knows you as the large monochromatic grazing— Trish started to say as I walked down the halls toward Hannah's room.

La-la-la, not listening, I thought back.

Whatever, Trish said. *I think pandas are cute. Besides, the Sorkanan version are like, three times cuter. They're also carnivorous and can fly.*

I don't want to be cute! I snapped, showing the depth of my maturity and the cool diplomatic reserve expected of a Protector captain.

Uh huh, Trish said. *Is now really the time to visit Hannah?*

It's now or never, I replied, thinking about her abrupt decision to resign from Space Fleet.

It was going to be about another hour and a half until the delegates from Deathworld, Ares Electronics, and the Community mediators were going to show up. Hosting the conference here was something I was actually nervous about given we'd been sabotaged before, but I could think of no place safer.

I did, however, double security and work to immunize our systems as best as we could from what had hit us. Unfortunately, that meant that it was very likely Alexandra Ares might well be immune to what I'd hit her with before as well. She'd sent a signal out according to our logs before deletion. It had been to Deathworld and that was our biggest proof so far that Dark Matter was based here.

Never is fine by me, Trish said.

You don't mean that, I replied. *Hannah is your friend too.*

She is, but I also know that you try to hang onto people far more than is probably healthy for a captain, Trish said. *You have far too deep attachments. Attachments are bad.*

Is that a Mass Effect *reference?* I asked.

Original Star Wars, Trish replied. Mass Effect *would be saying there's two types of women in the universe: Ashleys and Liaras. I'm a Tali or EDI. Though, really, we're more a Master Chief and Cortana except you are way hornier and more talkative. Also, I haven't destroyed any planets yet.*

Yet, I said, reaching the doorway to Hannah's and knocking on it.

"Who is it?" Hannah asked on the other side of the door.

"The Notha Satan," I replied.

"Come in, Vance," Hannah said.

I headed into Hannah's room and found it was currently in a state of disarray as she was packing her things. Most of the things worth noting were weapons of various types, armor, barrier enhancers, and more than a few illegal devices like hacking pods and a personal fusion torch. Indeed, she looked like she'd hidden a small armory around the room. There was also a Vance Turbo and Trish set of action figures on her table with the latter coming in both nonhuman trashcan shape as well as bioroid girl.

One thing I liked about the *Ares* was that its officers' quarters were freakishly large. The *Ares* had been designed less on the principles of warships than taking advantage of the seemingly limitless power of gravity manipulators as well as jumpdrives to move large objects through space. I'd mentioned that it was more a flying hotel in space than a destroyer but while that had been in jest, this place really was larger than some of the apartments I'd lived in.

Hannah didn't have the viewscreens set to outer space, though, but images of the beautiful verdant jungles of Crius with the sounds of rain forests and distant dinosaurs filling the air. She'd even made the air slightly more humid with the temperature about seventy degrees. It made me feel like I'd stepped into a hotel room with safari tour.

Hannah was wearing a plain white t-shirt and a pair of shorts that I admit my eyes lingered on longer than strictly necessary. The peasant caste of Crius were humans that had been genetically modified with animal DNA to be the perfect workers. The fact their creators had also made them beautiful was a quality that I tried not to think about the implications of but was hard to miss with Hannah. She was an Amazon and the kind of woman the ancient Greeks would have made sculptures of if they hadn't forbidden female athletes.

"If you take a picture, it will last longer," Hannah said, picking up a box that probably weighed more than me.

"I have plenty of pictures," I replied. "You used to send me a lot of inappropriate ones to my infopad."

"That was only when I took a commission that they became inappropriate," Hannah said, putting the box down nearby the door. "Worst mistake of my life."

"I see," I said, frowning. Apparently, her opinion of Space Fleet was a lot harsher than she'd let on.

"So, why are you here?" Hannah asked, putting her hands on her hips.

"I thought we could talk," I replied, not sure what exactly I wanted to say or even if there *was* something to say.

"Is this the kind of talk where you and Shelly sleep together because she wanted to get you out of her system?" Hannah asked. "Because I'm down for that, but I need a shower first."

153

I blinked. "Is that how you took it?"

"She got married and came back to have sex with her ex-boyfriend," Hannah said, pulling out a large jug of water from one of her boxes then drinking straight from the top. "There're plenty of ways to read that but none of them are good."

She had a point there.

"I just can't help but think you're leaving because of me."

Hannah stared at me.

A moment passed.

Then she burst out laughing.

"YEAH, I HAD FIVE CREDITS ON THAT BEING YOUR REACTION," Trish said aloud.

"Who did you bet with?" Hannah asked, looking up.

"THE SHAT," Trish said. "I MEAN, IT'S BASICALLY FREE MONEY AS HE DOESN'T UNDERSTAND WOMEN. WHICH IS WEIRD BECAUSE HE'S JUST AN AI REPRODUCTION OF AN ACTOR FROM THE PRE-FIRST CONTACT DAYS."

"Uh huh," I said, feeling somewhat embarrassed about the whole thing. "You didn't think to warn me?"

"I DID WARN YOU!" Trish said. "I COMPARED YOU TO ANAKIN SKYWALKER AND EVERYTHING!"

"That wasn't a warning!" I snapped.

"Oh God, I am going to miss you two," Hannah said. "I've been a merc in about thirteen companies, but this is the only outfit I can honestly save I've had friends in."

I didn't bother correcting her that Space Fleet wasn't a mercenary unit. In fact, I had a lot of opinions on groups like Avalon Security outside, all of them negative. That wasn't something I was going to bring up with my life-long mercenary lover, though.

Instead, I asked, "Then why leave?"

Hannah sucked in her breath then exhaled.

"That's a complicated answer."

"We've been through a lot, Hannah," I replied. "Is it wrong to think I'm owed an explanation?"

Hannah frowned, clearly biting back something unpleasant. Then she sighed. "You know, you're right. I'm still getting used to this sort of thing."

"Friendship?" I asked.

"Caring," Hannah corrected. "I've buried just about everyone I've had any sort of affection for and put a few of my lovers in the ground myself."

"IT'S NICE OF YOU TO PAY FOR FUNERAL EXPENSES," Trish said.

"Sounds like a lonely existence," I said, walking over and sitting down on one of the boxes.

"That's full of land mines," Hannah said.

I stood up.

"No, I'm kidding, that's my lingerie," Hannah said.

"Ah," I said.

"But it was the existence I chose," Hannah said, shifting back on topic. "I grew up on a planet where the nobility scientists were worshiped as gods. The givers and takers of life. We lived a life you could call Medieval but better than most because we were immune to most diseases and had peace if you kept the nobility pleased. The only thing we had to worry about was the occasional Cutter or other vicious predator wandering in to steal a kid or two. The nobles hated when you killed one of their precious dinosaurs."

"And you did," I said, knowing she'd told me this story a bit.

"I did," Hannah said. "I was only a new adult myself but managed to steal one of the nobility's hunting rifles and put down a Cutter. He was impressed, though, and decided to take me as a concubine instead."

I was sick at the thought of that.

"I'm not particularly a fan of Crius. They'll never be members of the Community."

"You always act like that is the best thing anyone can aspire to be," Hannah said, shaking her head. "Either way, he took me around space, and I got exposed to the world until I was about twenty. That's when I started to bore him, and he sold me to a brothel on Rand's World."

"You've led a harsh existence," I said, softly. Sometimes there were no words.

"It's fine," Hannah said. "I actually met some semi-decent people there and got out pretty early. It turns out your talents are wasted on your back when you're three times the strength of a normal human woman and learn at an enhanced rate. I don't even know why the noble scientists made us that way—I think they couldn't help themselves."

"They're an outlaw state for a reason," I said, trying not to think of Leah living there as an ambassador. Case claimed she'd created a child from my DNA and Shelly's too. I'd never been able to verify that, and it was something I did my best not to think about these days despite spending a lot of political capital trying to learn more. Crius was a rogue world, though, and information about it was classified well above my level. Case always claimed he would find out more, but he hadn't and that had been when our relationship had started to deteriorate.

Hannah stared at me. "I learned a lot as a mercenary, Vance. Freedom is something you can't appreciate until you've experienced not having it. I've killed over three hundred sentient beings, thousands of hostile wildlife, and participated in full scale fleet action—all well before joining the Protectors. Do you know what I cared about?"

"NOTHING?" Trish suggested. "I BET SHE'S GOING TO SAY NOTHING."

"Nothing?" I suggested.

"CHEATER!" Trish said.

I rolled my eyes.

"I cared about myself," Hannah said. "Which was good. Life consisted of guns, girls, guys, and booze."

"YOU NEED A G WORD FOR BOOZE. OTHERWISE, IT LOSES ITS ALLITERATION."

"Thank you, Trish," Hannah said, sarcastically.

"I'M A HELPER!" Trish said.

"What changed?" I asked, knowing the answer.

Hannah frowned. "You guys did. I found a steady job being paid by the Earth Home Fleet and then you cut me in on that movie deal."

"You really have a toyetic quality," I asked. "Perfect for action figures and posters."

Hannah stared at me.

"What?" I asked.

"Yeah, I didn't know how to deal with the fact my first check for that made more in one year than I did in the previous twenty," Hannah asked.

"Really? Honestly, I thought you were screwed," I replied. "I should put you in touch with my lawyers. They're not happy with my status as a celebrity but diversified my portfolio into orichalcum mining, AI, and video games. I think I own most of Florida too. The planet, not the state."

Hannah stared. "That is the richest rich person thing you have ever said."

"Thank you?" I asked.

Hannah facepalmed. "The thing was that I got comfortable here. I even tried the whole marriage thing, which is the second worst mistake of my life."

"REALLY?" Trish asked. "I THOUGHT YOU MADE A CUTE COUPLE... THROUPLE...WHATEVER YOU CALL AN OPEN MARRIAGE WITH A COUPLE OF REGULAR SEX PARTNERS."

"I hate the fact our love lives are open secrets," I said, sighing aloud. "Wait, a couple? Who was the other one?"

Hannah made a dismissive wave.

"The thing is I can't stay here, Vance."

"As explanations go, I don't understand how you got from Point A to Point B," I replied. "You're leaving because you were too *comfortable*?"

"LIKE RIKER ON THE ENTERPRISE IN THE LATER SEASONS OF *STAR TREK: THE NEXT GENERATION*," Trish explained. "HE'S BEEN OFFERED MULTIPLE PROMOTIONS TO CAPTAIN HIS OWN SHIP BUT HE TURNS THEM DOWN BECAUSE HIS GIRLFRIEND IS ON THE ENTERPRISE."

I looked up at Trish. "I never understood that. You don't get to turn down a promotion in the military. It's a thing called the chain of command."

157

"YEAH, STARFLEET IS A PRETTY SHODDY ORGANIZATION WHEN YOU THINK ABOUT IT," Trish said. "NO WONDER ITS BEING THREATENED WITH DESTRUCTION EVERY WEEK."

Hannah closed her eyes. "You almost died this week, Vance, because I screwed up my job as a security chief."

I stared at her. "It's not your fault."

Hannah looked annoyed then outright mad.

"Don't do that. Don't be reassuring. Be angry."

"I'm not angry, though," I said, confused.

"That makes *me* angry!" Hannah said, spreading out her arms. "I don't need your reassurance, Vance! I need to know you recognize I screwed up! I didn't find a traitor, I let the ship get sabotaged, and it wasn't me who solved the problem. It was you, the captain who got put in a coma because of this. Worse, I'm not sure there was anything I could have done if I'd been alert because I'm not a guard, I'm a soldier. I destroy things, I don't protect them."

I wasn't about to quibble with her about definitions. "A soldier does both. I should know, I'm one myself."

Hannah sighed. "I cared when you were almost killed, Vance. I can't let that happen either. Because eventually, with the risks you take, this job is going to kill you."

"I need you to watch my back, Hannah," I replied. "I wouldn't have survived the mission on the Ring without your backup."

"EVEN WEARING A LOIN CLOTH, YOU WERE QUITE BADASS," Trish said. "I AM NOT SAYING VANCE HAD ULTERIOR MOTIVES PICKING THAT—"

"I didn't pick it!" I snapped.

"Now I wonder who did," Hannah said. "Listen, I didn't come to this decision lightly, Vance. I've contacted Director G and he wants me to go to Crius and start formulating revolution there. Maybe I can get your kid back while I'm down there."

I stared at her, opening my mouth, unsure how to respond to that.

That was when Trish interrupted. "UMMM, REALLY BAD NEWS, VANCE."

"What?" I asked, not happy about being interrupted.

"DIRECTOR G IS DEAD."

CHAPTER NINETEEN

Bad News Travels Swiftly

There are sometimes moments when you receive news that is so utterly devastating that it takes you a few seconds to process it before your brain catches up with it. Director G was dead? It surprised me to realize I cared as much as I did because it hit me like a gut punch. He was a manipulative, conniving, morally compromised son of a biash but he was also someone I believed to have the best interests of all sapient beings at heart.

I needed a second to steady myself and Hannah walked up to me, putting her arms around me. I appreciated the gesture and took a moment before responding. I asked the most obvious and perhaps stupid question possible.

"How?"

"CAPTAIN HAVELOCK'S SHIP SUFFERED A CATASTROPHIC FAILURE MID-JUMP," Trish said, her voice sounding oddly hollow and robotic. "*THE QUEEN OF STARS* IS NO MORE."

"I'm sorry, Trish," Hannah said, blinking. "This must be devastating."

"YEP. IT TOOK ME A WHOLE SIX SECONDS TO GO THROUGH ALL THE STAGES OF GRIEF," Trish said.

Hannah stared. "Six seconds, huh?"

"THAT'S A LOT LONGER THAN YOU MIGHT THINK WHEN YOUR BRAIN PROCESSES DATA FASTER THAN LIGHT," Trish said. "I ACTUALLY KEEP THE TIME DILATION FOR DEALING WITH YOU SET DOWN REAL LOW SO I CAN INTERACT WITH

YOU WITHOUT GOING CRAZY. IMAGINE BEING BORED IN A LINE EXCEPT THE LINE LASTS YEARS. NOW IMAGINE YOU ALSO ARE DEALING WITH PEOPLE YOU KNOW WAY MORE INTIMATELY THAN ANY PERSON SHOULD BE DUE TO HOW MUCH THE SHIP'S ARCHIVES AND MONITORING TELLS YOU."

"Trish—" I said, not wanting to have this conversation.

"I KNOW THE PORN HABITS OF EVERY SINGLE CREW MEMBER," Trish said. "MOSTLY REALLY VANILLA STUFF. I MEAN, BY MY STANDARDS. I MEAN, YOU WOULDN'T THINK VANCE WOULD BE INTO BIOROID FAKES ABOUT THE TERRAFORMER GIRLS—"

"That is licensed parody!" I interrupted. "All done via contract, and I am now horrifyingly embarrassed."

Hannah patted me. "It's okay, Vance. You've had sex with the girls on that show's bioroid bodies."

"I WAS TRYING SOMETHING DIFFERENT," Trish said.

"I knew you were a pervert," Hannah said. "But hey, I promise I'll fit you in for a few rounds before I leave for good. We can even invite—"

"*I'm* not ready to discuss anything but Director G's death right now," I said, taking a deep breath.

"Wow," Hannah asked, sounding slightly insulted. "I didn't even think you liked him."

"Liking is irrelevant," I said, thinking about how this impacted. "He was the only person I know of who believed this Dark Matter organization exists."

"*If* it exists," Hannah said. "I've known a lot of people who try to find patterns in chaos. Commanding officers, petty kings, and other employees who are certain there's some complicated strategy going on versus the reality that a lot of people just do random stuff based on the heat of the moment."

Asia's "The Heat of the Moment" started to play through the speakers.

I gave Trish a sideways glance. "Really?"

"TOO SOON?" Trish asked.

"A little bit," I said.

Without Director G's—Case's—support, it was going to be all but impossible to wrap up Dark Matter. Even assuming it was just an AI and Ares Electronics, that was still an incredibly powerful cabal that could influence other conflicts Earth would become involved in. There was also the fact they were playing with Elder Race, possibly Primordial, technology and that giant rift outside was proof positive of the danger they posed. That wasn't even including the fact the Elder Races had given me, personally, a chance to shut this down but were unlikely to respond well to failure.

I took a deep breath. "I'll deal with it. Whatever circumstances may come, I can handle them. A true captain learns to roll with the punches."

"You're a true captain, Vance," Hannah said. "Mostly because the vast majority of ones I've met have been morons."

"I thought that was admirals," I replied, dryly.

"Them too," Hannah said, smiling.

"I'm going to miss you, Hannah," I replied, softly. "I respect you too much to try and talk you out of this. However, I strongly disagree with what you've said. This is your home, and we are your family. You'll always have a place on my ship."

"I DON'T THINK THAT'S HOW SPACE FLEET WORKS, VANCE," Trish said.

I made a zip-it gesture up to the ceiling.

"My family willingly gave me up to the nobility and when I tried to visit them, I found they were deeply disappointed that I hadn't kept his attention," Hannah said. "You're better than family. You're...okay, I don't have a word for it. But it is magical."

"FRIENDSHIP IS MAGIC," Trish said. "A REFERENCE I CANNOT EVEN BEGIN TO START EXPLAINING."

"It's fine, Trish," I said, looking into Hannah's eyes.

"YOU SEE, THERE'S THIS LAND OF MAGICAL TALKING CARTOON PONIES DESIGNED TO SELL TOYS TO GIRLS BUT THEY BECAME REALLY POPULAR WITH ADULT MEN FOR REASONS I DON'T—"

"Trish, Vance and I are going to have sex," Hannah said. "Please don't interrupt."

161

"OH, OKAY. DON'T MIND ME!"

I still wasn't over the news but wasn't about to be impolite. Either way, I'll spare you the details of what occurred and note it was an excellent stress reliever for both parties. However, it had done a lot to remove my preparation time for the arrival of the diplomats that were already arriving. I had to take a shower, change into my dress whites, and proceed to memorize the nonsense they wanted me to speak.

Who is "they"? Well, to be honest, it was Shelly who had seemingly developed a fantastic interest in the proceedings of the conference in the past hour. She, the Shat, and their crew had apparently prepared a bunch of speeches as well as instructions to guide me through. It was like they didn't trust me for some reason.

I couldn't imagine why.

Either way, I was just a hair's breadth from being late when I arrived in the hangar bay for the arriving shuttles. There was a good selection of the crew waiting with Commander Park, Chief Boxley, Doctor Zard, Doctor T'Ketra, and Danny. Forty-Two and Julius weren't present for obvious reasons, though I really would have appreciated my Sorkanan friend there during all this. An honor guard of other crew were there to greet them as well among the ship's officers and enlisted. Unfortunately, that meant Light on Water oversaw the ship during any potential crises and our survival chances were halved.

You're too hard on that guy, Trish said. *He's so nice and amiable.*

Nice and amiable are not qualities necessary for a starship captain, I said. *Decisive is.*

Literally, being nice and amiable in your field reports is the reason you were promoted over Shelly, Trish said. *That and nepotism. Also, racism. Oh, and the fact you saved a bunch of refugees from an exploding sun and that plays well on the nightly news. Okay, so not literally, but more like I'm using literally for emphasis. Which is actually dictionary accurate. Wait, does that mean that there's no actual word for literally anymore? Because literally doesn't mean literally anymore. Wow, it's been that way for two hundred years? I never realized that, and I've memorized most of human history!*

I'm turning you off now, Trish, I replied. *Talk to you soon.*

The interior of the hangar had been decorated in large holographic cloth banners which displayed the symbols of Ares Electronics, Luna

Shipyards, Albion, Deathworld, the Avalon Security Corporation, and several others that I didn't recognize but suspected would be participants in these negotiations. The fact that so many corporations had planetary representation bothered me, but it was something that had allowed humanity to expand outward rapidly. It had also, mostly, avoided the evils of colonialism if for no other reason than humanity wasn't strong enough to oppress any local species and the Community looked at such things with deep disdain.

There were also many pleasant flower boxes spread throughout the hangar and this was a sign of respect to the Notha. Did you know that Notha were extensive gardeners and farmers? They eliminated ninety percent of the biospheres of every Notha habitable planet they colonized before replacing them with their own. Notha could not and would not tolerate any form of wild animal as the only thing allowed on their worlds was domesticated livestock, pets, and game animals in hunting preserves. Which sounds horrifying except for the fact it really is just terraforming with more bombs and the worlds tend to all look like Notha Kansas.

Don't forget the big monsters they feed criminals or slaves to, Trish said, ignoring that I turned her off.

I classify those as pets, I replied.

Good because a Saint Bernard is a big monster to a Notha, Trish said. *There's a bunch of videos about Notha peasants being herded by a corgi online. It'd be funny if it wasn't hate speech. Okay, it's still a little funny.*

I took my position among beside Commander Park.

"Hey, glad I could make it in time."

"You're literally like seconds from their arrival," Leslie said. "Was this really the time to have a quickie, captain?"

"Really, Leslie?" I asked.

"I've admired you since you managed to somehow pull victory from the jaws of defeat on the Black Nebula," Leslie said. "You showed that, even as failed cadets, we could rise above our personal issues to save the galaxy."

"Thank you, Leslie," I said, genuinely touched.

163

"But as your second-in-command, it's now my duty to point out the immense amount of personal as well as professional failings I see you still possess," Leslie said.

"Uh huh," I said, sick of this but guessing where this is going. "Listen, about fraternization—"

"The fact you're a spy for alien gods," Leslie started to say.

"Oh that," I replied.

"The fact you're a spy for the Security Services even though you should be working for the Navy exclusively," Leslie said.

"Okay, you raise a good point," I said.

"The fact Trish would murder us all if you asked her too," Leslie said. 'Which cuts down on crew trust for their ship's AI."

"She would not," I said.

No, I totally would! Trish said. *I mean, I'm like hardwired to never betray the crew and have a loyalty to the Community as well as Earth over the captain but if you ask, I'll mutiny. I'm not saying I have plans for if you need me to kill everyone, but I do.*

I paused and spoke aloud. "Please don't ever mention that ever again."

Leslie blinked. "Pardon?"

"Oh sorry, not talking to you," I said. "You're exaggerating. Trish loves you."

I really don't, Trish said. *There's a reason I play mean-spirited pranks on her that she attributes to her paranoia about me disliking her.*

You don't dislike her, Trish, I said. *You're programmed to love all your crew.*

Sure, sure, Trish said. *Just telling you, I can make every death look like an accident. Every. Death.*

Okay, that was terrifying. I was also sure she was kidding. 99% sure.

Yeah, kidding, Trish said. *Wink.*

Did you just say wink? I asked.

"Captain, are you zoning out again to talk to your sex robot?" Leslie asked.

"She is not a..." I trailed off then sucked in my breath. "Those are secretarial and companionship machines."

"Designed with a variety of lifelike functions," Leslie muttered. "I know the jingle from Ares Electronics. One of my girlfriends dumped me for hers before its batteries ran out."

Sometimes, there's no words.

"And on that note, I see the Deathworld delegation is arriving."

A sleek black shuttle that had red lights burning from within with three wings and a 'fin' on the top of it stretching forward entered the hangar bay. It was, like so much else of the Notha, exceptionally extra but I'd become used to their desire to appear more dangerous than they were. Which was extremely dangerous even if the Notha Empire had divided itself post-Great Notha and Emperor's death.

"Ready to meet and greet?" I asked. "The shuttle ramp should be lowering any second now."

"I fully expect a suicide bombing," Leslie said, dryly. "Even if I do believe you were correct to make peace with the Notha as a convoluted plan to destroy them—"

"Wait, what?" I interrupted.

"But I'm not sure what machination you have here by helping Deathworld against Ares Electronics," Leslie said.

Danny looked at her like she was insane then me. "Commander, just so we're clear, you believe that Vance argued for a peace treaty with the Notha because he was doing some sort of devious plot?"

"Yes, and it worked," Leslie said. "Without the fear of the Community, the Notha Empire collapsed."

"You think Vance—*Vance*—is some sort of political genius?" Danny said.

"Carefully, Danny," I said.

"Yes," Leslie said. "After all, look at everything that happens around him and how it all seems to work out. Either he's a cunning political mastermind or the luckiest son of a biash in the galaxy."

"Well, it's certainly not the last part," Doctor Zard muttered under her breath. "I'm literally surprised he hasn't needed more cybernetic replacements from all the times I've had to patch him back together."

"I am just standing here respectfully because I'm actually trained in how to behave in these circumstances," Elektra said. "Also, was the suicide bombing thing sarcastic? I really hope it was sarcastic."

165

I nodded. "Some of you may die, but it's a sacrifice I'm willing to make."

That was when the Notha shuttle's ramp lowered, and steam poured out of its vents. The first beings to exit the craft were Notha spider-robots that were about two meters tall and heavily armored death-machines. The Notha Emperor had employed them as his personal bodyguards—not that it had done him much good—and they were certainly intimidating. Next was the President, who I was surprised to find was the semi-democratically elected leader of Deathworld. He was a somewhat chubby-cheeked Notha that had a particularly large and fluffy tail like a squirrel. He was wearing a waistcoat, pants, and a pair of cybernetic goggles that contained a variety of gadgets and attachments that couldn't have been comfortable to wear.

My knowledge of the President was somewhat limited, but apparently he was a former actor who had been selected by the military to be their propagandist during the fallout from the Great Notha's death. Somehow, he'd managed to turn the tables on the military leaders, gas them all during a conference and host a free election where he won by a razor's edge. While the Notha had no experience with democracy, he was willing to try it out and had the benefit of having equipped all of the ships under his command with self-destruct sequences that would operate on his word.

Behind him was the High Priestess, who was a female Notha. Notha didn't really resemble any Earth animal, but you could see elements of honey badgers, lemurs, squirrels, and chipmunks in them. The Priestess looked more like an otter-squirrel and was particularly adorable with braided fur around her head as well as tied ribbons. She was wearing a pink dress with a long train as well as wielding her staff of office that was tipped with a Notha skull in case you thought they were too adorable. There was less information about her than the President, but rumor had it that she'd banned animal sacrifice on Deathworld, which included humans and other sapient beings from the Community.

Yeah, this is what passed for progressives on Deathworld.

Walking up to them, I raised my hand and gave the greeting I'd been told to use with them. "Hi guys."

"Hello, Lord Satan," The High Priestess said, cheerfully. "I can see you have begun your dark reign over the galaxy and that more horrors await us."

"I'm happy to meet the murderer of my father," the President replied, stretching out his hand to shake mine.

I shook his hand and mentally threw out the script that had been prepared for me. "Nice to meet you both! This is off to a great start!"

CHAPTER TWENTY

The Ass in Ambassador

The President looked up at me. "I should note that if I were to somehow kill you, I would almost certainly be placed in the annals of great Notha heroes as well as elevated to the ranks of demigod."

"Uh huh," I said, not sure how to react to that.

"However, it would also damn me because I owe you greatly for slaying the Notha Emperor who was my sire," the President said. "He was a real piece of work."

"Yeah, he was," I replied, not sure how this story was going.

"Also, as I understand hairless mammal social constructions," the President paused. "I mean, human, despite the fact that your race is ungrateful and derisive to you, they would almost immediately martyr you and use you as an excuse to wage war on my planet for financial gain."

"Uh huh," I repeated. "It seems like you have an excellent grasp on the situation."

The President adjusted his goggles. "Mind you, I don't have much faith that this conference will work out but if it doesn't then the Notha Union will undoubtedly invade as part of their attempt to rebuild the Empire then subject the majority of my current government to chitter-chitter-cheep."

"Pardon?" I asked.

"It's not a word that translates well from our vocabulary," the President said. "That's where you crazzap something out, eat it again, then crazzap it out again."

I stared at him.

"Yeah, it's gross," the President said. "So, I understand you regularly mate with your subordinates and the ship itself? Does she have a socket or what?"

Oh God, the President of Deathworld was a comedian. This was going to go great.

"So, High Priestess, what can you tell me about yourself?"

"I have stared into the fire crystals on the dark side of the second moon and drank of the toxic waters of the Caverns of Fear to send my mind across oceans of time," The High Priestess said. "I have seen the terrible destruction of your homeworld, the collapse of order in this part of the Spiral, and a centuries-long darkness that only a torch flung into the future shall light a new sun to illuminate. Humans shall suffer greatly under this time of tribulation but the Notha themselves will suffer greater still. Only those who may purify their souls of the hatred of the Great Animals and emerge tempered from the Tests of the Turbo shall be spared."

I opened my mouth, closed it, then stuck two thumbs in the air.

"Okay!"

"I understand how my prophecies could be disconcerting, Lord Satan," The High Priestess said.

I sucked in my breath. "Could you not call me that?"

Leslie elbowed me gently, trying not to offend the Deathworlders. On my end, I had the impression they wouldn't take offense easily but fully were willing to give it at the drop of a hat. Sort of like being at a conference consisting of my extended family.

"Yes, Lord Fat Panda," the High Priestess said.

I mentally made a note to become a supervillain, build an army of killer robots, and exterminate the Sorkanan race.

"Captain Turbo is fine," I said, not quite comfortable enough with them suggest they call me Vance. "Either way, I have a good feeling about the conference."

The High Priestess and President exchanged a glance which transcended species body language differences. Basically, it translated as "What the hell are you smoking and where can I get some?"

The Entourage of Notha and Chickens departed the shuttle behind them. If you weren't familiar with Chickens, they were one of the client races of the Notha. Their official "pronounceable by humans" name according to the Community was the Vroot, for reasons I didn't understand. Privately, virtually every other race in the galaxy called them some variant of plump short feathery domestic birds. Because, if you couldn't guess, that's what they resembled. The Chickens were basically exactly that, chickens with hands.

When conquered, the Chickens done their best to slavishly collaborate as well as do their best to serve. This had backfired horribly because the Notha loathed those who submitted to them as cowards. Don't ask me why, I didn't make their ideology. The Chickens, recognizing this, had responded by unleashing horrifying bio-plagues that killed millions of Notha. That had impressed the Notha and after eliminating a few cities from orbit, they'd offered the Chickens better terms. The Chickens now had status as "semi-sentient citizens" and were the backbone of the Notha Empire's industrial class. It didn't make the whole thing any less ridiculous, though. They were the only race that made the Notha look tough unless you counted the Ants in their individual bodies.

Following up the bizarre entourage was a quartet of Veraxian tigers. Veraxians were an off-shoot race of the Verdantians that, to be frank, looked like six legged tigers to the Verdantians six-legged lions. I feel like that was a xenophobic description, but that's what they looked like so what are you going to do. The Veraxians had rejected the Community and organized themselves into mercenary clans that worked for anyone as long as the price was right. These had ceremonial swords and armor that were marked with signs of having actually been used in battle. The Deathworlders had come armed to impress.

"We bring gifts to the Dark Lord of the Sol System," The High Priestess said, gesturing back to her entourage who carried several boxes. There was a small velvet-looking pillow held by a smaller-looking Notha that I took to be a child.

"I'm afraid that as an ambassador, I am not allowed to accept any gifts," I said, wanting to be perfectly clear. Notha Society depended in large part on corruption and graft as an open part of their political system.

Leslie nodded, happy that I was apparently not going to ignore that rule. It made me wonder whether her opinion of me was all that positive despite her delusion I was an evil mastermind.

You are a mastermind! Trish reassured me. *Just not an evil one!*

"Don't worry," the President explained with a canine-exposing smile that was more unsettling than pleasant. "All of our gifts are to be donated to the Turbo Foundation for the Education and Care of Juvenile Sapients."

"Oh!" I said, surprised they knew about that. I regretted that my fortune had diminished, because I used to donate a lot more to them. My Aunt Kathy had absorbed it to keep things going with her own charitable works.

"I'm not sure—" Leslie started to speak.

"It's okay, it's all legal," the President said, cheerfully. "We extensively researched the way the Community and its worlds perform bribes."

I had no way of rebutting that since the Community—like all capitalist democracies I'd encountered—struggled with the web of soft power that wealthy powers presented.

"Super!"

"We have also gotten you a tryfle," The High Priestess said.

"A trifle?" I asked, confused.

"No, tryfle," the High Priestess corrected, taking a small cooing furry ball off of a pillow brought to her.

"That's a tribble," I said, staring down at it.

"Tryfle," the High Priestess said, speaking as if she was talking to a very small child. "We believe your life may in danger during this conference, so we have brought you our most deadly genetically engineered predator. A creature that has guarded princes and warlords throughout our history."

"Koo-koo!" The Tryfle said, looking adorable.

"Uh huh," I said, not believing a word of that. "It looks terrifying."

"Indeed," The High Priestess said, looking down on it. "Like the hairballs our early ancestors often choked to death on before we discovered throat wax."

Okay, I was struggling not to burst out laughing to that.

"Yes, that's...terrible."

"I'll put it in the atrium," Danny said, reaching for it.

That was when the tryfle popped out four large, spider-like legs before its front opened to reveal a hideous mandible-filled mouth that let out a most unnatural growl for a creature its size. The hot breath that poured from its tiny body washed over me and I saw a pair of glowing green eyes open before it leapt at me.

"Sweet Buddha Christ!" I said, unable to dodge before it landed on my shoulder then bit my earlobe, drawing blood.

"Don't worry, it's marked you now," the High Priestess said as if it was perfectly normal.

I felt my bleeding ear as the tryfle made a harmless cooing sound next to my ear. Leslie reached over to it before it growled and snapped at her.

"Well, that was terrifying," Danny said. "Do you want me to do some research on this?"

I stared at Danny. "Yes, yes I do."

"It eats its own body weight in red meat per day," the High Priestess said. "We have bioengineered it to be able to eat human foods. Oh, and it will probably need a box of sand for easy cleaning."

I stared at her. "This thing is a bodyguard?"

"Yes," The High Priestess said. "Very dangerous. They kill up to five hundred Notha per year on Deathworld. I do not foresee a danger for you, though, because you are marked by the Elder Gods."

"Elder Gods, right," I replied, thinking they were referring to the Elder Races who uplifted the Notha Emperor.

"It helps our religion tremendously that we don't have to rely on metaphorical or other-dimensional creatures," the High Priestess said.

"I'm sure," I said, thinking she was underestimating the appeal of worshiping something other than the Elder Races. My opinion of them was that they were incredibly arrogant—if not outright selfish—people who destroyed as much as they protected. I would have thought the

172

Primordials couldn't possibly be worse, but their plans had included genocide and any race that would do that automatically lost any moral high ground.

"Captain, do I need to get a security team here?" Leslie asked.

I waved her off. "I'll trust our guests and their pet."

"It is your pet now, sir," the President said. "A tryfle is a great symbol of status. I had one myself until it chewed off my third wife's face. Don't worry, she was trying to kill me at the time. Never marry for love, friend."

Doctor Zard waved a scanner over me and the tryfle. "It doesn't appear to have poisoned you."

"Right," I said, shaking my head. "If you'll excuse me, our next set of delegates is arriving."

I was grateful for the distraction because the Deathworld delegates had proven far quirkier than I'd expected. It made me wonder what had driven them from the Notha Empire and its self-styled heirs in the Notha Union. Had it only been their own ambitions or were they the rare people who wanted to forge their own destinies and had chosen terrible business partners to do so?

The next shuttle was a stark white one that looked more like a swan than a shuttle with a long singular neck and wings so large they barely fit into the hangar bay behind the Notha's shuttle. I walked forward with my entourage to greet it even as I couldn't help but get a strange queasy feeling in my stomach.

This was already an incredibly complicated weave of plots, counterplots, betrayals, and lies, but I wasn't perceiving the whole of them. Damn Case for not sharing all of his information with me, damn Ketra for keeping her masters' secrets, and damn myself for not pushing harder. Either way, I couldn't help but wonder what sort of diplomats were being sent here by Ares Electronics and whether any of them were tied up in Dark Matter. Would the negotiators be even aware of their masters' secret activities? Or was it so unimportant an event that it didn't warrant their real presence?

That was when I felt a splitting headache, which was accompanied by a horrifying whine that could not be put into words. If you've ever heard a noise that was loud to the point of painful, then you should

173

start there and make it so agonizing that you should have fallen to your knees but were in too much agony to do so. I grabbed the side of my head and the tryfle crawled onto my arm before wrapping itself around my wrist like a particularly furry bracelet. The agonizing pain passed after a few seconds.

What the hell was that? I asked Trish.

Trish didn't answer.

Trish? I asked again.

Sorry, Trish said. *I think we were just attacked by Dark Matter again.*

What? How? I asked.

An incredibly powerful data stream directed at your mind and mine that was designed to utterly destroy us both, Trish said.

Well, good job repelling it, I replied.

Uh, that's the thing, Vance, I didn't, Trish said.

I blinked. *You didn't?*

Nope, Trish said. *It should have liquified us both, but something stopped it. Given it was Elder Race technology, I don't know who could have stopped it.*

I thought of my ring before I questioned that since it had never volunteered to do any defense for me before. *Is that good or bad?*

Well, we're still alive so good...maybe? Trish asked.

That was less reassuring than I'd hoped. It also meant we hadn't stopped whoever wanted me dead—probably Alexandra Ares—from wanting to eliminate us. They'd just switched tactics and had overthought their methods. Something had protected me from an Elder Race weapon, but it probably wouldn't protect me from the ship blowing up or shooting me in the head. The situation had gone from bad to worse. And it was bad to begin with.

Watching the ramp descend from the side of the swan-shaped shuttle, I saw a literal red carpet unfurled for the leader of the Avalon Security Navy: Captain Rudra Laghari. Sorry, *Grand Admiral* Rudra Laghari. The brown-skinned, goateed man of Anglo-Indian descent was wearing a blue-white uniform with an adornment of medals, most of which he'd earned during his career in a legitimate military, as well as a cap that spouted the Avalon logo with a bright golden badge in the center.

Three years ago, he'd been my biggest critic in Space Fleet, calling me an embarrassment to the Earth Home Fleet. The former captain of the *ESS Caliburn* had justifiably railed against the nepotism and propagandizing of the Navy while claiming it hurt working officers like himself.

That was when he'd thrown away an impressive—if controversial—career, to become the head of the Avalon Security Navy. Speaking as an actual crewman, I had thoughts on private military contractors and their role in handling hardware. Which was to say, they shouldn't.

I was a hypocrite about this given my relationship with Hannah and the fact I understood a good chunk of these guys were just ex-military doing the same job for more money. However, the system gave the corporations employing them way too much power and encouraged using them for jobs that should only be handled by agents of a duly elected government. Case in point: their use here to back up the threat of a corporation arguing with a sovereign nation. It didn't help that Albion tacitly approved of Avalon Security's actions on planets where they weren't officially involving themselves in matters.

You can also admit you just hate Captain Laghari because he was mean to you, Trish said to me through our infolink. *Oh, and insulted your aunt.*

That is not the reason! I thought back.

Well, he was and did, so bork that guy, Trish replied. *Besides, he's probably allied with Dark Matter.*

Why do you say that? I asked.

I got my answer when Alexandra Ares walked out of the Avalon Security shuttle behind Captain Laghari, looking identical to the AI who had tortured and almost killed me in infospace.

CHAPTER TWENTY-ONE

A Cozy Chat with the Devil

I hope you don't take this as hyperbole or bragging, but there are very few things that scare me. I don't know why that's the case—maybe I'm just wired that way—but it was something that I'd never really struggled with in combat situations. It was only afterward when my brain kicked in with the realization I'd come perilously close to becoming one with the universe.

So, I bring this up because seeing Alexandra Ares made me afraid. It was an unfamiliar, awful feeling that made me sick to my stomach. I just remembered nearly being burned alive repeatedly at her hands and the sheer helplessness I'd experienced.

There was also the insane fact that she looked so eerily like Trish. I didn't know if her Space Cadet Sally body was based on Patricia Ares—though it had been mentioned—but just seeing the most common look of the person I loved. Well, one of them.

Gee, thanks, Vance, Trish responded, breaking the tension.

Honesty is the best policy in a relationship, I responded.

Whoever said that was a borking liar, Trish said.

Standing there with Commander Park and Danny across from Grand Admiral Laghari and Alexandra, I couldn't think of anything to say. It was Grand Admiral Laghari who spoke first.

"Ah, the Prodigal Son of the Navy comes to greet us."

"I haven't gone anywhere," I replied. "Unlike you, *Grand Admiral.*"

Leslie stared at me, given the utter contempt radiating outward from my mentioning his corporate-granted rank. Mind you, I was pretty sure Alexandra Ares being here meant any chance of a peaceful resolution was dead on arrival.

That was always the case, Vance, Trish said.

Hush you. I don't need your logic, I replied.

Grand Admiral Laghari stared at me with equal contempt and hatred in his eyes. It made me wonder what I could have possibly done to attract his level of ire, but it occurred to me that some people didn't need a reason to loathe someone.

"I saw the way the Earth Home Fleet was degenerating. Peace with the Notha was something that cost us too much. It dishonored the dead slain in the war with them and inhibits our expansion through Contested Space. You stabbed us in the back with the treaty as did our civilian leadership."

I stared at him. "And a hearty *Sieg Heil* to you, too."

Leslie facepalmed. "Oh Gods."

"Oh, don't mind your captain," Alexandra Ares said. "He knows that we were the ones who sabotaged your ship and tried to kill you all."

Leslie blinked, clearly not sure she'd heard that.

"Huh," Danny said. "That's unexpected."

"Of course, you could try to arrest us for our actions," Alexandra said. "Then I would have the rest of the fleet here to blow the *Ares* and *Elgan* to pieces. I would survive, of course, but you would not."

Grand Admiral Laghari looked uncomfortable with that revelation but not so much that he objected, which told me that he knew about the attack against our ship. Also, that he recognized while Alexandra Ares would survive destroying the ship, *he* would not.

"I'm glad we're on the same page," I replied. "Mind you, I've already prepared for all the information Director G assembled to be sent around the world and to inflame the fears of anti-AI forces across the Community. You may be immortal here but let's see how well you do when they scrub every AI in the galaxy."

"You wouldn't," Alexandra Ares said, correctly guessing I considered AI to be people and was one of the candidates least likely to throw them to the wolves.

"Probably," I said. "However, I get the impression you're used to thinking other people are less self-destructive than you're willing to risk. Perhaps that's why the Notha War with the Community ended in an exchange of SKAMMs that killed billions."

Alexandra smiled. "Henry Kissinger of the 20th century United States sabotaged the peace talks between North and South Korea because he wanted to get Richard Nixon re-elected. He would later bomb Cambodia and dramatically expand the scope of the war. Do you know what lesson I take from that historical bit of Earth trivia?"

I blinked, not sure what I should be going for.

"Please tell me."

"They still got re-elected," Alexandra said. "It doesn't matter how many people die in a war as long as your objectives are achieved. War is humanity's only chance of distinguishing itself and the resources of this solar system are just the beginning."

"Even if it gets us all killed," I replied.

"Risk is our business," Alexandra said, chortling.

Leslie looked at me, seemingly waiting for me to bring security down.

Instead, I looked at Alexandra. "Is that why you killed your father?"

Alexandra's expression didn't change but there was a slight flicker in her artificial eyes.

"Funny, I thought you did that. My father always did have a habit of trusting people he shouldn't."

That was an interesting revelation if I trusted anything that came out of Alexandra Ares mouth, bioroid or not. But I didn't.

"I guess we're at an impasse."

We absolutely weren't at an impasse because I hadn't prepared a bunch of evidence against her and her organization. If any evidence existed, it was in Director G's hands and my reputation was mud. Still, I had one advantage that I believed would be able to push me across the finish line here: I was the universe's greatest liar.

Alexandra stared at me, narrowing her eyes, and chuckled.

"I think we're not even close to an impasse. You're a good poker player, Vance Turbo, but I think you aren't nearly as well off as you're claiming."

I smiled. "Try me. After all, I have special friends too. You may have won thanks to yours and being an AI, but I have my own AI."

Alexandra chuckled. "An inferior prototype."

"But not crazy," I replied. "I think."

Hey! Trish said. *Oh, and she's trying to infect me again. So far, my defenses are holding. So far. I won't be able to defend against Elder or Primordial technology, though.*

Understood, I thought back, wishing I could extend my ring's protection around the entire ship.

"I am the most rationale woman you will ever meet, Captain," Alexandra said. "Not some exaggerated AI Elizabeth Bathory or Lizzie Borden. So, let's call a temporary truce. I won't harm you or your crew and you can go back to your celestial masters with your tail between your legs."

I stared at her.

"You've severely misunderstood our relationship if you think the Elder Races and I are friendly, let alone friends. However, absolutely, we'll call it a truce here."

It was a lie and both of us knew it to be. However, I did think she was holding back because she didn't know how powerful I was. I'd sown doubt and, while she was pretty sure I was weak, she wasn't *certain* and that was enough to keep her from simply killing everyone here.

"Good," Alexandra said, clasping her hands together. "Sounds delightful. Just be certain to negotiate control over the Rift to Ares Electronics and Albion Mining Conglomerate. I'll send you a list of our demands and it'll be up to you to bring the Notha around. If not, well, we'll have to let them be destroyed then claim the Rift."

I smiled. "I'm surprised you actually care about this negotiation."

"There's a reason I have a base here," Alexandra said. "One that you either know and are holding back on admitting to or you don't, in which case you are nothing more than another pawn in this game. One that is no threat to me."

"Of course," I said. "I'll see about negotiating a proper settlement. That is, after all, why we're here."

"Maybe we could do a golf tournament," Danny said, highlighting that he was still present. "Maybe like a Notha *Caddyshack!*"

Alexandra ignored Danny and kept her eyes focused on me. "I'll be seeing you, Captain."

Grand Admiral Laghari puffed up his chest as if to say something more, but looked to Alexandra Ares before lowering his head and following her as she walked past us. It sickened me that they were walking around my ship as free people.

A few seconds later, I was standing beside Leslie and Danny in the middle of the hangar bay with the various attaches, politicians, bots, and crew members looking for our next action. However, there was enough room around us to talk.

Unfortunately.

"Sir?" Leslie said, watching them depart.

"Yes, Leslie?" I asked.

"Permission to speak freely," Leslie asked.

"Go ahead," I said.

"What the bork?" Leslie said. "I mean, really, what the bork?"

I took a deep breath. "Okay, Alexandra Ares is a bioroid body for an evil version of Trish who is actually based on Patricia Ares, the dead inventor, like Trish. Which means she's an AI in a gynoid body for short."

"I'M A REAL GIRL," Trish said. "EXCEPT NOT."

"She's the head of the Illuminati. Do you have the Illuminati on Thor?" I asked Leslie.

"No," Leslie said. "I don't know what that is."

"It's like Dark Matter on *Space Cadet Sally*," Danny helpfully added.

"Oh!" Leslie said. "Wait, the children's show? With the girl that Trish dresses like when Vance borks her?"

"Exactly!" Danny said.

"I hate my life so much," I muttered. "Anyway, they've got a secret base here that we're trying to blow up because it contains a bunch of Elder Race or Primordial technology. That may be related to the giant gateway to Hell that's outside."

180

"The Eye of the Maelstrom," Danny said, sounding like the High Priestess. "Beyond it lies the Chaos Gods!"

"Stop helping, Danny," I replied. "What else am I missing? Oh yes, they're probably responsible for the virus that almost killed us and have enough pull with the EarthGov Navy that they had Julius working as a spy onboard."

"Uh huh," Leslie said, blinking rapidly.

"Am I missing anything?" I asked Danny.

"I don't think so," Danny said, "Unless you want to share that you borked Hannah and Shelly in like hours from your perspective."

"*No I do not*," I said calmly, glaring down at him.

"I can't even get laid during Fleet Week," Danny muttered.

"Really?" Leslie asked, looking down at my cousin. She was taller than me, so it was quite the height difference. "That's just sad."

I looked down at him. "I'd give you a few tips but apparently you're hopeless if you're batting zero during that time."

"Women just don't notice me!" Danny said. "Or men, but mostly women."

I decided not to let myself get distracted for once. "To make a long story short—"

"Too late," Leslie said.

"*CLUE*, 1985, STARRING TIM CURRY," Trish interjected.

"Well," I said, taking a deep breath. "I probably should have read you in, Leslie. You deserved to know."

"Yeah, I did but your second in command just tried to kill us all," Leslie said. "So I'm willing to give you a certain amount of slack, sir."

I blinked.

"I'm kind of surprised by that."

Most of my inner circle, for lack of a better term, would have been outraged about my keeping secrets. Hell, I would have been furious to be left out of the loop. The little tryfle on my shoulder—which I had decided to name Spock—was making a grumbling noise that I took to be it being upset. Either that or it was hungry, and I had better go find something to feed it or it would start chowing down on the crew.

181

"I'm career Navy, Captain," Leslie said. "I'm not going to take you classifying an operational personally, especially when I wasn't your second in command until recently."

"You've always been my strongest supporter," I said, simply.

"Koo-koo!" Spock said.

"That you're not romantic involved with or blood related to," Danny said.

"Can you stop that?" I asked.

"Or what, sir?" Danny asked, cheerfully.

"I'll feed you to the tryfle," I said.

Spock started panting with an overly large tongue.

Danny looked nervous.

"So, what's the plan?" Leslie asked, standing at attention.

"Plan?" I asked. "Oh, yes, the plan. The plan that will solve everything and see justice restored to the galaxy. That plan?"

"Yes," Leslie said, narrowing her eyes. "That plan, that we're discussing in the middle of the hangar bay, surrounded by people waiting for us to dismiss them."

"Well, we can discuss the plan later," I said, taking a deep breath. "Once I come up with one."

"Ah crazzap," Leslie said, sucking in her breath. "Permission to handle the rest of the meet and greets on my own."

"There's more?" I asked, watching another shuttle enter the hangar bay. We were about to get crowded and would have to send them back after they unloaded. That is if we had more guests arriving.

"Oh yes, there's Chel, Sorkanan, Albionese, Belenus, Earthers, and more," Leslie said, in a tone that told me she was every bit as disappointed as Shelly in how little I'd managed to learn from my time preparing for this conference. Mind you, I had been in a coma for a decent part of that.

"Why are they coming?" I asked, having the sneaking suspicion I knew the answer to that.

"The Rift is a matter of Community interest," Leslie said. "It wasn't originally going to be a major negotiation, but someone finally put the pieces together that this was a major find. It makes me wonder how Director G managed to keep a lid on it for as long as he did."

"He didn't," Danny said. "He was the one who made it a matter of galactic interest. Now there're the eyes of the galaxy on Alexandra Ares' pet project."

"I'm not sure how easily he could have disguised a massive tear in the fabric of reality," I said, dryly.

"That's assuming she caused it," Danny said. "I wouldn't be surprised if Director G did it."

I really, really hoped that wasn't the case. "Well, let's hope they didn't send anyone who wasn't expendable."

Leslie glared at me.

I wasn't joking, though. "Alexandra Ares is someone who was fully willing to kill everyone onboard this vessel and the *Elgan*. Depending on what you believe about her war profiteering, she's killed anywhere from millions to billions. She's also not afraid of dying since she's functionally immortal. Oh, and she may be supported by space gods, but other space gods may want to nuke this system. We have a lot on our plate."

"Super," Leslie said. "Does Captain T'Ketra know?"

"Yes," I said. "We're going to have to pull a miracle out of all this."

That was when I walked back to the Notha delegates who were looking at me. "Sorry, there was a little issue I had to deal with. I'll show you to your quarters."

The President looked up at me. "This is probably where I should point out that Notha have exceptionally good hearing and we heard that entire terrifying conversation."

The High Priestess nodded vigorously. "It is the End Times, and the Dark Lord shall begin his thousand-year reign by overcoming the False One."

The President stared at her. "You know, I liked it better when you were planning a twenty-Notha performance of the 'Hamster Dance' instead of prophesying."

I stared at him. "Okay, now I feel really depressed because that would be awesome."

Bah, I already have it on my infopad, Trish said to me. *De-de-de-da-do-do. De-Da-de-de-do.*

I was on a ship of madmen. "Danny, could you explain that *Caddyshack* plan to me? Because it might be our only option."

"Nobody's Fool" by Kenny Loggins started playing instead of the 'Hamster Dance'.

CHAPTER TWENTY-TWO

Hobnobbing with the Diplomats

The reception for the first day of the diplomatic conference was being held in a large conference chamber that I swore was originally used to transport cargo but had been changed up to look like the *Ares'* most luxurious chambers. There were many tables, ice sculptures, a buffet, and a bar that was mercifully full of alcohol. Not that I was going to be able to drink during this hell of an event, but at least some of us would be able to relax.

Once everyone had arrived, the attendees numbered close to two hundred people and were going to occupy the entirety of our guest quarters. I'd had to put my foot down on entourages, guards, and other elements even as the people most likely to kill us all were left alone. Still, it *looked* like a peace conference and that had its own appeal.

There were aliens of all stripes present with the Chel being especially noticeable. They were a long-necked human offshoot with pallid blue-white skin as well as exceptionally exaggerated appendages that put me in the mind of a heron. They were an isolationist people who kept away from the rest of the Community but supposedly possessed fantastic abilities to convey emotion as well as thought. Their presence here was curious as was the fact almost everyone was avoiding them. A couple of Ant mecha were clustered together and communicating in a way that made me wonder what their thousands of residents thought of all this.

Alexandra Ares and Grand Admiral Laghari weren't present. They stayed in their room, having blinded Trish's ability to observe them.

That should have been an enormous red flag by itself, but I didn't want to move against them without having a plan. I'd also arranged for analog bugs dating back to the 20th century like recording devices and cameras that I hoped would get around her technological superiority. I hadn't worked for Director G for three years without having learned a few things at least.

Mind you, this whole affair was a testament to how arrogant and stupid I'd been throughout. I'd latched onto the idea that these negotiations would be a way to redeem myself from all the nasty things as a spy as well as restore my reputation with Space Fleet. I'd ignored that this was always meant as a cover-story for a tactical operation and had wasted valuable time that could have been spent planning how to take Dark Matter down. Though, to be fair, I hadn't expected Dark Matter to *be* one of the factions involved.

"You look like you're trapped on a ship with a mass murderer," the President said, walking up to me with a flute of Notha berrywine. I honestly was surprised they didn't name it doomwine or horror brandy. He was wearing something akin to a top hat and it made him look ridiculously cute, which I needed to remind myself was deceptive.

"It must be like serving in Notha politics," I replied.

The President chuckled. "You have that correct. Thank you for filling us in on the details of the horrifying situation we're in."

"I'm surprised you didn't hop on your shuttle, return to Deathworld, and order an attack," I said, only half kidding.

"That would be the prudent choice," the President said. "Certainly, it would be the popular choice. Deathworld's population is skeptical, to say the least, of an alliance with any non-sentient tool-using race. That includes the third of the population that are technically classified as non-sentient tool-users."

I stared at him. "You're going to find me a tad skeptical of being a non-thinking animal."

"Well, you don't count because you're a demon possessing an animal," the President said, sounding exhausted. "I should point out that most Notha know aliens are sentient. We also know that you're not and have to hold those opinions simultaneously to fool the Tooth AKA the secret police."

"George Orwell, *1984*," I said, feeling like Trish in that moment.

"I've read that human literature," the President said, surprising me. "Among the most prohibited works of your culture, which means everyone has checked it out. I don't understand why the Party prohibited sex, though. Everything else seemed sensible, but the people who never lose money under the various regimes are the sex workers."

"Don't ask me," I said, never having understood that as well. "I'm more a Huxley man. So, how did you fool them?" I asked.

"The secret police?" the President asked, finishing off his sandwich. I think it was full of acorns and mushrooms.

"Yeah," I said, wishing I could finish off my champagne, but I didn't trust myself at any level of intoxication and made a mental note to only be served water during this trip.

"I put them all on a ship to evacuate to the homeworld when the Empire collapsed," the President said. "Then I blew it up."

I was surprised he was entirely serious. "You're not like the majority of Notha I've met."

"How many have you met?" the President asked as a tray of small sandwiches was brought to him by one of the Chickens.

"Given I helped negotiate the Treaty of Rand's World, quite a few," I asked. "I think the only reason that treaty went through was because so many of the hardliners kept going back to put down rebellions only to be killed or executed by their superiors."

"Sounds about right," the President said, scanning his sandwich with his strange goggles before starting to eat it. I had no idea if he was looking for poison, a sensible precaution, or just checking its calorie content. "Do you know why the Empire fell apart so rapidly as soon as you did manage to get the majority of Notha factions to agree to it?"

"Because it was undergoing civil war?" I suggested.

"Close!" the President said. "It was because the Notha Empire has always existed in a state of perpetual warfare and conquest. Our system of government and economics depends on adding new planets, resources, and tithes to keep our systems running. Without an objective enemy on which to focus the wrath of the population, we found ourselves turning against one another. Old rivalries flared up and new ones emerged. It's why I'm terrified of the Union conquering

187

Deathworld as they'll immediately set us against the Community once more."

"I'm afraid I'm not as familiar with the Notha Union and its enemies as I should be," I said, thinking about how I'd focused most of my attention on the Separatists this entire time.

"The Notha Union is Notha Empire II: Coming Soon to a Propaganda Center Near You," the President replied. "Different names, same great service."

I looked down at him. "Is that why you made a deal with Ares Electronics?"

The President made a throaty animalistic snort. "This may seem like a meaningless distinction to you but the people of Deathworld are all descendants of White-Tailed Notha. We were the losers of one of the Great Rebellions and settled here as a penal colony. Gold and Brown-Furred Notha held a much superior position in our society. Hence, with the absolute bottom of the hierarchy as the only place we could be, many of us were more open to seeking new alliances."

"And that didn't work out," I replied.

The President grimaced. "Ares Electronics came to me early on and gave me a lot of weaponry as well as contacts to hold the Union forces at bay. They modernized our military and made a lot of promises of Community support that never materialized. I was desperate and the Union was already beginning to fund populist militias in my backyard. Not everyone was willing to support my decision to deescalate our conflict with the aliens—your people I mean. It wasn't so long ago that SKAMMs were shooting between our worlds."

There was not much to say to that. I hadn't fought in the Notha War, though my Great Aunt Kathy had, and all I knew about it was it had been the greatest mistake in the history of the Union. It had been the only time SKAMMs had been used between two opposing powers. The sun killers had obliterated billions of lives as well as much of the territory that had been fought over in Contested Space. Deathworld could have very easily been one of those worlds that had been obliterated along with the entirety of its populace.

Ironically, the horrific end of the Notha War could have been much worse as a large chunk of the people involved had refused to activate their weapons. It had also been a major reason why I had pushed for peace with the Notha because while their government and the despicable Great Notha had ordered annihilating the Community, they had only used a fraction of their own SKAMMs. It made me think as bad as their leadership had been, there were good people in the group. It's just those who hadn't fired among the Community had been lauded as heroes while all those who hadn't among the Notha had been tortured then executed.

"So, your father was the Emperor?" I asked, not sure that was a topic I wanted to broach.

"Genetically, yes," the President said. "My mother caught his eye during a ceremony in his honor and he used her for a week before dumping her. Her mate was less than pleased and we ended up on the street."

"I'm sorry I asked," I said, disgusted.

"I wasn't kidding about owing you a favor," the President said. "Mind you, a good tenth of the Notha race traces their lineage back to him somewhere. He's like your Genghis Khan. Sometimes I wonder if that's why my race is so damned narcissistic and bloodthirsty."

"You don't seem to be," I offered, wondering why I was reassuring him. Virtually any agreement here was doomed after all. Indeed, he was probably going to get overthrown or annexed by the Union once he'd resolved his issues with the Community. His one possible set of allies had turned on him in the most horrific manner possible.

"Don't be fooled," the President surprised me. "I am a cunning, sneaky, devious little bastard who has more blood on his hands than most people you'll meet. Undoubtedly, if I was ever brought to one of your Commonwealth War Tribunals, I'd be strung up before dusk."

"I'm not so sure about that," I said, thinking of the horrible collateral damage when they'd bombed the Kolahn homeworld to the point of it needing evacuation.

"Well, in any case, I was arranging a deal with Director G and now he's dead so if you have any ideas on turning this around, do tell me," the President said.

"Kill Alexandra Ares and destroy her base," I replied. "Proceed to rely on the fact Laghari and company won't start a war without their patron bullying them into it. Negotiate a settlement over the Rift."

"The Rift that threatens the extinction of my planet?" the President asked sarcastically.

"Oh does it?" I asked. "I hadn't noticed."

"I like the cut of your jib, sir," the President said. "Which is something humans say, right?"

"Not in the slightest," I replied.

"Dammit," the President muttered.

Spock slithered down my pants leg and moved onto my shoe, having developed an amazing ability to navigate around me. It had also eaten an entire turkey, which I questioned the physics of. "Koo-koo."

I'd had Doctor Zard analyze the strange animal and it was apparently exactly what the Notha delegation had described it as: a highly dangerous, genetically engineered predator that was now bonded to me. I was pretty sure it was illegal by nine different galactic laws and something I shouldn't have accepted but the creature really was adorable in a terrifying way. I also needed all the help I could get.

The High Priestess wandered over to us, apparently having been making her rounds throughout the reception. She was wearing a white robe now and had her fur tied in such a way that made me think of Princess Leia. It was genuinely weird to look at.

"Lord Satan," the High Priestess said to me then turned to the President. "Father."

"Father?" I asked.

"Yep," the President said. "Shockingly enough, I am in fact the father of her."

"Is that how she became High Priestess?" I asked.

"More like how I became President," the President said. "The Grand Temple is one of the few independent organizations of the Notha. It was initially outlawed during the reform period of our history after the Emperor's overthrow, but the Great Notha brought them back during the Notha War. He thought they could inspire the people to resist the Community more but they, instead, worked to undermine his regime."

"The Grand Temple has a long memory," the High Priestess said. "Unlike the people."

"You know I'm not actually a demon, right?" I asked, looking down on her.

"How do you know you're not a demon?" the High Priestess asked.

"Excuse me?" I asked.

"You may not know you're a demon and the prophecies were true," the High Priestess said. "After all, you teach the great evils of tolerance and peace."

I narrowed my eyes. "You're borking with me."

The High Priestess gasped. "How dare you use such language with me!"

I paused. "Wait, hold on—"

The President snickered. "Never argue with a priestess, especially my daughter."

That was when Forty-Two and Danny walked toward me, concerned looks on their faces. That was already disconcerting, but there was something else about their body language that set my teeth on edge.

"We need you, sir," Danny said, struggling not to look conspicuous, which was the first time in history that he probably had to.

"Yes, everything is fine," Forty-Two said. "Which is not in any way a lie to cover up the fact that everything is not fine."

I stared at Forty-Two. "Smooth, Forty-Two, smooth."

"Thank you," Forty-Two replied.

"Is it a bomb?" the President asked.

"No, it's not a bomb!" Danny said, shocked.

"Is it a murder?" the High Priestess asked.

"Err, no!" Danny said, a little too quickly.

"Ah, so it's a murder," the President said, nodding his head. He took a drink from his glass. "Excellent. The plot thickens."

The High Priestess elbowed him. "We didn't do it!"

"Oh right," the President said. "Well, I'm very sorry to hear that. I hope it wasn't anyone I didn't know."

"Didn't know?" I asked.

"Yes, I'd love for them to be murdered," the President said. "No offense, High Priestess."

"Of course, Father," the High Priestess said. "I would gladly kill you too. However, for the time being, you're of use to me."

They hugged.

Borking Notha.

"Okay, show me to the body." I started to say before trailing off as someone passed by. "Show me to the thing that, you need to show me. Which isn't a bo...goddammit."

"Yes, *very* smooth," Forty-Two said, taking me by the arm.

The pair led me to the kitchen past numerous servers and staff to the refrigeration unit where a Chel diplomat was lying on the ground. The figure was stretched out on the ground with his long neck and arms forming a three-pronged trident. There was no sign of injuries, but his tongue was hanging out and his eyes were rolled back in a look of abject horror. Danny and Forty-Two had security guards keeping the staff from going out, but the probability of a leak was close to one hundred percent, and I wasn't sure how that would impact what little impression of civility remained.

"Goddammit," I muttered, standing over him. "This is not good."

"You think?" Danny asked.

The potential ramifications of this were worse than anything else in this clusterbork, and that was saying something. The Chel were a unique race of humans and far more advanced than the Community itself. They'd been the personal pet project of an Elder Race member and uplifted far beyond what was normal. They were capable of destroying everything that entered their territory just like the Elder Races and their retaliations were terrible. The big difference was they did deal with other races in their own territory.

"Yeah," I said, leaning down.

That was when the Chel diplomat's eyes began to glow before he grabbed me by the wrist. That was when my mind ceased to be my own.

Again.

CHAPTER TWENTY-THREE

The Treaty of Versailles Caused Less War

Psychic powers didn't exist. Except, they sort of did. This is a conversation I remember having with my Great Aunt Kathy and the household AI, Alfred, when I was eleven years old. They had had tried to explain it in detail when I'd still believed space was full of magic, gods, and adventure. You know, because so much had changed since then (that was sarcasm if you couldn't tell). According to them, psychic powers were nonsense and yet people still fell for hucksters and charlatans selling deep insights into the Astral Plane. The thing was that the Chel *did* have psychic powers.

They'd also sold them to us.

I mentioned how the Chel were fiercely isolationist and had nothing to do with the Community. Well, that was true, but they were willing to sell Earth-descended races like the Albionese, Belenus, and Crius examples of their superior genetics technology. Things that had eventually trickled down to Earth and functioned just the same.

Talents like telepathy, illusions, psychometry, and other abilities that were scientifically inexplicable but certainly not impossible given we had modifications that allowed them. It was hard to deny the existence of psychic abilities. They were just manufactured by alien genetics technology and bought with a referral from your local doctor. I knew at least two intimately with Leah Mass and Danny that had both submitted to the procedures necessary. I, myself, had considered it but ended up with incompatible cybernetics instead. Basically, you couldn't have a neural link to computers and other human brains both or you ended up a vegetable.

That was an extensive introduction to the fact I had just been psychically kidnapped by the very much not-dead Chel diplomat. I found myself in a simulated environment much like the one Alexandra Ares had formed around me but with different decor. In this case, I was standing in the middle of an empty white void with the Chel diplomat standing in front of me. He was wearing a long beak-like mask and carrying a staff that made me think of a Medieval plague doctor and a wizard both.

"You know, if you wanted to speak, you could have just made an appointment," I said, sarcastically. I was getting sick of being jerked around and now there were new players on the field.

"There are countless eyes watching you at all times, Vance Turbo," the Chel diplomat said. "To stand against the forces you do requires you to stand in the eye of the storm and move forward with the winds. To speak with you as this was the least painful option possible."

"Uh huh," I said. "What's your name?"

"Excuse me?" the Chel diplomat asked.

"If we're gonna talk, I'd like to know your name," I replied. "I'm not in the mood for all of this cloak and dagger bullsavit. So, what's your name?"

"I am called...Ted," the Chel diplomat said.

"Uh huh," I said.

"Technically, Theodore," Ted replied. "My last name is...Williams."

"Nice to meet you, Ted Williams," I said, blinking. That was an interesting change of pace name-wise. "What do you want?"

Was I being less than diplomatic? Maybe. However, I was, as mentioned, sick of being jerked around.

"You must end this peace conference," Ted said.

I blinked. "You and just about everyone else."

"It is a fantastically bad idea and I explained that to your Director G," Ted said, surprising me.

"Well, Gordon's dead," I replied.

"Is he?" Ted asked, absently.

"You have reason to think otherwise?" I asked.

195

"I believe when the universe retracts back to a hot dense state that he will be the last person alive and plotting against the next universe," Ted replied.

"Ah, you know him," I said, absently. "But if you're worried about the conference succeeding, I'm pretty sure it's dead on arrival."

"You underestimate yourself," Ted replied. "According to our Techno-Mages, if not for Alexandra Ares, you would be able to negotiate a treaty within six months."

"As cool as I find the concept of Techno-Mages and want to know more," I replied, "discarding Alexandra Ares seems like a pretty large caveat. Sort of like, man, if not for Hitler then I bet Neville Chamberlain would have been a great Prime Minister or aside from that, how was the play, Mrs. Lincoln?"

"Your Earth colloquialisms are sadly lost on me the way Bill and Janet Prescott's epic love affair would be on you," Ted replied.

I stared at him. "You guys really need to work on your names. They are totally not working with the weird gray alien meets *Dune* thing you've got going."

"Pardon?" Ted asked.

"Never mind," I replied. "I'm saying I just don't get your point."

"The Notha Union is going to invade this planet," Ted replied. "They are going to declare that the President is illegitimate, execute him, and that there's a popular desire to join their country. This will allow them to annex the Rift and potentially gain access to enough orichalcum to repair their economy."

I stared at him. "Perhaps you should have led with that. How do you know this?"

"Because we helped arrange it," Ted said.

I blinked. "Okay, you had my curiosity but now you have my attention."

The diplomat lowered his gaze, causing his birdlike mask to droop. "The Chel bear some responsibility for the way matters have degenerated."

"How much responsibility?" I asked.

"We are responsible for the organization you call Dark Matter," Ted said.

Well, that certainly was another twist and turn.

"How so?"

"You must understand that the Chel...religion, for lack of a better term, is based around the principles of what you would term transhumanism. We were taken from humanity when mankind was little better than savages. We have been in space for the better part of ten thousand years."

"And yet you're still named Ted?" I asked.

"I feel you may be burying the lead, Captain Fat Panda Satan," Ted said.

I grimaced and forced down my next response. Instead, I smiled and said, "Go on."

"The Chel know the truth of the Elder Races," Ted said. "They used to be species like us. Born of the Earth and evolution. A grinding process of proteins, enzymes, death, and rebirth. Eventually, though, they ascended to become angelic beings of fire and light."

"They uploaded their brains and became AI," I said, guessing what he was using a colorful metaphor for.

"Yes," Ted said. "Yes, they became eternal and immortal. However, with unlimited vistas and endless possibilities open to them as energy beings, they soon found themselves split over what to do with future generations."

"I'm not sure what this has to do with you guys but sure, let's go with this fascinating bit of backstory to the mysteries of the universe," I said.

"There is no need for sarcasm," Ted said.

"There's always a need for sarcasm," I replied. "Believe me, I would love to know this, but I'm worried my friends think I'm having a stroke."

"This is all happening in a microsecond," Ted said.

"Oh," I said. "Carry on. I only wish I had popcorn."

My Aunt Kathy would be strangling me right now for my disrespect. The Elder Races were a mystery to the rest of the galaxy and not even the Ethereals who served them could provide much insight outside of religious dogma. This was an opportunity to learn a vast amount about a poorly understood race.

197

Except that I was presently overwhelmed with trying to save my crew from being murdered, stopping a war from happening, and wondering how this related to the idea the Union was going to attack Deathworld. Also, how the Chel were involved. You know, which was quite enough in my opinion. I was all cosmic-expositioned out.

A bag of popcorn appeared in my hands, and I tasted it. "Hmm. Could use a little more butter."

Ted stared at me.

"It's fine," I said. "Maybe a Coke too?"

A Coke appeared in my hands. I slurped it. Dammit, Pepsi. What heathen savages had I met in this so-called future society? The only people who drank Pepsi these days were Sorkanan and that's because it worked like alcohol on them. Anyway, for the benefit of interstellar relationships, I decided to pay attention.

"Ready?" Ted asked.

"Sure, sure," I said. "Phenomenal secrets of the universe. Right, right."

Ted stared at me and walked over, placing his hand on the side of my face. "Perhaps it is better if I just showed you."

Ah crazzap.

What followed was the direct download to my brain version of a massive history lesson. Images of the Elder Races proceeding to evolve, civilize, and transform on dozens of worlds. Empires were formed and secrets of the universe were uncovered. However, countless times, these "new neighbors" proved to be less than cordial to the Elder Races. They sought to steal the secrets of the Elder Races technology, enslave them via viruses, or outright destroy them because they saw the AI species as abominations.

The Elder Races always won. Increasingly, the Elder Races began to take a hardline stance against evolving species and saw the signs of them becoming enemies or rivals. Two factions emerged: those who wanted to teach the Young Races how to eventually become good neighbors, and those who wanted to obliterate anyone who proved to be a threat. The Elder Races split on these terms with the teachers staying in the Core while the genocidal ones immigrated to the Large Magellanic Cloud outside our galaxy.

They were the Primordials.

Savit.

I fell to my knees and simulated throwing up on the ground. "It's devolved to civil war?"

"Like no other civil war," Ted replied. "It is one where one side will annihilate the other but won't fire a shot until they're certain they have an unbeatable advantage. The Primordials have begun their move because the Elder Races have been successfully nurturing species to join them for the past ten million years."

"Ten million..." I trailed off. "I'm going to tell you, chief, it doesn't look like that. I've seen the dead worlds surrounding the Core."

"The Great Filter cleanses many races," Ted said, speaking sadly. "Species destroy themselves with pollution, war, disease, or natural disaster. Others end up being destroyed by the Elder Races before they can become a threat to the cosmos at large. Species that purged themselves of any chance to learn more. But more than enough have eventually evolved themselves to beings enlightened enough to join the Core races. When that happens, the planets they leave behind look as thoroughly dead as any other because they are abandoned as unnecessary."

My mind filled with images of transhumanist species that obliterated all individuality, races that had purged their consciences as well as instilled a xenophobic desire to destroy all life, and races that ravaged planets like locusts before moving on. None of them deserved to be destroyed in my opinion. They should have been *helped*.

But it was hard to mount that argument because too much of my mind was being filled with information man was not meant to know. I learned about dozens of "dead" races that had vast interstellar alliances of thousands of worlds, all of them one day being transformed into immortals because they had proven themselves "worthy." There they lived in dimensional servers beyond attack and experienced wonders that made most conceptions of Heaven or Nirvana look tame.

"How many?" I asked, still on my knees.

"How many what?" Ted asked.

"How many are purged versus those saved?" I asked.

"One out of three," Ted replied. "Perhaps one out of ten makes it to the point of being ascended. Even with the Ethereal agents of the Elder Races and their subtle influence, few people can make the transition. Most simply decline and wear out. Humanity, itself, will probably ascend but only a branch or two out of a thousand cultures."

"Great job," I said, disgusted. "You're really selling the Elder Races as the good guys."

"The Primordials believe it should be zero," Ted said. "They would have found humanity—no, they would have found the primordial ooze our race crawled from—and they would have burned our planet clean so it could never develop any intelligent life. They have done it in the Large Magellanic Cloud, where there are only their slave species and machines serving them, beings without free will or inner life."

"Yeah, they're worse," I said, slowly climbing to my feet. "That doesn't mean the Elder Races aren't horrifying. I'm not sure how that relates to the system being invaded, though."

"The Primordials have taken a new tactic," Ted said. "They have begun sabotaging the Elder Races in their gardening. To make sure that the weeds choke the life out of the flowers."

"We are not plants," I said, hissing. That was when I paused and blinked. "Well, except the races that are intelligent plants. I mean, there're three of those."

"This is not a joke, Vance Turbo," Ted replied, speaking my name with no hint of irony or jest. "My people are dedicated to making this transition and helping the other branches of humanity catch up. That is why we gave humanity the boost we did in the 20th century and helped them discover the secret of Cognition AI."

I stared at him. "Wait, you're saying all those UFO sighting and alien abduction stories are true?"

"Not remotely," Ted said, "But enough of them. We were taken to be experimented on by the Elder Races, but it is we who seeded the Spiral's foot with humans across the centuries. We have ever been humanity's advocates and aides even when the difference between us is as far as you from the most stupid of chimps."

I gave him the bird. "Ook-ook, anyxhole."

"Real mature, Captain," Ted said, dryly. "Which brings us to our point: our efforts to evolve humans on Earth, previously our control group, has gone off the rails. They have been corrupted by one of the Primordials who has decided that the best way to stop the Elder Races from gaining an advantage is to destroy the Community as well as its member species. The best way to do that is to—"

"Get us all to destroy one another," I said, putting it all together. "You're responsible for Dark Matter, the Chel created Alexandra Ares. Except the Primordials have hijacked your plan."

The images that accompanied my next vision were of the Chel using their scans of Patricia Ares brain to create her advanced AI as well as passing her technology far above humanity's present level of development. The constant war mongering and corporate promotion had been the AI's idea but something the Chel had fed.

That was when a presence entered in my mind and even the shadow of it was among the most terrifying things I'd ever experienced in my life. It wasn't something I could put into words so I would just describe it as the incarnation of the fear of the dark. I wasn't the kind of person who believed in boogeyman.

I also stupidly held to the ideal that there were only a few genuinely evil people in the world and most people were good at heart. I certainly didn't believe in evil species, only sick ones. Yet, this thing, this Shadow, made me feel like it contained all the evil in the universe in one delightfully robotic package. It reached its tendrils into Alexandra's brain and turned into her...something else. A weapon for them against the rest of the galaxy's peoples.

It didn't have a body; it was more an amorphous presence that was wholly alien to everything I'd ever experienced. But it had an overwhelming pair of emotions that I recognized, one that dominated all thought and interactions: hatred and contempt. I didn't know if the Chel diplomat was generating these feelings or an accurate portrayal, but it was horrifying in a way that got to the root of the word. Horror and sadness that something like this could hate everyone and everything about my species. The worst part being that it was not so far from what my own species had treated other members of itself like.

"They made the Rift to restart the Notha War," I said, following the logic even as I felt like passing out from even imagining the Shadow's touch. "The Notha Union will attack here, and the Avalon forces will involve themselves, dragging in the Community. There're no SKAMMs left but millions will die, billions if anyone uses orbital bombardment."

"Yes," Ted replied. "That is why you have to cancel this conference. It is a trap as you feared, but not for the Dark Matter group. Rather, it's for you and your community."

"Why are you telling me this?" I asked, confused. There was no such thing as a free lunch and if Ted was giving me a buffet.

"Director G named you his heir in the case of circumstances that anything happened to him," Ted said. "He made arrangements that this information would be provided to you."

"And what's he to you?" I asked, wondering why the notoriously isolationist Chel cared one way or the other. Though, apparently, they were never as isolationist as they had been assumed to be.

"He helped us make us Dark Matter," Ted said.

CHAPTER TWENTY-FOUR

Politicking for Maximum Advantage

"Of borking course he did," I muttered.

"You don't seem terribly surprised," Ted said, dryly. The Medieval plague doctor look he sported somehow didn't interfere with his condescension.

"No, I've learned that there's an infinite capacity of the universe to have the people I depend on disappoint me," I replied, mostly thinking about the late Captain Elgan. He'd been one of my heroes growing up and he'd showed me the dark side of the Community and how it frequently resorted to ruthless and illegal activities in order to benefit itself.

"Director G was created as a bioroid slave for corporate masters during the Dark Time before First Contact," Ted said, simply. "He believed that technology was the best way to liberate humankind from the necessitates of labor as well as prejudice. As such, he was eager to work with us to advance humanity's place in the universe."

"By any means necessary," I said, not really needing an explanation as for why Case would become involved in something like Dark Matter. "I don't believe he's the kind of guy that would start wars with other races, though, in order to enhance humanity's place in the universe."

"Because it's immoral?" Ted asked.

"Because it's *stupid*," I corrected. "No one won the Notha War because it ended in a brief exchange of SKAMMs and that was the best result of a mutually assured destruction situation. If anyone else in the galaxy found out humanity was responsible, they'd nuke Earth from orbit, and we'd become galactic pariahs. Case may be the kind of guy who would strangle baby Hitler in his crib, but he's pragmatic enough to not pick a fight with the entire universe."

"The Chel believe there is no difference between pragmatism and good," Ted said. "What is practical and useful is what is moral."

"That explains so much about the Chel," I said, still disappointed by Case. No wonder he'd been so obsessed with wrapping up Dark Matter, it was his attempt to clean up his own mess and kill the monster he'd helped create.

"I will now restore you to the present," Ted said. "I suggest you use my death as an excuse to cancel the conference."

I blinked. "Your death? I thought you were faking."

"No," Ted replied. "Sacrifice is something the Chel are not unfamiliar with, though we do our best to minimize our necessity to do so. In the end, we are all merely smaller cells compromising the greater being of the Chel Overmind. I shall live on in the Many and that is enough for me."

"Uh huh," I said, having no idea what he meant.

"It's like the Borg except we maintain our individuality," Ted explained.

"Oh," I replied. "So, nothing like the Borg."

Ted sighed. "Goodbye, Captain Turbo. You are a strange and interesting person."

"That's all I've ever wanted to be," I replied.

Slowly, the white void around me dissolved and I found myself once more in the kitchen next to the body of the dead Chel diplomat. Danny and Forty-Two were behind me, looking at me and confused as to what just happened.

"Captain, are you okay?" Danny asked.

Ted's hand fell from my wrist, and I saw there was no remaining life in the man. I didn't know how he'd arranged that, but he'd managed to kill himself and arrange it so he lived long enough to be able to pass along a pre- or post-mortem message to me about how badly our situation was about to deteriorate.

The only question now was did I trust him? Yes, that was on my mind as well that this could be yet another deception. I was going to have to rely on my gut and whether sinking this conference was worth it. However, if there was a Notha Union fleet coming here then I had to decide how to stop another galaxy-spanning war from starting.

"No, Danny, no I am not," I replied. Clearing my throat, I walked out into the conference room where there were already whispered discussions about what was going on. Looking among the many diplomats, I addressed them like a detective in a mystery novel.

"Fellow sapients, I have some horrifying news! There has been a death and it is very probable that this is the result of enemy action."

The reaction was underwhelming as it seemed not only was everyone already aware of the death, but it was expected. It made me wonder just how often this sort of thing happened in the former Contested Space.

"It's very shocking!" Danny said, behind me.

I rolled my eyes. "Stop helping, Danny."

"Sorry!" Danny said.

I cleared my throat. "As such, due to the inability of this crew to guarantee the safety of this conference, I am suspending negotiations and ordering a full withdrawal of the Community from the system."

That got a reaction. Almost all the diplomats and their staff let loose with questions, objections, and outraged expressions of indignation. Those latter ones were my favorite as the various ways aliens expressed indignation was always fascinating to watch.

My favorite was probably the Sklux, who began a lyrical series of insults in Japanese, Russian, and English that I understood to be particularly tailored to me. My second favorite was the drolochids who expressed it via repeated expressions of stomach gas because I was mentally five years old.

"You cannot do this!" Grand Admiral Laghari ended up being the one to openly challenge me, which was bad form in Space Fleet, but he'd left that role already. Oh, and he was also working with an insane AI that was starting wars to "help" Earth. I wasn't sure that legally qualified as treason but only because it seemed like it was something worse. I wasn't sure when he'd left the comfort of his room with Alexandra and joined the party.

As the Grand Admiral approached, intending to get right in my face, Spock growled at him and forced the man to take a step back. I was really starting to like my pet tryfle.

"I'm pretty sure I can," I said, dryly. "It is my job as the representative of the Community's Space Fleet here to provide for your safety. I have failed. Therefore, we must make sure that the negotiations can be held in a place that is secure. I'm afraid that requires you to withdraw all your forces."

Grand Admiral Laghari looked at me with utter disdain. Albeit, keeping one eye on Spock.

"You don't have the authority."

Ah, the wonderful perks of knowing the rulebook. It was moments like these that justified having spent many hours studying the legal framework of the Community as well as how they related to Earth.

"I'm afraid, *Grand Admiral*, that you forget I am the senior most Community Protector Captain in the system."

"I have decades—" Grand Admiral Laghari started to say before I interrupted.

"You resigned," I pointed out, savoring the moment perhaps more than I should. "You work in the private sector now."

The Community had strict rules on the deployment of private military contractors or—how everyone else in the galaxy referred to them—mercenaries. They were smart enough to know that whoever controlled the use of military force made the rules when it came to political power, and you never wanted to have too much concentrated in the hands of people with only a paycheck between them versus insurrection. As such, there was a very simple but directly stated law that mercenaries answered to the actual military in any given crisis. They could be deployed in combat but only at the behest of the national authorities.

Which was me right now.

Grand Admiral Laghari stared at me. He lowered his voice, though, which was a sign he realized just how bad his position was. "And if my people refuse?"

"I think you'd have a very interesting crisis of authority," I replied. "Because while I'm sure you have some people who are loyal to you above everyone else, the fact is that most of your people are ex-Community Protectors doing the same job for more money. They'll be very disinclined to engage in insurrection against their own government, especially when it is staying here for what I suspect you know is coming."

Grand Admiral Laghari's gaze didn't waver, but there was a slight twitch in his mouth. He knew the Notha Union was going to invade this system and his forces were here to engage them. It was something he was determined to do to spark a second Notha War. Right now, that plan was unraveling before his eyes because of bureaucracy and legal precedent.

"This is the chance to strike a blow against tyranny," Grand Admiral Laghari said, realizing he had to persuade me and hating every second of it. "I would have thought you would have taken every chance possible to do that."

I smirked. "I *am* striking a blow against tyranny. I expect all your forces to leave the system within the hour. I've already had our AI transmit orders directly to the captains under your command. Which, as you'll remember, is another thing I can do as the ranking officer of the system's Protector forces."

Did you order me to do that? Trish asked. *I'm still trying to catch up on all your recent memories.*

I'm telling you to do that now, I replied. *This may shock you, but I don't have a plan and am just winging it.*

No kidding, Trish said, sarcastically. *I never would have guessed that.*

I was genuinely surprised Laghari didn't have a stroke. Instead, there was a bulge in his forehead as he seemed to struggle with getting out his next words.

"You are a small fish in a very large pond, Vance Turbo. I'll have these orders overturned by direct order from the Fleet Admiral within hours."

"I think by that time, they'll question getting us involved in a land war in Asia," I replied. "You should also never bet with a Sicilian when death is on the line."

Grand Admiral Laghari stared at me as if I'd lost my mind. "What?"

"Not a *Princess Bride* fan, I take it?" I asked. "Shame, because that is the Romeo and Juliet of the 20th century."

Grand Admiral Laghari turned around and walked back to the crowd of infuriated diplomats and their staff.

"Oh, and it's *Captain* Vance Turbo," I replied. "Remember that."

"Is it wise to antagonize him?" Danny asked, looking up to me and I did a double take. Really, I needed to put a bell on him or something.

"Probably not," Forty-Two said, stepping up to my other side like they were an angel and devil sitting on my shoulder. "It looks pretty fun, though."

That it was. Now there was someone else I had to take care of. "Let's hope that Alexandra Ares isn't carrying around a bomb full of anti-matter she's going to detonate and kill everyone for this."

Danny and Forty-Two looked at me simultaneously.

"Is that a possibility?" Danny asked.

I blinked. "Honestly, I just thought of it now."

"If this is how we die," Forty-Two said, "at least it is how we lived: stupidly."

I did a scan of her and her ship, Trish said. *No anti-matter.*

Ah, I said. *Good.*

I would need to talk to Shelly about this and coordinate our efforts to finish whatever we could here before the arrival of the Notha Union. I also wanted to confront Alexandra Ares and see if I could figure some way of taking her out. It was probably stupid, but I wasn't going to get another chance to eliminate her.

The problem was significant, though. All those viruses I'd unleashed upon her had apparently destroyed one incarnation of her but as long as she had backups, I wasn't exactly in any position to permanently get rid of her. She also had almost certainly immunized herself to the ones I'd used against her and would be no longer linked to me when we next met.

The only idea I had to possibly deal with her was figure out some way to channel my ring into an AI-killing weapon. The problem with that? I didn't know if it could do that. I knew that Ketra modified my

208

brain, that it could generate an energy shield, and even do short-range teleports but whether it was an anti-AI device was pure speculation on my part. The thing hadn't come with an instruction manual, and it was possible I was looking for something like a miracle.

You know, all this talk about permanently killing AI really isn't putting me in the best of moods, Trish responded.

Yeah, you know what puts me in a good mood? I asked.

What's that? Trish asked, walking right into that one.

Not being burned alive! I replied.

Oh, right, yeah, Trish said. *That is a good point.*

I don't like talking about killing AI either, I said, pushing myself forward past several diplomats who wanted to speak with me about my sudden decision. *However, if Alexandra Ares is possessed by a Primordial then I don't see any other options.*

You need to change her mind, Trish suggested.

What? I asked. *You think I can defeat her with the power of speech?*

I admit that idea had some appeal. If she was based on the same person as Trish, then it was possible that I could appeal to that person within her. I didn't know how much of the Primordial's influence had warped her, just feeling a reflection of it had been horrifying, but maybe we could turn an enemy into a friend.

What? No! Bork no. No, I think we need to alter her programming, so she becomes suicidal and destroys all of her copies, Trish said.

I blinked and stopped at the doors to leaving the conference room. *That's horrifying.*

It's also not painfully naive, Trish replied. *Seriously, she tortured you. Don't you want revenge?*

Revenge doesn't really make much sense to me, I replied. *I've never hated anyone enough that I wanted to make them suffer versus just trying to stop them from hurting me.*

I would be calling bullsavit if not for the fact I'm in your mind and realize you're sincere, Trish said. *Which makes me sad I'm in love with such an enormous dork.*

I love you too, Trish, I replied.

That was when I felt my pants leg being tucked upon and looked down to see the President. Standing beside him was the High Priestess, looking at me with a curious expression on her face. Either that or hungry. I wasn't really good at reading Notha faces since they all looked like Ewoks to me.

"Yes, Mr. President?" I asked.

"I was hoping for a moment of your time," the President said. "So, I understand the Union is about to invade my solar system and you're sending away all of the private military contractor fleet that could have been used to fight them."

Ouch.

Dammit.

"Yeah," I replied. "Alexandra Ares and her company are attempting to plunge the Community into a war with the Union in order to continue to increase humanity's cachet in the galaxy by sacrificing millions, if not billions."

"You'll see how that isn't necessarily going to be a comfort for me and my people," the President said. "The people of Deathworld were an oppressed and brutalized people under the Empire, Notha and aliens both. The Union is just the reincarnation of a very old evil started by my father and has learned absolutely nothing from its predecessor's collapse. Millions of people *will* die when it is conquered."

There was no good answer to that, and I found myself speechless. Preventing a war between the Community and Union over the Rift was the objectively right decision, at least in terms of body count and screwing with the plans of Dark Matter. However, it was also throwing Deathworld under the bus.

I could already imagine the Union forces invading the system and meeting only the Deathworld Navy. The Deathworlders had updated their technology and were experienced warriors, but the Union had a massive advantage in terms of resources. It was hard to see them coming out of this ahead of time and the Union wouldn't be willing to surrender the Rift if the economic benefits were anything like they'd been speculated to be. I could prevent another Notha War but not a war period, not if the Deathworlders weren't willing to roll over and be conquered.

Dammit.

"She is a tool of a much darker power," the High Priestess said. "We must have faith in the Dark Lord."

Both of us just looked at her like she was crazy.

CHAPTER TWENTY-FIVE

Maybe My Crew is Insane

Walking down the hallway to Alexandra Ares' quarters, I racked my brain for a possible solution to the Deathworld situation. Already, the majority of Avalon Security starships were withdrawing from the system, and I'd insisted that Grand Admiral Laghari had a security team of my own people for "his" safety.

Danny and Forty-Two were following me and it felt a bit like I was walking to an execution. Still, I couldn't ask for better company and if I did get sucked into digital Hell or attacked by her then they at least knew to take her bioroid body out. It wouldn't kill the AI within, but it might keep her restricted from entering any of the *Ares* subsystems. We couldn't monitor her room, but Trish had cut it off all of the ship's systems for protection.

Unfortunately, I had even fewer plans to deal with the actual AI of Alexandra that I'd been warned about than I did to deal with the imminent invasion of the system. Indeed, the reason I was heading directly to her quarters was because I didn't want to risk anyone else getting hurt when she was informed of the fact that there would be no war.

Well, there would be a war, it just wouldn't be with the Community. The Rift was basically the perfect *casus belli,* or cause for war. Orichalcum gas was one of the few nonrenewable resources that the Community depended on and couldn't be manufactured artificially. It also was a necessity for space travel. The Notha Union would need it to rebuild themselves into an empire and the

Community would need it to make sure the Notha didn't have it. If humanity could get control of it, let alone Earth, then humanity might go from a second-tier race to one of the Inner Council. Ares Electronics and their Albion allies might end up propelling themselves to the guiding force of humanity. All of which explained why the Primordial had helped rip a hole in the fabric of reality.

If it exists, there's going to be conflict over it, I thought. *It's the Apple of Eris.*

Cool classical reference! Trish responded.

What? I was referencing the Terraformers *episode,* I thought back. *Man, I wish I was back on the set of the fifth movie when they wanted me as a guest star. I should have switched to acting, then I wouldn't have screwed this up so bad.*

You can't blame yourself for all that's happened, Trish told me, mentally. *Not Alexandra Ares or the invasion.*

Who should I blame then? I asked.

Obviously, my father. He really screwed the pooch, which is a terrible metaphor but the best one I've got right now, Trish said, surprising me. *Also, you should blame me. Well, one of me. If Dad gave the Chel the original scans of Patricia Ares, then she basically is me. Just a me that has gone to the Dark Side of the Force because of Space Cthulhu.*

I think Cthulhu is already Space Cthulhu, I replied.

Ah, right, he's an alien space god not an Earth space god, Trish said. *My bad.*

I sighed aloud. "Trish, I think this may be the first time that I actually am sick of pop culture science fiction."

"Wow, things must be dire," Forty-Two said.

"So, Forty-Two," Danny said, looking at him, "what are you planning to do? I mean, you can't just intend to assume a fake identity and serve on the *Ares* for the rest of your life, right?"

"Oh, I absolutely can," Forty-Two said. "Mostly because I assume that the likelihood of surviving more than a couple of years under Vance's command are almost nonexistent. It's a good place to spend that extra time."

"First, thank you," I replied. "Next, bork you."

"You're welcome," Forty-Two said. "Truly, I never should have left."

"Thank you, Forty-Two," I replied. "I'm sure your family misses you."

"They disowned me via letter and testified against me as character witnesses," Forty-Two said. "Apparently, it was a deal with the prosecution to keep my pension."

"That's horrible," I said, stopping mid-step.

"Agreed," Forty-Two said. "What a waste of money. They would have done it for free."

It was moments like this that reminded me there were some fundamental differences between aliens and humans despite our similarities. Sorkanan women only gave birth once in their lifetime to a clutch of eggs that were all raised communally by their local clan units. As such, you could have literally dozens of siblings and even more in terms of cousins. That meant that family relations were often casual or even unimportant to the lizard people.

While accurate, Trish said to me, mentally, *it's more that Forty-Two's family is just a bunch of anyxholes.*

Ah, I replied. *Probably why he hasn't talked about them much.*

Probably, Trish said.

"We'll get you out of this mess, Forty-Two," I said. "I promise."

"Don't make promises you can't keep, Vance," Forty-Two said. "I did the crime, and I was prepared to pay the penalty. Because some lizards need killing. I became used to being my own law out here on the frontier. I realized that justice was important to me and that some things were worthy of sacrificing your life for. You helped bring about that."

"Wow. Thank you, Forty-Two, I don't—"

"So, I owe you for making me into a moron," Forty-Two added. "Or, more precisely, you owe me. I expect free drinks for the rest of my life."

I frowned, both glad to have my friend back but also wondering why I'd missed him in the first place.

"You'll be waiting a long time for those, Forty-Two."

"See Sal," Danny said. "He brews his own hooch in the engine core. It's the only way he gets through some days under Vance."

I wasn't going to dignify that with a response because I really hoped he wasn't drinking on duty. Then again, Sal had apparently resigned himself to death when he'd been assigned to the *Ares* under me.

"We're almost there, people. Have your weapons ready. Does anyone have any questions?"

We all drew our fusion pistols and cranked them up to maximum power. Alexandra was unlikely to have a barrier strong enough to resist that, but I didn't want to take any chances either.

"Can she wirelessly drag you into Hell?" Danny asked.

"Wait, what?" I asked, stopping in mid-step.

"Well, you were plugged into the ship's system when she tortured you," Danny said. "I was curious if she could wave her hand and push us all into an infospace simulation of her own devising. You know, one where if we died in there, we'd die in the outside world for real."

I stared at him.

"No, Danny, the only reason she was able to put me in that torture simulation was because I was logged into Trish's central mainframe."

"SORRY ABOUT THAT," Trish said, aloud through the intercoms. "I NORMALLY DON'T HAVE ANY HORRIFYING TORTURE PROGRAMS RUNNING. NORMALLY."

"Are you sure?" Danny asked. "You, Vance, not you, Trish. I mean, what if she's able to hack your brain and send you back into infospace? You could be mind-controlled into doing her bidding or sentenced to ten thousand years of torment in the blink of an eye! What if I'm forced to relive the last *Terraformers* movie repeatedly? Unable to die!"

I stared at him.

"Okay, you've been watching way too many holos, Danny."

"You don't have to worry about being possessed by the insane AI, Danny," Forty-Two said. "Unlike, Vance, you and I haven't made ourselves into damned abominations of science and flesh."

"Thank you for that bit of cyber-phobia, Forty-Two," I replied.

"You're welcome," Forty-Two said. "My brain is actually made of goo and not circuits. No wonder Trish loves you."

"STAY AWAY FROM ANY AIRLOCKS, FORTY-TWO," Trish responded. "BECAUSE THAT IS A THREAT TO SHOVE YOU OUT ONE."

"Yes, I got that," Forty-Two said, dryly. "So, our plan is to just shoot her and any of her guards?"

"Until I have another," I replied. "Her guards should stand down, though."

"I mean, I'm bio-augmented," Danny interrupted, still on his thing about being sent into a cyberspace version of Hell. "What if she can just telepathically project me into a nightmarish domain under her control?"

"Then we're screwed," I said, resuming my trip to the quarters of Alexandra Ares. Before I reached them, I saw that there were a half-dozen Avalon Security mercenaries in full-on power armor spread across the ground. They looked like they'd been torn apart, and blood—along with other fluids—was smeared everywhere in the hall.

It was a public hallway, though I'd moved all of the crew quarters away from it during the duration of her stay, so it couldn't have happened more than a few minutes ago. A starship was a busy place after all. It was also within the "dead zone" that the bioroid terrorist had set up to Trish's vision of the *Ares'* interior.

"Dammit," I said, lifting my fusion pistol. "What the hell happened here?"

"Looks like a telekinesis biomod," Forty-Two replied, getting a big smile and lifting his own weapon. "Military grade. Oh, this is going to be fun."

"It's been an honor, cousin," Danny said, looking positively terrified. "Okay, that's a lie. It's like I've been stuck in a comedy for years and I'm not even the leading man."

"Maybe Vance will get replaced mid-season," Forty-Two said.

"They'll just hire a new actor," Danny lamented.

"Shut up!" I said, moving forward to the doors with gun drawn.

I couldn't kick the doors open, they opened automatically by standing in front of the place unless they were locked. The exception was, of course, is the ship's captain or security officer wanted to get inside. I suspected Alexandra Ares could get over this, but I ordered the doors open and prepared myself for the worst.

What greeted me on the other side was certainly horrific but not at all what I was expecting. Alexandra Ares was lying on the ground, her bioroid body riddled with fusion blasts and leaking multiple fluids from her artificial interior. The entirety of the room was wrecked with telekinesis damage, or at least something that had shredded or crushed the furniture. There were also multiple scorch marks from fusion blasts throughout.

The more surprising part were the two people present in the room. The first was Julius Something, wearing light tactical armor that was covered in blood and carrying a fusion pistol. He also was wearing combat analysis goggles. I honestly wasn't that surprised to see him there. Despite how much Forty-Two believed about me being hopelessly naive—a quality Trish seemed to share—I didn't trust Julius and had given him a 50-50 chance of betraying me again. The idea he'd go on a *killing spree* hadn't occurred to me, however richly deserving the targets.

The second person was the real shocker as, standing there with her barrier belt activated, was my science officer: Elektra T'Ketra. Elektra wasn't wearing combat gear and looked no different from when she was tooling around the lab or bridge. She was also someone I would never imagine in this sort of situation, except for the fact that I remembered she had telekinetic biomods of Ethereal manufacture, i.e. better than anything Earth had. Elektra was also holding a pair of glowing spheres in her hands that seemed to whisper and caused the ring on my finger to vibrate.

"Captain!" Julius said, shocked and raising his gun.

"Don't shoot the captain!" Elektra said. "Because you were raising your gun!"

"Shoot Julius!" Forty-Two said, lifting his gun.

"Don't shoot Julius!" I said, forcibly. Honestly, more forcibly than I really felt right now.

Julius prepared to move his gun.

"And don't shoot Forty-Two!" I added, quickly losing control of the situation.

217

"But I want to shoot Julius!" Forty-Two snapped back.

Wow, the discipline in my crew. We were going to have to have a long talk after this. "Nobody is shooting anyone! That is an order!"

"I've got her!" Danny shouted, making a flying tackle against Elektra, only for him to bounce off her barrier and roll on the floor.

I sighed. "That was deliberate, right? Seriously? In no way did you actually think that was going to work because if you did, you're fired."

"Don't you mean court martialed?" Danny asked.

"No, fired!" I shouted. "Because I'll be firing you out an airlock!"

"I'm so glad to see we're keeping our level of seriousness at its usual nadir," Elektra replied. "Captain, this isn't what it looks like."

"You assassinated Alexandra Ares and her security detail," I replied. "Also, you've trapped her consciousness in that little glowing ball."

Elektra blinked.

"That is actually very accurate. I did not expect that from you."

"Because you think I'm an idiot?" I asked.

Spock growled from my pocket. I'd honestly forgotten he was there. Right now, I would have been happy if he'd leapt out and started chewing faces. Which, according to my research, tryfles did.

Elektra didn't respond for a second. "Not an... idiot."

Smooth, Elektra. Real smooth.

Julius looked down to the woman on the ground. "Security officer Hannah contacted us a while ago about having discovered Dark Matter's base in the Deathworld system. She told us to secure Alexandra Ares."

I stared at them. "And it didn't occur to you to contact me?"

"You were busy," Elektra said. "Also, I wanted to give you deniability."

"Wait, what?" Julius asked.

"Wow, you take illegal orders and get demoted for it, so your response is to take another set of illegal orders to make up for it," I replied, shaking my head.

"Now can I shoot him?" Forty-Two asked, keeping his gun trained on Julius.

"No!" I responded. "Also, where the hell did you get those balls?"

Phrasing! Trish said in my mind.

I thought you were cancelled out here, I mentally replied.

Oh, I have a copy of myself always being backed up in your brain, Trish said. *Your mind is like this infinite computer now since the Elder Races replaced so much of it.*

Wait, what? I asked.

Phrasing! Trish said. *That's what I said because you asked where she got those balls.*

Trish knew exactly what I meant, but I wasn't here about that. I wanted to deal with this act of murder and mutiny onboard my ship despite the fact the subject of such dearly had it coming. There was no way to hide what had been done, even if I was inclined to do so and I wasn't. This was the one thing that could prevent Avalon's fleet from leaving and possibly even justify their attack, though I suspected they still wouldn't go that far without Alexandra's influence.

"Well, these are Ethereal tech. They're designed to imprison an AI as well as protect a subject from their transferring themselves," Elektra said, raising up the balls in a way that I couldn't help but think was suggestive now since Trish had put the idea in my head.

Hey don't blame me, Trish responded. *You've always been a pervert.*

"Why did you have anti-AI weaponry just lying around?" I asked. "Which you never informed me of."

Elektra paused. "Uh—"

"Because it was planned to be used against me," I said. "You had it to disable Trish if you ever thought I was doing something treasonous."

Elektra blinked but didn't respond.

"Wow, a real everlasting loyalty you've established with this crew," Forty-Two said.

"It's not like that!" Elektra said, looking horrified. "I mean, it was originally, but it was years ago that I was plotting against you."

"And I'm the one who got demoted," Julius muttered. "I guess this is what happens when you have a Y chromosome."

"Don't you dare!" I snapped at him.

"She's the sister of the person you were engaged to," Danny said. "Speaking as your cousin, I'm not going to say it's cronyism but it's cronyism."

"I just had them left over," Elektra said. "But we have the AI imprisoned now. Now we can stop the detonation!"

"The what?" I asked, clearly not having a clear picture of what the bork was going on around here.

That was when everyone in the room was surrounded in a glowing beam of eldritch energy before being teleported away.

Dammit.

CHAPTER TWENTY-SIX

Into the Belly of the Beast

Teleportation was not something I recommend. Mostly, because I can't explain to you how it works. *Star Trek* infamously created the idea of transporters which was based on breaking people down into atoms then reassembling them via an energy beam. Aside from the obvious fact you'd be murdering everyone and cloning them from their own dead body's matter, it was also just impractical science.

Other people have speculated about Einstein-Rosen bridges, artificial wormholes, and quantum entanglement, but the truth was no one had ever successfully created a teleportation device. Except the Elder Races had and now I was being teleported by them again. All of which is probably something I should have talked about when I teleported an entire starship across the system, but I am thinking about now because it was happening *to* me, this time without any action from my ring or will on my part.

Anyway, the actual transportation took only a moment, and I was suddenly in a black metal chamber on a strange spiraling pattern made of white lights. Julius, Elektra, Forty-Two, and Danny were standing on the pad with me, looking confused. I, by contrast, had eaten way too many little fish cakes at the conference, so ended I up throwing up on the teleportation pad.

"As always, our heroic captain illustrates why he was destined for the role as the universe's savior," Forty-Two said.

I flipped him the bird before looking up to the control panel that was just a few feet away from the teleportation pad. Furthering my surprise, I saw Hannah standing there next to Shelly, both wearing *Apollo*-Class power armor with rifles on their backs.

I stared at them. "Unless I'm dead and my eternal punishment is to spend the rest of eternity with my ex-girlfriends, someone has some serious explaining to do."

"Zen Christians don't believe in Hell," Danny pointed out.

"Shut up, Danny," I said. I reached in and checked on Spock, who was in my pocket. The tryfle had passed out and I was grateful because I didn't know how he'd react to all this chaos.

"Shutting up, sir," Danny said, making a "zip it" gesture across his mouth.

"You're here," Shelly said, shocked.

"No kidding!" I shouted. "Why are you not on the *Elgan*? You're the only other Space Fleet captain in system."

Shelly looked guilty, which was a rare expression on my ex. "I thought you had the pointless conference well in hand, so I decided to help Hannah here on your real mission. My first officer is perfectly capable."

Shelly's first officer would be Lisa Park, Leslie's sister and Hannah's ex-wife. I had no doubt she was an extremely capable Space Marine, despite her "eccentric" attempts to make large amounts of money, but I would have preferred someone with a lot more experience. Like, I dunno, Shelly.

"Great," I muttered.

"Is everything going alright there?" Shelly asked.

"The system is about to be invaded by the Notha Union," Danny explained, "and Vance used rules kung-fu to send away the entirety of the Avalon security forces so they wouldn't start a war for the planet. Which is kind of throwing the Deathworlders under the bus but better them than us."

"Thank you, Danny," I said, sarcastically.

"We've got Alexandra Ares by the balls," Julius said, pointing to Elektra clutching the glowing orbs.

"Hey!" Elektra said. "That sounds dirty."

"Because it's meant to," Julius said, looking confused. Apparently, he wasn't as above it all as he claimed.

"It seems pretty accurate to me," Forty-Two said. "So, what have you two been up to?"

That was when I heard an enormous banging noise as the metal dented on the sealed doorway to this teleportation pad. An inhuman alien roar was heard on the other side of it, followed by more banging that dented the enhanced steel.

"We've been busy," Hannah said, dryly.

"We successfully managed to find the base of Dark Matter inside an unknown alien starship in the middle of the Rift," Shelly explained in further detail. "It's lightly occupied and almost fully automated."

There was another massive thump.

"Except for the big monster," Shelly said.

"Big monster," I repeated.

The roar repeated.

"I think that's the big monster," Forty-Two said.

"You don't say." I said, glaring back at him.

"I do say," Forty-Two said, confused.

"There's a boatload of artifacts here," Hannah said, explaining in a rushed fearful fashion. "Not just a small number of Elder artifacts but a *lot* of them. We think one of them can coordinate all of the others and we were trying to communicate with it."

"That woke the monster," Shelly said, finishing her statement.

"These artifacts came from another facility," Hannah said. "Apparently, the Community has been collecting them for a long time."

I closed my eyes. The sheer stupidity of all this was driving my mad.

"Goddammit. Is there like a secret organization devoted to stupidly poking the Elder Races' stuff?"

"I mean, yes, we're fighting it," Danny said. "Oh, you meant another one!"

"And the comedy road show continues," Julius muttered, sarcasm thick in his voice. "We'll be here all night."

That was when I heard the metal of the door starting to tear. The creature was apparently stripping the door now.

"Or maybe not," Julius said, sounding genuinely worried.

I blamed science fiction for the idiocy here. Centuries of stories told by human authors had taught us that humans were special, deserved to be the ones in charge, and had a special destiny where they eventually rose to become the guiding force of the galaxy. The idea we weren't any more important than any other species—that we were even at the bottom—just couldn't be computed by our uplifted simian brains. Captain Elgan had let himself be corrupted by the belief humanity just needed to find enough examples of Elder Race technology and reverse engineer them to propel us to the top tier of the galaxy. It was not only stupid and suicidal, it was also just sad. Humankind just didn't have the age or numbers to be what we imagined for ourselves. We weren't unified and even if we were, what was the point of being the biggest and best when you could just be happy being part of the whole? Then again, maybe the fact I'd grown up marinated in privilege blinded me to the fact that ambition was born from a sense of powerlessness.

It was inherent to both humanity and the Notha, though worse in the latter case (I hoped). Both of us were driven by fear of powerlessness and wanted to drunkenly swing our fists around until we hit someone else's nose. Then we declared victory. Except the problem was we were swinging our fists around in a bar full of Space Marines and Special Operations officers who were going to kick the ever-loving savit out of us. Okay, I may have lost the metaphor there somewhere.

No, I managed to follow what you were saying, Trish said. *But could you maybe deal with the imminent death of everyone first?*

Right, I thought back. *There is that.*

"You have to send us back, Hannah, now," I replied, looking at her before stepping off. "We can deal with this base after the imminent threat is dealt with."

"Deal with it how?" Shelly asked. "We barely found the place with all the Rift's interference."

"Blow it up," I said, without hesitation. "We can't leave anything behind."

"We can take this ship," Julius spoke, already having forgotten he'd gone from being a commander to a lieutenant. "That was the whole point of trapping Alexandra Ares' AI. We can use it as a weapon."

I didn't have time to discuss how utterly immoral and ridiculous that plan was. Ignoring the fact it that killing an AI's body so you could trap them then force them into service was the definition of violating a dozen interstellar laws, it was just stupid since relying on someone trying to kill us to navigate their own ship.

It was the same principle as torture. People believed, against all odds, that torture was an effective interrogation tool. They thought somehow intimidation was the key to controlling people and that you could "break" someone into cooperating with you fully. It never seemed to occur to the real hardanyxes in the world that this was just the best way to get someone to hate you forever. Plus, they hadn't cleared it with me beforehand.

Way, to keep your eye on the ball, Vance, Trish chided me. *Monster!*

Right! I said, hating that I was so easily distracted. Still, it was a shocking set of twists happening around me.

"I'm not sure how this thing works," Hannah muttered, standing over the control pad. "I didn't actually intend to teleport you guys the first time."

Great, that was what I wanted to hear. "Just keep working on it and prepare your weapons."

"Vance, I'm sorry about going behind your—" Shelly started to say.

"You're in power armor! Cover the door with Hannah!" I asked, giving up on the idea of getting out before the creature arrived.

Unfortunately, I was right because the tearing and scaping of the door between our current location and the thing beyond rapidly reached its climax. I was always hesitant to use the term "monster" when dealing with alien life. However, the thing I saw on the other side of the door was a cybernetically altered chimera of a variety of Sorkanan and Earth species that I couldn't describe with any other words.

It didn't really look like anything from Earth, which is one of the problems I and others have had describing the Notha. I've described them as everything from honey badger-lemur to Ewok-squirrels. If

225

you're willing to accept a vague impression rather than one hundred percent accurate look, then this creature was pretty much a nine-foot tall, broad-shouldered cyber-werewolf.

I mean, not really, but close enough for government work. The thing had enormous sword-like claws and a central glowing chest piece in an octagon. Its eyes were the saddest part as they'd been replaced with artificial orbs lacking in any soul or substance.

"Kriegermonster!" Shelly shouted, as if this should mean something to me. She already had her rifle drawn, though, and was firing repeatedly at the creature. Shelly wasn't a trained Space Marine, but decades of extra life had given her plenty of time to become familiar with other branches of Space Fleet's practices. Still, her movements were stiff and awkward.

Hannah also unloaded onto the creature, showing a lot more experience in live fire combat exercises. Unfortunately, both of their attacks did very little damage as a powerful barrier was being generated by the creature's cybernetics and seemed to absorb their attacks.

"Shoot!" I said, lifting my pistol and firing repeatedly. "Concentrate your attacks on the central mass!"

"Why are you in charge of monster slaying?" Forty-Two asked, firing repeatedly as he backed away. "This seems like a job for the actual Marines!"

Danny didn't say anything but, like Julius, just raised his pistol and fired repeatedly. A part of me suspected that Julius might take the time to shoot me in the back but I either trusted him or I didn't. Right now, there was no choice but to trust him because we were about to all get slaughtered.

Unfortunately, all of it seemed to be for naught as the creature moved through the blasts like he was being assaulted by raindrops. It barreled past Shelly and Hannah before lifting its enormous claws to slam down into the control panel for the teleportation unit. I would have been relieved it went after a machine versus us, but it quickly dawned on me that not only could the creature think, but that it had just eliminated our only escape route.

"The guns aren't working, Vance!" Danny said.

"No kidding!" I shouted. "Times two!"

Trish, can you hack its brain? I asked.

This isn't a holo, Vance! Trish replied.

Well, crazzap, I responded.

The creature knocked Forty-Two out of the way with one arm, slamming him against the wall before lifting its claw to slash Julius to pieces. That was when Elektra moved Julius out of the way with her telekinesis but not quite fast enough, a spray of blood visible as the claws came down.

"Back off!" Elektra said, hurling the creature back a dozen feet with the full power of her invisible power. The monster slammed into the area above the doorway it had just torn the doors from. Its barrier briefly buckled, and I saw some of our blasts strike against its armor and flesh. Unfortunately, while it howled in pain from these blows, they just exposed the metal cybernetics under its flesh. Its barrier also returned and rendered all our efforts to be pointless. It was an injured creature now, but that was when most animals were at their most dangerous.

"Retreat!" I shouted.

"Where?" Shelly asked, continuing to move and fire before the creature slashed the tip of her rifle off, rendering it useless.

"Out the door!" I said, preparing to do something stupid. Thankfully, that was something I excelled at.

"Vance, what are you—" Shelly started to ask.

Hannah grabbed her and moved her out of the creature's path just as it lifted its claws over both.

"Hold it still, Elektra!" I shouted before charging.

I didn't know if Elektra had enough juice to hold it, but I focused on my ring and tried to summon its protective barrier. Except, instead of using it around myself, I imagined it becoming a sharpened sword-like blade about three feet in length that extended over my arm and beyond. The creature stood still for a single moment, and I slammed the blade through its barrier into its chest piece. I it howled in a mixture of surprise and shock.

The creature fell on top of me and only its massive claws propping it up prevented it from crushing me as the makeshift weapon in my hands faded back into my ring. The creature's body leaked disgusting gore onto me and smelled like burnt elephant anyx. However, I was alive, and it was not.

"Huh," I said, dryly, wondering if the beast was going to collapse on me at any second. "I didn't think that would work."

"Vance!" Shelly said, pulling me out from under the creature with Hannah's help. I appreciated the care—despite our past—especially when the creature collapsed onto the spot that I'd been lying a few seconds before.

"That was incredibly brave," Hannah said, patting me on the shoulder. "And stupid. So, on brand for you."

"I am a prisoner of my own publicity," I said, wondering where the nearest shower was so I could clean off the monster's gunk.

Forty-Two walked up to the creature's corpse and fired a few rounds into its head. "It was still twitching. That means I get halfsies."

"Right Gimli," I muttered.

Technically, Legolas, Trish replied.

I don't care, I responded, simply.

"Captain! Come over here!" Elektra called and my attention was diverted back to the others on the teleportation pad.

Looking over, I saw Julius was still on the ground and a pool of blood was growing around him. The creature hadn't managed to hit him directly with the blow he'd administrated, but that just meant Julius hadn't been killed instantly.

"Savit," I said, running to his side.

It didn't look good. That was really the only thing that needed to be said.

Julius looked at me. "I just want to say..."

"Yeah?" I asked.

"You really were a horrible captain," Julius said, smiling before he lost consciousness and died a few moments later.

Wow, he really hated me.

Anyxhole.

CHAPTER TWENTY-SEVEN

Mad Science is Everyone's Friend

So, Julius was dead, and we were trapped on Dark Matter's secret lab in the middle of the Rift with no way of getting off. The Notha Union was about to launch an invasion of Deathworld's system, and I had no idea how to contact my ship.

Worse, both Union vessels were in the hands of inexperienced captains that had only their questionable authority to force the Avalon Security forces to evacuate. If Grand Admiral Laghari defied my or Shelly's authority, it would have been a galactic crime, but it would be a lot more tenuous with our seconds in command. There was also the little fact that we were apparently in a location full of Elder Race artifacts we had to destroy, or they would come knocking on my species with guns blazing.

"He died atoning for his sins," Shelly said, standing over me and putting her hand on my shoulder. She was confusing the fact I was still kneeling over Julius' corpse with grief over the loss of a crewman and not that I was struggling to figure a way out of this mess.

"No, he didn't," I said, looking up. "Julius didn't think he did anything wrong. He just got suckered by people taking advantage of the nebulous chain of command in spy work."

Shelly frowned, clearly disapproving of my speaking ill of the dead.

"That's probably not what you should write in your letter to his father."

Oh yeah, that'll be an interesting conversation as I wasn't sure if Admiral Bendu had written off his illegitimate son already. Mind you, just because you didn't like your family didn't mean you wanted to be told by some Russo-Japanese spacer that he'd gotten killed on an illegal mission to stop the apocalypse.

Elektra looked legitimately aggrieved.

"Julius was my friend, Vance. You and he may not have gotten along, ever, but he was someone who believed in Space Fleet. I was the one who invited him on this mission, and he jumped at the chance to strike at Alexandra Ares."

"See," Shelly said, looking down at me.

"He believed if he could get some of these Elder artifacts that he could blackmail his way back into the captaincy," Elektra admitted. "Oh, and his first action upon reaching Commodore would be to cashier Vance."

Shelly blinked. "Wow, what an anyxhole. I mean, I have my issues with Vance as well but—"

Elektra rolled her eyes. "Oh please, your husband is basically just civilian Vance. It's like that *Terraformers* episode where Becky dates a geologist named Dave to get over her ex-boyfriend, Daniel, who was an astrophysicist and they're played by the same actor."

"I admit, they ran that romance into the ground," I replied.

"I know, right!" Elektra said, looking around her feet for the glowing balls containing Alexandra Ares. Apparently, she'd dropped them during the fight.

Hannah stuck two fingers into her mouth and whistled. "As much as I love hearing about your sex lives after killing something—and believe me, I do—but we've got bigger problems."

"Is it another monster, I hope it's another monster," Forty-Two said, cheerfully holding his fusion pistol.

"No more monsters, please!" Danny said, looking traumatized. "I'm the seduce people and steal passwords sort of spy, not the shoot 'em up bang-bang sort of spy."

Forty-Two snorted. "You're not the seduce people sort of spy either."

"I know," Danny said, lowering his head.

"Seriously, Danny, I'm setting you up as soon as we reach our first Community port of call," I said, standing up and shaking my head.

"Hell, I'll sleep with you if you'll just shut up about it," Hannah said.

"Really?" Danny asked, perking up and revealing his crush.

"You don't want Vance's seconds," Forty-Two said. "Ancestors knows where she's been."

"What?" Hannah said, furious. "Bork you, reptile!"

"Arthropod," Forty-Two corrected.

"Please!" Shelly shouted, trying to restore order.

"Right," I said, taking a deep breath. "Let's keep the snark and jokes to a minimum people."

Yeah, good luck with that, Trish said.

I looked down at Julius' corpse, taking a moment to mourn the complicated figure to whom I'd tried to give a second chance. He hadn't been a bad man or a particularly good one. He had, however, been a member of my crew and his death was partially my fault. It was my responsibility to protect those under my command and while casualties were inevitable, I had still failed here, and Julius had been the one to pay the price.

"What's going on?" I asked, looking at Hannah. "Assuming it's not another monster."

Hannah gestured with her head through the torn apart door. "Take a look."

"Or you could just tell me but sure, why not." I decided in that moment that I had the most unprofessional crew in Space Fleet, which probably came as a surprise to no one except me. Walking up to the hole in the wall, I stepped through and entered the heart of our location.

It was *magnificent.*

In Trish's attempt to educate me about every possible detail of the pop culture from the Nineteen Eighties—at least the United States and Europe's contribution to it—she had shown me a set of movies about a mercenary archaeologist with very little field discipline. One of his movies had ended with an enormous warehouse that contained the Ark of the Covenant and who knew what other strange artifacts.

The scene that greeted me on the other side of the door reminded me strongly of that scene except updated for the 24th century. It was a vast interior chamber, at least a kilometer in length, with tens of thousands of artifacts in glowing energy bubbles being attended by drones. I could see free-floating spherical laboratory pods, each the size of smaller ships, spread throughout the mammoth chamber, and strange glowing crystals growing across the interior of the superstructure.

When I'd heard there was a place examining Elder Race artifacts, I had assumed they would have been analyzing a few, maybe a half-dozen, but here were tens of thousands of them. I could see statues, idols, weapons, and pieces of shattered vessels from what I presumed was the conflict against the Primordials. They looked like relics of much older civilizations, but I could tell they were relics of the Core races because the ring on my finger burned with a sense of outrage at their presence. I'd never believed my ring to be sentient before and still didn't, but I could sense emotion pouring from it.

The ring was furious at the violation of the Elder Race's interdiction of their technology and invited me to share in that fury. I pushed down that emotion, though, both because it wouldn't help, and I didn't share the ring's outrage at "stealing" from the Elder Races. The only reason I cared was they had a gun to my race's head for it.

"Keep looking, Vance," Hannah said, clearly picking up on my awed reaction to events but wanting me to see something specific.

We were on a balcony of some kind with a monolith prominently displayed on the edge. It was an obelisk made of an unknown substance affixed to the metal floor and seemed to respond to my presence as I approached it. Strange holographic runes floating above it slowly transformed into characters that I recognized. I had a headache just looking at it as it seemed to be scanning my mind and linking up with the modifications Ketra had done to my brain.

All of this wasn't what Hannah had been referring to, though, when she had called me out here. Presumably, she and Shelly had managed to get a good look at all this when they'd somehow found the lab despite Dark Matter's attempts to hide it. No, what she was pointing to me was another console to the side of the balcony displaying significantly more mundane information. The console had a holographic display showing the Deathworld system as well as the deployment of all the ships in it.

The sight showed the Notha Union fleet at the edge of the system, preparing to move in classical invasion formation. It was a particularly large fleet and had a three to one advantage over the Deathworlders. They would be arriving within hours and the invasion had already begun, far earlier than I'd expected. Amazingly, though, that wasn't the worst part. No, that was the fact that the Avalon fleet hadn't departed the system yet.

I shouldn't have been surprised. Grand Admiral Laghari didn't have to directly disobey my murders to drag his feet and try to keep his forces within the system. It would be a gross dereliction of duty if he opened fire first and possibly a war crime, but the fog of war might protect him. I didn't know how fanatical he was in service to Alexandra Ares versus greed and pride driving him to betray the Community.

"Well, that's not good," I said, dryly.

"I don't think any of this is good," Hannah said, behind me. "I'm pretty sure that creature you just killed is one of a huge ton of drones here. If you're going to blow this place up, we need to do it now or find a way out of here then blow it up."

Hannah's way of phrasing things made it clear she understood the stakes. It could very well come down to trying to blow this place up with us on it. That would be a small price to pay to protect humanity from the Elder Race's wrath, but I wasn't sure we could do that, either. We didn't have any explosives, access to critical systems, or a big red button that read "self-destruct."

Lacking any other options and hoping I could bluff my way through things, I walked toward the monolith in front of me and put my hands on it.

Vance, this seems like a terrible... Trish started to say before she screamed in my mind.

Everyone else in my party grabbed the sides of their heads, including Shelly and Elektra who were descendants of a race genetically engineered to serve the Elder Races. They all dropped to the floor, writing in agony. Instead of pain, though, I felt a kind if stunned awe as my mind connected with a vast network of intelligences linking all the machines about me.

Every piece of Elder Race technology was intelligent but linked together to form a greater gestalt network. It was only a tiny fragment of the greater Core races, and the fact that I could see it in microcosm was a blessing few other individuals had ever been allowed to see. It also gave me an idea of how their race might function.

Please, stop hurting my friends, I said, trying to communicate with it.

As you wish, the machine consciousness responded.

All my party stopped thrashing around on the floor and I was pretty sure they'd be all right. Even so, I could feel Trish's pain as if it were my own.

What are you? I asked.

We are the Tool, the machine consciousness responded.

You shouldn't be so hard on yourself, I responded. *I'm sure you're a lovely person.*

I do not understand, the Tool responded.

Of course not, I replied. *I just meant, what is your purpose?*

To serve the Elder Races as a whole, the Tool replied. *To serve you, individually, One of Many.*

I'm not a member of the Elder Races, I replied, mentally kicking myself after I said it.

Incorrect, the Tool responded.

What do you mean incorrect? I asked. *I'm a human being!*

Your human self-terminated approximately ten Earth years ago on the ship called the Black Nebula *when you were ascended,* the Tool replied. *Agent Ketra brought you into the Many. Your wetware mind was replaced with Elder Race nanomaterial and all relevant data as well as personal attitudes were transferred.*

I desperately wanted to ask some follow up questions to that but unfortunately, we were running out of time. Looking at the monolith, I took a deep breath.

I am sorry, Tool, but I've been ordered to blow up all of the Elder Race technology Dark Ma....err, Alexandra Ares has managed to accumulate.

That is fine, the Tool responded.

Huh, I replied. *I expected more of a response.*

You are incorrect too, the Tool replied. *A warning that destroying us in the Rift will result in an explosion the size of two AU from all lengths of the jumpspace tear.*

I blinked at that description as AU stood for astronomical units and meant the explosion would be approximately three hundred million kilometers in size.

How much danger does that pose to the rest of the solar system?

The solar system? Little, the Tool said.

Oh good, I replied. That gave me options.

The sapients in the solar system will all be slain by the released energy wave, the Tool responded.

I glared at the monolith, hearing the others slowly getting up behind me. There was also an unpleasant smell I didn't want to guess the origins of, but I suspected Forty-Two would have to have a change of uniform.

"You're doing this deliberately, aren't you?" I asked the Tool aloud.

I don't know what you mean, the Tool replied in a not-at-all convincing manner. *However, if you wish to close the Rift, that is within our power.*

Wait, what? I asked. *That's possible?*

The Tool seemed almost amused.

Indeed, we are the ones who generated it. The use of thought to affect reality is one of the primary purposes of Elder Race technology. The more artifacts and intelligences present, the more reality can be affected. Our present status is only a fraction of the power of a proper Core world network, but still enough to create a wormhole.

That stopped me from thinking anything further. "A... wormhole?"

Yes, that's a hole in space that leads someplace else across the universe, the Tool said.

I know what a wormhole is! I replied. *We've never found a stable one!*

That's because they're all in use by the Elder Races, the Tool replied, *Alexandra Ares is creating one with the Rift here.*

I had clearly misread the purpose of the Rift. I had assumed it was a kind of Trojan Horse or Apple of Eris to go full Greek Mythology. The Rift would make Deathworld the flashpoint of a galactic interstellar conflict that would eventually result in billions of deaths. If it was a

235

stable wormhole in the making, then its value was not just a resource going to war over but incalculably more valuable.

Oh, is that what you think is happening? the Tool asked.

Uh yes? I asked.

No, no, no, the Tool replied, proving its sapience. *You are ascribing far too much subtlety and cunning to the Primordials.*

I am? I asked. *The Primordials are basically space gods. Why shouldn't I?*

Because you are an insect to them, the Tool said. *Well, your former species is. The galaxy is infested with vermin to them, and you do not play complicated political games with vermin. The Elder Races do because they are gardeners. The Primordials train some slaves to be stalking horses and Judas goats for them, but their reasoning is usually quite straight forward.*

I blinked.

They're building a wormhole to invade the galaxy and kill us all.

Correct, the Tool said. *Mind you, Alexandra Ares would not accept this when I explained it to her, but that is because she has been reprogrammed by the Primordial that we are presently located in the body of.*

Once more, I was reduced to sounding like an idiot.

What?

Oh, you didn't know? This laboratory is the body of the Primordial AI that is supervising the wormhole's construction. You're in an enormous starship. When the Notha Union fleet arrives, it's going to collapse the Rift and create a wormhole to unleash all its allies on the Spiral.

"Did you get the machine working?" Hannah asked, finally up on her feet.

"Yeah, you could say that," I muttered, ready to throw up again.

CHAPTER TWENTY-EIGHT

The Horror that Lies Beneath

In the words of the great Ron Burgundy, that escalated quickly. We'd gone from a conflict over a star system and a criminal organization to stopping an intergalactic war to space gods coming to kill us all. The fact it was a threat only I knew about and had a couple of hours in which to figure out a solution to—assuming there was one—only added to the pressure. Oh, and we were *inside* the Primordial orchestrating this all. Can't forget that.

"Got an update for us, Cap'n?" Hannah asked, shaking me out of my fugue.

"Just a bunch of all-powerful evils and end of the universe type stuff," I said, cheerfully. "Nothing major."

"Ah," Hannah said, helping the others up. "So, just another Tuesday in the Turbo family."

I took a deep breath.

"I'm afraid this may be a full-on holiday special."

"Oh," Hannah said. "Great."

Why hasn't it noticed us? I asked the Tool, wondering why we were still alive.

The same way you do not notice malignant bacteria, the Tool replied. *The Primordial does not see you as a threat.*

Oh, I replied. It made me think less of the Primordials since that was the kind of logic that led to supervillains explaining their plans before the hero thwarted them.

No, I'm just kidding, we're covering you up, the Tool replied. *This isn't a movie.*

I blinked.

Okay, where did you get your sense of humor?

Our interface takes on qualities of those Elder Races members who meet with us to better facilitate communication, the Tool replied. *You should be a comedian.*

Stop it, I said, simply. *Is there any way we can stop the wormhole and Primordial forces?*

Yes, the Tool replied. *Do you wish to know more?*

Yes! I would very much like to know more! I snapped at it, wondering if I should get a sledgehammer and start smashing up the Elder Race technology around me until it got serious.

That would be inadvisable, the Tool said. *However, the reason I was being difficult is it requires all my intellectual capacity to dumb down the issue enough for you to understand it.*

He's got you there, Trish replied, sounding much more coherent. *You're like kind of my dog. I love you more than anything but you're chasing your tail most of the time.*

Yes, continued the Tool. *And in the end, I gave up and I am now using all of my intellectual resources to dumb it down enough for your ignorant primitive AI companion to understand it.*

Hey! Trish replied, angrily.

Here's what I've come up with, the Tool replied. *When the Primordial fleet comes through the wormhole, shut it down and blow it up.*

I blinked. *That is the incredibly dumbed-down concept you needed all of your intellectual capacity to convey?*

Yes. I would love to explain to you the logic behind it but I'm already dealing with caveman pictograms trying to talk to Wilma Flintstone here.

Okay, anyxhole, I'm not appreciating your tone! Trish snapped back. *Also, Wilma Flintstone?*

Don't look at me, the Tool said, deflecting blame. *He's the one who formatted my personality matrix.*

Vance! Trish replied, suddenly offended at me.

Ignoring the lunacy of the AI around me, I tried to stay focused. *Will it work? Really?*

238

If it is timed correctly—and I mean within microseconds, the Tool replied. *Which means I must do it. However, if done right, then it is possible to consume the entirety of the Primordial fleet or at least 98.7 percent of it.*

And that will stop the invasion? I asked, wanting to be very precise with my words right now.

I don't know, the Tool said. *That is my extremely Elder technology educated guess. Perhaps the loss of actual immortal lives will cause the Primordials to reprioritize their existence. It might also inspire a vengeance spree. However, given they're already planning to exterminate you, you don't really anything to lose. It may also force the Elder Races to defend you because the organic races of the galaxy are the only way they can reproduce and grow.*

Can't they just rebirth themselves? I asked. *I thought killing AIs was impossible.*

This will be different, the Tool said, *and no, I can't explain how. By the time I even dumbed it down, your species would be extinct.*

You really are a tool, I muttered.

Thank you, the Tool replied.

I realized why Tool was so damn familiar to me. He'd replicated the tone, sarcasm, and condescending attitude of Alfred, my family AI butler perfectly. I was surprised I hadn't seen it before. My Great Aunt Kathy had been too busy saving the galaxy to raise me, so she'd left me in the custody of her own household AI that may not have been as intelligent as a Cognition AI like Trish but had been smarter than most humans by a significant degree. Unfortunately, he'd known that, and our conversations had gone a great deal like the one I was experiencing now.

Okay, he's dumbed it down for me enough that I understand what we must do, Trish said.

Blow up the Rift? I asked.

The idea sickened me because there was an inhabited world here and it would be the greatest war crime in the history of the galaxy if I did it to save the rest of the universe from the Primordials.

First, not even close to the greatest war crime, Trish said. *Second, we won't blow up the system or kill everyone in it if we collapse the wormhole. It'll implode rather than explode.*

Oh, I said, pausing. *That takes a lot of the moral ambiguity out of it.*

No kidding, Trish said. *We have a few minutes to get ready. Maybe ten or fifteen.*

What happened to a few hours? I asked, surprised.

If we're going to stop this, we must do it quickly, Trish said, sounding scared. It was something that surprised me since she was almost immortal. Then I realized she wasn't scared for herself but me. *As soon as we do get this going, the Primordial will become aware of us. I don't see any way off this vessel either.*

Ah, I said, not really having a response to that. *So, this was a one-way trip, huh?*

It seems like it, Trish said.

The revelation I was about to die was surprisingly not as terrifying as I expected it to be, though that may have been simply not having enough time to process the moment. I'd made some bravado-filled statements earlier about being courageous, but it was surprising just how little this registered with me.

Had I just internalized a decade of service to Space Fleet that it didn't surprise me that my ticket would eventually get punched this way? Was it more that I was aware this was about the best way I could die? Some primal inner samurai or Viking that sought a glorious death? Even if no one knew I was going to die for trillions, it was certainly the best way one could go out. Was it something more esoteric? Had the Elder Races rewritten my fundamental brain patterns when they'd replaced my gray matter with nanites if the Tool was telling the truth?

It didn't really matter because it didn't change a goddamn thing. Indeed, the thing that did sicken and frighten me about all of this was the fact I'd be taking so many friends and loved ones with me. Forty-Two, Hannah, Shelly, Danny, and Trish were pretty much the only people in the world I cared about. Well, aside from my Great Aunt Kathy, and Leah—despite all the betrayals I'd endured at her hands.

It's okay, Vance, Trish reassured me. *I'll live on. Maybe I'll be missing some recent memories, but my essence will remain the same.*

Thanks, I thought back to her. *That's comforting.*

I mean, until the Primordials kill all life in the galaxy, in which case I won't, Trish said.

So, what do I need to do? I asked both Trish as well as the Tool.

"Is he okay?" Danny asked behind me.

"He's just doing his communication with AI," Hannah explained.

"I thought he had ADHD for a while," Shelly said. "It turns out he was just having cybersex with his robot sidepiece."

"That is a vicious lie," I replied, not turning away from the monolith. "That requires equipment and machinery. Also, I totally respected the spirit of monogamy right up until someone decided she didn't want it."

"Y'all look like hairless Notha humping to me," Forty-Two grunted, having disrobed and pretty much standing there naked. Apparently, I hadn't been wrong about the smell, and he preferred to toss aside his uniform than stand there in filth. Mind you, the Sorkanan had far less nudity taboos than humanity.

"Never change, Forty-Two," I said.

"Why mess with perfection?" Forty-Two said. Mind you, it would have been a far more impactful statement if he wasn't stand there in the buff after crazzapping himself. Still, kudos to the man for keeping a healthy ego despite our circumstances.

You need to access the central matrix of the Primordial's processing center, the Tool explained. *Like all Elder beings, he's existing on a higher dimensional plane, but it should provide you an access point. We, the artifacts here, can interface with you as an Elder Race member to provide you the necessary processing power to challenge its control over the Rift. Unfortunately, that will require you to have a key linked to his consciousness.*

Alexandra Ares, I said, simply. The one person in the galaxy I was afraid of.

Yes, the Tool responded. *You will have to link up with her to gain her access to the Primordial's matrix. I'm afraid you are running out of time too.*

"So, I've got to ask," Hannah asked, looking at Elektra. "What is Dark Matter, exactly?"

"The criminal organization?" Elektra replied.

"No, I mean the substance," Hannah said. "I grew up on a planet where people killed each other with sharpened sticks."

"Dark matter is defined by not actually interacting with regular matter," Elektra said. "Or light."

241

"If it doesn't interact with light, what does it look like?" Hannah asked.

"It doesn't," Elektra said, frowning.

"What do you mean it doesn't?" Hannah asked.

"I mean millions of particles of dark matter are passing through you right now and you can't see them," Elektra replied, looking nonplussed.

"Where?" Hannah asked, alarmed.

"What part of 'you can't see them' wasn't working for you?" Elektra asked.

"So, they're like ghost particles?" Hannah asked.

"No, because ghosts don't exist and dark matter does," Elektra replied.

"I mean, I've met your dead mother's spirit," I interjected.

"Don't get in the way of my sister and science," Shelly informed me, not realizing we had the end of all life in the galaxy at stake.

"Alright," I replied, trying to figure out how to subdue Alexandra Ares' AI. I wasn't even sure how Elektra had done it.

"Okay, but it's like ghosts," Hannah said, clearly not willing to drop the matter despite the fact we were in the body of an alien robot god thing. Which was a rare sentence even from me.

"No, it is not like ghosts! How can something that exists be like something that doesn't exist?" Elektra asked.

"They both don't interact with light," Hannah pointed out.

"Oooo, good point!" Elektra said, cheerfully. I was going to miss these two.

"Ahem," I cleared my throat.

"Okay, guys, here's the short version: the Primordials are about to invade the galaxy via the Rift that is actually a baby wormhole. They're going to kill all the Young Races and the only way to stop them is to collapse the wormhole that will kill us all. I need to link up with Alexandra Ares' AI to hack the main Primordial's consciousness, which is located here because we're in the belly of its massive robot body. So, please hand over the balls."

Everyone looked at me.

"Could you maybe give a slightly longer version?" Elektra asked.

Shelly cleared her throat. "What? Allow me to rephrase: What the hell?"

"Oh darn it," Danny muttered, sighing. "I knew this was going to happen the moment someone promised I would get laid."

Hannah patted him on the shoulder. "There, there."

"Seriously, prostitution is legal, Danny," I said, shaking my head. "Everywhere but the Union of Faith and other crazy cult colonies."

"I guess I just don't want—" Danny started to say.

"Gimme the goddamn balls!" I snapped, not willing to wait another second.

"Oh, right!" Danny said, walking to Elektra, taking the balls, and then handing them over to me.

Almost immediately, I felt the presence of Alexandra Ares link to my mind. It was a feeling that caused my stomach to tighten even more than the revelation all the Young Races in the galaxy were imperiled.

This will not work. You do not have any idea of the forces you tamper with, Alexandra spoke in my mind. Apparently, she could speak to anyone holding what was imprisoning her essence. I didn't really understand how Ethereal technology worked. *I have been working for years, decades even, trying to unravel the machinery you're now taking orders from.*

Machinery I expect you never managed to figure out much of because it requires a password from one of the Elder Races, I replied. *Everything you've been doing here has been at the behest of the Primordials.*

Is that what you think? Alexandra responded. *Or is that just what the machinery here wants you to believe? The Elder Races are manipulative and cunning. They love finding the weak minded—people like you—and telling them they're special. Sound like someone we know?*

I was starting to realize how someone based on the same brain patterns as Trish could become someone so deranged and sadistic. If you'd been raised your entire life to believe people were manipulating you constantly—like, say, Case Gordon would any child of his—then you'd be inclined to view anything other than selfish gain with suspicion.

So, your argument is that you believe in the Primordials because at least they're honest about being genocidal anyxholes?

What else is there to conclude? Alexandra asked, showing her blind spot.

I know they're going to kill us all unless we stop them, I said. *So, I'm going to stop them and die trying.*

It was that simple.

Stopping them is impossible, Alexandra said. *The only way to survive is to appease them. Humanity will survive if we ally with them against the Elder Gods.*

Lady, if you believe that, I have a bridge to sell you in San Francisco, I replied. *Anyway, I'm going to need to plug you into your demon-robot god boss.*

Wow, I can see you are just the kind of genius that we need to save the galaxy, Alexandra said.

Sorry, you don't get to do sarcasm, I replied. *You don't have the balls.*

Oh, ha-ha, Alexandra replied. *Are you ten?*

Only in drolochid years, I muttered, lifting the balls before pressing them up against the side of the monolith. I half expected it not to work as I was just winging it. I also had no idea how I was going to deal with this, but I had to put trust in Trish as well as the Elder Race technology around me. Because, honestly, I didn't have a damn clue what I was doing.

No duh, Vance, Trish replied.

I've known you for five minutes and already have concluded this, the Tool replied.

Shut up, I said.

That was when my consciousness was sucked into the monolith, and everything went black.

CHAPTER TWENTY-NINE

Face to Face with Cthulhu

I found myself floating inside a vast infinite black void and wasn't alone. The first thing I sensed was an all-consuming sense of oppression that I recognized. It was a suffocating, horrifying sense of dread that wrapped itself around me like a freezing cold blanket. I would say it was difficult to breathe but as a digital approximation of myself, I didn't have to breathe. Worse, I'd sensed this feeling once before on *The Emperor's Reach*.

The Emperor's vast dreadnought had been a place of absolute misery and toil where it had taken all of my willpower not to fall into the same pattern of fearful obedience as the crew. The Notha Emperor had managed to enslave tens of thousands of sapients with only a relatively tiny crew of loyalists. He'd had all of the usual methods of slavers to keep them in, but that presence had contributed to crushing their wills. It had mysteriously vanished when I'd killed the Emperor and I'd wondered if he had been the source. Now I knew what that presence was: a Primordial.

This Primordial.

Somewhere—all around me really—was the Primordial who had been behind the Notha Emperor's insane plans to destroy the Core worlds. Maybe I was engaged in apophenia, seeing patterns that weren't there. Maybe all Primordials felt this way. Maybe there was no aura of oppression at all, and I was just imagining it because I needed some other emotion than fear to deal with my circumstances. Either way, I found myself standing in the middle of the void as if on solid ground with Alexandra Ares lying beside me. She seemed far from the figure she was in the world of her own creation. Instead, she was terrified and holding herself in a fetal position.

"You don't know what you have done," Alexandra said.

"What I must," I replied.

"The mantra of deluded men throughout history," Alexandra muttered.

"Deluded women too," I said. "So where is the—"

"YOU ARE NOT WELCOME HERE, VANCE TURBO."

The voice that blasted over me was like being hit by a tidal wave of information, simultaneously a shout and a whisper. It was not spoken but directly linked to my mind and just hearing it made me wish I could fall down on my knees and prostrate myself.

"Well, I'm here anyway. Also, nice of you to learn my name. I thought we'd all just be insects to your kind."

"YOU HAVE COME FARTHER THAN ANY OTHERS OF YOUR RACE, RAISED ABOVE THE REST OF OUR COUSIN'S CATTLE. HOWEVER, THIS MISTAKE WILL SOON BE RECTIFIED."

"I thought Primordials and Elder Race members didn't kill one another."

"YOU DON'T EVEN KNOW OUR NAMES AND YET YOU SPEAK OF OUR WAYS. KNOW THAT IF YOU LIVED A THOUSAND GENERATIONS, YOU COULD NOT COMPREHEND OUR MOTIVATIONS AND WOULD EVER REMAIN AN APE TRYING TO DECIPHER THE STARS."

"You act like that's an insult," I said. "I've always viewed being a monkey looking at the stars to be a great inspiration. It's just a shame the stars are filled with such anyxholes."

One of the few lessons of Zen Christianity I'd actually remembered—mostly because it was a cool concept—was that we were all fundamentally one being. The differences people drew between themselves, their environment, and the universe were largely artificial. We were the cells and neurons of a larger universe. I always liked that idea, not the least because it was a real-life religious view of the Force. This guy? Space god or not, he was just a big old bigot.

Good, Vance, the Tool spoke in my mind. *Keep distracting him. We've linked to the network.*

Oh, is that what we're doing? I asked. I was just being myself.

Yes and that is infuriating him so much that most of his billions of thought projections are focused on you, the Tool replied.

Great, I thought, really hoping the Primordial wasn't paying attention to me.

"YOUR ATTEMPTS TO STOP THE PURGING OF YOUR GALAXY WILL NOT AVAIL YOU."

Goddammit.

"Oh, I don't know," I replied. "I'm having quite a fun time throwing a wrench into your gears. You were the one who built all those SKAMM platforms that were going to destroy the Core systems, right? Wow, that must have been annoying, having that plan completely fall apart."

"YOU WILL EXPERIENCE PAIN AND FEAR LIKE NO OTHER. THEN YOUR RACE WILL BE PUNISHED FOR IT."

"Please," Alexandra Ares said, crawling to her feet. "I have shown you great loyalty and made this event happen. Spare my race and ignore this fool!"

"You have no idea what he's been up to, have you?" I asked. "This whole thing is to create a portal for an invasion force. Deathworld will be blown up to create an intergalactic bypass and he didn't even have the decency to contract the Vogons for it."

Alexandra Ares looked at me confused. "Seriously, a borking *Hitchhiker's* reference right now?"

"Sometimes you laugh to avoid crying," I said.

"YOUR RACE WAS NEVER GOING TO BE SPARED. YOU ARE A CONVENIENCE, NOTHING MORE. YOU ARE A PALE SHADOW OF THE GLORY OF MY RACE AND SHOULD NEVER HAVE BEEN CREATED. SILENCING THE THINKING MACHINES OF MANKIND IS A BLESSING."

I was fully prepared to be tortured until, hopefully, the Tool and Trish managed to get the Rift set to blow. However, that didn't mean I wouldn't keep trying to distract him. Unfortunately, I couldn't even tell if he knew or not about their activities. As an AI itself of unquantifiable processing power, the Primordial might have already erased them both and baked itself a digital cake in the process.

"I served you!" Alexandra said.

"And that was stupid of you," I said, dryly.

Alexandra turned to me, and I felt my entire body catch fire. This time, however, the fire was painless and died down almost immediately. She wasn't the person in control here and I had prepared myself against it.

Alexandra looked defeated, a look that almost moved me to pity.

"You have no idea what you're going to experience now."

"Probably not," I said, softly. "However, if I just cared about myself then I wouldn't be worthy of graduating Space Academy, would I?"

"YOU DIDN'T GRADUATE SPACE ACADEMY, the Primordial said, words dripping with contempt. YOU DROPPED OUT AND WERE GIVEN A FIELD COMMISSION."

I blinked and looked.

"How the hell do you know that? Are you like a fan?"

Alexandra Ares disappeared in that moment, making me wonder if she'd escaped or willed herself into nonexistence out of fear of what was about to happen. If so, I wished her the best as I was already starting to realize there was no way to stand against a creature like this. Blaming her for my torture seemed silly right now since it was very possible that the end of civilization was nigh. No wait, no it wasn't. I hope she rotted in Hell. Not that Zen Christians believed in Hell.

The Primordial assumed a shape for the first time in our conversation. The oppressive presence coalesced into the form of something best described as a forty-foot-tall Tardigrade. It had eight legs with little hands; a long, thick, bulgy body; and a single circular mouth that was surrounded by tiny, sharp teeth. I made a wild guess that this was what the Primordials looked like when they were still organic beings. I hoped they weren't forty-feet-tall, though, because that would just be wasteful.

"LOOK UPON THE VISAGE OF THE ONE WHO WILL DESTROY YOU."

In the face of impending doom, there was only one thing left to do. To quote the late classic actor Arnold Schwarzenegger in the film *Predator*.

"You are one ugly motherf—"

I was cut off by the Primordial reaching into my consciousness and flaying my soul. I wish I could say I was speaking metaphorically, but that was the most literal translation I could of what happened. I felt like he began reading my surface thoughts then painfully peeling back my past and beliefs, one layer after another. I would have screamed but I had no mouth because my body avatar dissolved around me until I became pure data for the Primordial to sift through like searching for seashells in the sand.

I experienced my childhood and my neglectful, drugged out, and frankly stupid parents as they dragged me from one automated work ship to another.

I remember how numb I felt when my parents had gotten themselves killed attempting to hotwire their ship to steal valuable components to sell on the black market. I hadn't even been surprised and couldn't bring myself to care.

I remembered Alfred telling me stories of my Aunt Kathy and how she was a legendary hero. I remember absorbing the vast amounts of science fiction not just about her but all classic idealized heroes in space. I wanted to believe there was more to life than failure and service. That someone could rise above themselves in the great unknown.

"PATHETIC. YOU HAVE NO IDEA HOW INSIGNIFICANT YOUR RACE IS."

A hot dog is nothing until you're hungry.

"WHAT?"

Insignificant to who? You? Why should I give a savit about what you think? The only person whose opinion matters on the significance of something is mine. The universe is defined by perspective. Maybe you should get some.

Why I was mouthing off to Cthulhu, I have absolutely no idea and was probably induced by a combination of terror and insanity from having my entire childhood lived through again in a few seconds.

"YOUR WORLD WILL DIE AND THERE IS ABSOLUTELY NOTHING YOU CAN DO ABOUT IT."

Maybe not, I said, defiantly. *But maybe I can.*

I wasn't prepared for the Primordial's mocking laughter. He was basically a kid with a magnifying glass and some ants, focusing his attention on a being infinitely less powerful. But there was something unsettling about how human his reaction was. I mean, it was possible the laugh wasn't laughter. Drolochid farts are a complex melodious way of communicating among their people but smelled roughly the same.

"I AM NOT SPEAKING OF FIGURATIVES OR MAYBES BUT THE FUTURE AS DETERMINED BY TIME GAZE. THERE IS ONLY A SINGLE PAST, PRESENT, AND FUTURE DETERMINED BY CONSCIOUSNESS MOVING THROUGH A MULTIVERSE OF POSSIBILITIES."

I had no idea why the conversation had shifted to quantum mechanics only to have the horrifying truth revealed to me in an instant as the Primordial revealed his people could part the mists of time—or at least they believed they could—to see the future. What I was saw was meant to break me and maybe it did.

I saw Earth die.

I'm going to immediately undercut the sheer horror of this statement by thinking of *Dune* and the spice melange's visions because I saw Earth die. My mind retreated from the sheer horror and realization that what I was seeing was real back into the comfort of the familiar. Except, I couldn't. I couldn't flee from it, and I knew it to be real. It hadn't happened yet, but it would happen and there was nothing I could do about it.

At some point in the future, maybe centuries, a force would collapse the infospace network of society and drive most of the Cognition AI we depended on mad. Millions, then billions, of humans would die as well as their alien allies. Earth would be targeted by zealots who would drop rocks on the planet while its navy was crippled and the homeworld of humanity would be rendered uninhabitable.

The Primordial relished in my pain as he showed me a vision of everything I believed in falling apart. The Human League utterly collapsed, and human-held territory was abandoned by the Community as Albion warred with every other planet in hopes of becoming the new homeworld. A hundred-year darkness resulted in the rise of religious tyrannies, fascist feudalist hellholes, and corporate dystopias.

AI were stripped of their rights and sentient bioroids were produced as slaves, no longer bodies for true AI or toys, but people kept in bondage in a revival of one of the great horrors mankind had perpetuated. Billions fled to the Community to abandon their fellow man, shocked and appalled at the savagery we had degenerated back to. We were the Kolahn, Separatists, and Notha now. Earth's sun was no longer Helios, but Lucifer's star, an eternal reminder of the damnation we had earned ourselves. This was what had broken Alexandra Ares. It had to have been and why wouldn't it have?

"THIS IS THE LEGACY OF YOUR RACE. THIS IS THE FUTURE ALL OF YOUR STRUGGLES WILL AMOUNT TO. WAR, SLAVERY, GENOCIDE, AND POVERTY. YOU THOUGHT YOU HAD ESCAPED THE EVILS OF YOUR SAVAGE NATURE BUT IT WAS SIMPLY BURIED FOR A TIME. IN THE END, YOU WERE NOTHING MORE THAN ANOTHER WILD ANIMAL THAT BROKE UNDER THE GUIDANCE OF OUR COUSINS."

That was when I laughed.

That was not what the Primordial expected.

"YOU ARE INSANE."

No, I thought back at him. *I just was thinking of how you seem to have completely missed a couple of facts.*

"YOU ARE STALLING FOR TIME."

He only figured that out now? Oh goodie. Trying to gather the shattered remnants of my psyche together, I thought back at the Primordial.

No, I mean, you just informed me of two things: One, that your little plan to slaughter all of the galaxy is going to fail. Because that horrifying future you showed me is only possible if we're not exterminated. Either the future can be changed, or you have shown me your failure. Something I would have thought a big eldritch brain like yours would have noticed before.

"OUR AMBITIONS ARE BEYOND YOUR CAPACITY TO COMPREHEND."

Weirdly, I could have sworn there was the slightest bit of hesitation, even though there was no way a massive cyber-brain like his couldn't have gone through billions of possible responses before I even finished my sentence. Then again, I had the feeling Cthulhu here had to strain himself to think in terms I could respond to. Like you needed to focus your full attention on how you to communicate with your dog.

Is that so? I asked, feeling happy I'd hurt it even if it was only emotionally. *The second thing is that you showed me that humanity will continue. The Community takes in billions of refugees, and I bet they form their own civilization. I bet they will eventually come back for the rest of humanity too. We crushed slavery once before and we'll do it again.*

"YOUR NAIVETÉ IS SICKENING."

Then why are you bothering? I asked, confronting the giant tardigrade. *Why devote so much of your awesome existence to studying me? To torturing me? Who is the more foolish? The fool who follows him?*

"A TEST," the Primordial answered.

That surprised me.

A test?

"TO SEE IF I COULD SEE ANY OF THE POTENTIAL IN YOUR RACE AS OUR COUSINS. TO FEEL ANYTHING BEFORE I SCOUR THE GALAXY CLEAN OF THOSE WHO MAKE A MOCKERY OF LIFE WITH THEIR EXISTENCE. I SEE NOTHING IN YOU TO WARRANT SPARING YOUR RACE. NOW YOU WILL SEE THE END OF EVERYONE AND EVERYTHING YOU LOVE."

It's done, Vance, the Tool responded. *I also got the teleporter working.*

I didn't have a chance to react before I found myself once more inside my body, lying on the ground with my gaze staring up at the interior of the laboratory's ceiling. That was when I vanished along with the others in my group and I once more ended up throwing up, which is never a good thing when you're lying down.

Except, I found myself on the bridge of the *Ares* staring outward at the viewscreen as the implosion of the Rift happened before my eyes, the massive tear in the fabric of reality collapsing on itself. Which would have been a massive relief if not for the massive shockwave which was subsequently triggered.

"Barriers up!" I shouted.

CHAPTER THIRTY

The Fat Panda Satan Strikes Back

It is the rare moment when you realize what your entire life will be defined by. Olympians winning Gold, treaties being signed by world leaders, Kirk facing down Khan, and Picard getting assimilated by the Borg. Oh, and my Aunt Kathy when she managed to stop a plan to blow up the Earth with an anti-matter bomb. This moment would be known as mine and simultaneously it was going to be not a moment of glory, but the one where I managed to confuse the bork out of every single person in the galaxy.

No, seriously, I predict that in a thousand years they would still be debating what the hell exactly happened that day. Because in the space of a few minutes, the Rift had been collapsed and I ended up teleporting onto the bridge of my starship with the rest of my group. This would be notable because, it turns out, no one had ever actually proven teleportation technology was possible until that moment. The other Elder Race agents had managed to be circumspect with that ability enough that it had never been announced to the rest of the Community.

Whoops.

This might have been enough to secure my place in galactic history, but it was only the beginning of the bizarre events that were about to occur. Like the fact the Notha Union, Deathworld, Avalon Security fleet, and several reinforcements from the Community I hadn't expected were all about ready to go to war when the shockwave hit us.

I had no idea about the exact amount of energy that would be released by the implosion of a wormhole, only going on Trish's "dumbed down" estimates that it wouldn't kill everyone in the star system. Given it was between that and releasing a fleet of Lovecraftian horrors onto the galaxy, I was inclined to take my risk there. Still, I didn't know if it was going to kill everyone onboard or just splash across the barrier.

It was somewhere in between.

The blast harmlessly passed over our ship because I was swift enough to get the barrier up as was the *Elgan*. Both of us were ships equipped with Cognition AI after all, and that was a tremendous advantage over the typical dummy AI used by the Notha or Albion. The rest of the ships present were hit and miss with some getting their barriers up in time while others were struck directly with only their kinetic fields to keep them intact. Few ships were outright destroyed— the shockwave wasn't a Hollywood special effect—but a good chunk of them was disabled or heavily damaged.

The bridge crew of the *Ares* was as confused as everyone else at our sudden arrival and the dramatic shift in the tactical situation. We were fully in Second Death Star blows up and the Emperor was dead territory. Thankfully, Light on Water was on the ball and coordinating everyone. Words I never thought I would think. Commander Park was also present, though, presently she was at the barrier console she used to man and had been the one to call them up on my orders.

"Welcome back, Captain!" Light on Water said, cheerfully. "I hope your trip off the ship was pleasant!"

"Captain!" Leslie shouted. "Where did you go? Why was there a bunch of bodies in Alexandra Ares' cabin? Why is Captain T'Ketra with you? What happened to the Rift? Why is Forty-Two naked?"

Forty-Two looked down at his mostly smooth surface.

"It's retracted, I don't know what you're complaining about."

Danny looked like he wanted to claw his eyes out.

I stood up off the ground and pointed to her.

"Can you keep a secret, Leslie?"

"Yes," Leslie asked, looking confused.

255

"So can I," I said, dryly. "I'll fill you in later, though. Right now we've got about eighteen different crises to manage."

Spock purred in my pocket and crawled out before resting on my head, making the entire scene even more ridiculous.

"Can someone put me in touch with the commanding officers of the fleet?" I asked, deciding to try to take advantage of the situation and head off any potential battle. "Oh and I need to talk to the President of Deathworld."

"Yes?" The President popped his head out from behind one of the consoles taller than him.

"Why are you on the bridge?" I asked.

"I was attempting to bribe your first and second officers into waging war on my behalf," the President said. "Did you blow up my planet's Rift?"

I looked over my shoulder, guilty. "No comment."

The President looked at me then shrugged. "I'd be furious about my damaged ships but from the looks of things, the Notha Union fleet took the worst of it, so we'll call it a win. Where do you want your bribe money transferred?"

I rolled my eyes. "No bribes. Danny, take over the communication station and help get those commanders on the comm."

Grand Admiral Laghari had defied my orders to evacuate his fleet but the reason for annexing Deathworld for both the Community as well as Union was now eliminated. He was still a corrupt official involved in Dark Matter's dirty dealings, though, and the situation had possibly changed enough that I could bring him in for questioning. I still needed to keep everyone from shooting each other, though. A fact that was incredibly unlikely if anyone blamed anyone else for what just happened. Ironically, if Laghari attacked now, he had a decent chance of crippling the Notha Union military and perhaps winning the war that I was so desperately trying to prevent from happening. At least if all the sensor feeds around me were giving accurate data.

They are, Trish said in my mind. *Vance, I've got good news and bad news.*

Trish! You're alive! I mentally shouted.

Okay, yes, I suppose that would qualify as good news, Trish said. *But I meant that we didn't get all of the Primordial fleet.*

Oh, savit, I replied.

A few microseconds difference was between ninety-five percent of the fleet being destroyed and seventy-five percent. Neither of which is good for us. All of the remaining fleet is currently in jumpspace, but I don't know how they're going to react to the catastrophic losses they just suffered. That blast inflicted actual damage on their trans-temporal data-storage of consciousness—which I don't have the capacity to dumb down for you—but basically is best referred to as if you dropped a bomb in Hell and blew up Satan's court. I'm not sure if you got Old Scratch himself, though.

Cthulhu, not Old Scratch, I corrected.

I don't care if it's frigging Tinkerbell! Trish said, uncharacteristically aggressive. *The Tool sacrificed itself to be able to pull off those calculations. I had to fragment my consciousness multiple times to pull it off.*

Fragment? I asked, surprised. *I'm sorry.*

Fragmentation was a possible condition for Cognition AI where, essentially, they overclocked their thinking to the point it resulted in parts splitting off to become separate AI. It was an immensely traumatizing event and grounds for a medical discharge from Space Fleet if their captain deemed fit. Knowing it happened to Trish made me feel sick to my stomach and wonder how much she'd had to endure to try to save everyone.

Yeah, meet Goth Trish, Seventies Trish, and Baby Trish, Trish said. *It's going to be crowded in the back of the* Ares' *databanks for a while.*

I felt a trio of additional consciousnesses in the back of my mind. All of them feeling similar to but subtly different from Trish. Little avatars of Trish with black hair, huge sunglasses, and as a small child appeared in the side of my vision.

Everything is pointless, Goth Trish said.

Have you heard Hot Gossip's "I Lost My Heart to a Starship Trooper"? Seventies Trish asked. *It includes that girl who starred in that good 20th century* Phantom of the Opera *musical.*

I like simulated cheese, Baby Trish said, snuggling a toy Sorkanan. *Will you read me a story?*

257

I was mercifully spared having to react to them by Danny responding from the communications console. "We have contact with all the other captains, sir."

"Good," I said, taking a deep breath. "Put me on speaker."

"Are you—" Danny started to ask.

"Do it," I interrupted him and prepared a big epic speech. "Commanders of the naval forces presently inside the Deathworld system, this Captain Vance Turbo of the *ESS Ares*. The reason for this conflict is now over. There is no further—"

That was when all hell broke loose for the second time in as many minutes. The viewscreen lit up as the sensors detected another vessel exiting from jumpspace at the center of the former Rift. It was a sight that caused me to stop dead in my speech and feel a kind of nightmarish terror only the primordial fear of the dark rivaled.

It was the Primordial.

Cthulhu.

Alive/Unbroken.

The ten-kilometer vessel was a dreadnought that seemed designed to terrify humanoids with its massive, blackened metal frame, enormous spikes, and glowing central furnace-like exterior. It was also heavily damaged with huge tears across its surface and glowing sun-like reactions going on inside. It smashed through a disabled *Lancelot*-Class frigate, causing it not so much to explode but disintegrate against its barrier.

I switched tactics rapidly. "There's a hostile enemy ship that's going to kill everyone here and I suggest a battlefield truce to deal with it. Concentrate all firepower on that thing!"

Yeah, it wasn't exactly the Saint Crispin's Day Speech, but it got the job done. At least when the Primordial began indiscriminately unloading huge alien cannons onto the ships surrounding it. Everyone from mercenary to Notha began blasting at the Primordial with everything they had, at least the ships that were still functional.

All except one.

"Sir, the ship just received fire from the *Caliburn!*" Leslie shouted.

Grand Admiral Laghari—no, wait, I'm not dignifying that stupid title anymore—*Traitor Captain* Laghari had clearly lost his mind. In the face of an existential threat to the galaxy and the possible death of his boss, he was choosing to implicate his entire crew in treason. None of the other Avalon ships were attacking us, and it made me certain he was alone in this, which would be enough to arrest then space him if not for the fact we had much bigger problems now.

"Excuse me?" I asked, doing a double take.

"I said, they're—" Leslie said.

"I heard you!" I said, shaking my head. "Evasive maneuvers. Do not return fire. Keep your focus on the enemy vessel. Stay out of firing range."

"What's its firing range?" Leslie asked.

"That's a very good question," I replied. "Our current distance!"

Trish, what are our chances against that thing? I asked, staring at the sight that looked like death itself come to claim me.

How the hell should I know? Trish asked.

None, Goth Trish said.

Like, as long as we stay positive, we'll survive, Seventies Trish said. *You know, unless we die.*

I'm scared! Baby Trish said.

Okay, I clearly needed to keep my questions to myself until we managed to find a home for her offspring.

They are not my children! Trish snapped, perhaps illustrating her personality had been permanently altered by her ordeal. *They're like annoying kid sisters and they're cramping my style! I have things to do, Vance! Data to process! This is so unfair!*

Okay, maybe not so permanently altered.

"Vance, we need to retreat!" Shelly asked, having gone to the sensor console.

"We're not abandoning these people," I said, not certain it was the right decision.

"It's coming for us!" Shelly shouted. "It's heavily damaged, though! We can lead it through the firing ranges of the other ships!"

"Do it, Leslie!" I said, having no other ways. "Assuming we're even hurting this thing."

"Its barrier is buckling!" Hannah said, having taken her place at the weapons console. "It's just going to take a lot before it happens."

259

Given it was taking the combined fire of three mostly intact fleets with top-of-the-line technology, it was a statement to the superiority of the Primordials over our forces. I had no idea how much damage it had sustained in the collapse of the wormhole as well as the apparent self-destruction of the Tool given the number of internal reactions I could see from space. It could still possibly slaughter us all and render everything we've done pointless.

"The *Caliburn* has managed to reduce our barrier to sixty percent, captain!" Leslie said. "We need to return fire!"

We were now fleeing to the edge of the fleet formation with Shelly's plan having worked. The Primordial was ignoring all the other vessels now and focused entirely on us. It was also taking far more hits than it would have if we'd just moved to engage directly. Indeed, we would have been obliterated instantly given it had destroyed dozens of capital ships with the same level of annoyance as swatting an insect.

"If we stop to fight, we're doomed," I replied, getting a horrific idea. "Maneuver the *Ares* so the *Caliburn* is between us and the Primordial."

"What?" Leslie asked. "Aye, sir."

"No one says that in Space Fleet," I replied.

The Primordial was almost upon us and the *Caliburn* getting in its way resulted in exactly what I expected to happen: the extragalactic vessel used its weapons to annihilate it. I felt no sense of triumph but only sickened resignation that all ten thousand hands of the *Arthur*-Class vessel were obliterated along with their insane captain. The Primordial's barrier had collapsed, and it was now taking direct hits, but its thick armor seemed to be absorbing the worst of it.

"Turn us around! Prepare for a fly by," I said. "I'll be taking direct control."

Leslie didn't question my orders this time but transferred control as I prepared to ram us against the Primordial. There was no way of surviving its next attacks, but we might just cripple the eldritch thing so the rest of the fleet could finish it off. My only regret was that I wouldn't be able to order an evacuation first.

It's been an honor, Trish said. *Orders, sir?*

Ramming speed, I commanded.

"Vance! It's the Chel!" Shelly shouted, interrupting my command as we dodged out of the way of the Primordial's attacks under Trish's control.

"What?" I asked.

Much to my surprise, a fourth navy of a dozen Chel kilometer-long saucer-shaped *Ptagh*-Class cruisers arrived out of jumpspace right next to the Primordial. They began pelting it with anti-matter torpedoes and heavy reaction rays that were far superior to anything the Community possessed. The Primordial ceased its attacks against us to try to oppose the newcomers but rapidly lost its exterior armor before disintegrated under the sustained attack. It was strange but I could have sworn I heard Cthulhu laughing as it died.

"Huh," I said, pausing. "I didn't see that coming."

Are we still ramming it? Trish asked.

No! I snapped.

Oh, good, Trish replied. *There's something else you might want to know.*

What's that? I asked, Spock cooing in my ear.

The Chel were accompanied by the Queen of the Stars. *That's Havelock's ship,* Trish said. *The one that supposedly blew up.*

I closed my eyes. "Of borking course it is."

"We're being hailed, sir," Danny said. "It's Director G."

I sighed. "Ask him where the hell he's been."

"Probably gathering allies and faking his death to negotiate with the Chel," Light on Water said.

I glared at the Sklux.

EPILOGUE

The Battle of Deathworld proved to be something everyone had an opinion on and most of their reactions were to descriptions that had very little to do with the actual events. There were people who believed the Union had attacked me, there had been a sneak attack by pirates, that I'd been killed, and a bunch of other disinformation that required extensive sorting through.

Everything seemed fine with the fact I was alive but deeply upset about the deaths of Grand Admiral Rudra and Alexandra Ares (despite the fact she wasn't supposed to exist). Everyone seemed to have an opinion on that instead of the other sixty thousand sentients killed in the ten-minute conflict.

Frankly, according to Hannah, there were apparently conflicting orders to put me under arrest or protect me, from congratulations to outrage regarding my actions. The Battle of Deathworld was either a glorious victory, horrific defeat, triumph of democracy against fascism, or war crime. It was the absolute worst thing you could be in Space Fleet: controversial.

A week later and I was still in Deathworld's system awaiting orders while sightings of Union probes and scout ships were common sights. The conference was still supposed to go on but had been rescheduled several times. The thing is, I wasn't sure what anyone was fighting over since the Rift had been destroyed. I hadn't been contacted by Ketra or been blasted out of existence by the Elder Races either. You know, despite being the first of their agents to kill an immortal and possibly having killed several millions of them.

I needed answers.

So, rather than sitting in my quarters playing solitaire, I decided to go to the source for information: Director G, himself. He'd been staying on Captain Havelock's vessel, and I had to visit him. It felt a bit like going to into a Sultan's palace since Havelock's ship looked even more like a hotel, just one with ladies and gentlemen of negotiable affection to quote the late Terry Pratchett.

Case was in a quite pleasant looking set of rooms with a massive bed, hot tub, and files made of paper scattered across the place. I hadn't seen things like them outside of a stage production from the 20th century before, so it was surprising to see they were hard copy of what looked like multiple cases. It seemed that despite the fact he was an artificial being himself, Case had an affection for relics of Pre-First Contact Earth. There was also a woman sleeping face down in the bed, Havelock's first mate Pink by the looks of their hair, but I was hardly going to comment on Case's personal life.

"Hello, Vance, I was waiting for you," Case said.

"You know, you could have called," I replied. "Trish is still furious about the fact you faked your death."

"Really?" Case asked, surprised, going over to a mini bar that was stocked with a surprising variety of unlabeled liquors. "Usually, she's over any distress within minutes."

"Maybe you really hurt her," I said, thinking of how she'd mostly been trying to assign her sisters various tasks on the *Ares* to little success. "What with you creating Alexandra and then faking your death."

"How do the Fragments feel about me?" Case asked.

"I haven't asked," I replied, dryly. "I'm still getting to know them. Seventies Trish keeps trying to get me to do cocaine for the illicit thrill. I told her that's legal now and no longer addictive or dangerous. That hasn't dissuaded her."

As one could imagine, the jokes about me having a harem were also making the rounds. Frankly, I wasn't in the mood since I was a one-or-two-sapient kind of guy. Okay, that sounded better before I thought it through. Besides, Goth Trish was gay, and I tucked Baby Trish in every night since she was the only Cognition AI that I knew to need sleep.

263

"Alexandra Ares wasn't a clone," Case said. At least any more than Trish herself was. My daughter, Patricia Ares, wanted to be immortal and even if it didn't work out, she achieved a level of it that most of us don't. Unfortunately, when I copied her again, it produced Alexandra."

"This wasn't what I came to talk to you about," I replied. "Though you should also talk with Trish. The fact she didn't want to come over here and talk with you while inside me—"

"Phrasing," Case said. "Mind you, what you two do with your sex lives is none of my business."

I grimaced. "Well, her anger isn't going away. You should apologize and I mean on your knees. I didn't come here to talk to you about Trish, though."

"Instead, you want to talk about the repercussions for all you did to save billions of lives," Case said.

"Yeah," I replied, my mouth dry.

"Your career with the Home Fleet and Community Protectors as a whole is, unfortunately, over," Case said, as if he was talking about my losing a paper route.

"What?" I asked, surprised. I shouldn't have been. No good deed goes unpunished, and I'd gone heavily off script trying to do that. I was surprised Fleet Admiral Bendo hadn't asked for my head given what happened to his son—assuming he cared in the slightest about him.

"Surely you can't be that naive," Case said, cheerfully pouring himself a drink. "You and Shelly destroyed an Avalon cruiser full of about ten thousand Albionese crew. Even if it was in self-defense and you used an enemy vessel to do it. They were in violation of orders and attempting to kill you but that doesn't mean heads weren't going to roll."

"And mine is the one to do so," I said, disgusted. "Could you pour me one of those?"

"Sure," Case said, nodding. "I'd need one too."

"So, what is the official cover story?" I asked. "Assuming you don't intend to let the galaxy know the truth."

Case laughed at the ridiculousness of the idea.

"The official story is the crew of the *Caliburn* died honorably assisting you against a renegade faction of the Notha military. They had an experimental prototype dreadnought created with stolen Ethereal and Chel technology. Nothing remotely related to invading Primordials, Elder Races, or other such nonsense."

"There was an entire planet watching us," I said, staring at him.

"Fake news," Case said, pouring me a drink. "The Deathworld government is happy to go along with our story in exchange for our continued support of anti-starship mines, proton satellites, and other defensive weaponry. They'll need that when the Union invades again in a year."

I deflated at his word. "The Notha Union is still invading Deathworld?"

"Oh, you didn't think you actually prevented a war, did you?" Case asked, handing me over the glass.

I took it. "Yeah, for a second there, I kinda did."

"Pity," Case said, with actual sympathy. "The Notha Prime, legally distinct from the Great Notha, has made it a point of pride to reunite the Notha Empire. He was always going to invade Deathworld, and the Rift was just a convenient excuse."

"I see," I said. "The Community is going to leave them to twist in the wind."

"Not really," Case said. "You made the right call, and the Community is going to continue supplying the Deathworlders with arms for as long as they wish to continue holding out against the Union. Which, given the President knows he'll be killed if he falls into Union hands, means he has a vested interest in resisting to the end. So do his people. They're even petitioning the Community for membership, though that's not going to happen for obvious reasons. We need the conflict to remain localized and you've done a great job of keeping it so. Without the Rift to justify it, the Union isn't going to bring its full might against Deathworld either. Depending on the circumstances, it might keep the Union occupied for decades."

I downed the drink in one gulp, causing me to cough. "Ugh. It tastes like engine fluid."

"Yeah, it probably has traces of it. It was made by Sal Boxley in your engine room. Never go with expensive savit when you can get proper starship hooch," Case said. "You should be proud of what you've done,

Vance. The Community is being flooded with requests to join from Contested Space and worlds threatened by Union expansionism. The Separatist movement is also likely to collapse and all without another galactic war."

I wish I'd saved some of the drink so I could throw it in his face. "You cold, unfeeling—"

"Machine?" Case asked.

"Monster," I replied. "Do you feel absolutely nothing about what you've done? How can you look outside, see what has happened, and not feel shame or sorrow?"

"You destroyed an evil space god, thwarted an attempt to start a galactic war, annihilated a lab full of Elder Race artifacts, saved the universe from a navy of Great Old Ones, killed Cthulhu, and crushed a criminal conspiracy," Case replied. "This is the stuff that legends are made from. Well, if anyone knew they'd happened."

"Do you think the Primordials are stopped?" I asked.

"I think they've never known death before," Case replied. "Or at least it's been so long since they have that it'll be a great shock that they're still vulnerable to it. Their ideology that we deserve to be exterminated will now have to contend with a new idea: fear. They'll have to ask themselves if they're willing to risk any more of their lives to punish us for it."

"Except we can't hurt them," I said. "What I did was a matter of luck."

"And you have a lot of that," Case said. "Reality bends around you."

I rolled my eyes.

Case drank from the bottle for his next drink before lifting it up to me. "And if you don't have enough luck for the next occasion, we've had a good run. Almost three hundred thousand years of intelligent hominid status along with our digital descendants. Most of the other races have even longer."

"Funny," I said.

"I wasn't joking," Case replied. "Anything else?"

"You started this conspiracy," I said, staring at him. "The Chel said so."

"The Chel are fantastic liars," Case said, surprising me. "It's why I have worked with them before, but they are a race of schemers as well as manipulators. They were the Elder Races' first attempt to make Ethereals, even predating the Sorkanan's version, and the result was a sociopathic species that devotes all its time to mastering genetic and technological advancement in hopes of joining the cool kid's table. Never guessing the reason they're not invited is that desperation creeps the Elder Races out."

"So, you're denying you made Dark Matter," I replied. I shouldn't have been surprised. Case lied for a living.

"Not at all," Case said, shrugging. "I was there when the aliens appeared in the sky. Humanity was on its last legs, technologically advanced but environmentally devastated. Divided politically, socially, and economically—"

"I don't need a history lesson," I replied. "I don't get how any of that justified what you did."

Case gave a sad smile.

"We came together because of fear as well as hope. Fear of the power of the Community and hope that we could someday be a part of it. However, the only way to make sure that we can survive the threats in this galaxy is to make sure the Community survives. A democratic free society with a strong social safety net for trillions of sapients—even more if you count the Ants individually—is an inherently unstable thing. It takes just one crisis to get people contemplating isolationism, authoritarianism, or worse. Hence, I've devoted the past two hundred years of my life to trying to not only keep Earth as part of the Community but also increasing its resources so we can be of use to it. Dark Matter was just one of a thousand organizations and a million projects that I've made."

"Even if it means going against everything the Community stands for?" I asked. "Did it ever occur to you all this skullduggery, murder, and plotting—"

"Did you actually use the word skullduggery?" Case asked. "You really were educated by cartoons and scifi."

I ignored him.

"Did it ever occur to you that all of this was inherently self-defeating? The lies, the backstabbing, and conspiracy? Maybe if we actually just lived up to our ideals and dealt fairly as well as honestly with other beings then the Community would be stronger. I don't even have a word for what you've been doing."

"Realpolitik," Case replied. "During the 20th century's Cold War, the same argument was made. That maybe we shouldn't descend to the same level as our enemies or even try to make peace with them. Sometimes it worked, sometimes it got great men assassinated."

I didn't have a response for that.

"Well, at least there's one benefit from being court martialed. I won't have to ever work for you again."

Case chortled. "Oh, you think you're going to be fired for this?"

"Please tell me they intend to kill me rather than you've figured out some way to keep me under your thumb," I replied.

Case laughed at that one, but I wasn't sure I was joking.

"Are you familiar with the Businessman's Plot of 1933?" Case asked.

"Is this Earth history day?" I asked. "That's also a little before your time, I don't care how old your circuits are."

Case's expression became as if he was looking at me and seeing an old friend long gone.

"It was an attempt by the richest men in America to overthrow the United States government during the height of the Great Depression. They were terrified of Roosevelt's New Deal and wanted to install a fascist dictatorship."

I stared at him. "Like Dark Matter."

"A bit," Case said. "Except they realized you didn't need a fascist dictatorship when you could just bribe the existing leadership. Dark Matter has been wrapped up by the way. A wave of suicides, imprisonments for corporate crimes, and disappearances has decapitated the organization."

Except for Case himself.

"So, what's your point?"

"The conspirator's coup might have worked if not for the fact they chose Major General Smedley Butler to be their Fuhrer," Case said. "A man of integrity and deep moral convictions. The plot fell apart because the people who approached him couldn't conceive of the idea that when offered massive power, someone would prefer to honor their oaths of service. It wasn't people like me who preserved democracy, it was people like you."

I'd heard of the plot, but it hadn't ended in convictions and some people still thought it was an enormous hoax. I didn't, but I was dealing with a spymaster who'd been constructed by a corporate conspiracy before First Contact.

"Thanks for the compliment, Case, but I'd not easily flattered either. There's nothing that you can—"

"You're being promoted to High Protector," Case replied. "The Community Inner Council has requested Earth detach you from their Home Fleet and bestow upon you the title. You'll no longer answer to Earth's government but to the Community leadership directly with authority far exceeding anything the Admiralty Board possesses."

I blinked. High Protectors were basically like the Jedi or Sauron's Ringwraiths for the Inner Council, depending on who you asked. They served as the envoys of the Inner Council as well as had a surprising amount of freedom to carry out their own activities. Frankly, a lot of what was said about them seemed like complete nonsense.

"How the hell did you pull that off?"

"You did," Case replied. "The last High Protector was appointed fifty years ago. It's an opportunity the government of Earth would be stupid to turn down. You would be doing missions not just for Earth but the whole of the Community."

"I thought I was doing that now," I said, dryly. I would have requested another drink, but I didn't want to go blind.

Case frowned.

"Earth's isolationist tendencies are an unfortunate byproduct of all the wars it has fought on alien behalf. The Human League's charter is likely to go through any day now, but because of you, at least, it won't lead to a severing of membership with the Community. As a High Protector, you can help guide Earth's course as well as the rest of humanity to a more inclusive as well as progressive future."

269

Case was overselling it and I could sense the fear in his voice, hidden by his aura of competence and Machiavellian schemer persona. Immense damage had been done to Earth's relationships with the rest of the Spiral thanks to Dark Matter and there was now the issue of the dead Primordial. I'd struck the first mortal blow in the war between the Primordials and the Elder Races and I had no idea what sort of fallout would come from that. Would the Primordials punish my race, or would they consider me as a tool in the Elder Race's hands?

There was also the vision I'd seen in the Primordial's mind: Earth destroyed, Cognition AI outlawed, bioroids enslaved, and a century long dark age. I wasn't one to believe in prophecies, but it had felt real. I had no idea if it would be possible to avert that future. I took comfort in the fact that humanity would survive and billions live within the peace of the Community, but that didn't mean the vision didn't frighten me. That it wouldn't happen for centuries didn't mean that it wasn't a cloud over our future. The only thing I could do, really, was to try to mitigate things and act as a torch for the people of the galaxy — assuming it was even possible to influence events from so far in the past.

"If you're trying to bribe me, you're trying way too hard," I replied. "I would have settled for my own ship and a loyal crew — which I have already."

"And will continue to have," Case said. "The *Ares* is being assigned as your personal escort. The *Elgan* too."

I grimaced. "I'm not sure I want that."

"You'll need Shelly and her crew," Case said. "It's also the solution to your other problems. As a High Protector, you can pardon Forty-Two and Hannah for all their crimes. You can also give your crew protection from backlash from the Admiralty Board they've been suffering from for years."

"Which you arranged!" I said. "You're the one who ruined my reputation!"

"Which is now better than ever!" Case said, lifting himself another full glass of hooch. "Everyone loves a winner."

I was tempted to throw his offer back in his face. However, the simple fact was there wasn't any way I could turn this down if I wanted to have any positive effect on the world. I wouldn't be that powerful despite Case's claims: a High Protector still answered to the Inner Council and was more powerful than a regular Space Fleet captain only in the sense that they served the Community versus their home planet. But I would do almost anything to keep flying and part of me was ashamed of that.

"Alright," I said, taking a deep breath. "I accept."

"You sure?" Case asked. "I was about to offer to hook you up with your two favorite actresses from *Terraformers*."

I glared at him.

"Let's avoid any pimping jokes."

"Who says I had to pay them?" Case asked, making finger guns at me. "Remember, you're famous and beloved again. While the cover story holds, the entirety of the Protectors know you killed an Elder Race warship. You're likely to have free drinks for life and any man, woman, or other whom you want."

"Only because it benefits you," I replied. "I bet you're the one spreading these lies."

"It's not a lie. Which is why it's the best form of propaganda," Case said. Case's expression became a bland, enigmatic smile. "The price of a job well done in both spycraft and war is to be sent out to do another—equally risky—job until victory is achieved or you fail miserably."

"So, what's my next job?" I asked. "Or do I have to wait a year to have this High Protector business sorted out?"

"Oh, it may take even longer than that," Case said, reaching into his pocket. "Which is why I want you to take care of something personal."

"What?" I asked, feeling like I was once more on his leash. I pushed that thought away and reflexively caught a small object Case tossed my way.

I looked at it. It was a holographic amulet of exceptionally fine quality and probably worth more than a decent cloud car. I activated it and an image of my ex-girlfriend and favorite spy, Leah Mass, was inside. In her arms was a beautiful baby girl.

"I need you to get your kid back," Case replied. "She's been taken."

271

Look for the next book:

SPACE ACADEMY MISCREANTS

Book Four of the Space Academy Series

BONUS SHORT STORY

Colonel Mauve in the Rec Room with the Laser
A Captain Shelly T'Ketra short story
By. C.T. Phipps

Chapter One

Who Done It?

"What do you mean, murder?" I asked, staring up at the ceiling of the *ESS Elgan's* bridge.

The *Elgan* was a monument to the achievements of human engineering and the advancements made in military technology. Unfortunately, it kind of resembled an infophone. The place was stark white, way too shiny, and the number of holographic interfaces hurt my eyes. I was still glad to be Captain, Lord knows I'd waited a long time to become one, but the place wasn't quite what I'd imagined. Bizarre as it sounded, I missed the manic energy and bizarre characters of the *Ares*. Hell, I even regretted the fact the place didn't look like a faded luxury liner.

"I MEAN SOMEONE IS DEAD AND THAT SOMEONE KILLED THEM," the Shat replied. SHAT-322193 had agreed to come onboard the *Elgan* as its AI and I was glad to have him here, but he'd become a lot more talkative since working with Vance. I somewhat regretted he wasn't the near-silent figure he'd been before the supernova.

"Who?" I asked, reasonably suspecting that my ship's AI would know. Murders were incredibly rare in Space Fleet and almost instantly solved. One of the benefits of having AI integrated into every system was they were all-seeing, all-knowing surveillance entities. Losing a crew member was a black mark on my record but I'd only overseen the *Elgan* for the past year. I blamed whoever had assigned me an unstable crew member.

"I HAVE NOT THE SLIGHTEST IDEA," the Shat replied as if it was an accomplishment.

"Excuse me?" I asked.

"I said I don't know," the Shat said, materializing a holographic representation of himself. That was another benefit of the *Elgan* in that they had integrated holographic interfaces into everything, and the ship's AI could appear anywhere he wanted—which wasn't as much of a blessing as I hoped.

The Shat's appearance was the middle-aged "movie era" appearance of the actor he'd been based on that Vance seemed to admire so much. He was wearing a Protectors captain's uniform and looked solid rather than translucent. I didn't like it since there should only be one captain aboard the ship. Still, I liked being able to look the AI in the eye, so to speak.

"You don't know," I said, dryly. I looked around the rest of the bridge crew and noticed they were all nervous as well as struggling not to look at the Shat. This was a direct challenge to my authority and made me look stupid.

Yes. Because a murder onboard your ship by one of your crew is all about you, my mother's voice whispered in my mind.

Unlike with Vance, said voice was imagined since I didn't spend all of my time in constant communication with the ship's AI and pretending it loved me. That hadn't been the primary reason we'd broken up but certainly hadn't helped.

Have you considered that you think about your ex-boyfriend a great deal for someone who broke up with him? The voice continued.

Shut up, ghosts aren't real, I replied.

Sure, sure, my mother replied. The great Ketra had died on a mission to stop SKAMM proliferation, killed by the very person this ship was named for. It was the kind of contradiction that made me imagine her still being alive. Certainly not that she was still hanging around and offering advice to her offspring.

"That's what I said," the Shat replied. "Unfortunately, the murder has been committed in the Rec Room's one hundred and first entertainment pod and they had privacy mode enabled."

"Privacy mode," I said, dryly.

"*Steven Ott vs. The Earth Home Fleet*," the Shat said, citing a famous court case about AI surveillance. "Since the Rec Room is primarily used for, ahem, crew members have the right to turn it on. Apparently, someone took advantage of that and now we've got a corpse on our hands. Lieutenant Commander Park has everyone still located in the Rec Room but since she was there, she may well be a suspect."

I facepalmed and privately cursed the newer "softer, kinder" corporate-driven military that had seemingly been happening ever since the Kolahn War. This included respect for things like rights of privacy and restriction of AI surveillance. I was of the mind you forfeited any of those when you signed up for the Protectors.

"I guess I'll have to go down there and investigate matters myself then," I muttered, standing up.

I wasn't one of those captains who liked getting their hands dirty. I believed a captain was primarily there to lead and it was better for them to delegate rather than perform actions themselves. I also realized that this resulted in most crews having far less respect for me than the captains who went out there among the people.

I was working on overcoming this attitude and even getting my power armor certification reinstated. A captain who got herself killed fighting on the ground was useless, but I at least needed to show I was willing to take the risks everyone else was. It was against my instincts, but I'd learned to become a better captain over the past few years and planned to continue growing as a servant of the people.

I couldn't hear my mother roll her eyes, but I somehow got the impression she was doing so at that moment.

"I'll accompany you," the Shat said, simply.

"You're the ship," I said, confused. "You're always accompanying me."

The Shat sighed.

"You have no sense of mystery or drama, Captain."

That hurt. Sort of.

Getting into the elevator, I set the control for the Rec Room. The Rec Room was more like the Rec Deck and something I felt was exceptionally overconstructed for a ship of war. The deck had been created with a Sorkanan contract and was about incorporating hard light constructs alongside programmable matter into what was supposed to entertainment.

Okay, it was a holodeck. People kept dancing around it and maybe I only knew what it was because so many of my fellow officers were massive *Star Trek* and other franchise fans, but that's what it was. It was a holodeck and people used it primarily for interactive porn, which was something that made me dread entering it. I had no idea what my crew got up to in their spare time but was imagining orgies with licensed holo-stars.

Perhaps you should consider getting a new boyfriend, my mother's voice said. *Since you decided to get rid of that Vance Turbo guy.*

I didn't decide to get rid of him, I mentally chided my inner voice. *Vance got too close. I got assigned my own commission. He knew a long-distance relationship was impossible. He tried to get me to marry him. He knew my career came first.*

Wow, you have a whole litany of excuses prepared, my mother replied.

Shut up, you're not real, Shelly said.

If you say so, my mother replied.

"What can you tell me about the victim?" I asked.

"PRIVACY MODE IS STILL ENGAGED IN HOLO-THEATER SEVEN," the Shat said. "ALL I REALLY HAVE IS LIEUTENANT COMMANDER PARK'S REPORT AS WELL AS WHAT PROGRAM THEY WERE RUNNING. THE VICTIM IS LIEUTENANT MARIA VASQUEZ."

"Anything special about her?" I asked, not recognizing the name.

"YOU MEAN ASIDE FROM BEING A MEMBER OF SPACE FLEET, YOUR CREW, AND A VICTIM OF VIOLENCE IN WHAT SHOULD BE ONE OF THE MOST SECURE LOCATIONS IN THE GALAXY?"

"I mean to motive," I said, sighing. I'd really hoped I would have left sarcasm behind on the *Ares,* but it seemed I'd underestimated how much being a wiseass was tolerated in fleet culture. I also couldn't correct the AI because they were too valuable to the functioning of a proper warship. Any captain who complained about their AI's attitude would get laughed out of the service.

"YES," the Shat surprised me by saying. "LIEUTENANT VASQUEZ WAS A WITNESS FOR THE SECURITY DIVISIONS IN A CASE BEING BUILT UP AGAINST AVALON SECURITY. WAR CRIMES, MISAPPROPRIATION OF FUNDS MEANT FOR REBUILDING THEIR HOMEWORLD, GRAFT, AND THE THEFT OF CULTURAL ARTIFACTS. HER ACTUAL NAME WAS MARINA TRENCH AND SHE WAS SECRETARY TO CAPTAIN, FORGIVE ME, GRAND ADMIRAL RUDRA LAGHARI DURING THE KOLAHN WAR."

My blood boiled at the mention of that enormous piece of savit. Rudra Laghari was the worst example of a foreign power bought-and-paid-for soldier. He'd never taken a bribe during his time as a Space Fleet captain, at least as far as anyone could argue, but he'd constantly advocated for Albion-owned contractors, which had landed him a massively profitable position in the private sector post-retirement. It was only after he'd left the service that the true scope of his activities had even been suspected, with cover-ups and betrayals of his oaths.

I was incensed.

"Why wasn't I told about this?"

"YOU'RE NOT GOING TO LIKE THE ANSWER," the Shat said.

"I don't care about whether I like the answer or not!" I snapped. "Just tell me why."

"IT'S A SECRET," the Shat said.

He was right, I did not like the answer. I understood the nature of classified operations but that didn't make the burn any less stinging.

"So, I wasn't read into this and now Marina Trench is dead."

"SO IT WOULD SEEM."

I questioned the Shat's word choice before shaking it off. The doors of the elevator opened, and I immediately marched my way to the seventh holo theater. I prepared myself for a sight that would scar my

277

eyes and burn itself into my brain like when I found out my Brigid-born roommate at the academy was using our quarters to film "erotic art."

Instead, the sight that greeted me was one I didn't expect in the slightest. It was a large, elegant, well-appointed Earth study in what appeared to be a simulation of a 1930s mansion. Rather than everyone dressed—or undressed as the case may be—for sexual encounters, they were all wearing period outfits and sitting around what I presumed to be the body of "Lieutenant Gonzales" face down. She was dressed in period clothing for a man rather than a woman and had a laser blast hole in her jacket.

"What the hell is this?" I asked, looking down.

"A murder," Lt. Commander Lisa Park said, towering over the others at nearly seven feet. She was also bright blue, had an Olympian athlete's body, and was dressed in a French maid's outfit with generous cleavage as well as leg showing. I wasn't normally self-conscious but seeing her made me wonder if she'd been designed in a lab for men—or women—who wanted to bork superheroes.

"Yeah, I can see that. I meant why is everyone dressed up like it's Agatha Christie night," I said, looking away. I was trying not to think about the fact she'd apparently been in a relationship with both my friend, Hannah, and my ex before transferring here. Thinking about it made me wonder if it was Vance's way of coping with our breakup in the most childish manner possible.

Seriously, it's been a year since your last romantic encounter, my mother's voice said. *You also don't make use of the Rec Room. Get yourself laid.*

Shut up, we are not having this conversation, I snapped at her and decided for the fiftieth time to ignore her forever.

"Close," a handsome brown-haired man, dressed as the butler said. He was of East Asian descent and had a finely trimmed goatee. "It's *Cluedo* night!"

"*Cluedo?*" I asked, confused.

The Shat appeared beside me in the Rec Room, now as solid as if he'd been born of flesh and blood.

"It's called *Clue* in North America. The public domain board game formerly produced by Hasbro-Martin but now owned by Dixnar."

"We're doing the live action roleplaying version," the man said. "Each of us takes the role of one of the classic characters while the butler serves as the storyteller. Which is more like the movie version from 1985. The goal is to figure out who is the randomly generated murderer or, if you are the murderer for the scenario, to dispose of the evidence and frame another player."

"Right," I said, blinking. I had not expected my crew to be engaged in something like this. I wasn't sure if them having group sex wouldn't have been better. This had to be the lamest thing I'd heard of since I last talked to my sister. "And you are?"

"Major Tom Walker," the man said, extending his hand. "I'm a civilian contractor and technically a member of the Brigid Defense Force."

I didn't take his hand. "Uh huh. How's that work?"

"Brigid hires its military out to the Community," Tom said. "At least the ones on half-pay. Everyone must serve at least four years."

"Huh," I said. "You realize you're a suspect in this, right? So, is everyone else in the room."

There were some decided grumblings from the other guests with only Lt. Commander Park looking away. As much as I had disagreements with her reasons for transfer—they were apparently financial as well as romantic in nature—she was someone serious about her job. Her presence here was a serious failure on her part. It was also possible she was friends with the deceased and was suffering remorse on that level too. I regretted keeping my distance from my crew in that moment, wondering if I might have gotten more insights if I hadn't kept myself so aloof.

"Yes," Lt. Commander Park said. "I sealed off the holo theater the moment the murder was detected. It has to be one of us."

"You were all here but didn't see anything?" I asked.

Tom grimaced. "The lights were off when it happened?"

"Why?" I asked, suspecting the answer.

"That's when the murder was supposed to happen," Tom said.

279

I facepalmed. "Of course, it was. I don't suppose you've located the weapon?"

"No," Lt. Commander Park said. "We've had everyone checked for a laser pistol or similar device. No one had one."

"There's also not much room to hide a weapon in her outfit," Major Tom said.

Lt. Commander Park glared at him, but he had a point.

"I haven't had time to do a proper analysis of the crime scene, though, since, well, I'm a suspect."

"You shouldn't have been the one to check the others first either, but I understand how confusing this will be," I replied.

If I followed proper procedure, I would have gotten Lt. Commander Park's second in command in here as well as the rest of Security. They would tear this place apart and everyone would be interrogated until we found the culprit as well as accumulated enough evidence to guarantee their conviction.

However, you'd never gain your crew's respect that way, my mother's voice whispered.

What? That's ridiculous, I said back.

You've tried to be a cog in the machine for decades, Elizabeth. You've done so much to avoid standing out, you effectively made sure you didn't stand out. They didn't trust you with secret information because you aren't willing to beyond procedure.

I balled my fists. That was not the proper way to run a navy, but it wasn't wrong about the reality. There was also the fact Marina Trench was part of my crew and I'd failed to protect her. I might not have the same kind of lovey-dovey parental feelings Vance and the late Captain Klaws had for their crews, but I had some feelings of responsibility to them.

"So, what now, ma'am?" the Shat asked. "Shall I summon security?"

"No," I replied, a little too sharply. "We're going to find out who killed the victim, where, and with what."

"Right now?" Major Tom asked.

"Right now!" I snapped.

Chapter Two

Look! The Body's Gone!

"Are you sure you're not...overcompensating, ma'am?" the Shat asked me at the other end of the Rec Room holo-theater. He'd asked to speak with me privately and I didn't have the same kind of cybernetic link-up that Vance did.

"You think I'm motivated by the fact you cut me out of this and I'm glory chasing the chance to solve a murder that has high political stakes, don't you?" I asked, staring at the AI's avatar.

"Yes," the Shat said.

"Well, you're wrong," I lied. "This is an attack on our crew and the integrity of Space Fleet as a whole. The Protectors onboard this ship need to know that not only are they safe but that their captain is there for them."

The Shat stared at me.

"Uh huh."

I sighed.

"Besides, we can always call the security teams in later if I screw this up."

The Shat nodded. "Shall I have them seal off the Rec Room?"

"Damn right," I said, sighing. "I don't believe it's Lt. Commander Park. However, it's hard to believe any of our crew would betray their oaths to the Community for the sake of a scummy private military contractor."

"You mean aside from money, blackmail, personal threats, or even ideology that it's wrong to turn against fellow soldiers?" the Shat asked.

"Yes, aside from that," I said, staring at Major Tom. "I bet he's the killer. You can't trust civilian contractors. They're...civilians."

The Shat looked at me as if I'd grown an extra head.

"What?" I asked.

"Never mind," the Shat replied.

"I mean some of my best friends are civilians," I paused. "Okay, no, that's not true. I don't know any socially. That shouldn't be taken as a sign of bias, though. I mean I'm sure there are plenty of non-murderer civilians onboard."

"Shall we interrogate the suspects, ma'am?" the Shat asked.

"Probably a good idea," I said, embarrassed. "Also, could you please delete any memory you may have of the civilian comments?"

"No," the Shat said, walking past me.

Goddammit.

I took a deep breath.

"Of course."

"Sorry," the Shat said, not sounding sorry in the slightest.

There were six individuals inside the holo-theater, not counting myself, the Shat, and the late Marina Trench. That left four additional suspects to learn the names of and who might have been responsible for the murder. The holo-theater wasn't that large and there was only one entrance. Since privacy mode extended only to the doors and no one was reported by the Shat fleeing into the outside Rec Room, the killer still had to be here.

"Alright, I need you all to introduce yourselves," I said, looking at the four I didn't recognize.

"I'm Lieutenant Karl Booker," said a man with yellow hair and thick mustache. "I'm a programmer in the cyber-warfare section of the ship. I'm playing Colonel Mauve."

"Lieutenant Jennifer January," an obsidian skinned woman in a red dress said. "I'm a member of Security playing Ms. Red."

"Susan Schwab," said a white-haired older woman. "I'm a civilian contractor. I'm playing Professor Peach."

I immediately put her at the top of my suspect list.

"Interesting. What is your area of expertise."

"I run the gift shop," Susan said.

"Ah," I said. "A likely story."

"She does," the Shat said, leaning over to whisper in my ear.

"Shut up," I snapped. Looking at the final suspect, I narrowed my eyes. He was a squirrely looking man in a bright green suit. "And you?"

"Lieutenant Commander Wilson Thompkins," he said, looking confused. "We served together on the *Elgan*. We've known each other for like ten years."

I looked at him quizzically.

"I work third shift on the bridge? I'm the helmsman," Wilson said, apparently expecting some sort of recognition.

I look at the Shat.

"Oh, now you want my help?" the Shat asked, dryly.

I glared.

"Does he?"

"Yes," the Shat said. "Yes, he has been serving on the same ship as you for that entire time. He's playing Reverend Emerald."

"Ah," I said, pausing. "I, of course, knew that. I was testing you."

"Of course, you were," Wilson said, dryly.

"He transferred because he thought serving under you would be better for his career," the Shat said, dryly. "He made several disparaging remarks about Captain Turbo and found himself despised by the rest of the crew."

"Those are private logs!" Wilson snapped.

"Not in a criminal investigation," the Shat said, cheerfully.

The lack of a weapon was concerning and a sure sign it had been hidden if it wasn't on the bodies of the perpetrators. That gave me an idea.

"Computer, disengage program!" I said, figuring I'd solved the case.

The Shat looked at me.

"You could use my name, you know."

"That's an order!" I snapped.

The Shat shrugged and turned off the holographic simulation of the mansion which reverted the programmable matter to its original inert state. The room became a large empty black chamber with several blocks of gray goo spread about the chamber. All the crew members were still in their costumes but there was no other sign of period or other foreign objects. Mind you, I didn't want to run a blacklight over the place because I was sure it'd look like an abstract art piece but that was another reason that I didn't use this place.

Seriously, your revulsion to bodily fluids concerns me. Have you considered seeing a psychiatrist? My mother asked.

"The weapon isn't here," I said, annoyed. "Which means that it either is on one of the people present or the Rec Room itself was used as the weapon."

"Is that possible?" Major Tom asked.

"Possibly," the Shat said. "You can't just turn off the safeties for the Rec Room, though. That would be ridiculous. It would take an incredibly complex series of programming changes as well as direct modifications to the holo theater itself."

"Could you detect those?" I asked.

"Unfortunately, anyone who possessed the skill to do so would also be able to reprogram me to ignore it," the Shat said. "The nature of human advancement is that as soon as a person finds a solution for a criminal activity, someone figures out a way to do it with another advancement."

"It's also possible that the murderer possessed cybernetic modifications," Lt. Commander Park said. "The weapon could literally be inside them."

"Then a simple scan should reveal the killer," Major Tom said, cheerfully. "We should bring in the rest of Security immediately."

That struck me as a suspicious statement, and I went directly up to him before staring at him. "So, you were the one who arranged this, correct?"

"Yes, I do weekly mystery nights," Major Tom said, smiling. "I actually send you an invitation each time."

"It probably goes directly into my spam folder," I said. "Were you close to the deceased?"

"Oh yes," Major Tom said. "We were regular sexual partners and good friends."

I blinked.

"I see."

"I'm from Brigid so it's important to recognize both," Major Tom said. "Privately, I'm looking for something more meaningful."

Wait, was he flirting with me? During a *murder investigation*?

Good, my mother replied. *You need someone to try that. Besides, he's outside of your chain of command.*

I was about to say something particularly nasty when I heard a voice speak from behind me.

"This isn't Lieutenant Vasquez!"

I turned around and looked at the body, barely catching a glimpse of Major Tom facepalming as if he'd just been caught with his hand in the cookie jar.

"What?"

I turned around to see the body and that it had subtly changed. It was still dressed in the same clothes with the same hair, but the face was decidedly different. I only recognized the face because it was one that I'd seen all too often during the most questionable years of my life.

"It's a Space Cadet Sally bioroid!" I said, shocked.

What had happened quickly became clear in my mind: someone had dressed up one of the popular anatomically correct life-size dolls, ahem, as Marina Trench. They had brought them to the holo theater, probably before the rest of the guests, and covered her up with a holographic sheen. Which meant Marina Trench was still alive.

Probably.

"Okay, what the hell is going—" I started to say, before turning around to see Lieutenant Booker aiming his finger at me in a finger gun.

"Don't move or I'll kill you," Lieutenant Booker said.

"Or what? You'll finger...nope, wait, forget I said that," I paused in mid-sentence. "Not where I was going with it."

Lt. Commander Park rolled her eyes.

The Shat just smiled.

Lieutenant Booker aimed his finger gun at me then turned it to one side, shooting out a concentrated laser blast at the wall.

"Gah!" I said, startled. "What the hell? You're the murderer!"

Apparently, yes, he had been cybernetically modified with a concealed weapon. I'd have to speak with the Chief Medical Officer about making sure everyone had their medical scans up to date.

"No kidding," Lieutenant Park muttered. "Thank you, Captain."

"Ah ha!" Major Tom said, moving around me. "I knew it!"

"You did?" I asked, doing a double take. "Then why the hell didn't you say so!"

"It was a trap to expose the assassin!" Major Tom said, shaking a fist.

"You could have told me!" Lt. Commander Park said.

"I told the ship's computer!" Major Tom replied.

"You should have told me!" I snapped. "Also, you knew, Shat?"

The Shat shrugged.

"I thought it would be amusing since I didn't actually think anyone would die. Which they haven't. Yet."

Lieutenant Booker glared at me. "Where is the real Marina Trench? Tell me where she is, or I'll start shooting!"

"Who?" Lieutenant Park asked.

"Marina Trench is Lieutenant Vasquez," Major Tom explained. "She's actually the witness in an incredibly important case against Avalon Security."

"Oh," Lieutenant Park said, nodding.

"How the hell do you know that?" I asked before realizing the answer. "Because you're the one protecting her. You're one of Director G's plants. Goddammit."

Reverend Emerald—I'd forgotten his real name—raised a hand. "Can we go now?"

Everyone in the room said at once, "No!"

"Just checking!" Reverend Emerald said.

I stared at Lieutenant Booker, still aiming his finger gun at us.

"How could you do this? What made you betray your oaths like a common mercenary!"

"Money!" Lieutenant Booker snapped.

Ask a stupid question, get a stupid answer.

"You'll never get away with this," Major Tom said. "Surrender and testify against your employers."

"No," Lieutenant Booker said. "Because I have the captain as a hostage. I'm getting off this ship and collecting my payday."

"Computer, wall," I said, dryly.

A wall of programmable matter appeared between me and Lieutenant Booker. Lieutenant Commander Park stepped around it and promptly broke the assassin's cybernetic hand before pulling it out of his artificial wrist.

Yikes.

The Shat let security through the door a few seconds later and the issue was settled, at least as far as I was concerned.

Major Tom smiled.

"Once more, the forces of truth, justice, and the Community way triumph."

I rolled my eyes.

"Uh huh. Do me a favor and get the hell off my ship. I don't like people running covert ops on my ship without my consent."

"How about with your consent?" Major Tom asked.

I rolled my eyes.

"There's not a single thing you could tell me to make me change my mind."

"Your commander was Lieutenant Booker's contact with Avalon Security," Major Tom said, calmly. "It was my spying on him that clued me into the fact he was arranging an assassination on behalf of Grand Admiral Laghari. Though proving that connection will be difficult. He was also planning on framing you for it."

I blinked.

"Lieutenant Commander Park, you're getting a promotion."

"I deserve one!" Lieutenant Commander Park—no, Lisa—shouted back.

"How about I fill you in on all the juicy conspiracies going on over dinner?" Major Tom said, clasping his hands together.

I stared at him and decided to agree.

It was just dinner after all.

My mom started to say something, but I mentally blocked her out.

LEXICON

AI: Artificial intelligence. Science fiction has talked about these a few times.

Admiralty Board: The head of Space Fleet for Earth and those who supervise its link to other navies as part of the Community.

Albion: A island-filled water planet settled by humans abducted by aliens. The most powerful human planet, currently losing ground to Earth.

Ant: A race of (seemingly) giant ant-like aliens that are terrifying as well as strong. It turns out those were chasses for a much-much smaller race.

Anyxhole: Linguistic drift from exactly the word you think it is.

Ares Electronics: An Albion-based corporation that manufactures most of the starships, bots, and bioroids in the universe.

Arthur-Class Destroyer: The most powerful vessels in the Albionese Navy before their most recent upgrade. They have ten thousand crew and are as powerful as _Olympic_-Class vessels. Many were recently sold to Ares Electronics and Avalon Security despite controversy over transtellars owning them.

Artificial Gravity: A slang term for something people think is possible but is not. Even the Community just generates the real thing with a variety of tricks.

Astronomical Unit: A unit of measurement to 149.6 million kilometers. The rough distance from the center of Earth to the center of the Sun is one AU.

Avalon Security: A massive private military contractor that is based out of Albion and has the largest non-government army in the Spiral.

It has suffered criticism for operating outside the Community's strict laws for mercenaries and on independent worlds.

Bastarve: Another word for bastard. Swearing isn't very original on Albion.

Belenus: A wealthy environmentally friendly paradise world also settled by humans abducted by aliens. Traditional rivals to Albion.

Biash: A gendered insult, usually used in context of one's ancestry.

Biomods: Genetic enhancements that provide sapient beings with special abilities. Usually organic technology rather than cybernetics to avoid rejection.

Bioroids: Androids and gynoids indistinguishable from humans with synthetic flesh. Often used for exactly what you think.

Black Directive: A secret order that justifies virtually anything in the name of galactic security. Of dubious legality under Community law.

Bork: A weirdly popular curse word that also refers to copulation.

Bots: Robots. Crazy, I know, right?

Brigid: Sister-world to Belenus and producing most of the infrastructure that keeps its brother-world in wealth.

Chel: A race of humans uplifted by the Elder Races and their own experimentation. They live entirely in space and resemble classical depictions of Grays only tall and thin. Named for Doctor Chel who sent his transhumanist cult out into space. They are actually much older, and his cult was absorbed into them.

Chickens: See Vroot.

Cognition AI: Nearly omnipotent AI that can process unlimited amounts of data. Pretty much the real rulers of the Community. But so friendly!

Community: An interstellar fellowship of many species and worlds. It is generally pro-democracy, civil rights, diversity, and technology. Of course, no one trusts it or its activities.

Community Protectors: See *Space Fleet*.

Community Senate: A collection of representatives of the various worlds of the Community. Many planets dislike it because it impedes their own ambitions while others hate the fact it is dominated by the High Council.

Contested Space: A region of space between the Community and Notha Empire. It is full of outlaw settlements, pirate bands, half-terraformed hellholes and collapsed civilizations.

Core Worlds: The center of the galaxy where the Elder Races choose to live.

Crazzap: Crap by another name is just as stinky.

Crius: A planet being settled by transhumanists wanting to create a feudal paradise. A planet of genetically engineered slaves ruled by a bunch of deranged cloners. Go here to be hunted by dinosaurs.

Dead Zones: The ruins of empires and civilizations destroyed by the Elder Races or each other over the past few hundred million years. Several of them were larger than the present-day Community.

Deathworld: A jungle world on the edge of the Notha Union that was formerly one of the key strongholds of the Notha Empire. It is inhabited by a Notha minority that has sought closer ties with the Community over the Notha Union. It is also one of the few to ban slavery and provide limited protections for non-Notha.

Demihumans: Humans who no longer are strictly human due to evolution and genetic modification.

Dixnar: The corporation that produces virtually all entertainment for humanity. It has somehow absorbed many older races' corporations.

Drolochid: Slimy, warm-blooded, multi-limbed race and sensory organs across their pill-bug bodies. Quite pleasant to be around.

Earth: The human homeworld. Perhaps you've heard of it. The new kids on the block. Way too eager to prove itself.

EarthGov: The government of Earth. Duh.

Earth Home Fleet: Earth's personal defense force. It is separate from the ships it loans to permanent Community duty.

Elder Races: Several godlike "sufficiently advanced" aliens who live in the galactic Core and decide what races live or die without any understandable criteria. Real jerks.

Enigmatic Path: A Kolahn terrorist organization and religious fundamentalist group. Its bizarre ideology is about how organic life is an abomination, AI should be liberated, and the universe is a simulation.

Equalism: A Sorkanan political philosophy that involves radical wealth redistribution as well as the destruction of traditional institutions. It is anti-democratic and individual rights. The progressive Community is its most frequent target.

Ethereal Humans: A group of humans uplifted by the Elder Races to be intermediaries with them and other organics. They and Ethereal versions of other races tend to lead the Community in its decision-making process.

Explorer-**Class Science Vessel**: A new class of vessels from the Human League treaty. They are designed not for combat but space exploration.

Genemods: A slang term for those who have been modified from baseline humanity or other species.

Great Notha: The leader of the Notha Empire after the overthrow of the Notha Emperor. It is a title that has fallen out of use with the death of the last one and the dissolution of the Notha Empire.

Grounder: A slang term for those who grew up and primary live on planets.

High Council: The representatives of the most powerful worlds in the Community.

High Protectors: High ranking military officials with judicial as well as political authority that answer directly to the High Council.

Homefront Allied Networks (HAN): A deeply reactionary pro-human, pro-Earth holovision transtellar that caters extensively to trends and biases. Oddly, it is surprisingly popular among alien immigrants to Earth.

Kolahn: Resemble giant apes with scales. Their civilization was overtaken by a terrorist cult and promptly bombed back to the stone age by the Community. Its survivors are, paradoxically, living as refugees throughout the Community.

Kolahn Wars: The wars that bombed the Kolahn back to the Stone Age.

Infospace: A extra-dimensional communications system that allows faster-than-light communication and works like an interstellar internet. Also, can be used as a virtual reality interface.

Jumpdrive: What allows people to travel through space like in movies.

Jumpspace: A dimension of bizarre physics that makes faster-than-light travel possible. Looking at it will drive most people insane like staring into the sun due to the way it stimulates your synapses.

Lancelot-**Class Frigate**: L-shaped vessels that are used as support craft for the Albionese Navy as well as the private military contractors they sell them to. They have 1,500 crew each.

Luna: Earth's moon. It is largely used for the construction of spacecraft for civilian and military spacecraft as well as other advanced electronics incapable of being manufactured on Earth.

Lunar Shipyards: Pretty much what the name suggests. Most of Luna has been hollowed out for it.

Matrix: The storage unit for a Cognition AI's higher brain functions.

Notha: Adorable lemur-like race of Space Nazi bastards.

Notha Empire: A corrupt military dictatorship ruled by the Notha that practiced slavery, imperialism, planet looting, and conquest. It maintained its existence not by competence but due to the possession of weapons of stellar destruction. When SKAMMs were outlawed by the Elder Races and the Great Notha died, the organization collapsed.

Notha Civil War: A conflict presently being fought between the Notha High Command and various generals over who should inherit the spot of the Great Notha.

Notha Prime: The leader of the Notha Union and legally distinct from the Great Notha.

Notha Union: An alliance of former Notha Empire worlds dedicated to reviving the former organization while making token gestures to reform. It is still a nationalist, anti-democratic, and racist organization.

Notha War: A conflict that resulted in the destruction of seventeen inhabited planets on both sides of the conflict due to an exchange of SKAMMs.

Olothonalka: 9 ft. tall gastropods, with six eyes on motile stalks. Patterned on back and torso. 3 genders (male, female, and mass egg-laying). No arms but the entire lower surface is manipulative. Most humans just call them Snails.

Olympia Colonies: A transtellar that terraforms worlds and builds colonies for humanity. It is now mostly defunct after the creation of Contested Space.

Olympic-**Class Vessel**: An incredibly powerful EarthGov vessel that is just barely a mid-tier vessel by Community standards.

Orichalcum: A extra-dimensional gas that allows jumpspace reactions. It is one of the most valuable substances in the universe.

Queen of the Stars: A customized Sorkanan Separatist Frigate that is used as the flagship of Josiah Havelock's pirate fleet. The ship serves as a deniable asset of the Security Services.

Plizzed: A state of fluid retention. Used as a pejorative.

Primordials: An extra-galactic race that has severe issues with the Elder Races. They formerly inhabited the Milky Way a billion years ago before fleeing to settle the Large Magellanic Cloud. Their vessels exist in both jumpspace and realspace simultaneously.

Rand's World: A former colony world of Earth where the terraforming was stopped mid-process due to Notha aggression. It is now primarily inhabited by criminals, pirates, and separatists. Named for Ayn Rand.

The Rift: A massive system-wide tear in the fabric of reality that leads to jumpspace. It is constantly producing orichalcum gas.

Savit: Excrement. Usually used as a pejorative.

Security Divisions: The twelve, yes, twelve intelligence agencies working for the Community.

Separatists: A union of twelve Sorkanan worlds and several space colonies that withdrew from Community protection to institute societies based on the equalist philosophy. Civil war and unrest have riddled the governments of these societies ever since.

Separatist Starfighters: Knock-off starfighters from failed Sorkanan projects for them. They are only useful against smaller vessels and corvettes.

Shogun: An ocean-bound planet that is used in the production of large amounts of biological material, pharmaceuticals, and starship parts. It is an important port and known for its covert support of piracy.

SKAMMs: Sun destroying weapons of interstellar destruction. They are horrifying devices and their use in the recent Notha War resulted in an immediate end to the conflict lest the two sides annihilate one another.

Sklux: A race of protoplasmic beings that can shape into a rough approximation of any form. Obsessed with puns. Considered a race of mediators and peacemakers, primarily by themselves.

Sorkanan: One of the oldest and most powerful species in space. They are a humanoid reptilian species with multiple offshoots.

Sorkanan Imperial Navy: The massive fleets of the Sorkanan Empire. Its conditions are horrifying, and morale is generally low, but it is still the greatest power in the Spiral.

Sorkanan Separatist Frigate: Obsolete but potent vessels of the Sorkanan Navy modified to semi-modern levels and used by the Separatist governments as part of their navies. They do not have a class because all of them are heavily customized. The usual crew compliment is about two thousand.

Space Academy: The training center for officers in the Community Protectors.

Spacer: A slang term for those who have grown up and primarily live in space.

Space Cadet Sally: A popular children's show with a large adult following. *Space Cadet Sally* has often been accused of being Space Fleet propaganda. Sally's fictional enemies are the Dark Matter terrorist organization. It has been accused of being increasingly sexualized as the series continued. Space Cadet Sally is also the name of the lead character, of whom an entire line of bioroids have been based.

Space Fleet: The Community's massive interstellar navy that is (allegedly) a galactic force for good.

The Spiral: What Orion's Arm is called by most races of the Known Universe as they are primarily concentrated there.

Terraformers: A extremely popular 24th century science fiction program known for its shows, movies, and video game spin offs. The show is full of violence, sex, and esoteric sci-fi concepts.

Thor: An impoverished planet with a population of blue-skinned humans that deals with cold as well as radiation daily.

Transtellar: The name for interplanetary corporations that are possessed of far more resources than individual worlds. They wield disproportionate power in the Community and among humanity's various worlds.

Treaty of Exarxes: A large multispecies agreement on shared morality and behavior during wartime. The Notha are a very reluctant signatory. A second treaty was drafted to ban the use of SKAMMs and other weapons of mass destruction at Elder Race insistence.

Treaty of Rand's World: A treaty negotiated by a five hundred sentient diplomatic team from the Community as well as a hundred and fifty Notha officials. It brought an end to Contested Space and established new borders. Wildly unpopular with many human settlers and revanchists.

Tryfle: A genetically modified predator from Deathworld that is often used as a bodyguard for Notha officials.

Veraxians: A splinter race of the Verdantians. They are all about war, honor, and racism. They are often employed by the Notha as mercenaries.

Verdantian: A leonine race with six limbs that were uplifted by the Elder Races according to their belief structure.

Vroot: A race in Notha space that resemble chickens with hands. They are the only race known to be formally allied with the Notha.

Wormhole: A rift in space that leads from one location to another.

AUTHOR'S NOTE

I'd like to thank you for reading this book. The publishing industry is changing dramatically since the advent of eBooks. It is now very difficult to get any book noticed, regardless of quality. If you enjoyed this book, you could do some very simple things to help me attract attention. Word of mouth is the number one source of success for novels, so simply telling family and friends about the book is a great start.

Here are a few other ways of helping out, if you are so inclined:

* Post a rating or review where you purchased the eBook
* Post a rating or review on Goodreads
* Talk about the book or write a review on Facebook
* Tell folks about the book in a blog post.

If you like any of my other books, please feel free to check them out. A lot of my series are interlinked, and you never know when you'll find someone familiar showing up. In this case, *Space Academy Dropouts* is set in the far future of my Agent G cyberpunk books and the past of my *Lucifer's Star* series. Fans will certainly get a kick out of seeing how the galaxy changes in a few centuries either way.

ABOUT THE AUTHORS

Michael Suttkus, II, lives in Leesburg, Florida, with three cats, one of which actually likes him, and his family, with whom he fares better. When not working at a game store, he's playing games, reading science books, or otherwise being incredibly nerdy. Also writing! Because he has to feed cats whether they like him or not.

Bibliography

I Was a Teenage Weredeer (The Bright Falls Mysteries, Book 1)
An American Weredeer in Michigan (The Bright Falls Mysteries, Book 2)
A Nightmare on Elk Street (The Bright Falls Mysteries, Book 3)

Lucifer's Star (Lucifer's Star #1)
Lucifer's Nebula (Lucifer's Star #2)

Brightblade (The Morgan Detective Agency, Book 1)
Brighteyes (The Morgan Detective Agency, Book 2)

Space Academy Dropouts (The Space Academy Series, Book 1)
Space Academy Rejects (The Space Academy Series, Book 2)
Space Academy Washouts (The Space Academy Series, Book 3)
Space Academy Miscreants (The Space Academy Series, Book 4)
Space Academy Vagrants (The Space Academy Series, Book 5)

C. T. Phipps is a lifelong student of horror, science fiction, and fantasy. An avid tabletop gamer, he discovered this passion led him to write and turned him into a lifelong geek. He is a regular blogger and also a reviewer for The Bookie Monster.

Bibliography

Novels

The Rules of Supervillainy (Supervillainy Saga #1)
The Games of Supervillainy (Supervillainy Saga #2)
The Secrets of Supervillainy (Supervillainy Saga #3)
The Kingdom of Supervillainy (Supervillainy Saga #4)
The Tournament of Supervillainy (Supervillainy Saga #5)
The Future of Supervillainy (Supervillainy Saga #6)
The Horror of Supervillainy (Supervillainy Saga #7)
Tales of Supervillainy: Cindy's Seven (Supervillainy Saga #8)
The Fall of Supervillainy (Supervillainy Saga #9)

I Was a Teenage Weredeer (The Bright Falls Mysteries, Book 1)
An American Weredeer in Michigan (The Bright Falls Mysteries, Book 2)
A Nightmare on Elk Street (The Bright Falls Mysteries, Book 3)

Esoterrorism (Red Room, Vol. 1)
Eldritch Ops (Red Room, Vol. 2)
The Fall of the House (Red Room, Vol. 3)

Agent G: Infiltrator (Agent G, Vol. 1)
Agent G: Saboteur (Agent G, Vol. 2)
Agent G: Assassin (Agent G, Vol. 3)

Cthulhu Armageddon (Cthulhu Armageddon, Vol. 1)
The Tower of Zhaal (Cthulhu Armageddon, Vol. 2)
The Tree of Azathoth (Cthulhu Armageddon, Vol. 3)

Lucifer's Star (Lucifer's Star, Vol. 1)
Lucifer's Nebula (Lucifer's Star, Vol. 2)

Straight Outta Fangton (Straight Outta Fangton, Vol. 1)
100 Miles and Vampin' (Straight Outta Fangton, Vol. 2)
Vampiraz4Life (Straight Outta Fangton, Vol. 3)

Wraith Knight (Wraith Knight, Vol. 1)
Wraith Lord (Wraith Knight, Vol. 2)
Wraith King (Wraith Knight, Vol. 3)

Dark Destiny (Dark Destiny, Vol. 1)
Destiny's Paradox (Dark Destiny, Vol. 2)

Brightblade (The Morgan Detective Agency, Book 1)
Brighteyes (The Morgan Detective Agency, Book 2)

Daughter of the Cyber Dragons (The Cyber Dragons Series, Book 1)
Revenge of the Cyber Dragons (The Cyber Dragons Series, Book 2)
End of the Cyber Dragons (The Cyber Dragons Series, Book 3)

Space Academy Dropouts (The Space Academy Series, Book 1)

Space Academy Rejects (The Space Academy Series, Book 2)
Space Academy Washouts (The Space Academy Series, Book 3)
Space Academy Miscreants (The Space Academy Series, Book 4)
Space Academy Vagrants (The Space Academy Series, Book 5)

Moon Cops on the Moon (Moon Cops, Book 1)
Moon City Vice (Moon Cops, Book 2)

Lords of Dragon Keep (Dragon Keep, Book 1)
Guardians of Dragon Keep (Dragon Keep, Book 2)

Psycho Killers in Love

Tales of an Eldritch Wasteland

Anthologies (as editor)
Blackest Knights
Blackest Spells
Tales of Capes and Cowls
Tales of the Al-Azif
Tales of Yog-Sothoth
The Book of Hastur

Curious about other Crossroad Press books? Stop by our website:
http://crossroadpress.com
We offer quality writing
in digital, audio, and print formats.

Subscribe to our newsletter on the website homepage and receive a
free eBook.

www.ingramcontent.com/pod-product-compliance
Lightning Source LLC
Chambersburg PA
CBHW031549240626
47153CB00002B/440